KT-462-124

A ROSE IN FLANDERS FIELD

1917. Driving an ambulance through the mud in Flanders, aristocrat Evie Creswell is a long way from home. At Oaklands Manor she was expected to look pretty and make a good marriage. But with the arrival of World War One everything changed. Evie shunned an aristocratic husband and instead wed artist Will Davies, who works as a butcher's apprentice. As she struggles to transport the wounded to hospital, avoiding the shells and gas attacks – her privileged home life, and her family's disappointment at her marriage, are a lifetime away. While Evie drives an ambulance in Belgium, Will is in the trenches in France. Can their marriage survive this terrible war?

A ROSE IN FLANDERS FIELD

A ROSE IN FLANDERS FIELD

by

Terri Nixon

Magna Large Print Books
Long Preston, North Yorkshire,
BD23 4ND, England.

British Library Cataloguing in Publication Data.

A catalogue record of this book is
available from the British Library

ISBN   978-0-7505-4547-1

First published in Great Britain 2014 by Carina
an imprint of Harlequin (UK) Limited

Cover illustration © Collaboration JS/Arcangel by arrangement with
Arcangel Images Ltd.

Terri Nixon asserts the moral right to be identified as the author of
this work

Published in Large Print 2018 by arrangement with
Harlequin Books S.A.

Magna Large Print is an imprint of Library Magna Books Ltd.

Printed and bound in Great Britain by
T.J. (International) Ltd., Cornwall, PL28 8RW

I would like to thank everyone who has continued to support me over this past year, and I hope this new offering has been worth it! Special thanks to my youngest son, Dom, for his patient indulgence as I look blankly at him over the lid of my laptop while my mind struggles to re-connect with day-to-day reality.

Thanks also to my agent, Kate (Kate Nash Literary Agency), to my editor, and to everyone who has worked towards getting this book to publication; the support, professionalism and advice has been invaluable.

I would also like to publicly thank the editors of Lady Under Fire on the Western Front, (the wartime letters of Lady Dorothie Feilding) which I read over and over again while planning this book, along with many other first-hand accounts of those at the 'sharp end' during the Great War.

And finally, to all those fallen during that conflict, and those who gave everything to help them; a sacrifice beyond imagining, a debt beyond measure.

To my wonderful parents: Anne and Eddie Deegan. Your encouragement has been unstinting, as has your patience with my relentless blathering. This one's for you.

Chapter One

Flanders, Belgium, February 1917.

The explosion was more than a noise, it was a pressure, and a fist, and a scream that started in the pit of my stomach and flashed outward through every nerve. Pulsing light from relentless shelling afforded glimpses through the dark of the uneven road ahead, and I had long ago learned to use this sinister glow as I guided the ambulance between dressing station and clearing station, but tonight it seemed Fritz was sending over all he had. Our chaps would give it back twice as hard though – at least that's what I told myself, what we always told ourselves, and what we always made sure to tell the boys who looked to us for reassurance that their suffering was not in vain.

The wheels slid on half-frozen mud, and all my driving experience melted into mere hope; on a night like this it would come down to luck as to whether we stayed on the road or pitched off into the even rougher ground beyond, and luck has a famously capricious heart.

It occurred, not for the first time, that less than three years before, my prayers would have been no more intense than the wish that my mother would stop trying to marry me off to one of her friends' 'perfectly charming' sons. Even then I'd had no interest in, or need of, a husband, but it was a sobering thought that most of those adventurous and brightly confident young men would now be entrenched in mud, and finding their own prayers much altered.

Those who still lived.

I blinked hard to relieve my eyes from the strain of staring at the road, and a second later my heart faltered as I identified the cause of this latest, and loudest, of explosions. A moment later Kitty, the new girl, cried out in dismay as she saw it too: the large house ahead, and the sprawling collection of tents and outbuildings in its grounds that served as the casualty clearing station, was ablaze. Part of the roof was gone, a gaping mouth from which flames belched and licked ravenously at the overhanging trees, setting even the wettest canvas of the nearby tents alight. The painted red cross had collapsed inward, and while many of the staff retained their sense of duty, many more did not – chaos had the night in its grip now, and it was each man for himself. The two sister-stations, one empty and waiting and one already taking the overspill from the house, were in danger of catching too, and panic was evident in every silhouette that stumbled in search of safety, and in every cry that transcended the roar of flame and the crack of wood and glass.

Time was short, and I turned the wheel before we reached the road junction, sending silent but heartfelt apologies to my wounded, and then we were bumping over the roughly pitted grass towards the burning buildings. The moment I pulled to a stop, Kitty was in the back urging those more able to bunch up to make room, and

14

explaining we must go another ten miles to the base hospital in the town. Exclamations of dismay followed me as I jumped down, and I understood every one of them; the men would have been blessing every turn of the wheels that brought us closer to help, and now they must hold on a little longer. There was little doubt that, for some, it would prove too long.

The intense heat stung every exposed inch of skin as I ran towards a group of evacuees, huddling as far away from the billowing smoke as they could get, and I drew a deep breath in readiness for shouting, feeling the moisture stripped from my throat the moment my mouth opened.

'Two! We can take two—' I broke off, coughing, bent double with it and unable to shout again, but one of the orderlies had seen me and when I rose, gasping and teary-eyed, he gestured me over.

In the end we took three; two more in the back, and one sitter up front with us, a boy no older than Kitty herself by his looks. He had just begun treatment for shrapnel wounds to the arm and shoulder, and moving at all must have jarred him terribly, but as soon as he was settled in his seat he began talking, with cautious relief, about being shipped back to England. I exchanged a glance with Kitty, and we both found wan smiles for what he considered his good luck before we rolled off once more towards the town. There was a harsh jerk and a new rattling sound as we rejoined the road, and I wondered how many more trips we could make before something else fell off the ambulance, or broke, and I would be required to spend the rest of this freezing night lying in the

15

mud with my tool box.

When we got to the hospital we found one of the new blessés had died, and the shrapnel-wounded boy's relief fell away, leaving him paler than ever and deeply subdued; I gathered they had been friends. We covered the dead man with his blanket and the boy hitched a breath, and there was no more talk of Blighty while the VAD led him away to have his wounds redressed. Kitty and I hurriedly sluiced down the inside of the ambulance, and set off back to the dressing station for one more trip.

And one more.

When the night's grim work was finally over we returned to our little cottage, and I went over the ambulance with my torch, checking carefully underneath. Gertie, as we'd named her, had been a godsend, but she was fast reaching the end of her useful life as an ambulance, and must soon be retired before she became a danger rather than an inconvenience. Rather like myself, it seemed at times. By the time she had been emptied of blood-soaked blankets and stretchers, there remained precious few hours in which to steal a bit of sleep.

Kitty went gratefully to the room we shared and fell into bed immediately, but I sat at the kitchen table, pen in hand, and a blank sheet in front of me. I never told my husband what I had been doing; he had his own worries, and his own dark stories, and to heap mine upon him would be cruel and unnecessary. Instead I wrote that Kitty Maitland was an absolute treasure, although nerves made her clumsy and she still kept knocking things down. Naturally we had immediately

16

nicknamed her Skittles. I wrote that the weather here was as vicious as it was in France, and that I hoped he was making good use of the warm scarf I had sent him. I told him some of the girls in the ambulance corps were jealous of us because their commandant was utterly hard-hearted, and they wished they had set up alone as we had. I wished him a happy thirtieth birthday.

Then I laid my pen down, folded the letter ready to post, and burst into tears.

Chapter Two

Oaklands Manor, Cheshire, New Year's Eve 1911.

I paused at the foot of the back stairwell and carefully rearranged my expression, then pushed open the kitchen door. Instantly all talk ceased, and only began again, in hesitant tones, as I nodded demurely in greeting and crossed to speak to the cook.

Mrs Hannah looked up. 'Miss Evangeline. And what might we do for you this morning?'

'I'm sorry for disturbing you,' I said, in my most timid voice, 'but I was just on my way out and Mother has asked me to pass on a message.'

'Why ever didn't she ring down?'

'She knew you were busy, I expect,' I said, gesturing at the table laden with vegetables.

'Well, she'd be right,' Mrs Hannah agreed, 'and if Mercy leaves, like she's saying, things will soon

17

get even busier.'

I glanced at the scullery maid, who was on her knees with her head in the grate, and lowered my voice. 'Poor Mercy. She was never happy here, was she?'

'Ideas above her station, should you ask me,' the cook opined, not bothering to match my discreet tones. If Mrs Cavendish had heard she'd certainly have given her one of her special 'Head-Housekeeper' looks that usually sent the recipient scuttling away, although Mrs Hannah always ignored them. I liked Mrs Hannah.

She was looking at me now, knife paused mid-chop. 'The message then, Miss Evangeline?'

'Oh, yes. Well, you know how mother has given you that recipe for the loaf her grandmother used to make?'

'The fruit loaf, yes.'

'And you know how she specifically told you to follow it to the letter?'

'I do.' Mrs Hannah's eyes narrowed, but I kept my expression carefully blank.

'Well, it appears she made a little mistake. Where it says dates, it should say raisins. And where it says half a cup of sugar, she has asked me to make it particularly clear that she meant to write one whole cup.'

'I see. Is that all then?'

I pretended to think for a moment. 'There was one other thing, now you mention it. You'll see Mother has specified almonds to be laid along the top?'

'I expect you'll be saying she didn't mean that either.'

'She didn't, no.'

'Would she have meant glazed fruit, do you think?'

I beamed. 'Exactly. And it's most important you don't forget about the sugar, Mrs Hannah.'

Mrs Hannah raised an eyebrow and favoured me with a rare, amused little smile. 'Don't worry, I'll be sure to follow the instructions to the letter.'

'Thank you,' I said, although I wasn't sure if she meant to follow the original instructions, or my own amendments; only time would tell, but I had done my best. Mother's cake ideas always looked wonderful on their plates, but it was best they stayed there if the illusion of perfection was to be maintained. I paused on my way out, and turned back to make sure Mrs Hannah was absolutely sure about the swapping of dates for raisins, but was distracted by a knock at the side door.

Ruth, the kitchen maid, hurried into the hall to answer, and returned followed by two men. I recognised Frank Markham, the local butcher from Breckenhall, but behind him stood a young man I had never seen before; an attractive boy of around twenty, with tumbled brown hair and a faintly bemused look on his face. He was bowed under the weight of a large wooden box.

'Morning, Ruth. Mrs Hannah.' Mr Markham ushered the young man forward. 'This is Will Davies, my new apprentice. He'll be helping with deliveries from now on, so don't you ladies go giving him a hard time.' He winked at Ruth, who ignored him and greeted the apprentice with a good deal more enthusiasm than was proper; I saw Mrs Hannah roll her eyes, but she said nothing and went on with her work. I hoped someone would take Ruth aside one day soon, she was becoming quite the little madam from what I'd heard.

Will staggered to the table to relieve himself of his burden, and as he stood upright again his eyes found mine. It was hard to see what colour they were from this distance, but they crinkled when he smiled, and a dimple deepened in his cheek. I blinked in surprise at the casual nod he gave me, then realised he wouldn't know I wasn't just another of the kitchen staff, wearing my plain outdoor coat as I was. It was an interesting notion.

I watched as the apprentice went through the delivery order, enjoying the way he kept stealing glances my way, and that dimple kept reappearing. But before someone could address me by my title, and ruin the fun, I slipped back out into the corridor and up the stairs to the main front door, exploring the unexpected tingle I had felt when our eyes had locked. I'd quite liked it.

A week into the new year I saw the apprentice again, and this time there was no hiding who I was. I was wearing my best coat this time, and getting into the car with Mother and my younger brother Lawrence to go to church, when the butcher's van rattled up the drive. Will was seated beside Mr Markham, wearing a fixed look of terror at the older man's driving, and I hid a smile in my glove as I pictured how much paler he'd look if I was behind the wheel; the illicit lessons I begged whenever I went to stay with the London family were going well, but I tended to pay little attention to the words of caution that came with them, and people were starting to find urgent business elsewhere when they saw me approaching them with a hopeful expression.

Will's eyes widened slightly on seeing me, and I saw realisation slip into place, then he grinned at me and winked. The tingle woke up again, stronger this time, and I was unable to prevent an answering smile from crossing my face. Just before I turned my head away I saw his expression soften, and he settled more happily back into his seat, all sign of nerves gone as the van pulled to a stop by the back gate. I glanced at Mother, but she was accepting the footman's assistance into the car; neither the butcher nor his apprentice held any interest for her. It already felt like a rather delicious secret.

I found my thoughts straying to him more and more often. I'd look out for the van from my window and suddenly find some reason to be downstairs, or wandering along the drive, and when we glimpsed each other the smiles were quick to come, slow to fade, and warmer every time. Then one bright day in early March, the day before I was due to leave for London for two months, my mother's maid and I were in Breckenhall, buying last-minute gifts for the London family.

Behind us was the open-air market, full of tantalising smells and sounds, brightly-coloured clothing, and bric-a-brac and old books. I compared it to the imminent wait in the stuffy post office while Alice bought stamps for about a hundred thousand letters, and eyed the busy stalls longingly.

Then I stiffened my backbone. 'I'm going to

just walk around by myself for a little while thank you, Peters.'

Peters was used, by now, to my impatience to be off alone, and it never seemed to ruffle her rather elegant feathers when I suggested it. But she had her orders. 'Of course we'll visit the market, but Lady Creswell told me I must stay with you.'

'I'm sure she doesn't mean you're to be glued to my side,' I protested.

'No, of course not, but–'

I reminded myself of the difference in our positions, although I felt guilty doing it. 'Just ten minutes,' I said firmly. Then my façade slipped, and I reverted to the child I had been and, in her eyes at least, still was. *'Please,* Alice? After tomorrow I shan't have a single minute to myself what with all those boring parties and dinners. People fussing over me morning, noon and night, dressmakers measuring–'

'All right! Ten minutes.' She looked resigned, but wore a reluctant smile. 'I'll be waiting by the cake stall.' I was already walking away, and she raised her voice to call after me: 'Just don't tell your mother you were able to talk me into it!' As if I would give Mother any reason to stop me coming into town.

After a happy few minutes spent enjoying the freedom, and sampling breads at a particularly delicious-smelling stall, I rounded a corner and saw, just ahead, a small boy standing alone. He looked to be around five years old, and he didn't appear upset at first, but, as I watched, sudden realisation of his lonely state seemed to hit him and his lip began to tremble. I took a step closer

22

but another figure appeared from behind a stall and crouched down in front of him, and my heart skipped as I recognised Will. He looked calm and competent, and, wrapped up warm against the hours he spent standing around in the early spring chill, he seemed older than I'd first thought.

The little boy was crying in earnest now, but Will paid no attention to the tears and instead kept up a cheerful chatter as he peeled the outer page off his newspaper. Still talking, his fingers worked quickly for a minute or two and then he held something out. The boy stopped snuffling and took the paper boat, and a bright smile spread over his face as he mimed its passage through an imaginary rough sea before showing it to a harried-looking nursery nurse, who seized his hand and pulled him away. She threw a brief 'thank you' at Will before vanishing into the crowd, and I went over to him, and found my voice.

'Hello again.'

Will jumped, but when he turned to look at me there was no nervousness in his expression, just unabashed pleasure. Up this close I could see his eyes were a clear and lovely blue, beneath eyebrows a few shades darker than his hair, and his features were stronger and leaner than I had thought at first. Will Davies was evidently something of a charmer, and I found myself for once unable to think of anything else to say. I could only twist my fingers together and hope he would speak first.

He did, but it didn't really help. 'Miss Creswell,' he said, nodding.

'Mr Davies. That was ... very clever, what you

23

did for that little boy.' He looked at me for a moment, and his eyes narrowed just a little bit and he took another sheet off his newspaper. He unfolded it, then his nimble fingers went to work again and a moment later he was handing me a rose, barely out of bud, with the petals curling outwards in the first welcoming hint of the full bloom to come.

I took it, and the expression on my face must have been much the same as the little boy's. The fact that the rose was black and white, with smudgy print and a flimsy stem, meant nothing; it had appeared seemingly out of nowhere, just for me. 'Thank you,' I said, and tucked it into the band around my hat. 'That should annoy Mother quite satisfactorily.'

Will laughed. The sound was lower than I'd expected it might be, and my response to it was a faint but pleasant confusion.

'Talk in the kitchen says you're off to London,' he said.

'I leave tomorrow. I'm expected to attend an awful lot of very dull parties with an awful lot of very dull people.'

'Oh, I'm sure you'll have fun when you get used to it.' But his expression said, clearer than words, that he hoped I would not. Something clicked into place between us in that moment, but it remained unspoken. It sat, quietly glowing inside me, and in him it manifested itself in a forced lightness of tone. 'What time is your train?'

'Well, that's the good part, at least,' I said, 'I don't have to sit on the train and breathe in all that cigar smoke. Uncle Jack is going to be taking me down in his motor car.'

'The Silver Ghost?' Will whistled. 'You are a very lucky girl, Miss Evangeline.'

'Call me Evie.' It suddenly seemed important that he not think of me as one of the Creswells, after all he wasn't one of the servants. If I had expected a modest protest from him I was pleasantly surprised.

'Evie,' he said, pretending to mull it over. Then he nodded. 'I approve. As long as you promise to call me Lord William, and to bow each time you see me.'

'My Lord,' I said, dropping into an elaborate curtsey. Rising, I saw his smile, just before it faltered and we fell into silence. We both looked away, casting about for something to say to prolong the meeting, and with a sinking heart I remembered my arrangement with Miss Peters.

'I have to go. Although I would have loved to stand here all afternoon, even in this faintly awkward silence.' Turning it into a joke made it a little easier, at least, and he was surprised into a laugh. 'Thank you so much for the sweet gift,' I added, my voice a little softer. I wanted him to know I meant it, that I wasn't merely being polite.

His smile slipped, leaving his expression defiantly hopeful. 'I'll never make one for anyone else.'

'Good. I'm glad.' I looked at him for a long moment, and then, obeying an instinct deeper than both etiquette and good sense, I stepped close and placed a quick kiss on the edge of his mouth. I paused, then said, 'I have a feeling I'm going to miss you, Will Davies. Why is that, do you suppose?'

'Because I'm irresistible?'

I smiled. 'Have a lovely spring, I'll be thinking of you. And when the new scullery maid starts in a week or two just make sure you're not *too* irresistible.' I briefly wondered at my own boldness, at both the kiss and the implication behind my words, but it was an exhilarating feeling nevertheless, and the look on his face told me it was not unwelcome. When I left him standing there I was determined not to look back, but felt the weight of his gaze between my shoulder blades like a warm hand, and the smile on my face made people glance twice at me and give me quizzical little smiles in return. But it was with Will that my mind stayed from that moment on.

Those two months felt like two years. The London Creswells were charming company, and the house magnificent, but it wasn't Oaklands. In the same way, there had been plenty of potential suitors, many of them handsome enough, all without a doubt extremely wealthy, and some of them even amusing, but there had been no Will Davies among them. Not one of them made me smile the way he did, or caused my chest to flutter the way his touch had. I arrived back at Breckenhall on a warm day in the middle of May, and would have loved to have found some reason to wander around the town, and past Frank Markham's shop window a few times, but the train had been delayed so we were late arriving. At least I was back in the same town, and might see Will at any time, and I would have to be content with that for now.

Uncle Jack, who wasn't my uncle at all but an old friend of my deceased father, was dressed in his usual casual clothes that we both knew would make Mother wince, and it cheered me so much to see him that disappointment was pushed to the back of my mind. My attention was taken up, for the moment, with the opportunity to put some of those clandestine driving lessons into practice: here was Uncle Jack in his marvellous motor, and no Mother to put her foot firmly down on the fun. But he was not to be moved.

'Absolutely not. Your mother would never allow me to set foot in the house again if anyone were to see you. And as for what she would do to you, well–'

'Then we shall keep each other's secret.'

'We shall do nothing of the sort. And you don't know how to drive anyway.'

'Oh, don't I?' I couldn't help grinning.

'Evie...'

'For your information, Uncle Jack, I've been driving a good deal whilst in London.'

'Why did you have to tell me that?' he groaned. 'Now I can't pretend any more that I'd no idea.'

'You knew?'

'I'd heard. But if your mother knew she'd have you confined to your rooms until you turn sixty.'

'Then it's a good thing I know you won't tell her,' I said, though with less certainty than hope. 'Besides,' I went on, eyeing him up and down, 'someone who dresses as you do can't possibly tell tales to my mother and expect them to be believed.'

'What's wrong with the way I dress?'

27

'Honestly, you *never* wear the right clothes! It's why I love you, of course.'

I stopped as we reached the car, and stared in surprise. A girl of around my own age sat huddled in the back, looking at me with wide blue eyes, and a terrified look on her face.

I wasn't quite sure what to say, but I had to say something, if only to make the poor girl feel better. 'Hello, whoever you are! Uncle Jack, have you been out collecting waifs and strays, or are you going to tell me this is your latest conquest?'

'Don't be ridiculous, you should know who this is, she works for you after all. In fact I'm taking her back to work now.'

I frowned, looking again at the girl. 'I've never seen you before, and I do know the staff rather well, unlike my mother.'

'I'm n-new. I've only been at Oaklands for two months.' She must be the new scullery maid. Her voice was soft, a little husky-sounding, and had a very rustic accent.

'Well then.' I turned back to Uncle Jack in triumph. 'You see? For all your disapproval, this girl began work after I'd already left for London.' I looked at the girl again. 'You're very pretty, but you're a skinny thing. We must make sure Mrs Hannah feeds you up. What's your name?'

'Mar ... Lizzy.'

She'd been about to say Mary, which must have been her real name, but she'd have been made to change that, of course, since our housemaid was called Mary. 'Mare Lizzy?' I deliberately misunderstood, smiling. The smile faded as I considered that the girl might well find an audience

28

for her escapades today, and that word would almost certainly get back to Mother. I should nip rumour in the bud now.

'Well, Mare Lizzy, I know how words are thrown around in the kitchens, and when they're caught they're often fumbled. I'd hate for anyone to be under the mistaken impression I'd gone against my mother's wishes whilst in London.'

'Of course not,' she responded promptly. 'I'm sure I shan't remember a thing of our meeting once I'm back at work.'

Our eyes met and held for a moment, then my smile returned. 'I have a feeling I can trust you, Mare Lizzy.'

'I'm just Lizzy.'

'I know that, silly,' I said. 'Uncle Jack, if we don't hurry I shall be late for tea, and Just Lizzy will be late for work.'

'I'm not the one standing around gossiping,' he said. 'And I do wish you wouldn't call me Uncle Jack. It makes me feel ancient.'

'You *are* ancient!' I winked at Lizzy before climbing into the front seat. She was looking quite terrified both of the motor car, and of me, but I instinctively liked her, and although our paths didn't cross again for quite some time I often thought back to that short journey, and the way she had sat in silence once the car had begun to move, embracing the new experience with quiet but intense enjoyment, her natural fear falling away to leave her breathless and bright-eyed as we parted company. I made Uncle Jack stop at the bottom of the drive, and turned around, genuinely regretful.

'Lizzy, I don't want to sound mean but I really

29

think it might be better if you walked from here. Mother will hear the approach of the car, if she hasn't already, and will certainly come to meet us at the door.' I shrugged, not sure how to put it without causing offence. 'She doesn't approve of family and servants mixing company I'm afraid. Terribly old-fashioned, of course, but I must respect her wishes.'

'When you're in her house at least.'

As the words left her lips to hang unretractably between us, Lizzy looked at me as though she wished the car would burst into flames around her. My own stunned surprise faded into realisation that she was absolutely right, and I almost laughed outright but managed to contain it; I must appear to possess some dignity at least. So I turned away instead, nearly putting my teeth through my lip in my effort to appear stern. I daren't look at Uncle Jack, who'd clearly had the same thoughts, and was staring straight ahead as if he had never been up our drive before, and was trying to see right up to the end of it.

Lizzy slipped from the car to begin her walk, and I saw her miserably embarrassed gaze following the car, as it roared up to the house with far more haste than was necessary. Neither of us suspected for one moment that we had just met the dearest friend each of us would ever know.

Chapter Three

The summer limped on. It seemed I had no time to myself, no opportunity to be looking out of the window for sight of Frank Markham's van, and certainly none to be walking around Breckenhall in the hopes of seeing Will. There was a faint disappointment that he wasn't seeking me out either, but I admitted I was being unreasonable; how could he possibly? Nevertheless, I began to wonder if I'd imagined the connection and growing warmth between us, and the sense of anticipation that had been coiling in my stomach since my return home was replaced by niggling doubt, and even faint embarrassment.

August was creeping towards its end, and my childhood with it. I would be eighteen on the twenty-third, and after that my life would be even less my own than it was now; strange how I had always envied the grown-ups their freedom, never suspecting that they were as much fettered by expectation as Lawrence and me. I found my interest in the Suffrage movement increasing; the sense of change just around the corner found an anchor in some frustrated corner of my mind, and began to pull ... more than once Uncle Jack and I talked about it – he had reservations, not about the principle, but about the way the cause was gathering momentum; too fast and potentially dangerous. But to me it sounded not only exciting

31

but inevitable and necessary, and I began to read as much literature as I could on the subject.

A few days before my birthday, thoughts of politics, and even of Will, had been swamped in importance by Mother's insistence that I behave according to my new status and take a personal maid. Everyone seemed certain the kitchen maid, Ruth, would be chosen. I didn't want a maid, could think of few worse things than having a little shadow, of any shape or size, but that it was likely to be the awful Ruth Wilkins was too much, and I said so.

'I am not asking you for your views,' Mother said mildly. 'I am simply telling you what is expected of you. Besides, you will find a maid utterly invaluable, and, since we will be entertaining more now, Peters will not be at your disposal any longer.'

'But does it have to be Ruth? She's ... well, she's not at all the kind of person I can turn to if I need anything.'

Her voice became firmer. 'Your maid is not your friend, Evangeline, and in any case, you know nothing about Ruth. She is an exceptionally good worker, according to Mrs Cavendish, and keen to better herself. I think she should do quite nicely.'

I sighed. Mother didn't know I spent more time talking to the staff than I did my own family, so I was not supposed to know anything about the girl. But I did, of course, and I didn't like any of it. She might well be skilled, and on the surface appear a dedicated worker, but in reality I knew her to be lazy, rude and selfish, with one ambition only: to move 'upstairs'. I had never trusted her, and if I couldn't trust my maid then surely it was better not to have one. But Mother waved my argument away, and I was on the verge of resorting to begging, and even promising to behave more like a young lady, when Uncle Jack spoke up from where he sat in the corner.

'Lily, perhaps Evie might be permitted to make her own choice from the staff? And then whoever she chooses might be allowed to either accept or decline.'

I turned in indignation, to demand he explain why anyone would be likely to decline, and caught the ghost of his grin. 'That's a wonderful idea,' I said instead, refusing to rise to his teasing. 'What do you think, Mother?'

Mother sighed and glanced at Uncle Jack, who nodded encouragement. 'Oh, very well. Although Ruth will be disappointed; she has long been the certain choice.'

'Not mine!' Seeing her expression I realised I was in danger of upsetting everything, and made myself stop there.

'You have until Friday morning,' Mother said. 'Please, darling, do choose wisely.'

'But my birthday is Friday, I'll need someone to—'

'Whoever you choose will still be needed up until Saturday morning at least,' Mother said. 'There are lots of preparations to make for the party on Saturday night. But don't worry, Alice will see to you on Friday. Now do go for a walk while you think about it, your pacing up and down here is giving me quite a headache.'

'I'm sorry. Yes, I'll do that.'

'If you see Lawrence while you're out, tell him

he's late for his lessons yet again. Mr Stoper is in danger of losing his patience.'

'I will. And I'll come and tell you as soon as I've chosen.'

I wandered down the drive and out onto the Breckenhall road, my mind ranging over the staff as I went. The second housemaid, Emma Bird, was sweet, but she had a dreadfully intense and obvious crush on Uncle Jack, and since they would see each other often it might be embarrassing for him. I smiled to myself; that might be reason enough to choose her! But it wouldn't be fair on poor Emma to use her for such sport.

Mary Deegan, the other housemaid, was lovely. She was kind and hard-working, rather serious much of the time, but I was sure she would soon unbend once we got to know each other. Yes, Mary was a good choice. Anyone would be, except Ruth! Emma said she hadn't improved at all and had taken an instant dislike to the new scullery maid.

Lizzy! I stopped in the road wondering why I hadn't thought of her straight away. She might be new, but Mother had said I might have my choice, she hadn't said it must be someone who had worked here a long time. I thought back to my first sight of the girl as she huddled in the back of Uncle Jack's car, hatless, with dark hair that had started out merely cloudy, and had ended up a terrific mess from the wind that whipped it into tangles. She had been looking at me then as if she thought I might dismiss her on the spot if she opened her mouth, and yet she had spoken up, with blunt honesty. Just Lizzy. Yes, perfect!

A rumbling in the road behind me made me look back. It was Markham's van, crawling along no faster than I was walking, but the butcher himself was not driving it – instead Will Davies sat behind the wheel, squinting through the glass and concentrating on the road so hard he had not recognised me. I stopped walking and waited until he drew alongside, then I waved, and his expression was so comically startled that I couldn't help laughing. But I didn't laugh for long.

The van lurched to the right, tugged that way by Will's determination to keep control of the vehicle despite lifting his left hand to wave back to me, and, as he realised what he had done, he grabbed the wheel again and sent the van careering across the road. It cut in front of me, and as I cried out in shock at the near miss, the van toppled into the ditch, precariously balanced on two wheels, and its driver spilled over the half-door to land sprawled beside it.

'Will!'

He raised his head and looked at me, dazed, and I saw he was moments away from being crushed. He saw it too, and scrambled to his feet, and I grabbed his hand and pulled him away a bare second before the van crashed onto its side. We stood there, both of us staring at the van, and then at each other. Will opened his mouth to say something, but instead turned back to the van that had chuntered into silence. We were both breathing hard and I realised, at the same moment Will did, that we were still holding hands. He didn't let go.

Instead he said in an awed voice, 'I think you might have just saved my life.'

It gave me a strange feeling to realise he was right. On the other hand... 'Well, it was my fault you crashed. Will Mr Markham fire you for this?'

'No, I'm too good at my job.'

I was about to tease him about his lack of modesty, but such was his confidence I was certain he was justified in it. 'What will you do now?'

'Walk.'

I stared at him, and he stared back, and then, out of nowhere we both erupted into laughter. It sounded wonderful in the summer air, free from hysteria, and unforced, and Will was still smiling as he stood back and let go of my hand.

He walked around to the back of the van and grimaced, then glanced at me curiously before bending to pick up one of the empty boxes that had fallen out. 'Why are you walking alone, anyway?'

'Mother was getting a headache.'

He blinked. 'I'm sorry?'

'I was driving her to distraction, as usual, pacing up and down.' I went to help him and, with an odd mixture of pique and amusement I realised he wasn't going to say, 'No, Miss Evangeline, you mustn't.' I hid my own smile as I dragged an empty box out of the ditch and placed it on top of the one he had laid beside him.

'What prompted all the pacing?' he asked.

It did sound silly, and petulant, even to my own ears, and I sighed; 'It's my birthday in two days. I'm expected to take a maid, although I don't want one.'

'It certainly looks as though you don't need one,' he observed, as I helped him lift another box.

I gave him a wry look. 'Apparently it has little to do with ability, and everything to do with tradition. Besides, Mother says I won't have Alice to help out any more, since we're going to be having a lot more house guests from now on.'

'Finding you a husband?'

'Don't, please!'

He leaned on the underneath of the van. 'So you'll be eighteen then,' he said, and the way his eyes locked onto mine was both unnerving and deeply, viscerally, exciting.

'Yes. Mother wanted me to have Ruth Wilkins.' He winced, and I couldn't help laughing. 'Do you know her?'

'Not as well as Frank Markham does,' he said. 'The two of them have been carrying on at least for as long as I've known him, probably much longer.'

Clearly none of the other staff were aware of this or Ruth would have had her marching orders, good worker or not. But I was trying to appear a woman of the world, and so I tried not to let my surprise and distaste show. 'Well, I don't like her,' I said.

'You're a good judge of character then. I don't think even Mr Markham likes her, particularly.'

I didn't want to think about Ruth; the more I heard the more I realised I'd had a lucky escape. 'I've made my choice anyway,' I said, still pleased with it, 'and it's most certainly not Ruth. It's the new scullery maid.'

'Lizzy Parker?'

'Just Lizzy.' He looked puzzled, and I grinned. 'It doesn't matter. Yes, Lizzy Parker. She seems a lively sort, and I'm sure we'll get on famously.'

'She's an angel,' he agreed, and I was ashamed to feel a tingle of jealousy at his warm familiarity, but when I glanced at him he was looking back at me with an odd look on his face and I didn't think Lizzy was on his mind at all at that moment.

Something about that look made me ask, 'How old are you, Will?'

'Older than you think, probably,' he said. 'Most people think I'm about twenty.'

'I thought that.'

'I was twenty-five last January.'

I studied him closely, noting, for the first time, the way he held himself; there was none of the gawky awkwardness of a young man just growing into his body, he was comfortable and at ease with his own strength. He was having an increasingly unsettling effect on me and I sought refuge in teasing.

'That seems a little older that I'd have expected for a butcher's boy,' I observed, hoping the flush did not show as vividly as it felt.

Will moved a step closer. 'I'm no boy, Evie.' He brushed his hand over my wrist, and we both watched as my fingers and his twined together, capturing each other in wordless acceptance of the attraction between us. Once again we each sought something to say, our eyes still on our linked hands as if they might say it for us. Will took a deep breath, and his free hand rose to my face, but before he could speak again we heard an alarmed, childlike voice from the other side of the van.

'Mr Markham? Are you all right?'

We froze, staring at each other. My mind raced;

Lawrence was decent enough, for a brother, but if he saw Will and me together by the stricken van he might easily let something slip during his inevitable telling of the story later.

Will leaned in close, and his breath brushed warm on my cheek as he whispered, 'I'll tell you more about my life one day, and how I came to be working for Markham. If you'd like that?'

'I would.' We both took a step back, and I smoothed down my skirt with hands that shook and still felt Will's warmth. Lawrence was still on the other side of the van and hadn't seen us, so I moved away, stepping over a patch of mud. My foot came down short of my intended spot, and I slipped. Quick as lightning Will's hand was at my waist, steadying me, and I caught my breath, hoping he would keep it there. But with Lawrence so close it would have been foolish to risk him seeing us, and Will let go of me as soon as my footing was secure once more. I wondered if he felt the same twinge of disappointment as I did.

There was no possible way to avoid being seen; Lawrence was having a good look around the van and it mustn't seem as if we were hiding. Ignoring Will's horrified look I stepped out into the road, in full view.

'Lawrence! Thank goodness.' His face, open and honest and very young for fifteen years old, went blank with astonishment at seeing me there. 'I'm afraid I've caused a terrible accident,' I went on. 'Luckily no one was hurt, but it's entirely my fault Mr Davies crashed the van.'

'Yours? How?'

'I wasn't paying attention, and walked right out

39

in front of him. If he hadn't been so quick he might have run me over.'

Lawrence looked awestruck. He was a sweet boy and I felt bad for deceiving him, but this was an event he would be telling everyone about for some time, and I couldn't risk asking him to keep quiet about my being here, he was too excited.

'It wasn't entirely your fault, Miss,' Will said, emerging from behind the van to stand behind me. I couldn't see his face, but he had managed to inject a note of annoyance into his voice and it was hard not to smile.

'Oh, you're too kind, Mr Davies, but it was.' I turned to him. Sure enough he was scowling, but I was close enough to see the flicker of amusement in his eyes, and the dimple came and went quickly. 'You must be very shaken. Come back to the house, Mrs Hannah will be pleased to make you a warm drink.'

'Thank you, Miss. Sir.' Will nodded at Lawrence, who smiled at the address. He would have to get used to it; he was heir to Oaklands after all, and people would soon be accepting him as more than just 'the little boy at the Manor'.

Will and I were careful to keep our distance as we walked back up the long driveway, allowing Lawrence to walk between us and ask Will all kinds of questions, about the van, and about driving in particular. Remembering Will's fierce concentration as he drove, I was sure I could have answered those questions with more detail, and certainly more enthusiasm, but I let them chatter, and instead concentrated on the way my feelings towards Will had intensified during my time away.

It was impossible to ignore the way he'd looked at me just before Lawrence had arrived and, while it might be socially unacceptable, there was no longer any doubt in my mind that Will and myself had a path to travel together at some point.

I reluctantly let Lawrence take charge of directing Will to the kitchens, and found Mother in the hall saying goodbye to Uncle Jack. Because of his government work he was often away for long stretches of time, and he didn't even live with us, but it was difficult to remember that and always a wrench when he left. This time though, I knew he would be back in time for my party on Saturday, which made it easier to see him off cheerfully. I wished I was going too, and that we could both stay away until after Saturday; as excited as I was, part of me still dreaded this party and the way my life would change after it.

Although my birthday was on Friday, the Saturday-to-Monday that followed would be when I was presented with my birthright, the Kalteng Star. Most thought it a thing of beauty: a blue diamond mined by the first of the wealthy Creswells at the turn of the last century, and upon which all future family wealth was built. But all it represented to me was discord and upset. Our family, and our distant cousins, the Wingfields, had been at loggerheads for years over that stone, and on Saturday I would become its sole custodian. I wouldn't even own it, it was simply mine to use, to create more wealth, until the last Creswell heir died, taking the family name with him. Beautiful, yes, set as it was into a plain gold band and worn on a fine chain, but still it was destined to bring nothing but pain, until it passed out of our lives forever. That day could not come soon enough.

Putting it out of my mind for now, I followed Mother and Uncle Jack out to the front door again and tried not to look around for Will – it was strange knowing he was in the house talking to other people, and I felt a new twinge of envy for those who ensnared his attention now.

Uncle Jack hugged me goodbye. He really was more like a father than my own had been, and I looked forward to his return; he seemed to bring a breath of adventure and mystery with him every time, and I enjoyed our long discussions, even though they almost always turned heated. Maybe even because of that. He never underestimated my intelligence the way most of Mother's friends did, and while we disagreed on many things, including my intention to adopt the purple, green and white uniform of the Suffragette, he never once made me wish I had not expressed an opinion at all.

I didn't know how he would feel about my latest decision, though, so I waited until we were all standing in the sunlight outside the front door and he would have less time to retract his suggestion. On the other hand, if he left before I had mother's agreement, I would have no ally at all. Simon was lifting the familiar, single bag into the back of the Silver Ghost, and the August sun glinted off the metal as he closed the door. It was now or never.

'I have decided who I'd like as my maid,' I announced.

Mother turned to me, a look of wary hope on her face. 'I don't suppose you've seen sense about Ruth?'

I shook my head. 'I thought about Mary Deegan.'

'Ah yes, now she would be an excellent choice,' Mother said, and her voice turned warm, but I was about to ruin this rare moment of approval.

'She would, but she's such a good housemaid, I thought it might be hard to replace her.'

'That's true,' Mother said. I saw Uncle Jack looking at me with a little lift to his eyebrow; he had guessed I was going to say something unexpected and was waiting, with clear amusement, to see what it was.

'I've decided I want to ask Lizzy Parker,' I said. Another glance at Uncle Jack showed a brief look of surprise, quickly followed by understanding, and then a smile.

'Lizzy Parker,' Mother mused. Then her eyebrows shot up into her hairline. 'The scullery maid? What do you know about her? She's only been here for a month.'

'Six months,' I pointed out. 'And we did meet once, on the day I came back from London. I'm sure if I ask Mrs Cavendish I'll hear nothing but good reports about her.'

'She did seem polite and well-mannered,' Uncle Jack put in. Mother looked at him in surprise and he explained how we'd offered Lizzy a ride home. 'I got the impression she, ah...' he broke off and his mouth twitched a little bit, 'she seems to have a burning desire to do well.'

It was an odd thing to say, but he didn't elaborate. 'Anyway, I liked her,' I said to Mother, 'and you told me to choose carefully. Well, I have.'

Mother was, thankfully, too distracted with

other things to argue. 'Very well, if you insist. I will speak to her on Saturday morning.'

Our attention was drawn to the quiet click of the tall wooden gate that led into the kitchen gardens, and Will nodded respectfully before striding off down the drive. My brother rounded the corner of the house, calling out to his new hero, and that envy flickered again as Will turned, smiled at Lawrence, and waited for him to catch up. Mother frowned and started to protest at the way her son was behaving with the tradesman, and I hurriedly kissed Uncle Jack goodbye and went back indoors, wondering how long it would be before that breathtaking smile was once more directed at me. Wondering, too, about what Will had been about to say before Lawrence's arrival had stopped him.

My birthday party, and Lizzy's first day as my maid, blurred into a mess of riding, dressing, catching the envious eyes of family members – particularly the Wingfields – as they watched Uncle Jack hang the wretched blue diamond around my neck, and the relief that I had, without doubt, made the right choice in Lizzy. She was attentive, gentle and funny, and with a sharp intelligence that I already knew would question everything, weigh up the answers, and then reach her own conclusions anyway. A girl after my own heart, and, despite what Mother had said, I knew she would be a good friend.

Shortly afterwards, when all the fuss had died down, my thoughts turned once again to the man who had laughingly dubbed himself 'Lord William'. I tried to convince myself I'd been wrong about that path we were to travel, that he was a distraction, nothing more, but even as I acknowledged it I felt my heart squeeze a little at the thought of his hand on my wrist, his breath on my skin, and his voice, low and soft, speaking my name. Distraction or otherwise, the need to see him again was growing, and it was something I could not ignore.

It was market day in Breckenhall. Sitting in my room, looking out at the sunshine and at Lawrence larking about with our cousins on the tennis court, I knew I couldn't wait a moment longer, and changed into the plainest of my dresses, left a note for Lizzy and, unable to find anyone to drive me, I walked into town.

Despite my eagerness I moderated my pace, deliberately keeping my mind on banal things; diary appointments, the next time I might ride to hounds, and what to buy Lawrence for his birthday. As I drew closer to town, however, my feet began to overtake my patience, and when I began hearing the sounds of the busy market drifting down the road it was all I could do not to break into a run. Once in the square I steadied myself, feeling the heat in my skin that I tried to tell myself was just a result of my fast walk. Will was manning Mr Markham's stall, urging customers to go across to the shop before all the best cuts were sold, and after the first lurch of excitement at seeing him I held back and watched him. I enjoyed hearing the laughter of the crowds as he kept up a running line of banter, folding small bits of paper into intriguing shapes to give to the children. Word had spread from the delighted recipients to their friends, and there was a small queue waiting; I watched his hands, busy at work as he spoke to his customers, hardly sparing a glance downwards, utterly confident in his creations.

Eventually he looked around and saw me, and the look on his face jolted me severely. I had hoped for a smile, one of those grins that lit up his face, but he looked as if someone had reached into his chest and stolen his breath. His words faltered and he gave the crowd a distracted smile, but his eyes were pulled back to mine again immediately. I felt my own heart stuttering, and couldn't look away, no matter what propriety dictated. His patter faded and the small group dispersed, so I made my way over to the stall and, making sure he was still looking, stepped between the backdrop and the high wall of the town hall. A moment later he was there and before I had time to blink I was in his arms. *I'm no boy, Evie...* I knew it for certain when he held me, and the way he breathed my name made me tremble.

'Lord William,' I murmured in return, and felt him laugh. I pulled back and looked up into his face, suddenly shy. 'I didn't know if you... I mean–'

'Does this reassure you?' He lowered his face to kiss me, and the rest of the world slipped away to become nothing more than a background hum and a vague awareness of a breeze in my hair. Will's lips were gentle but firm as they moved over mine, and my mouth opened without any conscious decision on my part. Our hands moved restlessly as they sought a closer hold, and as the kiss deepened I felt the sharp, hard nip of his

46

teeth and returned it.

When we finally broke apart, both more than a little shaken by the intensity of the moment, he stepped back and raised a questioning eyebrow. With an effort, I remembered the question.

'Well, yes,' I said, a little breathlessly. 'That was very reassuring indeed.'

He smiled and leaned in for another kiss, a softer one this time, our lips barely brushing. 'Good.' Then he made a small sound of annoyance and glanced at his pocket watch. 'Frank will be over in a moment. Quick, when can I see you again?'

He peeked out from our hiding place to check both the stall and the imminent arrival of his employer, and I thought fast. 'I ride alone when I can. Up behind Oaklands and towards the quarry. I try to go out on Sundays, usually as soon as I've changed after church, and stay out until teatime if the weather's dry.'

Will touched my cheek and I leaned into his hand. 'Well, there's a rare bit of luck; Sundays are my afternoons off. I'll be waiting by the quarry after lunch.' He frowned slightly, but it was a happy kind of puzzlement. 'I know this is ridiculous, but I have the vague suspicion I might have fallen for you.'

'Ridiculous,' I agreed, but my eyes stayed on his and I felt the pull between us, impossible to ignore. I daren't press my lips to his again, for fear we'd become lost in time, so I let them linger against his jaw instead. It was almost as hard to break away. 'This has to be our secret, for a while at least.'

He nodded. 'It's not that I'm ashamed of you,'

he said solemnly, 'but, you know, a man of my social position has his reputation to consider.' I cuffed his arm and he smiled. 'Don't worry, I won't tell a soul.'

'One day we're going to be able to tell everyone and not think for one minute they wouldn't approve,' I said. 'Things are definitely changing.'

He studied me for a moment. 'I hope you're right, I honestly do. In the meantime, not a word, I promise.'

'Not a word,' I repeated, and he drew me close again, his hands locked in the small of my back, only the contented sigh stirring my hair telling me his happiness matched my own.

Five months later he was holding me again, but neither of us was happy.

Chapter Four

Breckenhall Quarry, January 1913.

On New Year's Eve, my worst fears about the Kalteng Star had come true. It had gone missing during the huge party mother had thrown, and although I'd fully believed in my own desire to be rid of it, the shock rippled through all of us. Mother was obviously distraught, although to others I knew she made a vast effort to appear coldly calm, and I felt the guilt lying over me like a terrible weight throughout the fruitless search.

But in the end the blame had fallen squarely on

Lizzy, and nothing we had been able to do had persuaded the jury otherwise. The so-called evidence had built and built, and I had watched even her fiery determination crumple in the face of it, until she stood, shaking and helpless while they delivered the verdict.

Mary Deegan, who had formed a closeness with Lizzy from her first day, had defied etiquette and put her arm around me as the words fell like rocks into the silence, and Lizzy had looked back at us both as they'd taken her down. Her face was white and stunned, her eyes looked bigger and bluer than ever in contrast as she no doubt prayed for a last minute intervention, and then she was gone, to begin a ten-year prison sentence in Holloway Women's Prison, London.

We returned to Oaklands in silence. Mary was fighting tears but she wouldn't let them fall in front of me. That was another way in which she and Lizzy were different; had it been the other way around I know Lizzy would have been unable to control her distress. But I could tell Mary wanted to be alone, and so, after a brief word of mutual comfort, and a heartfelt promise to do everything I could to get Lizzy freed, I let her go and went to my own rooms to try and make sense of what had happened.

I had not gone downstairs at all that night, and Mother had not tried to persuade me. She too was in a state of shock, but for her it was more to do with the loss of the Kalteng Star than the terrible injustice that had befallen my friend. She told me Ruth would take up Lizzy's position first thing in the morning and I nodded, too wrung out to argue. I fell into bed, and lay awake with burning eyes until the early hours, wondering what Lizzy was doing and if she was all right.

When I awoke from a shallow and unsatisfactory sleep, I had taken advantage of the fact that I was temporarily without a formal maid to leave the house unnoticed. I asked the stable-boy Billy to saddle Orion, and rode up to the quarry. Even though it wasn't a Sunday I knew Will would not let me down. Sure enough he was there, and clearly had been for some time; he was freezing cold and shivering in the biting January wind, and came down the hill to meet me. I slid off Orion and into his arms, and we clung together, leaning into the buffeting wind while I wept out all the anger and despair I'd kept hidden in front of everyone else. When I eventually wiped my eyes, he took my hand and we walked in silence up the hill, over the wet grass, to the big rock at the top.

'I'm so sorry I wasn't there yesterday,' he said as we sat down, heedless of the puddles in the uneven surface. 'Markham said he wanted to go to support Ruth, if you ever did, and someone had to keep the shop open.'

I shook my head, dismissing the apology. 'I knew that diamond was going to cause upset. I told Lizzy so myself the night I got it.'

'Who do you think really stole it?'

'I have no idea. I would suspect the Wingfield boys if they hadn't been seen elsewhere at the time.'

'What about their mother, Clarissa, isn't it?'

'She was questioned by the police, and lots of people saw her too.' I sighed; it had all been going

50

around and around in my head for so long I was dizzy with it. 'I'm going to write to Uncle Jack as soon as I get home. He works for the government, he must be able to do something.'

'Darling, he's a diplomat, he's not part of the–'

'It doesn't matter! I have to do something!'

Will pulled me against him and tucked my head beneath his chin. 'I'm sorry. Yes, you're right, he might at least know someone who can help.'

'We have to try everything,' I said, and I felt him nodding.

'We will.' He paused, then went on, 'Evie, I know she's closer to you than your own family, but trying to absorb Lizzy's unhappiness won't ease it for her. Can you imagine how cross she'd be if she knew you were spending your days worrying and crying over something you have no power to change?'

I drew back, suspicious. He sounded awfully selfish, and it surprised and unsettled me. He frowned, then realised what was going through my mind and shook his head. 'I'm not suggesting you forget about her, that you ignore your feelings or that you be cheerful for anyone's sake but your own, and hers. All I'm saying is that, when you write to her, you hold on to that determination we all love about you, and don't show her a moment's doubt. Do your crying with me, cry all the time if you need to.' He touched my cheek, and his face was earnest, and more than a little helpless. 'I don't want to see you sad, but if you must be sad with someone, let it always be me.'

That afternoon when I returned home, I wrote to

Uncle Jack, and then to Lizzy, keeping Will's words in mind and forcing my determined cheerfulness onto the paper.

'Dearest Lizzy.

I have written to Uncle Jack in the hopes he may help secure your release, I don't know how, but he does seem to know some terribly important people. I await his response, but will write to you immediately as soon as I hear he is on his way, for I am sure he soon will be!

Yr loving friend,
Evie.'

As I reread the words before sliding the paper into the waiting envelope, I felt them wrap themselves around the despair in my heart and soothe it; there was nothing more I could do, but Uncle Jack would ride to the rescue, there was no question about it. Lizzy's fate now lay in his hands, and my own rested in mine and Will's; it had come as a breathtaking shock to discover how suddenly everything could change, and I realised I must treasure every fleeting and fragile moment of joy while it was still within reach.

The spring of 1913 was dull and wet, and gave way to an equally dull, but dry summer. Will and I continued to meet each Sunday; it was difficult to find any more time since mother had realised I would soon be turning nineteen, and was in danger of becoming the spinster of the parish. Of course, the loss of the Kalteng Star was having an effect on the number of potential husbands that crossed the threshold of Oaklands Manor, but there were still plenty for Mother to urge in my direction, and to question me over after I had returned from whichever dinner or party I had been whisked away to.

I played my part, of course. I danced with fathers, spoke glowingly to mothers of their sons' fine qualities, befriended sisters and curtseyed to grandmothers. I laughed with suitors and allowed a brief brush of lips on my gloved hand when we parted, and told Mother I'd had a wonderful time and would very much like to see that young man again. Then I went to my room, dismissed Ruth, and lay in the dark thinking of Will.

The day after a particularly excruciating party was a Sunday, and despite a strong breeze it was a rare sunny one. With Orion loosely tethered to a bush and munching at the grass, I climbed onto the high rock and looked across the valley to see Will, striding up over the hill with that eagerness he never tried to hide. His dark hair blew back from his face, showing strong, clean lines of jaw and cheekbone, and I enjoyed watching the unconsciously graceful ease with which he moved across the uneven ground towards me.

I stood up and waved, the wind whipping at my skirts and threatening to tug me right off the rock, and he shouted at me to sit down before something awful happened but instead I began to dance from foot to foot, just to make him walk faster. It worked; he began to run, laughing, until he was able to spring up beside me and press his smiling mouth to mine.

He tasted cold and fresh after his walk, and his

skin was flushed with good health and contentment. I could tell he was going to say something momentous and romantic, and I waited with impatient and growing anticipation, while he searched for the right words.

Eventually he took my hand, and fixed his eyes tenderly on mine. 'You've got a hole in your jacket.'

I blinked at him, then gave him a look of mock annoyance. 'And here I was thinking you were about to declare your endless devotion.'

'Oh, that too,' he said with a grin, and tugged my hair gently. 'Ruth not up to Lizzy's standard then?' My humour faded, and I sat down. He sat beside me and put an arm around my shoulder. 'I'm sorry,' he said. 'I didn't mean to remind you.'

'It's never far from my mind anyway. I do wish Uncle Jack would write back, no one's heard from him since the turn of the year.'

'Do you think he'll be able to help?'

'I'm sure he will. He must be owed a favour or two, after all he's always shooting off at a moment's notice and it can't be all his own choice.'

'And Ruth?' He waggled his finger through the hole in my jacket pocket.

'She's a disaster, of course. She might have been a good kitchen maid but her skills don't extend any further than that, and she doesn't seem at all disposed to learning. She doesn't have Lizzy's deftness of touch, and doesn't notice when something needs doing. I have to ask her half a dozen times at least.'

He grinned at my grumpy tone. 'But is she as

cold as ever?'

'More so, I would say.' But I didn't want to waste our time talking about Ruth. 'I'm thinking of telling Mother I don't want a maid at all.'

'You'd want one if Lizzy was still here,' he pointed out.

'She was very good, but I miss her friendship more than her skill with a needle. Besides, I can dress myself. And,' I added drily, 'I could mend my own clothes a sight better than Ruth Wilkins. I can't help feeling it's time to let go of all that nonsense.'

'So you're still convinced everything is going to change,' Will said, staring out over the hills. Then he swung back to face me and stared at me closely. I was ready for him to tell me I had a smudge on my nose, or a leaf in my hair, but instead he said, 'I want to marry you, Evie. One day. When we can, without upsetting your family. Will you let me?'

I felt a smile creep across my face and saw it answered in his own. 'Never mind my family,' I said, 'it's not them you're marrying.'

'What sort of an answer is that?'

'It's a resounding, thunderous yes!' I stood up again and cupped my hands to my mouth, bellowing down the valley in a most unladylike manner, 'Mother, can you hear this? I'm going to marry the butcher's boy!'

I turned back, still laughing, but Will had stood too, and was looking at me oddly. He folded his arms across his chest, tucking his hands into his armpits, but it seemed less as a way of keeping warm than of keeping his distance.

My own laughter died. 'What is it?'

55

'Why did you say "yes", Evie?' he asked quietly, his words almost whipped away in the summer wind.

'What do you mean? I said it because I want to marry you!'

He blew out a breath and looked down at his feet, and I could see he was struggling with something he didn't want to say aloud, but felt he must. Eventually he looked back at me, and there was a confused kind of hope in his expression.

'Are you sure you're not saying it just to upset the apple cart, and you'll change your mind later?'

'No! Why ever would you ask such a thing?'

'In the market, when I gave you the rose, I thought it was sweet and funny that you put it in your hat-band and said it would annoy your mother. I told myself it was because you were, I don't know...' he shrugged, embarrassed, 'a little bit moved, maybe, and couldn't think of anything else to say.'

'I was! That was exactly it. Will, don't–'

'No, listen. Just now, when you agreed to marry me, shouldn't your first reaction have been to come to me? To kiss me? But no, you stood up and, well yes, *gloated* that you were going to marry the butcher's boy. Not me, not Will Davies. The "butcher's boy".'

Remorse struck me as I stared at him, at his usually open, cheerful face, now tight-jawed and frowning. I couldn't blame him for his anger. I wanted to go to him, as I should have done before but it would just look false now – it was far too late. I simply didn't know what to do.

I looked at him helplessly, hoping my regret

would show through my wordless inability to move. He looked back, his face pale, his own silence begging me to contradict what he'd said, but I couldn't find anything big enough, and significant enough, to say. The feelings were swelling inside me, but they couldn't find a way to be expressed. Eventually I found a tiny voice and managed, 'Do you still want to marry me?'

He let his arms drop, but he didn't hold them out to invite me closer. 'Of course I do,' he said, gently enough, then went on in a firmer voice, 'but I won't be your toy, a means of annoyance to your mother.' He shook his head, his expression touched with exasperation now. 'I don't understand you sometimes. You clearly love her, but you have this need to push her to the limit of her endurance. I can't just be another weapon in your armoury.'

That stung. 'This is about you and me, Will, no one else.'

'And what of your mother?'

'Well, of course I love her, even though she's sometimes hard to love.' I saw a way to convince him then, and hurried on: 'And yet I'm prepared to risk hurting her to be with you. Doesn't that tell you all you need to know?'

'You torment her at every chance,' he pointed out, but he had softened his stance and now took a hesitant step closer. 'Look, I know you've always been a bit of a tearaway, but you're growing up fast, and Lady Creswell needs to get to know the young lady you've become. She'll never like me, I understand that, but when she sees you're serious she might give us her blessing.'

I shook my head. 'She won't. And it's not because of who you are, because if she knew you she would love you as much as I do. It's because of who you're not.'

He slumped a little then, but my words seemed to reach him and he accepted my tentative embrace. We stood for a while, on top of the rock, while our first ever moments of discord gradually slipped away into the breeze, and began to appreciate, once more, this precious time alone together.

I ran a finger over the back of one of his hands, noting the slender strength of his fingers and remembering their dexterity with the paper sculptures. 'You never did tell me: how did you end up working for Mr Markham? And what do you want to do, really?'

'I suppose if you're going to marry me you ought to know something about me,' he conceded. 'I have no deep, dark secrets, but you're right, butchery was never my first choice.' He jumped off the rock and turned to me, hands outstretched to help, but I'd been jumping off this rock for years and, with a withering look at him, I managed it quite well again today without his help. He grinned and took my hand, tucking it around his arm as we walked up towards the big quarry pit that lay over the hill.

'Dad wanted me to take over the business. He worked seven days a week, but that wasn't why I left, I've never been afraid of a full working life. I just felt as if I had no time to do what I loved most: sculpting wood.'

I should have expected this; his eye for crafting

beautiful things was clearly echoed in the skill of his hands. 'I had a friend,' he went on. 'Nathan. He lived in Blackpool too, but he had family in Breckenhall. Quite well off, I think. We both shared this...' he looked down at his free hand and flexed the fingers reflectively, 'this need to create, I suppose.' He glanced down at me, a little embarrassed, a little defiant.

'Go on,' I said, delighted to be learning about him at last. 'Where is Nathan now? Oh, and what was the family business you couldn't wait to get away from?'

Will stopped and withdrew his arm from mine to shove his hands in his pockets. 'You'll laugh.'

'I won't, I promise.'

'Cross your heart?'

'Absolutely. I will not laugh.'

His eyes narrowed in warning, then he shrugged. 'All right. It was a butcher's shop.'

I bit my lip, but it was no good, and although I didn't laugh outright I did feel a wide smile on my face that made him roll his eyes, pull my hat down over my ears and stalk off. I chased him, letting the giggles out at last, and caught his hand. 'Wait! I want to hear the rest!'

'I'll tell you the rest if you promise not to say the word "butcher" to me once more today.'

'I promise,' I said again, with the proper solemnity, and he sighed.

'Might as well get the grass to promise not to grow,' he grumbled. 'Anyway, Nathan was – is – an artist. A proper artist, not like me; I just like to make things, but he's a painter.'

'I don't see why that makes you less than a

'"proper" artist,' I protested.

Will shook his head. 'He had *real* talent, everyone said so. He was offered a studio here in Breckenhall, one of his family left it to him. So he asked me if I wanted to leave Blackpool, come here and set up with him in business. He would take commissions, I would work on my carvings and sculptures, and we would sell them at the market.' He shrugged again. 'It all sounded wonderful. I was just in the way at home, anyway.'

'In the way? How could you be?'

'I'm the youngest of five. There were plenty of others to take my place beside Dad.'

I tried to imagine how anyone could make him feel anything less than special, but I couldn't begin to. 'So the two of you came to Breckenhall, set up your studio, and what happened then?'

'Nathan's dream carried us for a while. I sold a few pieces and we set ourselves up using our savings. But we'd not thought it through really; frames, oils, canvas, brushes ... it all cost much more money than we'd allowed for.'

'But you owned the studio outright?'

'Yes. We partitioned it off and slept in one half, worked in the other. It was fun, those few years,' Will said, smiling in remembrance. 'We got on well, and we were able to spend all our time doing the thing we each loved the most. I was able to get by without spending too much on equipment; I walked to the forest and gathered hardwoods there, so all I had to do was keep my blades sharp. And eat and keep warm, of course.'

I wished I'd known him then, it gave me an odd feeling to think he'd been there all this time, I'd probably even seen him selling his carvings in the market without noticing him ... it didn't seem possible now. 'Sounds heavenly,' I said.

'Well, I knew things were difficult, but I thought we were muddling through. Then one day Nathan stayed up late to finish a project he was working on, and when I woke up I found a note. He'd gone.'

'Gone? Where?'

Will shrugged. 'Just ... gone. He'd been struggling for a long time, borrowing from friends and family, until he found himself in so much debt he couldn't pay it back. Not even his family could help. I had no idea things were so bad.'

'What about the studio?' I said, aghast, 'Couldn't you sell that?'

'He'd already sold it, without telling me, and now I owed rent to the new owners.'

'What on earth did you do?'

'I sold everything I could to pay the back rent, found a smaller room above the fruit shop, and just when I thought I would have to go back to Blackpool with my tail between my legs, I saw the note in Frank Markham's window.' He looked at his hands again and gave a rueful laugh. 'It seemed I'd learned more from my father than I thought, Markham was very impressed despite my "advanced age". He gave me the job there and then.'

'Well, thank goodness he did,' I said, 'or I'd never have met you.'

Will stopped and turned me to face him. 'Thank goodness,' he echoed, and I stood very still, breathless, thinking how close I had come to driving him away with my childish need to provoke my mother.

'I'm sorry,' I blurted. 'You had every right to be angry.'

'I wasn't–'

'Yes, you were.'

He smiled, suddenly. 'Yes, I was. Bloody angry, actually. There was I, baring my soul to you, and all you can do is start yelling down the valley.'

'Sorry,' I said again, then gave him my wickedest grin. 'You do look very handsome when you're angry though, I must remember that. Perhaps I should begin a list of all the things that make you cross.'

He growled, and lunged for me, but I danced back out of reach and sat down on the grass. 'You're so easy-going, what *does* make you angry?'

'Apart from young ladies reacting incorrectly to proposals of marriage?'

'Apart from that, yes.'

He sat next to me, and pretended to consider. 'Grown-ups sulking,' he said at last. 'I find that more annoying than almost anything.'

I lay back and rolled over, letting out the biggest, grumpiest sigh I could manage. He chuckled, and I felt his hand on my back, but although I smiled into the crook of my elbow I didn't roll over. I liked the feeling of the persistent rubbing of his hand through the thin material of my dress, and as he lifted the hair away from the nape of my neck I knew what would happen next. Sure enough, his lips touched the newly exposed and tender skin and I bit my arm to keep from letting out a sigh of pleasure; I wasn't ready for this to end yet, and as I gave another grunt of feigned annoyance I felt his mouth curve against my neck in a smile that I knew would be wide and beautiful.

'I'm getting very angry now,' he whispered, and the warmth of his breath sent a shock of longing through me that I wasn't prepared for. My play-acting ceased immediately and I lay very still, aware of the heat of his hand at my shoulder, and of the cool shade of his body. He kissed my neck again, and his hand moved gently down my side to cup my hip, then roll me gently towards him, brushing across my body to rest at my waist. I found myself unable to speak, but it didn't matter; his face blocked out the sun, and as his lips touched mine, I knew this time things were different.

Our afternoons had always held the *frisson* of forbidden pleasure, and, while I knew the attraction between us had been growing, I had never, until now, felt the almost painful need to take our innocent kisses any further. Now, as he drew back and looked down at me, his breathing suddenly shallow, I felt a sweet, tugging sensation in the pit of my stomach that grew stronger the more I studied him. I noticed every single thing about him; the way his hair flopped untidily across his brow; the stray lash that lay beside his left eye; the slightly reddened skin along his jaw where he'd shaved in a hurry before coming out to meet me. I felt his hand slide up from my waist and across my ribcage to lie tentatively beneath my breast, and then his thumb moved to caress the swell there and he closed his eyes.

I kept mine open. His collar was open in the August warmth, and I saw the muscles move in the strong, smooth column of his throat, and the pulse beating rapidly below the angle of his jaw. I smelled grass and soap, the faint tang of moorland animals, and my own light perfume, all mingling in the dry air, and then his mouth was on mine and as my lips parted I felt him sigh against me, and I was lost.

I came to only moments later. Will jerked away from me as if I had slapped him, and I stared up at him in mortified astonishment before realising he had not moved voluntarily. A tall shadow fell over us both, and even as I recognised the angry face of my cousin David Wingfield, Will rolled away from me and came to his feet. Before he had gained his balance David shoved at him and he stumbled back, but recovered in time to deflect a blow that would otherwise have crashed into the side of his head. His own fist came up with a short, quick motion and connected with David's jaw, and from where I lay I could see David go sprawling backwards.

Will turned back to me, stunned, and crouched down. 'Darling, I'm so sorry, are you all right?'

'What on earth is going on?' I said, putting my hand in his.

He pulled me to my feet. 'I have no idea why he's here, but you'd better–'

Before he could finish, David's foot rammed into the back of his knee and he staggered into me, carrying me back to the ground with a grunt, and my teeth clacked together painfully. He only just avoided landing on top of me by rolling onto his side and, off-balance and worried about me, he failed to move out of the way quickly enough and David's next kick took him below the breast-bone, knocking the breath from his body. He slumped, gasping, but the next time David's foot flew out he caught it and tugged hard, spilling David onto his back again.

Will climbed to his feet, pale and still dragging painful breaths, and waited until David was up-right again before advancing with his fists ready. I stared at them both, dizzy with the suddenness with which everything had changed, and wanting to go to Will and make sure he was all right. But he was completely focused on David now, and as David lunged, he easily dodged and clipped David on the point of his chin.

I watched, my heart slowing as the panic eased; Will was older, and easily the most agile and stronger of the two, and, despite the bruising kick, he was breathing more easily now. I wondered what had brought David up to the quarry in the first place, and, hot on the heels of that came the more urgent question: how could we prevent him from telling everyone what he had seen?

The two circled one another like wolves, the twenty-six-year-old and the seventeen-year-old, but David had already lost and we all three knew it. He eyed Will warily; Will had pushed his sleeves back to reveal forearms made strong by the hard work he did six and a half days out of seven, and the muscles flexed beneath his skin as he tightened and relaxed his fists. There was a gleam of sweat along his brow, and his eyes flashed bright blue in the sunlight, but now they weren't friendly at all.

David cleared his throat and stepped back, dropping his hands back to his sides, an act I reluctantly admitted took courage. Defiantly, he raised his chin and I could see the red mark that would bruise nicely later. 'I'll have you arrested if I catch you anywhere near Miss Creswell again.' His gaze flicked to me, and although I was quite respectably dressed I felt as if Will's warm hands had left blazing prints all across my summer dress, and that they must have shown. Then he looked back at Will, clearly relieved as Will also dropped his guard and assumed a more relaxed position.

David's tone turned rather snooty and I lost the fleeting sympathy I'd felt. 'Who are you, anyway? No gentleman, that's for sure. A gentleman would never assault a lady while she was out riding.'

'What do you want, David?' I said, moving to Will's side. 'Just say what you came for and then leave.'

'I came to see you, as a matter of fact,' he said. 'Your mother invited me to dinner.'

Whatever I had been expecting, it wasn't that. 'What on earth for? And how did you know where I was?'

'Everyone knows where you come to get away from everything, even your stable-hand. It's a good thing I came, if you ask me, another few minutes and that low-born thug might have done anything!'

'Watch who you're calling a thug,' Will said with deceptive mildness, but I saw him tensing up again.

David did too, and stepped back, his voice betraying his nervousness. 'Whatever you claim to be the case, you cannot deny I came along just in time,' he said. Privately I couldn't help agreeing, but for a very different reason. I found my eyes drawn once more to the muscular arms that brushed mine as we stood side by side, and knew that if they were around me right this minute I would have surrendered everything, wholly and without a second thought.

'Are you going to tell anyone what you've seen?' I wanted to know.

'Well now, I don't know what I've seen, do I?' David looked cunning suddenly, and I wanted to slap him. 'It's hardly your fault if some ruffian attacks you while you're sleeping in the sun.'

Will and I looked at each other, and I could see he was going to admit to exactly that, if it meant maintaining our secret for my sake. I spoke quickly, before he could. 'That isn't what happened, David, you know it isn't.'

'Evie–' Will began.

'No, it's not and you can't pretend it is either. You'll lose your job and Mr ... your employer will suffer too,' I said, almost naming Markham in my hurry to make my point. Mother would be certain to discover who Will was, and that would be the last time he or Markham would be delivering to Oaklands. Not to mention Will's reputation being torn to shreds. I could not allow that.

I turned back to David, who was glancing from me to Will and back again. 'David, I know you're going to run back to your mother and tell her what you saw, but you need to know that won't make any difference at all.'

'Any difference to what?'

'To us.' I slipped my hand into Will's and, after a glance of mingled exasperation and pride, he raised it to his lips. 'Nor to what you came here for,' I added, and David flushed.

'I merely came to dinner,' he reminded me. 'At the invitation of your mother.'

'And the instigation of yours,' I said acidly. 'She must be quite sure I will get the Kalteng Star back one day, and what better way to ensure it goes back to the Wingfields than if you and I were to marry?'

'The diamond is gone,' he protested, but there was no conviction behind his words; he clearly believed the same as his mother, that Lizzy would soon break under the terrible conditions inside Holloway, and tell someone where she had hidden it. Except I knew she hadn't taken it to begin with, and with any luck we would never see it again.

'Then Clarissa won't be too disappointed to learn that I have no intention of joining our two families again,' I said.

'Aren't you two related anyway?' Will said.

'Only distantly. David's great-grandmother was my great-aunt Catherine.'

'So it's legal for you to wed?'

'Legal, but not in the least desirable,' I said, 'particularly after the way he helped convict Lizzy.'

'I simply came to dinner,' he repeated stubbornly. 'Please allow me to escort you back, Miss Creswell.'

'I have Orion,' I reminded him, profoundly grateful for the excuse. 'And it's nowhere near time to eat yet. At least Mrs Hannah will have plenty of notice of your cancellation.'

David's jaw dropped. 'Are you refusing me the hospitality offered by Lady Creswell?'

'Not at all. Do stay, if you wish. I hope you enjoy talking to Mother.'

'Won't you be there?'

I smiled sweetly. 'I expect I shall have a head-ache later. It's probably best if I take a tray in my room.'

Will's hand tightened on mine as he choked back a laugh, and I gripped hard in return. David looked at us both, searching for a way to save face. In the end he simply turned on his heel and strode off down the hill, no doubt aware of the picture of dignity he made. This was spoiled slightly as he had to take a sudden side-step to avoid the in-evitable sheeps' leavings, and his ankle turned; his disappearing silhouette cut a rather less dashing figure from that moment on. Will and I leaned on each other in relief at being alone again.

'Do you really think your two mothers are conspiring to have you married off?' Will said. I was glad of the distraction, even if it meant discussing such an unsavoury thought; I was too conscious of the silence, of the peace that had fallen over us, and of the heat of his body.

'The Kalteng Star does funny things to people's minds,' I said. 'I wouldn't be at all surprised.'

'But, as you said, it's gone. We don't know who stole it, and it's fairly certain you'll never get it back.'

'Thank goodness, although Clarissa must think differently.' I realised something then, and smiled. 'Do you know, Lord William, that never once in all the time I have known and loved you, did it occur to me that you might have had your head turned by it too?'

He gave me an amused look; it had obviously never occurred to him either. 'Not even when I told you how much I'd struggled before, to make a living from sculpting?'

'Not even then. Besides, you're here with me now even though I don't have that fortune any longer.'

'You're still a very wealthy young woman,' he pointed out. 'Although the first time we saw each other I think we both knew we would be standing together one day. That was back when I thought you were kitchen staff at Oaklands, of course.'

'But I knew who you were.'

He put his arm around my shoulder. 'And it didn't make any difference to you, so why should it to me? The way I see it, loving you comes with a great deal more complication than loving me could ever do.'

'You're right,' I said a little glumly, making him smile. 'You have my sympathies. Promise you'll never give up on me?'

'I promise. I only hope David is too embarrassed to tell his mother, or yours, what he saw up here.'

I had to speak of it, now the moment had passed and I felt safe from my own unexpectedly fierce desire. 'Will, about before, when David found us–'

'I'm not going to tell you I'm sorry,' he interrupted, but I shook my head.

'But we can't ... you know. We shouldn't. And today I felt...' I was struggling to find the words, but he was there with his own and, as always, they cut straight to the heart of things.

'Only a word from you would have stopped

me.' He held my shoulders and ducked down so his eyes were level with mine and there was no hiding. 'And you wouldn't have said that word, would you?'

'No,' I confessed in a small voice. What did that make me? But the sudden, brilliant smile on his face banished the question and replaced it with the knowledge that it simply meant that this man and myself were meant to be together. As we'd both known from the start.

'Come on,' he said, tugging my hand, 'it's almost time you were back home.'

'Just a bit longer?' I pleaded. Despite the faintly tainted atmosphere that drifted around what had, for so long, been our private haven, it was such a heavenly day I hated to think it must end, and that I wouldn't see Will again for a whole week. He was breath and life to me now, how had I survived so long without him? Soon it would be even longer between chances; the year was aging rapidly and there were few places we could meet without risk.

'Just a few minutes then.' He made it sound as though he were doing me the greatest turn, but his eagerness to sit down and draw me down next to him gave him away. I smiled and looked down the hill towards Oaklands Manor. Beautiful it might be, bathed in the reddish gold of the late afternoon sun, but I couldn't wait for the day when I could move out and set up home with Will.

As if he could read my mind, he slipped his hand into mine. 'Don't you think we ought to set a date then?'

'What about my mother?'

'Tell her, or don't. Only you can decide, but

71

you'd better decide quickly.'

'Oh there you go again, getting all cross and handsome.'

He scowled and turned to press me down into the grass, and kissed me until I could barely breathe.

'God, Evie ... I can't wait much longer.' He rolled away to lie staring up at the sky.

I understood he was not blaming me and suddenly, out of nowhere, I whispered, 'Then let's not wait.' I immediately panicked when he looked at me long and consideringly, and wished I hadn't said it. It would be unfair of me to change my mind now, and I wasn't even sure I'd be able to, but I felt a churning, nervous wariness at the thought of what I had suggested.

His finger traced a gentle line from my temple to my jaw. 'Listen. I love you desperately, and you know I want you, but this shouldn't be something we may someday come to regret. It's too precious.'

I nodded, part of me relieved, the rest aching like never before, and lay back down, close to his side, reluctant to break contact. 'Then let's do something else. Something exciting.'

He gave a soft laugh. 'Such as what?'

'Go somewhere. Away from Breckenhall, somewhere where people aren't interested in us, and we don't have to pretend we're not mad about each other.'

'Are you mad about me?' he teased.

'Yes, but only a little bit.'

Still smiling, he twisted towards me and kissed me. It did little to dispel the sense of longing but I couldn't help smiling in return, and returned his kiss with renewed enthusiasm; now we had agreed to wait, it felt safe to do so. As we broke apart I felt his strong white teeth tug gently at my lower lip, and it was difficult not to pull him close again. 'So,' he said, in a voice that had turned faintly husky. He cleared his throat and tried again. 'You think we should go somewhere we can walk together and hold hands, right in front of everyone?'

'It sounds silly when you say it like that, but don't you think it would be wonderful? We could go to the seaside–'

'The weather won't last more than another few days.'

'Then we'll go as soon as we can. We can take a picnic lunch.'

Will sat up. 'Why don't we go to Blackpool?'

'Blackpool?' I tried not to sound disappointed; it was his home town, after all. But I'd hoped for somewhere a little more romantic.

'Do you remember last year, when they lit it all up? Absolutely thousands of lights. For Princess Louise when she opened the promenade.'

'Oh, yes, Ava Cartwright was there with her aunt. She did say it was beautiful,' I conceded.

'Well, Frank told me yesterday they were so successful, they plan on doing it again this year.'

I nodded, warming to the idea. It didn't really matter where we were, after all, provided we were together. 'All right, we can travel separately, but on the same train, then spend the day and evening at the Pleasure Beach. We'll see the lights, then be home before anyone's even noticed.'

'I'm not sure when I'll be able to get away, but I'll try.'

'You're looking a bit peaky,' I said, putting a solicitous hand on his forehead.'

He affected a look of deep suffering. 'I believe you're right. I feel a rather uncomfortable sickness coming on. Possibly in a few days.'

I laughed. 'How will I know when you're going to be laid up with this awful illness?'

'I'll leave a message in the summer house, as long as Mr Shackleton's not looking.'

'He spends most of his time in the sheds at this time of year,' I said. 'I'll check the summer house every day. Now I believe it's time to return, and face the rather off-key music that's waiting to accompany dinner.'

David had left before I returned, declining dinner on the grounds that the walk in the sun had left him with a headache. I couldn't help feeling cheated that he had appropriated my own excuse, and I was forced to dine *en famille* after all. Dinner was an awkward and silent affair; Mother kept looking at me narrowly, no doubt she had seen the blossoming bruise on David's chin, and noted how he favoured his right ankle as he walked, and she clearly suspected I had something to do with both. Quite what she thought I had done, I didn't know, but those looks across the table were enough to convince me she had her notions anyway.

I missed Uncle Jack more than ever that evening; he was always the one to keep up a lively conversation and to dampen any signs of discord. I missed his gentle teasing, and the way he would coax Mother, in even the most morose of her moods, into a reluctant smile that made her beautiful and familiar again. He hadn't been home since New Year's Eve, almost nine months ago, and I was once more growing worried about Lizzy; the days were flying by for me, but every day she spent in that awful place must feel like a week. Mother clearly felt Jack's absence almost as keenly as I did and I wondered, not for the first time, if the two of them were closer than they had led us to believe. I fervently hoped they were; there was no one I would rather have as a step-father than Jack Carlisle.

Lawrence sensed the tension in the silence and kept raising his eyebrows at me, but I studiously ignored him, and he pouted when he realised he was being left out of something yet again. Subsequently he requested to leave the table the moment his last forkful was taken, and to avoid the inevitable questions I did the same. But Mother took the rare step of coming to find me later.

'Evangeline,' she said, sitting down at my dressing table without being asked. I felt my stomach turn over nervously; she never came to my rooms unless it was something serious, the last time had been the day the diamond had gone missing.

'If this is about David–'

'Darling, I understand. I do. It can't be easy for you.'

'Easy?'

'But you mustn't worry. If you didn't actually ... if he didn't...'

'Didn't what?' I knew, of course. I just wanted to see how much David had told her.

'If you were both still fully clothed,' she said in

75

a rush, her face looking as hot as mine felt.

I chose to misunderstand, just in case. 'Why would either David or myself be otherwise?'

'Not David!' Mother tensed further as she realised she'd have to explain. 'The other young man. Were you both dressed when David found you?'

Relief welled up, and the dark thoughts about how she would react were swept aside. 'We were,' I said. 'Nothing happened, and I'm very very happy.'

She looked a little surprised at my sudden change in temperament, but she smiled. 'Then so am I.'

I bent to put my arms around her, and when she hugged me in return all the years fell away, and I was a little girl again and my mother loved me even though I was such an effort for her. I felt horrible for assuming she would rather see me unhappy than wed to the man I loved.

'You should have told me,' she said, her voice muffled against my shoulder. 'I wanted you to tell me yourself, and waited for it. I'm so sad you felt you couldn't.'

'I didn't think you'd understand,' I confessed. 'It was hard to know where to begin.'

'Of course I understand, darling, you mustn't feel at fault. Now, what did he look like?'

I stepped back, with the prickling suspicion that all was not well after all. 'What did who look like?'

'David would only describe him as a thuggish sort of a man, with messy hair and a fierce look in his eyes. Blue eyes, he says, which may help but not much. I gather there was quite a struggle

76

so he might be bruised as well. We must call Inspector Bailey of course. And you're to stop riding out alone.'

I couldn't speak. Quite aside from the exaggeration about Will's appearance, and the 'struggle', I couldn't believe David had told that story after all, it would achieve nothing. Was it simply revenge?

'Mother, what David told you is a lie,' I said at last.

'I beg your pardon?' It was only then that I saw she had been battling her own emotions, and there were tears in her eyes for my presumed suffering. I could have wept myself, the one time we had found a kind of bond in far too long, and now I must shatter it again. I felt a fleeting urge to allow her mistaken belief to continue, just to maintain that bond, but it wasn't fair on Will.

'I wasn't being attacked,' I said, 'I was lying down with ... with a man. We *were* dressed,' I added quickly, as the colour drained from her face. 'We were kissing. But that's all we were doing. I promise, it was nothing more–'

'Who was it?' Her voice was flat, and my own anger kindled.

'It doesn't matter. It's someone who makes me happy and who loves me as much as I love him. But he's not of "our class", so I already know what you're going to say.'

'Who?' she repeated.

'I'm not going to tell you,' I said, trying to sound stubborn, but instead I heard pleading in my tone. 'Mother, I don't want to upset you, but–'

'Upset me?' She rose, smoothing down her skirts

with shaking hands. 'I don't know what makes you think you can upset me now. Letting your maid steal our family's fortune, your own birthright, *that* upset me. This?' She gestured blithely, but her jaw was tight. 'This is nothing. It will pass.' But she paused at the door, and her tone softened a little. 'I assume he's a handsome boy?'

Man, I wanted to say, but didn't. 'Some would say so.'

'Then be careful. A boy's demeanour rarely matches a pleasant appearance, and the handsome ones are often the cause of more heartache than the plain ones.' Her expression turned reflective for a moment, and I wondered again about her and Uncle Jack. Then she shook the thoughts away. 'Don't forget your choices are more limited now you have lost the Kalteng Star.'

'I didn't lose it, it was stolen. And W ... he's never been interested in my fortune. Even when I still had the diamond.'

She looked startled. 'How long have you and this boy been courting?'

'We met in the spring. But have only properly become close since the end of last summer. *After* my birthday,' I added pointedly.

She came back in, and a shadow of that bond I had wanted to prolong reappeared as she took my hand. 'Sweetheart, I'm sorry. I assumed this was some fleeting bit of nonsense, some momentary loss of control.' I remembered how close that had been to the truth, but again held my tongue.

Mother squeezed my hand. 'I don't want you to be unhappy, of course I don't. And this sounds terribly old-fashioned and you'll hate it, but thanks to the terms of John Creswell's will, the future of our family depends on your match, not Lawrence's. You will never be asked to marry against your wishes, but if the Kalteng Star is ever returned to us, then whoever you *have* married must be worthy of it. You do understand?'

'Yes,' I said. Better to let her think she had convinced me, and to keep her warmth and sympathy, than to lose everything. But I was not going to give in entirely, even on the surface. 'I won't marry David Wingfield though.'

Mother looked at me for a moment, with pursed lips. 'Our two families make poor enemies,' she said at last. 'I've always known that. However, you will not find me pushing the matter any further. It was Clarissa who suggested this advance of his, not me.'

'Is that your way of trying to say you don't blame me?'

A reluctant smile crossed her lips and I loved her again, in that moment. She leaned in close and whispered, 'He's a terrible little oik, and his mother's frightful.'

She smiled again as she opened the door, and now there was an understanding between us that I could feel all the way across the room. Will was right; I was no longer a wayward, rebellious child with too much energy and too little patience, I was a woman, as Mother was, and she was ready now to help me find my way through the often dark and frightening maze of adult relationships and obligations.

There was a touching similarity between this acceptance, and when Will and I had kissed goodbye earlier. There had been no question of his being the friendly, funny butcher's boy, consorting in secret with the heiress; when Will Davies kissed me at Breckenhall Quarry that day, he was the young man with strength in his hands, and nothing but goodness in his heart. The same hands and heart for which I would defy anyone, and in which I willingly placed the rest of my life. I had no idea, in the happy, heady arrogance of youth, that I would have to fight so hard to remain there.

Chapter Five

The train was quite full. I couldn't even be sure Will was on it at all, and spent the entire journey in a state of agitation until I saw his dark head bobbing on the crowded platform by the second-class carriages. For the first time, I had the complete freedom to walk up to him in public, and I noticed one or two people looking twice at us and felt a second's uncertainty, but they were only reacting to the sight of two excited youngsters and I made myself relax. The wind tugged at my hat, and I knew it wouldn't be long before my neat curls were tumbling about my face, despite the care I had taken with them that morning; I had wanted Will to see me looking glamorous for once, instead of my usual windblown self, but he didn't appear to even notice my efforts and I was caught between exasperation and amusement. His own dark hair was already whipped into spikes, and I hoped he would never decide to start using oils on it and tame that fresh, clean look that was so typical of him.

He took my hand and tucked it beneath his arm. 'Where first?'

'I am desperate to go on that captive flying machine,' I said eagerly, pointing to the huge apparatus in the distance. 'Ava went on it last year and screamed all the way around, so she said. Can you think of anything more exciting than screaming in public and not being glared at?'

Will laughed. 'I might have guessed you'd make a beeline for that. Let's go!'

I could quite see why Ava had screamed her head off. I did too, to start with, but then I just laughed, thrilled to be so high up, secured by the huge, spider-like arms that were, in turn, fixed to the central frame. Nestled against Will, his arm about my shoulder, I abandoned any attempt to hold my hat on and held it in my hand instead while we whizzed around in the chilly air, listening to the yells of the other riders.

We staggered off a little while later, still breathless and barely able to speak, but both of us grinning with delight. I put my hat back on, fiddling with the loosened hair-pins but it was a pointless exercise and Will removed it again, and bent to kiss me.

'Now, tell me again how clever I am, and what a wonderful idea it was to come here.'

'I suppose I could come to like it,' I said, and ducked away as he swiped at me with my hat.

The day passed in a blur of sightseeing, paddling

and funfair rides, and looking around the Winter Gardens, and eventually we even stopped looking over our shoulders. It was almost perfect. We had an early dinner then went for a walk, admiring the glittering beauty of thousands of lights against the night sky, and I finally admitted to Will that his idea was the best possible one, and that we must return to Blackpool one day soon. I had thought he might have wanted to visit his family, but the subject did not arise, and I didn't want to make him feel obliged either to them, or to me.

The shadows lengthened and we had, by unspoken agreement, begun walking towards the train station, but I wasn't ready to end the day yet. 'Why don't we see what's showing at the theatre?'

'We're too late,' he said, though reluctantly. 'Whatever it is will have started by now.'

'Well, there are a lot of people over there,' I observed, pointing. A large group, mainly women, I noted, had gathered at the entrance to a small theatre across the street. 'Perhaps there's a late play. Come on, we can always get the last train.'

It wasn't until we had crossed the road and were outside the theatre that we saw what had drawn the crowds, and Will frowned. 'It's anti-suffrage,' he said. 'Come on, let's leave it.'

'No, we're here now. I'd like to hear what they have to say.'

'Evie–'

'I'm open-minded, it's only fair,' I pointed out. I was interested in seeing how this movement could possibly dispute the need for women's votes; it was preposterous to think they might have a valid argument, and I knew I'd go away fully convinced of the rightness of my beliefs, but there was a sense of fair play that niggled. I wanted to hear both sides.

'We'll just stay for a short while,' I promised.

'All right. But no lecturing me on the way home,' he warned. 'You have a habit of preaching to the choir.'

'No preaching,' I said solemnly. 'You have my word. Let's go in.'

We were jostled on our way through, quite roughly, and seeing the purple, green and white badges and sashes I belatedly realised the majority of people were not here to listen to the speeches, but to protest them. It was tempting to tell them that I was on their side, that there was no need to shove, but Will pulled me through quickly and I made do with nodding understandingly at their colours instead.

Inside, I was surprised to see a generous crowd, with standing room only at the back, and as my eyes adjusted to the gloom I began to feel uneasy; there was an air of menace about some of these women, their expressions were not open and interested, as I believed mine was, but hard and determined. I hoped any heckling would not work against the cause, but acknowledged the movement had grown more and more militant over the past few years. Emily Davison's death at the Derby back in June had fuelled things no end, and I'd heard awful stories about what went on at rallies.

I faced the front again as the first of the speeches began, and before five minutes had passed I knew I'd been right to come in. The anti-suffragists might well have supported women's votes in local elections, but what was the use in that, if we were to have no say in Parliament? Nothing had changed, after all. I turned to Will to tell him we could go now, and as I did so, out of the corner of my eye I saw a small, tight band of women in WSPU colours move into the aisle and towards the stage with firm, purposeful strides.

One was holding a bucket of water which I assumed would soon be flung at the speaker, but two more waved an anti-suffrage banner, which surprised me until a flare of light made it all horrifically clear; a fourth Suffragette had touched a lighted match to the edge of the banner, and the flame took hold quickly. More quickly, it seemed, than the two ladies holding the banner had foreseen, and one of them dropped it with a shout. She stumbled backwards into the woman holding the bucket ready, just for this purpose I now realised, and the bucket thudded to the floor, spilling its contents.

'Drop it in the water!' someone cried, and the woman threw the burning banner towards where the carpet was wettest, but the water had soaked away and the fire burned greedily across the carpet and licked at the legs of the chairs closest to the stage. Panic was rippling through the people close enough to see what had happened, and although the fire was not a big one, it was spreading fast. Those who'd been seated closest to the aisle scrambled over their neighbours' knees, while those who hadn't fully grasped what was happening merely stared about them, bemused and in the way.

Will had seized my hand and started pulling the

84

moment the banner had landed, or we wouldn't have stood a chance. Someone shoved into me from behind and I nearly fell, but managed to keep my feet, and from behind me I could hear shouts and screams, and someone yelled that they had the fire extinguisher, and to stand back. But it was too late; panic had swept the room, mostly through those who couldn't see what was happening, and although the fire was quickly brought under control, hysteria propelled people towards exits that were soon jammed.

The next time someone hit me from behind I knew I wouldn't fall; there was nowhere to fall into. I, in turn, barrelled into the person in front, a woman who turned and shrieked into my face. Luckily I couldn't hear her words or I might have let my own anger loose. Will's arm came around my shoulder and I took comfort from his presence, while fighting the urge to shove with all my strength, to get through, to find a clear space and fresh air.

The noise level had risen by now to a deafening, shrill cacophony of voices, some begging for calm, others, like the woman in front of me, simply screaming in fearful frustration. Will's strength held firm beside me, and he lowered his mouth to my ear so I could hear him without straining.

'Steady, and keep moving. Don't let go of me.' He wrapped my arms around his waist, and whenever I stumbled he tightened his grip on my shoulder and kept talking to me in a low, steady voice to calm my shredded nerves. A crash sounded from up near the stage, and we turned to see the front row of people had tried to exit

85

through the back of the stage, but brought down one of the scenery pillars which had been supporting the proscenium arch. The whole thing collapsed, and now the screams were terrible, and people were lying beneath the fallen scenery.

We were at the door now, bruised and shaken, but as I stumbled out into the blessed freedom of the lobby I felt Will's hand drop away from my shoulder and he eased me away from him, holding my arms.

'Go out onto the street,' he said, urgent now. 'I'll meet you there.'

Before I could question him, he'd fought his way back into the auditorium, thrusting his way through the people still spilling out, who nevertheless parted instinctively to let him past. I was about to follow when a weeping voice stopped me, and I looked around to see a young girl in WSPU colours, sobbing and holding her arm across her chest. I felt a flash of anger towards her at first, then remembered my own recent, passionate beliefs in the movement, and drew her carefully out of the crowd where I could help her better.

For the most part my mind was with Will as he went back inside to help where he could, but I was able to lend half an ear to the girl, who was Scottish, very pretty, and about my own age. Her sobs, it turned out, were not for her injured arm, but for her little sister.

'Please help me find her!'

'How old is she?'

'Twelve.'

My anger flooded back. 'What on earth were you thinking, bringing such a young girl along to a rally?'

'I wanted her to understand how important it all is,' the girl said earnestly. 'She needs to learn how the–'

'Stop!' I held up my hand. 'I don't need a lecture, you little idiot! Wait here, and don't go anywhere. What's her name?' I looked around, but couldn't see any children.

'Helen. She has black hair and is wearing a green dress.'

I placed the young Suffragette firmly in a corner, where I could be reasonably sure of finding her again, then I followed Will's example and pushed back into the auditorium.

Inside all was still chaos in the aisles, although most of the rows of seats were free of people now. I looked helplessly around, realising a twelve-year-old girl would be almost impossible to spot. Then I had an idea, and climbed over the back of the rear-most seats onto the ones in front, scanning the crowds as I went. From my vantage point I saw Will, helping a hobbling woman to a seat, and judged by the way she half-rose and then settled down, that he'd convinced her of the relative safety of staying where she was.

Taking my cue from his common sense, I climbed back down and began speaking to the people nearest me.

'The fire's out! It's safe here, don't push! Just sit down and wait, and you'll get out quicker, and without injury! Sit down, just wait...'

Gradually the word seemed to filter through, and the shoving eased off. I began to ask people if they'd seen a twelve-year-old girl in a green dress but no one had. Just when I was starting to despair of ever finding her, and assumed she must have made her way outside after all, I saw a crumpled form near the edge of the stage. It was dressed in green. I scrambled back over the seats, my skirts held high, not caring who was watching, and yelled to Will, pointing with my free hand. We reached her at the same time, and I laid my hand on her back.

She jerked upright, gasping and terrified, and I could see blood matting her dark fringe.

'Hush, Helen, it's all right,' I soothed.

She stared at me. 'How do you know my name?'

'Your sister has been looking for you,' I said. 'Sit still a moment, let's make sure you're fit to move.'

Will and I helped her to a sitting position, and I looked her over carefully. 'Did you faint at all?'

'I was hit on the head by something, but I didnae faint. I was a'scairt the rest of the scenery would come down on me, so I stayed curled up.' The little girl had a lilting accent just like her sister's, and would grow into a similar beauty one day. For now though she was tear-streaked and frightened, and hiccupped her way through a list of her bumps and bruises. None of them seemed serious, but Will asked her if she'd mind if he carried her anyway, just to be sure. She looked at him in awe and shook her head, and he scooped her up, carrying her easily and carefully through the thinning crowd.

I found the elder sister where I'd left her, and she swooped down on Helen with a cry of relief as Will lowered her carefully to the floor. 'There y'are ya wee rascal! What did I tell ye about staying close?'

'She was hit by some falling scenery,' Will said, and the reproach in his voice halted the girl's harangue. 'I'm sure she's fine, but you should get a doctor to look at her, she's cut her head.'

'I'm all right,' Helen said in a small voice, and smiled shyly up at Will. I looked at him too, seeing him through her eyes, and felt a stirring of hero-worship myself. I met his embarrassed eyes and gave him a little smile.

'We have a train to catch,' I said. The two girls thanked us profusely, and as we left we could hear them talking excitedly about what had happened, and heard the older girl make Helen promise not to tell their parents what had happened.

Will grinned down at me and took my hand. 'How about you, Florence Nightingale, are you all right?'

'I'm better than that,' I told him, 'I'm a little bit more in love with you than I was before, if that's possible.'

He laughed and waved a dismissive hand, but I was serious. I'd seen another side to him today: a courage that balanced the fun-loving side, and a calm strength that settled him just a little deeper into my heart. Walking beside him back towards the station I wanted everyone to know the bone-deep beauty of this man, and what he was capable of. I wanted people to look at me and envy me, and I wanted him to know how unutterably proud of him I was.

But if the day had shown me a new Will Davies, it had also shown me a new Evie Creswell, and I

89

wasn't sure how I felt about her. On the train, sitting close to him, I broached the question that had been bothering me. 'Will, am I different?'

'Different?'

'To what I was. To the way you saw me.'

'I don't understand.'

'It's just, today...' I hesitated, wondering if I was courting trouble even putting the thought in his head. 'I mean, all this time you've told me you admired me for my beliefs, and principles, and the way I could make you believe things too. Lizzy was the same. But now, after what happened, I feel as if ... how could I let something like this shake those beliefs? But it has.'

He twisted in his seat and took my hands. 'Evie, listen to me. We're still growing into what we will eventually become. If everyone waited until they believed they were fully formed before deciding they loved someone, the human race would die out. We're never "finished", so of course our ideals will change, *we'll* change.'

'But do you think we'll change too much?'

'Do you mean will I stop loving you? Tell me this, will you stop loving me if I change?'

'No!'

'And nothing will ever make me think you're not worth my whole life, Evie. I will never, ever give up on you, and I want you to promise the same.'

I looked at him, I saw the earnest truth in his face, and I spoke from the heart, not suspecting how the weight of the words would return one day to reshape our lives. 'I pledge my life on it.'

Chapter Six

'Will you go?'

'Yes, if they call us.'

I shivered, despite the warmth of the day. The news from Europe was increasingly disturbing, and I could tell Mother was becoming more and more concerned about Uncle Jack. His letters had been scarce, and very short, but if it hadn't been for those brief notes it would have been more worrying still. Now, though, my attention was fixed closer to home, and I looked sideways at Will, who sat with his knees raised and his hands drooped between them.

'It may not come to it,' he said, feeling the weight of my gaze, and turning to me. His eyes held mine and we both knew he didn't believe that any more than I did.

'If you go, I'm going to find a way to volunteer, too,' I said. The words were out of my mouth before I'd realised I was going to say them, but the determination took hold nevertheless. 'If all the boys join up, the girls will have to pitch in and take up the slack.'

He grinned. 'I can just see you up to your elbows in pig entrails,' he said, and threw a handful of grass at me.

'Well, maybe not *your* job,' I conceded, and

91

returned the favour, hitting him squarely in the mouth with a lucky throw. While he spluttered and spat out the grass, I lay back and stared up at the sky, wondering how something as perfect and clear, and such a beautiful, rich blue could be looking down on a world so full of uncertainty and fear.

'I've been thinking,' he said, and something in his voice made me raise myself onto my elbows again.

'What? You sound nervous.'

'Not nervous exactly. It's just ... with what's probably coming and all, don't you think–'

'Yes.'

'You don't know what I was going to say!'

'Yes I do.' I smiled and sat up all the way, slipping my hand beneath his knee to link my fingers with his, and said it again, slowly. 'Yes. I do.'

He returned my smile, and the tension left him. 'Well then, now you'll *have* to tell your mother.'

'No. I mean, yes, I will, but I'm going to tell her afterwards. I can't give her the slightest opportunity to put a stop to it.'

'How on earth will you keep it from her? The vicar at Breckenhall is bound to say something.'

'Then we won't marry in Breckenhall. We'll find somewhere further away. I hope Uncle Jack comes home in time, he'd be pleased to give me away.'

'Even to me?'

'Especially to you,' I said. Jack Carlisle would take one look at Will and me together, and not a single question would pass his lips about suitability or income. And if I asked him to leave it to me to tell Mother, he would do it. 'I'll find somewhere with a discreet minister, and we can set a date for sometime before Christmas. That's bound to give us time, and maybe the Kaiser will call off the show and leave Russia alone, and it will all come to nothing.'

But just two days later, on the first day of August, Germany declared war on Russia. The news came over the radio that, in order for them to remove France as a hindrance, they had asked for permission to move their army through Belgium, and, while the world listened with bated breath, Belgium held her ground and refused.

'But what does that mean?' Mother fretted. 'For us?'

'It means that, if the Kaiser doesn't withdraw his army, we're going to have to go in and make him,' I said. I felt quite sick and, despite my calm words, I was having a great deal of trouble straightening my thoughts to really understand what it all meant.

'Why do we have to do it?' She glanced over at Lawrence, and I could see the worry on her face. 'It's got nothing to do with us, surely?'

'Evidently it's to do with a treaty made back in the 1830s,' I said, not adding that it was Will who'd told me about it. 'Perhaps the Germans will withdraw when they realise what they've done, and that they can't win.'

But of course, they hadn't. Our government sent an ultimatum that was ignored, and by eleven o'clock on the night of the fourth of August, we too were at war.

To begin with, nothing seemed different. The sun still shone; night and day still came and went; people still went to work, only now their expressions slipped too easily from cheerfulness to shadowed fear. But gradually the little changes that were happening all over the country began to make themselves felt in everyday life. Shops closed as their owners answered the call to arms; the government put out a further call, for one hundred thousand volunteers, and Will joined the reserves. I tried to hold on to the common belief that the war would be short-lived, maybe even over before Christmas, but it seemed more and more evident now that this would be a protracted struggle, and that our men were being sent into a special kind of hell; the thought of Will joining them made me break into a cool sweat and pray constantly for the war to end before it was too late.

One afternoon in late August, Will met me at the quarry with an unusually sombre expression, and his face was pale. I saw immediately what he held, and my breathing sharpened into something painful.

'When?'

'Tenth of September.'

'Oh, God. Oh, God, Will...'

He seized me roughly and pulled me to him with a strange, sighing sob. All the enthusiasm when he'd spoken of joining up, of doing his duty, of protecting the innocent, had fled as we held each other, and I felt him shuddering under my fiercely gripping hands. It made the way he finally squared his shoulders and stood straight all the more courageous in my eyes; he was not naïve enough to think he was riding into glory, the shining hero of the tale. He understood some of what he was going into, and he was terrified, but he would still do it.

'I must marry you before I leave,' he said, and touched my face. 'I must.'

I thought quickly. 'We'll go to Gretna. Mary will be a witness, and you must find one too.' I spoke fast, hoping the trembling in my voice wasn't as obvious to him as it was to me. My mind was not on weddings, though, it was on the letter I'd been mulling over for a week or more, applying for a post with the Red Cross, and I hesitated no longer; if Will was going overseas in defence of another country, I could do no less in defence of his own.

Gretna, Scotland, September 1914.

'This is Martin Barrow,' Will said as he drew me into the little sitting room. 'He's taking my place as Markham's apprentice, once ... well, once I've left.'

'Very nice to meet you, Martin,' I said.

He shook my hand, a tall, earnest-looking young man with a friendly face. 'Miss,' he said. He glanced at Will, and then back at me, and to my surprise he looked a little shamefaced. 'I'd have joined up too, if I could,' he said, and it was only when he limped over to close the sitting room door that I realised why he hadn't. I wished he didn't look so guilty over it, but it wasn't my place to presume how he felt, I might have read

95

him wrong.

I gestured to my own companion. 'This is Mary Deegan,' I said. 'I understand you'll be travelling back to Breckenhall together on the same train.'

The two nodded to each other, and as Mary went over to introduce herself properly, Will slipped his arm around my waist. 'I can't believe we're doing this,' he said, nuzzling my ear.

'And I can't believe I haven't told Mother,' I said, and sighed. 'I know she'll take it badly but it's not you, it's...'

'It's what I'm not,' Will said, but he didn't sound resentful. 'Darling, I know all that, let's not go over the same old ground. Not today.'

'Come upstairs, Evie,' Mary said, coming over. She was smiling and I glanced past her at Martin, who was trying to pretend he hadn't been staring after her. 'Let's get you changed.'

I kissed Will lightly, our very last chaste kiss as single people, and followed Mary up the winding hotel staircase to the little room above. I looked at the bed nervously and felt my insides do a slow roll, but there was excitement there too, heightened by the memory of his breath on my skin.

My dress was quite simply cut, but when I'd first tried it on I knew that, of all the glorious and expensive gowns I'd worn in the past, this one was the one I would keep forever. Mary had made it from some ivory lace I had found in Breckenhall market, and since she was the only person, other than Uncle Jack, who I'd told about the marriage, I knew it had been made with pleasure and secrecy, which gave it a feel of something very personal. And tonight I would remove it in front of my husband. That nervous roll came again and I took a deep breath to calm the shaking that had suddenly seized my fingers and knees; would I please him, after all this time of waiting and anticipation?

Mary helped me dress and I wished, with a familiar sweep of sorrow, that Lizzy could be here too. In my mind I could hear her amused voice teasing me about how excited I was, and I could see her long dark hair tumbling out from beneath her hat as she tried, yet again in vain, to tidy her appearance before Mother saw her. It was too painful to think of what she might be doing now, and although I hated myself for doing so I tried to put her to the back of my mind and concentrate, instead, on this perfect day.

'Promise me you won't tell anyone,' I said to Mary, for the hundredth time.

She nodded. 'I do promise, Evie, you know that.'

'Not even Lizzy.' It seemed my friend would not stay in the back of my mind after all.

'Of course, if you say so, but why haven't you told her yourself? She'd be so happy for you both.'

'I wanted to, but I can't. If someone reads the letter before it reaches her, and passes the news back to Oaklands, it will hurt Mother all the more.'

Mary finished off the simple garland I wore around my head, and straightened the short veil. 'I won't say anything, not until you're able to. It's not my place anyway.'

'Thank you.' I touched her arm gratefully. I'd made up my mind to tell Lizzy as soon as Mother knew, but the trouble was I had no idea when that would be. That I had been lying to her was the worst part, but it had seemed necessary at the beginning, and the longer it went on the harder it had become to stop. Now she would be devastated, not only at my deceit, but also at the fact that she had been excluded from her only daughter's wedding.

'Please give me a moment alone,' I said to Mary when we were satisfied with my appearance, or in my case, almost satisfied. Mary stepped outside and I went to my suitcase and withdrew a small black box. Carefully I opened the lid and took out a battered, black and white paper flower, which I lifted to my lips and kissed before twisting the stem around the belt of my dress. It lay against the beautifully cut lace, incongruous and grubby-looking, and I knew I'd been right to wait until Mary had left the room; she would have tried strenuously to convince me not to wear it, and I would have resisted, and we would have wasted a good deal of time – time neither Will nor I could spare now.

I stepped out through the door, holding my small bouquet against my waist to hide the rose, and only moved it aside when I drew level with Will. The movement drew his eye downward, and then he looked back at me and there was deep and complicated emotion in every line of his face. He kissed his own finger and touched it to the half-uncurled petals, unknowingly mimicking my own gesture, and then he smiled into my eyes and I felt my heart turn over.

The service was quick and simple; those who

conducted it were well used to situations like ours, and not an eyebrow was raised even though Mary and Martin were our only witnesses. I remembered standing on the rock above the quarry and yelling to the world that I was going to marry this man, and here we were. Within ten minutes we were legally wed, and back out in the autumn sunshine, hardly able to believe we had actually done it.

After the glorious summer, the weather remained warm. It seemed impossible to think that tomorrow Will would board a train for the coast, and a day later he would be on foreign soil. A shadow seemed to cross the blameless blue sky and I shivered; yes, it did seem impossible, but with every minute that passed we drew closer to the moment when it would become a dark and terrifying reality. What had seemed a wildly romantic notion might have also had the uncomfortable taste of something we had been using to keep the fear at bay, but looking at my new husband and his slightly bemused air of giddy happiness, I knew it was more than that; planning the wedding had provided a welcome distraction, but that did not lessen its importance, or the joy we felt that we were finally together. I also allowed myself the pleasure of having seen Martin steal more than one fascinated glance Mary's way, although I was sure she herself had not noticed.

They left after tea, and by then Mary had begun returning Martin's attentions; it seemed they shared an interest in travel, and Martin had grown up in India with his family, so they had much to discuss. She also seemed to be flushing and laughing a good deal more than I was used to seeing. Will noticed too, and after we had waved them off on their return home, he smiled. 'Do you suppose they even still remember who we are?'

I smiled. 'Does it matter?'

'No,' he admitted, and took my hand. 'It's still early, Mrs Davies. Shall we walk up the lane before supper?'

The sun was just beginning its slow descent on this, the happiest day I had ever known, and as we reached the top of the hill, Will pulled me to a halt. I turned to see the orange-gold light setting his eyes on fire and burnishing his skin, and an intensity in his expression that I knew would be mirrored in my own. Without a word passing between us, we turned to go back to the hotel, a new urgency in our steps and all thoughts of the earliness of the hour banished.

In our room he took me by the shoulders and brushed his lips against my forehead with the most gentle of touches that, nevertheless, shot straight through me, leaving a trail of heat in its wake. He stepped back and removed his jacket and shirt, and, unable suddenly to look at his face, and instead keeping my eyes on his surprisingly compact, muscular body, I eased my gown over my shoulders. When we moved close together again I had only my petticoats on, and the friction of the fine silk sliding between us ignited that heat and made us both gasp.

But we were not yet close enough, and when he raised my arms and slipped the last remaining barrier away my hands went to his chest, as if by the touch of my fingers on his skin I would finally realise he was mine. He pulled me closer, and I let my hands drift down his sides, over the strong swell of his ribcage, feeling him tremble with the lightness of my touch. I wondered if he was as drawn to my body as I was to his or whether, now he saw me without the mystery and flattery of my clothing, he might be disappointed.

The question must have shown in my face because his hand came up to touch my jaw. 'Evie Davies, you are, without doubt, the most beautiful creature on this good earth,' he breathed, and then his mouth came down on mine.

Eventually he broke the kiss and led me to the bed. I lay down and he looked at me for a long, delicious moment before stretching out beside me and, easing one hand beneath me, he lifted me closer. He raised his free hand to my breast and I arched towards him, longing for the complete possession that seemed to hover so close, yet still danced out of reach. All the while he was kissing wherever he could reach, along my cheekbones and down to my jaw, his lips blazing across my face to my eyes as if he couldn't taste enough of me all at once. Thrilled at the thought that I excited him so much, I let my hands choose their path across his broad back and down to his hips, and my teeth nipped gently at his shoulder, my lips moving hungrily over the smooth skin.

Nervousness almost stole my pleasure as he moved across me, and I tensed as he positioned himself so that his entry was as smooth and painless as it could be, his eyes on mine in silent apology. But after a brief flash of pain my hips rose of their own volition to meet him and I didn't even have to think about matching his rhythm; all thought seemed to be happening on another level of my consciousness and there was only sensation now. Our movements grew more urgent and I tried to pull him deeper inside me, knowing that, as wonderful as it was, there was something more and I had to either have it or die.

All at once the warmth I had always felt in his presence – in my heart, on my skin, in my stomach – was now concentrated in one place and growing. Just as I thought I could bear it no longer, that elusive feeling I had sensed before rushed through me to meet that warmth, and the collision was everything. It was glorious. With every beat of my heart the sensation pulsed more heavily in every part of me, only fading away as Will, spent and exhausted, sank down to lie beside me.

After a moment he rolled towards me again, supporting himself on one elbow. I opened my eyes and smiled, and he looked relieved and brushed away a curl that had stuck to my cheek. His fingers were trembling. 'It didn't hurt too much?'

I could feel his thundering heart as his chest pressed against my arm. 'It was awful,' I said, 'I never want to go through anything like that ever again.'

Will laughed, a shaky, breathless sound, and dropped his hand to my hip. 'Never?' he asked in a low voice.

I scratched my short nails lightly across his stomach. 'Never,' I breathed, and kissed his shoulder, moving down across his chest, tasting the light, salt sweat of him and loving it. 'Not for at least ten minutes.'

It turned out ten minutes was a lot shorter than I'd thought.

In the morning we left that magical place behind forever, and to my embarrassment Will showed me he had taken some of the paper from the little supply in our room. 'I'll write to you on this, so we can remember,' he said. 'Whenever you see this hotel crest,' he traced it with one finger, 'you will know it's you I'm thinking of. I'm going to kiss every single page,' he grinned, warming to his promise as I rolled my eyes in disbelief, 'and whenever you get a letter from me on this paper, you will think of our wedding night.'

Despite my teasing look, I was unbelievably touched; Will was not what I would have thought of as a particularly romantic young man, but I had no doubt that he would do exactly as he'd said. And when he left later that same day to join his unit, I thought of the ridiculous little stack of paper tucked into his shirt, and wished I could have taken its place.

Waiting with him at the station was a strange, hollow affair. He wore his uniform now – an oddly plain, muddy-green, ill-fitting affair of rough wool – and carried a hessian kit-bag; it was as if he were going to stay with a friend for a week, nothing more. That we were surrounded by people in the same clothes, and that some of them openly wept, only served to heighten the sense of unreality.

As the train pulled into the platform, the mood changed. It became charged with a brittle air of patriotic fervour, men straightening their backs and declaring it time to 'get over there and sort the Bosche out'. Someone slapped Will's shoulder, and he gave them a mechanical grin and slapped back. They had never met before, yet now they were quite likely to be living side by side and entrusting their lives to one another. Someone, somewhere down the platform began to sing 'It's a long way to Tipperary', and a few disjointed voices joined in.

My heart suddenly, and finally, accepted that he was going, and it stopped beating for a breathless, terrifying moment. The thought flashed into my head: what if it doesn't start again? But of course it did, and the racing, sickening feeling made me dizzy. I looked up into Will's face and he seemed more dear to me then, more precious and more fragile than I had ever seen him. These people didn't know him. How could he go off with them when they didn't understand him? Didn't realise that, beyond the cheerful smile and the clear, friendly blue eyes, he was a man of warmth and wit, and a quiet, fierce intelligence? Would they ever have the chance to realise how lucky they were to be with him?

His voice, when he spoke, wasn't raised to shout over the cries of others. Instead it was pitched low, easily cutting beneath it and straight into my aching heart.

'Evie, my impossible, exasperating wife, I love you so very, very much.' He faltered, searching for words when we both knew there were none. At last he sighed. 'Promise me you'll be careful.'

'I will if you will.' I was trying hard not to cry in front of him; there would be time for weeping, so much time, but this was not it. So I smiled, but

104

the movement loosened the tears that had gathered in my eyes, and they spilled anyway.

'I promise.' He bent to kiss my forehead and the warm press of his lips almost sent me spinning into hysterical pleading ... *don't go!* But he drew himself upright and away from me. He stood tall and straight, somehow making that awful uniform look like a thing of honour, touched my cheek once, and then he was gone, heading for the coast, and God alone knew what awaited him there. I stood with countless others, long after the train had pulled out of sight around the bend and, as the chuffing faded and voices started to filter back in, I blinked, swallowed, and let out a shaky breath. Soon I would be leaving too, to begin my Red Cross training; each of us had answered the call to arms in our own way, and I could only pray that, when I saw him again, it was not as a shattered, broken echo of the man he was now.

Back at Breckenhall I made my way to the fruit shop above which Will had taken his rooms. He would have to surrender them, or be faced with a dreadful debt when he returned... I emphasised the *when*, which kept trying to change itself to *if*. It would help no one to think of that. In the meantime all his things would stay at Oaklands, and I needed to know how much there was to bring across.

I knocked on the landlady's door and introduced myself; she knew me only as one of the Creswells from the manor, and I told her I had come on behalf of Will's family, to pay rent in advance and remove his belongings so she could let the room out again. In all the time we had been together I had never come here, it had been too much of a risk. The stairs were narrow and dark, and I pictured him climbing them at night, exhausted from his work, looking forward to a wash and a quick meal before bed – where perhaps he might have lain and thought of me, as I did of him. Through the pain of missing him, the thought made me smile, just a little. Even the smile hurt, made me feel disloyal.

The landlady unlocked the door and I gave her the two weeks rent money I had brought. 'I can take just a few things now, but I'll send for the rest tomorrow.' She nodded, already used to her tenants' sudden departures. I waited until she had gone back down the stairs, then turned to take my first look at where Will had lived for the past three years.

The room was not a big one and the first thing that struck me was the clutter, although a second look revealed it to be no mess, but rather a collection of paintings, carvings and sculptures. The largest of these stood on the table, half-covered by a carelessly thrown sheet which I drew back to reveal a statuette, standing around a foot high and carved in dark wood. It was the shape of a woman, her hair escaping her hat and shaped into wild curls that blew across her face, hiding the features, but I didn't need to see them; I raised my hand to my own face, tears thick at the back of my throat.

The statuette wore the roughly outlined symbol of the Red Cross on her front, standing out against her uniform dress, and her legs were not yet shaped, just a solid block of wood. It felt as if my own legs were the same; just an unmoving lump, unable to take another step. The care that had gone into the carving of this piece sang from every notch and scrape, and the knife he had used to craft it lay on the table beside it, curls of wood littering the table as if he had been called away from his work suddenly. As I looked closer I saw, in the girl's hat, a tiny rose carved out of the same block, and with a sharp pang I remembered his face when he'd seen the paper rose at my waist just yesterday. The rose itself was back in its box, and would go with me to Rugby, and from there to France, or wherever we were sent.

This piece was the one I would take with me tonight. I glanced around: the majority of the space was taken up with paintings, most of them facing the wall, and when I turned one or two of them around I understood at once why Nathan had been so unsuccessful towards the end. It wasn't a lack of talent, far from it, but the paintings were dark and tortured-looking, full of deep reds and blacks, and swirls of mashed colours in thick oil that seemed to leap, screaming, from the canvas. Bodiless faces; roaring rivers; tall, black buildings; a huge, Golem-like creature bearing down on a tiny, helpless man ... symbols of the trapped terror the artist was feeling for his debts, no doubt.

Disturbed, I turned these paintings back to the wall. It was little wonder Will had faced them that way, it would be impossible to sleep in this room otherwise. I looked at one or two others and they were calmer, presumably painted during earlier, easier days, but of less artistic merit that I could discern. It was ironic that Nathan's best work had emerged as a result of the lack of success of these lesser pieces, and that gave me a pinch of sadness for Will's unknown friend, but it was followed by frustration that he had given Will this dream, and then left him alone with the nightmare.

I went back to the table and picked up two of Will's small pieces: a miniature cottage no bigger than my hand, but intricately carved in soft, pale wood; and a daisy of around the same size – both unpainted – and then I wrapped the statuette in the cloth again and tucked her under my arm. I would have everything brought over to Oaklands tomorrow, but for tonight I would have these things to remind me of my husband when I lay down in my bed, alone once again.

I slipped off my wedding band before the car arrived, and on the way home I rehearsed my cheerful lies; I'd already said I was attending a wedding, giving the impression it was a friend from London who was getting married, and fixed the description of my own gown in my head, ready to attribute it to the fictitious bride. The way the lies fell from my lips, cheerful or otherwise, disturbed me, but I wasn't ready yet to place this burden on Mother's shoulders; she was already distressed about my imminent departure to the Red Cross. Neither was I ready to turn this joyful news into something cold and hurtful, to be argued over rather than held tightly and treasured.

I tried once more to tell the truth before I left, but my mother's despair at my stubborn insistence on going overseas, instead of serving in

England, stole any inclination I had to heap more woe upon her, and it simply grew more and more difficult to tell her the truth. It seemed easier, and kinder, to let her believe I had too much to think about to waste time on hopeless, and un-suitable, romantic entanglements.

My training began in St Cross Hospital, Rugby, on a chilly October day. The hospitals were already taking in wounded from the various fronts and, although I knew I'd have heard if Will were hurt, I still felt my heart clench every time I went to the docks. When I realised he wasn't among them, I fought the guilty relief and threw myself harder than ever into helping those who were, to make up for it. I know I wasn't the only one to feel like that, and I soon bonded with a cheerful, freckled girl named Barbara, who was in love with an airman and talked about him non-stop. One day I called her "Boxy", for "Chatterbox" during one of our regular one-sided conversations, and it stuck. It suited her surname, Wood, too, and soon everyone was calling her Boxy but they didn't know why. It was our joke; a small thing, but in our situation it was the small things that could sometimes get you through the most difficult times.

Boxy Wood shared my interest in motor vehicles and their workings. She told me what it was like in the ambulance corps; her sister had gone out two months before to join a convoy in France. 'Hon-estly, Davies, it's the most awful sort of torture you could imagine. And I'm not talking about the wounded, or even the driving. Clara says their commandant waits 'til they're all falling asleep after a fourteen-hour shift, then blows her damnable whistle for inspection. And woe betide any poor girl with a mucky uniform; punishment duties are dreadful.'

It did sound awful. On the other hand the War Office had been calling specifically for young ladies of good breeding to go out there and do their bit. 'We have to go,' I said. 'They need people like us, and it doesn't look as though the war will be over by Christmas after all.'

She sighed. 'I know, poppet.' Then she looked at me with a little glint in her eye I was starting to recognise, and I felt a smile twitch at my lips in anticipation.

'What are you cooking up now?'

'All right, listen. We've missed out on our chance to go out with the Munro corps, correct?'

'Correct. Unfortunately. Why do you suppose Doctor Munro only took six in the end?' We'd both been keen to apply to Hector Munro's exciting-sounding venture; working with the support of the Red Cross, but independent of their strict regimes, closer to the lines, and right in the thick of things.

'Well, he had to pick the cream of the crop, and Mrs Knocker and Dorothie Feilding are certainly that.'

'They're so lucky,' I grumbled, 'avoiding all the huff and puff of inspections, uniforms and rotas. Doesn't seem at all in the spirit of why we want to help.'

Boxy nodded. 'Even worse since we've paid for our own training. It galls rather, doesn't it? So, why don't we just set up by ourselves?'

'What?' It was such a casual comment I wasn't sure I'd heard properly.

Boxy warmed to her suggestion, and became more animated. 'Look. We just have to find a base, some building no-one's using, and you can be sure there'll be plenty of those. We'll find a place as close to the lines as we can get, and move forward as they do so we're always within reach with emergency help. We'll do a bang-up job, I know it. If we're going to suffer I'd much rather it be on our own terms, wouldn't you?'

I would, of course, but there were practicalities to think of. 'How on earth would we get passes to work up near the lines, if we're not attached to the Red Cross?'

'We'll just have to prove they need us. Think about it, are they really going to turn us away if we arrive with our own vehicles, and fully trained to boot? You and I are just what they need out there.'

The more I thought about it, the better it sounded. We could take our own ambulances, or cars if we couldn't get them, and act as whatever was needed at the time; stretcher-bearers if they'd let us, ambulance-drivers if they wouldn't, both if we possibly could. Boxy wrote to the commanding officer of a unit just outside Dixmude, a friend of her airman, and he wrote back advising caution, but hinting that an independent ambulance base would be just as welcome as another Red Cross one.

Later, as he realised we were serious, Lieutenant-Colonel Drewe offered to arrange passes for us, provided we were certified and able to supply our own vehicles, and so we continued our training, knowing there would be little back-up once we were out there and making doubly sure we were proficient in all we could be.

Between us we raised enough cash through savings and donations, and bought a rattly old ambulance that we named Gertie in honour of an amusing pig we had seen on a postcard.

'She *sounds* rather like a pig,' Boxy had said, as we drove a noisily snorting Gertie off the ferry and onto French soil. 'A splash of pink paint and who'd know the difference?'

I rolled my eyes and laughed, a tingling excite-ment was making me feel a bit giddy despite the very real fear that was taking hold now. 'Barbara Wood, we are *not* painting her pink!'

The cottage in Belgium was a decent enough place. We had to give it a number, so as to identify it with the ambulance convoys and the hospitals nearby, so it became Number Twelve. Abandoned shortly after the Yser Canal had been flooded, to stay the German advance in late October, it sat alone in its own little courtyard, miraculously whole and quite the ugliest place I'd ever seen. But oddly beautiful at the same time. We loved it from the very first. Although it was just a one-bed-roomed cottage it had a roomy cellar, perfect for converting into a small ward, and with room for seven beds and an equipment store. We, and those we planned to help, would be safe down there from shellfire, and it was somewhere to administer basic first-aid before moving the wounded along to the Clearing Stations once they were more likely to survive the journey.

Not being part of an officially designated field ambulance division meant we lacked mechanical backup, so I was grateful Uncle Jack had always been firm with me, and shown me the basics of engine maintenance when he'd heard about my clandestine driving lessons.

'No good just learning to drive,' he'd said when I'd pulled a face. 'You need to know what to do if something goes wrong. You'll like it, once you get going, I know you.'

He was right and, even better, I discovered I had an aptitude for it; I couldn't help grinning with delight the first time I was able to correct the problems he'd deliberately caused, and I was glad he'd persisted – especially now, given the work Gertie was putting in over increasingly rough roads.

We'd arrived in November 1914, and collected as much bedding as we could find, but the luxury of gathering equipment, and setting up what we'd fondly imagined would be our sweet little dressing station, with comfort and curtains, and hot drinks for the Tommies, was not to be. We were thrown into it right away, attached to the military unit a couple of miles away, and, with no field telephone, we quickly grew accustomed to the shrill whistle of the runner on his bicycle as he summoned us to duty. Days blurred into long, cold nights, and weeks into months, while we battled extremes of boredom and terror, and we faithfully wrote our sunny 'gosh it's exciting being in the thick of it!' letters home so our parents could boast about us to their friends. Heaven forbid they should find out what we actually did, night after night, I'm not

113

certain Mother would have sat quietly at home if she'd known.

Our own tentative excitement had been crushed out of us after the first, awful night. With nothing of our own base ready we'd volunteered our services at least, and turned out to help the Red Cross convoy, lining up with the other drivers at the railway station. The trains had come in; old, rattling things in these early days of war, filled from end to end with wounded. Weeping men; silent men; angry, bewildered men; men numbed with misery and mute with horror ... *dear God, was Will in danger of becoming one of these?*

We'd sat, still and shocked, while the orderlies loaded us up and barked our load: *four stretchers, one sitter,* and then driven, somehow, to the sergeant at the gate. 'Four stretchers, one sitter,' I repeated, stumbling over the impersonal words that were supposed to somehow explain the softly moaning, tangled mass of humanity I was carrying.

He consulted his clip-board. 'Number Five.' He waved us through, and we were on our way. Where was Number Five? I was utterly lost, both mentally and geographically, but we found Number Five hospital mercifully quickly and were unloaded. Then it was back again; the train was still crammed with men awaiting their turn. Or their deaths. As dawn raked the sky with glorious pink rays that belied the tragedy beneath it, Boxy and I returned, in trembling silence, to our beds. Different women. Grown up in the space of a few horrific and nauseating hours.

The next morning, after we'd opened the

ambulance doors to begin cleaning, and instead contributed to the mess, we looked at one another, wiped our mouths and both of us had broken down in tears. It was the last time we did so as a result of our work, and since that night our bond had been unbreakable and if ever one of us wavered in her determination to stick it out, the other would simply touch her hand and walk away, leaving her standing alone. It served to remind us how the fighting men felt, away from the comradeship of their unit, hurt and frightened – it was why we were there.

But it was not all terrible; there was a certain amount of freedom we'd never have experienced if we'd joined the Field Ambulance, or were tied to the other units. There were a couple of friendly girls who came over now and again to spell us: Anne and Elise were based near Furnes, at a unit with which we often joined forces when things got especially hot. They enjoyed the chance to spend some time away from their slightly more regimented atmosphere too, and were keen to give us the opportunity to go into town now and again.

Will was with the 19th brigade of the 2nd Division at the start, and they rarely seemed to remain in one place for long. Letters were scarce – sometimes weeks would pass and then three or four would arrive at once; those were days I'd take myself off and find a quiet place to read, and read, and read, hearing his voice in my head as clearly as if he were sitting next to me. Except when I was particularly exhausted, when I sometimes struggled to remember what he sounded like, and then I had to put the letters aside or risk smudging the ink with tears of terror – what if I never heard him again? What if this was all I had left of him, only I didn't yet know it? How would I cope?

In June 1915, he was stationed a mere two hours away from me in Northern France, and towards the end of the month he wrote a hurried letter telling me he was due a weekend leave and would arrive at the station in Cuinchy on Friday afternoon. He would be staying at a hostel nearby, the name of which he jotted at the foot of the note, and he desperately hoped the letter reached me in time.

It arrived on Saturday.

Boxy and I had been working solidly for sixteen days; late April had seen the first use of chlorine gas, and the results were so shocking it was difficult to comprehend such a thing had been invented by human beings. We spent long days at the hospital, and longer nights collecting wounded and gassed soldiers from the dressing stations, barely snatching three or four hours sleep and eating very poorly indeed. We'd reached that point of exhaustion where you don't quite feel you're there at all; drifting around each other, avoiding collisions more by luck than judgement, and taking it in turns to clean and disinfect the ambulance and the two cars we'd been loaned by the Belgian Red Cross. When we received our visit from Anne and Elise, with instructions to 'flipping well get out of it for the day', we both threw guilt to the four winds and seized the chance.

Boxy and her airman, Benjy, were unable to meet, but she had friends stationed at the nearby hospital and went off to see them. No doubt she would be called into service there, so it was not much of a holiday. I was luckier; our saviours had blown in the day I received Will's letter, and I was able to shake off my tiredness and drive to Cuinchy in time to meet him before the cycle began for him again; front line, support, reserve, rest ... then back to front line.

Walking into the hostel, I didn't have to ask at the desk to find him. The place was filled with uniformed men, most in high spirits, and some singing – under the influence of some dubiously obtained wine, no doubt – but over by the window there was a small group, making the kind of appreciative noises that pushed long-distant marketplaces to the front of my memory. I felt the smile on my face before the instinct had solidified into fact, and my feet had already carried me halfway across the room, but I stopped short of drawing his attention, preferring to watch him for a moment, unnoticed.

He sat with his back to me, his dark head was bent to his work, and my fingers itched to brush gently across the back of his exposed neck. There were, perhaps, eight or nine men standing around, calling out suggestions, and the tallest of them was writing busily.

'Unicorn!' one man shouted, and the tall man rolled his eyes.

'Did you 'ear that, Davies? Bleedin' unicorn, he says! Look, mate, he might be good, but he ain't no Leonardo da Vinci!'

'Two toffees for a unicorn,' insisted the soldier.

'Oh, I can manage that all right,' Will said, and at the sound of his voice, this time for real, my entire body tightened with anticipation. I waited, curious to see how he could fulfil this lucrative commission. He worked quickly, and in less than a minute he stood up, turned to the soldier, and planted a narrow cone of paper firmly against the man's forehead.

'Unicorn,' he said, and the soldier's friends hooted laughter, clapping the newly created unicorn on the back, and taking over possession of the horn in order to fasten it to the man's helmet.

Will stepped back, smiling, and in that moment he saw me. His tall friend followed his suddenly still gaze, and he nodded to me, and squeezed Will's shoulder.

'I'll be busy tonight, mate,' he said softly. 'Room's yours.'

The two-bed room was tiny, but clean. Will closed the door and locked it, and then his hands were at my waist, pulling me against him. Urgency gripped us both, quite suddenly, as though we were two different people from the shy, hesitant newly-weds of last year; this was the first time we had been together, alone, since that night. Romance was the farthest thing from our minds; need was everything. The narrow, single bed was chilly, the sheets felt slightly damp on my bare skin, but Will's warmth covered me and I gave it no more thought. He gave me the most cursory of kisses, bruising kisses, the kisses of a man fighting for control, and I returned them equally savagely. I bit his shoulder as he entered me, and we both cried out at the same time, rocking together, pulsing heat between us and growing warmer with

118

every beat. We hardly moved, either of us, just stayed locked together until the sensation of mutual release faded and our hearts regained their normal rhythm. Will eased away, as far as the small bed allowed, and we both lay there, searching for the words to express the complicated and contradictory feelings of gratitude and despair, but eventually fell into our exhausted dreams without saying anything at all.

Sometime in the night he woke me with a press of his lips on my forehead, and, wordless, we danced again – this time with slow, sweetly drawn out touches and kisses, and when we next fell asleep it was in a tangle of limbs, and with our heads close together on the single pillow.

All too soon it was morning, and the end of Will's leave. The tall soldier from yesterday met us at the station with a girl in tow, and Will introduced him as 'Private Barry Glenn, Lothario and souvenir-collector extraordinaire. Does a good line in German helmets, but no lady's honour is safe, from Reims to Nieuport.' Barry grinned good-naturedly, flicked Will's ear, and left us to our last half an hour together.

Looking at him across the table of the café, where we sat clutching our mugs of weak tea, I tried to pinpoint what exactly it was that made him look different now. His eyes had not lost their sparkle altogether, but it had dimmed, and his smile was still wide, beautiful and with the hint of the impish charm from before. But a hint was all it was. He looked older and leaner, and the dark stories he kept locked away had put circles beneath his eyes, but he was still unmistakeably my Lord William and I loved every new line and shadow that graced his face.

'When are you expected back?' he asked. 'Will you be in trouble if you're late?'

'Not really, since I'm not governed by Red Cross rules. But Anne and Elise will be missed if they're not back at their unit, and I don't want to leave Boxy on her own for too long. I'll begin the drive back as soon as your train leaves, it's only a little over two hours.'

'Do you have to go back?'

The question came out of nowhere, but when I looked at him, startled, I could see it was something he'd been thinking about for some time. He stared back at me with cautious hope, as if the very suddenness of the plea might surprise me into giving the answer he wanted.

I shook my head. 'You know I must.'

'Yes,' he said quickly, and gave me a little smile. 'But you can't blame me for trying.'

'It's safe there,' I insisted. 'Safer than you'd think. We're very well looked after, and as soon as we hear any sign of shells we can get down into the cellar. It's quite exciting sometimes–'

'Stop it,' he said, and reached across the table to run a finger over the back of my hand. 'You're not as tough as you like to pretend.'

'Will, these boys need us. We do good things, we're not just playing at this.'

'I know! It's just... I know.' He sighed, and turned my hand over to lie beneath his, palm to palm. 'And to be honest, if I was sent down the line I would want someone like you pulling me out and getting me patched up.' He let go of my hand and forced a smile. 'But I'll never stop worrying about you, not until you're safely back in Cheshire driving Mrs Cavendish mad.'

'I'm saving up something special to torment her with,' I promised, relieved he had not continued pressing until we argued; it would have been awful to part like that, not knowing when we'd see each other again. I deliberately silenced that voice that still insisted, *if...*

He picked up his mug and swilled it around, pulling a face at the contents. 'Have you heard from Lizzy?'

'A short letter now and again. She's had a bad chill but she's a little better now. She's horribly uncomfortable, and I hate thinking of her in there, but at least she's safe.'

'How about Jack?'

'I had a few lines. I don't think he's had my own letters, because he never addresses anything I've said to him. Not even about Lizzy, and I know they got on famously and he would want to help. If it wasn't for the fact I recognise his handwriting I might think it wasn't from him at all. Presumably the censors have been on his mind; all he said was he's gone overseas.'

We finished our drinks, now stone cold, and I noticed people starting to move towards the door. It was almost time.

'You seem to have made a real hit with your paper-folding,' I said. Anything to prolong the conversation.

He laughed. 'It's so strange. These are men who are brilliantly skilled, back home they build houses, and mend *telephones* for goodness sake!

Some of them know the law of England like the backs of their hands. They perform complicated medical procedures every day of their lives. But watch a butcher fiddle with a piece of an old newspaper for two minutes and they're completely flabbergasted!'

I smiled at the honest puzzlement in his voice. 'I brought the rose with me to Belgium. I can't bear to be without it,' I added, suddenly shy in case he should think it was funny rather than touching.

But he looked pleased. 'It must be a shocking mess by now.'

'It is. But all the same...' I really needed him to understand, but it was hard to find the words to explain it, even to myself. 'When I look at it, it doesn't just remind me of you, it's almost as if it *is* you. It's both of us.' It sounded silly, and didn't even really say what I wanted it to, but watching his mobile mouth soften into a smile, I realised he understood, and was moved to lean across the table and kiss him. There was a chorus of whistles from the table of Tommies in the corner so we didn't stop, giving them the show they were so clearly enjoying, and not even caring if we were reported. When we broke apart we were both breathing faster; the memory of last night seemed very close at that moment.

'You keep hold of that shocking mess if it makes you do that,' he said with a grin. Then the grin faded and he grew serious as he rubbed his thumb gently over my cheek. 'Some of the lads have asked me to make one for their own sweethearts. I'll make them anything they want; cars, boats, houses ... any other flower. But the rose

122

will only ever be for you.'

On my twenty-first birthday Boxy and I threw a party, and invited anyone who could come. Some of the officers from the local company had made themselves known to us, and were pleased to be invited. They brought as much contraband as they could manage, and we ate like kings and queens, and sang songs until well past midnight. The night was a cloudy one, for which we were all grateful; far less chance of an offensive than when the moon shone brightly, and when the party tapered off Boxy and I sat outside, waving off our guests and enjoying a rare quiet night. The guns still boomed in the distance but there was none of the harsh, screaming wail that signified a serious shell attack. We finished the last of the chocolate cake brought by the officers, and took quiet pleasure in the chance to talk as we went over Gertie at our leisure for once.

I had still not told Mother about Will, and although Boxy confessed to finding it quite funny and romantic, she urged me to take the bull by the horns.

'Come on, Davies, it's not really fair. She has every right to know. Don't you think she'll adore your lovely man?'

'It's not a question of what she thinks of him,' I pointed out, kicking at a loose board on Gertie's runner. 'You know that every bit as well as I do.'

She shook her head. 'Well, no matter what she thinks of the marriage, you're going to have to brave it one day. Think how much happier you'll be when you don't have to think so hard about every letter you send, just so you don't let anything slip.'

'That would be easier,' I admitted. Unspoken between us lay the other truth; should something happen to me, it would all come out, and mother would have an awful sense of betrayal to add to her grief. 'All right. I've got some leave coming up next month, I'll write and tell Mother I'm coming home for a few days.'

'And you'll tell her?'

I sighed, and crossed my heart. 'I promise. Now belt up and hand me that spanner.'

Chapter Seven

Cheshire, September 28th 1915.

Oaklands Manor in the autumn was one of the more beautiful sights with which I had grown up, and it had never palled. The huge oaks were cloaked in the glorious hues of red, gold and bronze, and the light that shone through them set them on fire against the bright blue sky. I stood, for a moment, looking down the long avenue of trees, remembering the day, three years ago, that Uncle Jack and I had driven away, holding in our laughter – not well enough – while Lizzy stood looking after us in the gloomy belief she had committed a terrible faux pas.

Abruptly the date hit me, it was Lizzy's birthday. She too would turn twenty-one today, and while I had spent my birthday with my new-found friends and comrades, drinking wine, singing songs and eating cake, she would spend hers locked away from the world, and from those who loved her. A cloud seemed to pass over the brightness of the day, although the sky remained unchanged, and I turned away from the glory of the gardens; I couldn't enjoy them while Lizzy was suffering.

I was still aching for the youth Lizzy had lost, when I stepped over the threshold into the big hall. Always so familiar, it now looked like something someone had once described to me but I'd never really seen. I looked around it with new eyes, and saw nothing but grand emptiness.

'Evangeline!'

I turned to see my mother, her arms outstretched, coming towards me from the morning room, and it was so unlike her to seek me out that I dropped my bag and went to meet her. She had always appeared so tall, statuesque almost, and myself so small beside her, but now she seemed to have shrunk until I was the stronger of the two of us. She hugged me close, and it was more than her usual affectionate, but slightly impatient embrace.

Dodsworth had picked up my bag and waited patiently, but mother, still with one arm around me, waved her free hand for him to take the bag upstairs. Then she drew back and looked at me, her face pale.

'How are you? You look tired. Come and sit down, I have something to tell you.'

Bemused, and a little worried, I followed her into the morning room, her favourite place in the entire house. Instead of sitting down at her writing desk, she paced the room in much the same way as she had insisted gave her a headache when I did it.

'Mother, what's wrong? Has something happened?' I went cold as the thought hit me: Uncle Jack?

Mother took a short, sharp breath. 'It's Lawrence. He's left. Gone.'

'Joined up?' Surely he was too young ... but no, as strange as it was to realise, he had turned eighteen a few months ago. 'Where is he?'

'He's taken a commission and gone to France. Somewhere called Courcelette.' It sounded as though the words hurt her to say, and, for a fleeting and unfair moment I wondered if she had even once spoken of me with that same frightened note in her voice. But I shook the thought away; it wasn't the same thing at all. Lawrence was her baby, the sole heir to everything she had struggled to hold onto since the theft of the Kalteng Star, and he was directly in the midst of the action. There was a second's pride in the fact that he'd volunteered, and I thought of his cousins, the Wingfields – I doubted if either of those boys would see a moment's conflict over there unless they were forced to. But the pride vanished immediately, replaced by shame: after what I had seen, was I really just as bad as all those parents who saw their sons off to die, and then proudly claimed they had contributed to an assured allied victory?

The next thought was that I should tell Will, he had always liked Lawrence and, of course, Lawrence still hero-worshipped him. I looked at

126

Mother and realised I couldn't tell her yet about Will and me, she had enough pain to cope with, without adding my deceit to the weight of it.

I hugged her again. 'He'll be fine,' I said, sounding firmer than I felt. 'It'll be ages before he's put somewhere really dangerous, and the war could end at any minute.'

She sagged against me with a little sigh of gratitude. 'Are you sure? Ages?'

'Absolutely positive.' I was no such thing, but it would serve no purpose to worry her further. 'They have lots of training, and if he's taken a commission he's quite likely to be based with the general staff at HQ. That's miles behind the lines, honestly. Try not to worry, but if you can't help it then at least don't let him know it.'

She eased away from me again and gave me a smile. 'You're right, it won't do to let him see we're upset, he'll have enough to think about.' She looked calmer now, and it occurred to me to simply blurt out my news just to get it out of the way. But I still couldn't. Not yet.

'I'd like a bath, if I may?'

'Of course. I'll ask Mary to run you one.'

'How is everyone?' I asked as mother reached for the bell. 'I heard about Billy Duncan, the poor boy.' As I spoke I realised what I'd said, and steeled myself for Mother to consider Lawrence's dangerous situation again, and lose her carefully regained equanimity. But she merely looked puzzled.

'Billy Duncan?'

'The stable boy.' I tried to suppress my impatience; Mother was not cold-hearted, but she'd never been one to take too much notice of those who worked for her, particularly those she rarely saw.

'Oh, yes. Of course. Billy.' I looked closely at her and decided she was too distracted about Lawrence to concern herself, but I felt a prickle of the old exasperation. 'I gather Mr ... uh, the gardener's son was killed in a gas attack earlier this year,' she went on, and I had the rather uncharitable feeling she thought I should be appreciative of her knowledge.

I nodded. 'Poor Joe.' Then I added pointedly, 'That was his name, Mother, Joe Shackleton.'

'There's no need to be snappy, Evangeline.' But her words didn't have the same bite I was used to.

I spoke softly now. 'You're right. I'm sorry.' Lawrence's absence loomed between us, and I felt almost as if I should apologise for not being him, but, again, I knew that was unfair. I wished I could switch off that new, antagonistic part of me, but something about being here, instead of working, had taken the guilt I felt and turned it into a defensive kind of anger. It wasn't Mother's fault, but I couldn't make her understand through my letters alone, and unless she saw it for herself she would believe only what she heard on the news. She wouldn't come out and visit, although I offered to arrange passes, and so she remained encased in her bubble of misinformation. We were growing further apart every day, and I couldn't see a way back.

Mary's pleasure at seeing me was evident, which buoyed my spirits a good deal. She took me upstairs and ran my bath while I changed out of my travelling clothes, and we arranged to meet after dinner and toast Lizzy's birthday. It would be something to tell her the next time we wrote, and might help her to know how much we missed her and thought of her. On the other hand, would it simply serve to accentuate her isolation? I would have to think carefully about it, but I couldn't let the day go unmarked.

After my bath I walked the three miles into Breckenhall, enjoying the chance to stretch my legs after being cramped up on the train for so long; it was still too early for dinner, and I thought Martin might like to know how Will was getting on. The afternoon was still bright, although the day was rapidly cooling, and I enjoyed the sunlight that flickered through the trees and onto my face. It felt so peaceful here, a million miles away from the hollow boom of the guns, and the chorus of pain that was my life's usual accompaniment. It was with this quiet enjoyment still painting a smile on my lips, that I pushed open the door to Markham's shop.

'I say, here's a pretty thing,' a voice said, and I looked around. Behind me, also about to step into the shop, was a young man a few years older than me. He wasn't very tall, but he had an impressive bearing about him nevertheless, and his smile, when he bestowed it on me, was undeniably dazzling. I nodded acknowledgement of the compliment, but did not invite conversation and stepped over the threshold, aware he was following rather more closely than politeness allowed.

'What's your name?' he went on, and something about the way his eyes roved over me quashed my natural tendency towards friendliness.

129

'I'm sorry, I don't see that being any business of yours,' I returned, quite coolly, but he just laughed.

'Quite right too. My apologies, I can tell you're a lady of breeding.'

'Accepted, and thank you.'

Martin had looked up as the bell on the door rang, and warmth crossed his rather pale face. 'Evie!'

'Martin, how lovely to see you,' I said, and crossed to him. We weren't close friends, but the fact that he had been part of mine and Will's secret made it natural that I should stretch across the counter to give him a quick hug and a peck on the cheek.

'How's Will?' was his first question.

I gestured behind me. 'Perhaps you'd like to serve this customer first, and then we'll have the chance for a proper chat.'

'Good, I'd like that.' Martin looked past me at the only other customer; the man who'd followed me in. 'Can I help you, sir?'

'No thanks, I'm just looking,' the man replied, and began peering at the trays in the window.

I swallowed an irritated grunt, and turned back to Martin. 'Will's in reserve at the moment, I was hoping he'd be able to come with me on leave, but they have an awful lot of work on. Digging, at the moment, mostly.'

'Where?' It was the stranger who asked, and I snapped my mouth shut over an automatic response, and my need to share what Will was doing just for the excuse to talk about him. This man was far too nosy for my liking, and we'd all

130

seen the warnings about spies.

'I'm sure you realise I can't tell you that,' I said, then added rather pointedly, 'Are you on leave at the moment?'

'I am,' he said. 'Been at the Front from the off. France.'

'Really?'

'Really.' He smiled again, showing very good teeth and clear, untroubled, hazel eyes. He really was quite handsome, but something about him irked me, and I instinctively mistrusted him; had he really been out where Will was, the chances were those eyes would not be shining quite so brightly. Even if he was stationed a long way back from the lines, and had managed to avoid being involved in any direct action, it would still have left its mark.

'Are you from Breckenhall, Mr...?'

'No. So, tell me, Miss, is Will your husband?'

I thought he had something of a cheek asking so personal a question when he had rudely cut my casually polite one short, so I ignored him and turned back to Martin. 'How are things with you, is business going well?'

'As well as you could expect,' he said with a little shrug. We talked for a little while longer, and all the time the stranger hovered nearby, taking advantage of any lull in the conversation to ask something about me, or about Will – questions I either side-stepped or ignored completely. Unnerved by the whole thing, I wondered whether I ought to tell someone. If Uncle Jack were here, he'd tell me what to do. Mother might know how I could reach him, and I'd send another plea for

Lizzy too; I was still convinced he would know of some way to help her.

After a short while another customer came in, and I said goodbye to Martin, promising to pass on his greetings to Mary, and to Will the next time I wrote. To my relief the good-looking stranger stayed behind in the shop, and I only hoped Martin would adopt my stance and ignore those probing questions. I went straight into the café, where I enjoyed my first really good cup of tea for ages, before I noticed the evening had already begun to make its appearance and I ought to begin my walk back. This afternoon it had seemed a wonderful idea, to walk instead of being driven, but now I was regretting it as I came out of the café into the cool air and shivered. I drew my coat tighter about myself, then looked up at the sky.

'Can I drive you somewhere?'

I turned, already disliking that voice, and shook my head. 'No, thank you. I'll enjoy the walk.'

The young man looked at me consideringly, his head tilted slightly, that smile still playing about his lips. 'You've taken a strong dislike to me, haven't you, Miss Creswell?'

I frowned. 'I suppose Martin told you my name?'

'No, the lady who came in just before you left. She was terribly impressed to see you, I gather you're one of the family from the big manor house?'

'Excuse me,' I said, and went to walk past him, but he caught at my arm.

'Miss Creswell, listen. I'm sorry I've made myself objectionable by my questions. I understand you're a lady of high standing, and I'd like you to accept my apology in the spirit with which it's expressed.'

'Accepted,' I said. 'Now if you wouldn't mind letting go of me?'

He dropped my arm as if he'd only just realised he was still holding it. 'Again, my sincere apologies. Won't you please let me drive you back to the manor?'

'No, thank you.'

He crossed his arms over his chest, and pursed his lips. 'Your reputation precedes you, I shouldn't be surprised you're so rude,' he said.

I just gaped at him, then turned and walked away. My reputation? I had been abrupt today, certainly, but in my defence I had been provoked into suspicion. The opinion of this stranger had no impact on my conscience, but I didn't like the thought that people in town considered me anything but pleasant and easy-going.

My mood soured still further as I arrived home and saw our dinner guests for the evening just getting out of their motor. David's grandfather, Samuel Wingfield, brought out the worst in me, and always had. His wife Lydia, and daughter-in-law Clarissa, rated no higher in my good opinion, and I had to force myself to smile at them as they alighted. Matthew, David's father, seemed the only Wingfield who had any natural friendliness about him; the others were well-armed in social graces, but behaved as though they owned every-thing on which they stood at any given time.

Matthew, quiet and pleasant-looking, gave me a genuine smile and spoke softly. 'Evie, sweetheart. We've heard all about what you're doing out

133

there. So proud of you.'

I returned his smile and nodded my thanks, and took his arm when he proffered it, letting him lead me into the house. 'Will your boys join up?'

'Robert will, I think. David seems to have some deep objection on moral grounds.'

I looked at him but his face was fixed ahead, and I saw his brow drawn down. I decided not to press him on it. 'How about yourself?'

'I leave next week,' he said. 'Defence of the Suez Canal.'

'Ah.' I had read about this, and it was nice to be able to get the opinion of one who was going to play a part. 'Why do you think they took that decision? To put such a large force in place, instead of despatching the troops where they're needed most?'

Matthew looked at me with a little smile. 'I can hear echoes of Jack Carlisle in that question,' he said, with real warmth. 'The fact is, we can't tell whether the Turks have given up, or whether they're just waiting for us to redeploy to Gallipoli before they launch another offensive.'

'But surely, with things going so badly already at Gallipoli, the sensible thing would be to do just that? I mean, the Dardanelles Committee–'

'Evangeline!' Mother's voice cut through my words. 'Leave Matthew alone, dear, I'm sure he'd rather have a drink and some peace and quiet than talk about military strategy.'

Matthew waited until she'd passed us by, then winked at me. 'We'll talk about it later, and I look forward to it,' he said in a low voice, and squeezed my arm before letting go and following mother to the sitting room.

I went upstairs to change for dinner, and Mary helped me. I found this very hard to get used to; since I had first left home almost a year ago, and I so often slept in my clothes now, it felt like a dreadful waste of everyone's time to have someone ready my gown and sort my jewellery. Once dressed, I sat before my mirror and looked at my reflection with a rare twinge of sadness for what I saw. There had been shock and dismay on Mother's face when, on my first home leave and removing my hat, I'd revealed short, clumpy-cut hair.

It had seemed such a trivial thing to make her react in such a way, that I'd grown cross and simply said, 'Lice, Mother,' before realising her reaction to something she could actually see was only representative of the way she felt about my chosen wartime role. To soften the air between us I made sure to dress my hair as prettily as I could while I was at home, and she had wordlessly shown her gratitude by helping me.

But tonight it was Mary's job, and by the time she had finished adding little sprays of feather and beads, I actually felt quite feminine again and I wished Will were here to see it; the wide, belted waist of my gown fitted neatly and I knew he would have loved to feel the suggestion of curves beneath the fringed silk, tantalisingly separated from his touch by the smooth material. The small heels I wore raised me a little higher, but I would still have been shorter than him, my cheek would fit in the hollow of his shoulder, my head brushing his jawline. If he was here to hold me now, I would

135

slide my arms around his neck and, clothing or not, no part of me would be separated from him, not one inch of me left cold and alone.

But Will wasn't here. While I stood in this bright, clean room, dressed like a princess and with my eyes closed in sudden yearning, my husband lay in a field in another country, in a muddy uniform and wet boots, weighed down with weapons and wire-cutters, rations and rifle, blanket and bayonet. He might be talking with his fellow soldiers, taking his turn at sleeping, or playing cards. He might be thinking of me, he might be thinking only of somewhere dry and warm to sleep, not caring if he was alone or with twenty others. He might be using those strong, talented fingers to write me a love-filled letter, or to craft some piece of scrap paper into a boat, or a tree – never a rose – or he might be using them to load mortars or clean his gun.

But whatever he was doing, he wasn't here.

'He'll be fine, Evie.' Mary's voice cut through my sudden, tight-throated dismay at the direction my thoughts had taken. I felt a tear slide onto my cheek, and wiped it quickly away.

'I know. I'm as sure as I can ever be that he's safe at the moment. But he's...' I trailed off, shaking my head.

'Too far away,' Mary supplied gently, and I gave her a trembling smile, and nodded.

Dinner started off as the usual stiffly polite affair it always was when the Wingfields came. I gathered they were still regular visitors, as if they couldn't quite trust Mother to run Oaklands properly now Uncle Jack had gone away, but I was passionately relieved that neither David nor his younger brother Robert saw fit to join them.

'Are you all set for your travels?' Mother asked Matthew. He nodded and opened his mouth to answer, only to be pre-empted by Clarissa, who seemed unable to pass a single comment without using it to needle me in some fashion.

'Quite understand the men going off to fight, but surely not the place for a well-bred young lady.'

'On the contrary,' I said, keeping my voice even. 'It's the perfect way for us to contribute. Free up others who might be better suited for helping with war work, or doing the men's jobs. I know I'd be useless at that.'

'That's not the only choice, of course.'

'What do you mean?' But we all knew.

'Well, you're twenty-one now, isn't it time you were thinking about marriage?'

I raised my glass and caught the eye of Simon, who stepped forward and poured me some more wine. For a moment I concentrated on thanking him, while I composed my reply. 'I'm sure there will be plenty of time for that when the war is over,' I said at last, somewhat evasively.

'I wouldn't be too sure. All the young men are disappearing rather quickly,' she said, waving her glass at Simon, too. 'The last thing you want is to be left at home, with only the weak, the enfeebled and the cowards to choose from.'

I couldn't help it. 'When do David and Robert join their units?'

Matthew coughed, drawing our attention, and I saw his face had gone red as if he'd swallowed his food too quickly. As I began to turn back to Clarissa, however, I saw the grin that touched the corners of his mouth, though he raised his napkin to hide it; it was his turn to remind me of Uncle Jack now, and I wondered how Samuel and Lydia had managed to produce such a thoroughly decent son.

Clarissa scowled at her husband. 'Those are your boys she's mocking, Matthew.'

'You ought to be pleased they're not going,' Mother said, and shame crept over me at the sudden desolation in her voice.

'They have rather too much to contribute at home to go gallivanting overseas,' Clarissa said. I daren't look at Mother, and even Samuel flinched.

'Now, dear,' he said. 'Lily's son's a fine young man, doing a very brave thing.'

'Of course,' she said quickly, and reached out to squeeze Mother's hand. 'I didn't mean to imply otherwise, darling. Please forgive me?'

Mother inclined her head and removed her hand from Clarissa's, pretending she wanted to pick up her wine glass. I remembered her telling me what she privately thought of Clarissa, and my topsy-turvy feelings towards her swerved back to warmth once again.

Clarissa returned to the attack. 'Of course, now the Kalteng Star is missing, your choices will be far more limited,' she went on, wiping my smile away before it had fully formed.

'Clarissa!' Matthew's hand hit the table, making us all jump, but she turned a calm face on him and spoke quietly.

'I'm only saying what we're all thinking.'

138

'It's not your place,' he told her tightly, and for the first time I saw his eyes harden as he looked at her.

'She's right though,' Samuel said. 'You're a pretty enough girl, Evangeline, but you might think about growing your hair again. Gentlemen don't like to think they're paying court to a tomboy.'

I didn't know what to say, and looked to Mother for support, but she had turned inward as she drank her wine, too fast, and I don't think she'd even heard anything after Matthew had thumped the table.

'I'm not trying to attract gentlemen,' I said, allowing some of my own anger into my voice. 'I have a job to do.'

'And I'm sure it's a lot of fun, playing glamorous nursemaid to those soldiers,' Clarissa said, 'but you won't find a husband among the rank and file. An officer now, that would be quite acceptable.'

'I don't want an officer! I'm–' I managed to choke the word off just in time. I might have been tempted to blurt out the truth earlier, to Mother, but not in front of the Wingfields. 'I'm keen on someone already.'

Samuel raised an eyebrow. 'Oh? What's his family?'

Matthew sighed. 'What does it matter?' He looked at me with an apologetic half-smile, which I didn't return; nice or not, he was a Wingfield, and I was too angry with them.

Lydia had so far been silent, but I could feel her eyes on me now, although she was speaking to her son. 'Your father's right, Matthew. What if that awful maid of hers owns up about where she's hidden that diamond, and it comes back into the family? Whoever Evie marries–'

'Must be worthy of it, I know!' I said, my voice rising. 'But Lizzy didn't steal the diamond, and I hope it never turns up.'

'But this man you're talking about has the right–'

'He doesn't want it!'

'He knows about it?' Samuel said, leaning forward, suddenly eager.

'Yes, he's always known about it. He loves me even without it, and I love him.'

Now Mother seemed to swim back from her dark thoughts about Lawrence, and take note of the conversation. 'Is this the same young man you were seeing before you went away?'

The truth was pushing at me from inside, desperate to escape in its complete form, but all I would allow was, 'Yes. His name's Will Davies, he was the butcher's boy before the war.'

There was a silence that stretched and stretched, and then Clarissa spoke. 'The butcher's boy. Frank Markham's?'

'I didn't know you knew Mr Markham.'

She didn't reply, and began eating again, and I wondered where she might have crossed paths with our local butcher, living in Shrewford as she did. But the question was pushed aside as Mother spoke.

'I thought you'd seen sense where that boy was concerned, Evangeline. He's never going to amount to anything, Mr Markham has a new

140

apprentice now, and he'll be the one who takes over the business if Markham doesn't come back from the war.'

'He has a new apprentice because Will is away fighting!' I was finding it hard to keep my temper. 'He's over there right now, risking his life for–'

'Yes, yes, all very admirable,' Samuel broke in, 'but you need to be concerned with this family, and how it will go on. Especially now...' He seemed to realise he must not complete that sentence, and coughed into silence.

Mother pushed her plate away and stood up. 'I'm going to lie down,' she said in a trembling voice.

'Lily, darling, don't be silly,' Clarissa said. 'Samuel didn't mean anything. Did you?'

He cleared his throat, and stood up too, speaking more gently. 'No, of course not. Young Lawrence will do splendidly over there, and then come back, marry a nice girl, and the Creswell family will march on.'

I looked around the table. At Mother, standing on legs I knew would be shaking beneath her expensive gown; then at Lydia, her face directed down at her plate; at Clarissa, eyes on her father-in-law, who stood with his hand outstretched towards his hostess; and at Matthew, white-faced and still as he looked at his father. Why was I here? I felt Flanders calling out to me, as surely as I heard the heavy ticking of the hallway grand-father clock cutting through the silence in this room.

At last Mother reached out and accepted Samuel's conciliatory touch. 'Perhaps I shall just

141

go to the sitting room and wait for you there,' she said.

'Don't you want dessert?'

She shook her head, and Samuel laid his napkin down. 'Then none of us shall have it.'

'Why ever not?' Mother said. 'Mrs Hannah has been working very hard, she'll be most upset if you refuse it now. I'll go and wait, you stay and finish.'

I didn't want to stay either, and I was surprised at the strength of my longing to be back at Number Twelve with Boxy, even freezing cold and exhausted. If I had the choice between that, and sitting here being served exquisite food on fine bone china, surrounded by the Wingfields, there would be no hesitation.

But I stayed, if only to ensure they didn't make off with the silverware.

Later, after an excruciating evening listening to all the reasons why Will Davies would be the ruination of me, and having to bite my tongue several times to avoid snapping that it was too late and I didn't care what anyone thought, the Wingfields left. I was at the end of an extremely short tether by now, and as Mother prepared to retire for the night, I stood up and said, 'We're married.'

She looked at me blankly for a moment, then went absolutely white, and sat down. 'What?' she whispered.

'Will and me. Married. We got married right before he left for France.'

'But ... why didn't you tell me?'

It was not the question, or the reaction, I'd expected, and I didn't know how to answer.

'Because of this,' I said at length. 'Because of how you would react, how it would make you feel. I couldn't bear to think you might try to stop it, and then the longer it went on, the harder it was to tell you the truth.'

Mother shook her head. 'You thought I would try to stop you?'

'After what you said, yes.'

'What I said?'

'The same as Lydia said tonight. About my husband being ... worthy.' Anger bubbled to the surface. 'Will Davies is worth a million Kalteng Stars!'

Mother held up a hand. 'I understand, but you've chosen to risk our future by marrying someone who, if he lives, and of course I hope he does, will return to you with no livelihood, no money and no prospects.'

'He's got a profession.'

'He was still the apprentice when he–'

'He's a skilled man, an artist.'

'An artist?' She rose again and began to pace in her agitation. 'What on earth are you thinking? What kind of life will you have, the two of you? No Kalteng Star to win your way into society, a marriage so far beneath you as to be laughable, and your defence is that he's an *artist?*'

'He creates beautiful things,' I said, and the memory of the joyful innocence we'd known twisted my insides tighter. 'I'll show you.'

'I'm sure he does,' she turned to me, and her voice gentled. 'Darling, listen to me. Artist or not, talented or not, he's not right for this family. Your loyalties are to *this family.* You have to put an

143

end to this.'

'No.'

She looked at me helplessly, and with a surge of relief I saw something battling in her eyes: she understood. She really did, deep down. But she was scared. Everything was falling apart, and she was just plain scared.

I took her hand. 'I'm glad I've told you at last,' I said softly, 'and I'm sorry for the pain I've caused you. But I love Will, I've loved him for three years, and he loves me. I don't care how hard it is for us after the war, we'll make our way as best we can. We'll live where we can, work where we can, and we'll be happy.'

It seemed too quiet without the distant shout of the bombardment, and I wondered if I would ever get used to total silence again. Mother looked down at our hands, hers pale and elegant, mine rough and reddened, with chapped knuckles and splintered fingernails, and she raised them to her lips.

'I hope I'm wrong, Evie,' she said quietly. 'And I hope he knows what he has in you.'

'He knows me with all my faults, and he still loves me,' I said. 'That's all I could ever hope for.'

She nodded. 'I'll see you at breakfast,' she said. 'Sleep well, and perhaps tomorrow we can talk a little more.'

I left her, feeling more than a little wretched despite the relief of having told her at last, and I suspected that tomorrow she would revert, at least in part, to the cool, detached woman I knew so well. But tonight she was just my mother, and I had broken her heart.

Mary and I sat together in my rooms and drank the hot toddies she'd brought up. We toasted Lizzy, and I told her about the dinner, and then about the conversation with Mother when the Wingfields had left. 'She's bending to my way of thinking, but it won't last, I know it.'

'She's been under so much strain lately,' Mary said. 'Ever since young Lawrence accepted his commission. You can't help but feel for her.'

'I know. Everything's changing.'

'You always said it would.'

'But I didn't think it would take something like the war to make it happen. I thought it would be thanks to the suffrage movement.'

'You don't seem to be as favourable towards the Suffragettes as you were,' she observed. 'Why's that?'

I shook my head. 'I went to an anti-suffrage rally once, before the war, just so I could reinforce my beliefs. But things got quite nasty and I had cause to rethink things. I still believe in the movement, that hasn't changed, but I'm not so sure about the methods anymore.' I shrugged, and smiled faintly. 'It seems we might find a better way to express ourselves than setting fire to buildings and committing suicide.'

'Put like that,' Mary agreed with a little laugh, 'I'm sure you're right. Lizzy said she had to clean Sylvia Pankhurst's cell once, after she was forcibly fed. Said it's absolutely horrible what they do to those poor women.'

'Then there must be a better way. I hope we can find it. But first, there's the small matter of a war to win. As for the war with Mother,' I looked into my empty glass and sighed. 'Object achieved, and a new Front's been established.' I handed the glass to Mary, who put it back on the little silver tray. 'She called me Evie.'

'She did what?'

'Only once, but I think we only need to hold our position now, in order to declare victory.'

'She's not really the enemy,' Mary said with mild reproach.

'No, but sometimes it's your own troops who have the capacity to hurt you the most.' I looked up at her, with sadness pulling at my heart. 'I'm going back tomorrow.'

Mary pursed her lips, but I could see she understood, even if she didn't like it. 'I'll make sure you're breakfasted well,' was all she said.

And so, only a day after I'd arrived in what should have been the warm and welcoming safety of my home, I was back on the ferry to Calais. Mother had accepted my decision with, I was dismayed to see, something close to relief. I had no doubt that she worried, and that she missed me, but if my coming of age had been difficult for her, then the way I was now had drawn an even heavier curtain between us and she could no longer fight her way through the folds. So I was returning to the only life that made any sense now, looking forward and not back, regretting nothing.

It was less than a year later that I got the telegram.

Chapter Eight

July 14th 1916.

First there was the letter.

My darling Evie,

We are dug in at a place called Bazentin-le-Petit, having enjoyed an easy victory in this and Bazentin-le-Grand, and are resting while we await further orders. If our COs are to be believed I will be able to write again very soon, and at length. Hopefully without the censor stamping all over it either! We are optimistic at last, and I have only a few minutes, and little ink, but wanted to tell you again that you have been my heart's constant companion throughout this war.

How we have survived this long apart is a question I have long since stopped asking; I only know that when I see you again, and taste your kiss, nothing less than the threat of death will drag me away from your side.

Boxy's hand on my arm felt as if it were separated by thick winter clothing rather than the light cotton blouse I wore, and I looked from letter to telegram, with eyes that refused to believe what they were seeing. My gaze fell on the qualifying comment, below the rather stark information that Will had been "posted as missing" on July 16th 1916.

The report that he is missing does not necessarily mean that he has been killed, as he may be a prisoner of war, or temporarily separated from his regiment.

Official reports that men are prisoners of war take some time to reach this country, and if he has been captured by the enemy it is probable that unofficial news will reach you first. In that case, I am to ask you to forward any letter received at once to this Office, and it will be returned to you as soon as possible.

Should any further official information be received it will be at once communicated to you.

I am,
Sir or Madam,
Your obedient Servant

The telegram marked the beginning of four months of an exhausting mixture of anguish and hope, and more than ever before I longed to be able to just pick up the telephone and speak to Uncle Jack.

'What could he do, though, even if he knew?' Boxy asked, sensibly. She touched my hand, and I flinched away without really knowing why, except that any touch that wasn't Will's was the wrong one. I looked at her with a silent apology that she waved away. 'Davies, listen. You go and search wherever you can. Ask at the hospitals and clearing stations, you need to do that. Take as long as you need, I'll ask the chaps at HQ if they can get another pair of hands drafted in here.'

'I'll take one of the Belgian cars,' I said with difficulty, my throat was tight with gratitude for her understanding and her brisk practicality. 'I'll leave Gertie for you.'

'Thank you,' she said, and her dry tone made me smile, despite everything. 'Go on, poppet, get organised.'

But I couldn't do much, after all. The dirty, bloody job of protecting the front was relentless in its throwing away of life and limb, and would not stop simply because one woman's husband had gone missing.

Last November the 19th brigade had gone over to the 33rd division, newly arrived in France, and consequently Will had been with them at the rout that was High Wood, and it was the last time he'd been seen. The censors, at least for mail going between military units, had not deemed it necessary to block out the name of the town where they had dug in immediately after the successful raid at Bazentin; neither of the places he'd named were military targets. This, at least, gave me somewhere to start, but I couldn't afford to keep putting fuel in the borrowed car, so all I could do was drive to Bazentin and volunteer at the nearest hospital, in the hope someone might remember seeing him.

Aware I was only a few miles from where Lawrence was stationed at Courcelette, I tried to find time to visit him. We managed a single, half-hour encounter before he had to leave again, and in that time I saw the beginnings of the changes that would break our mother's heart all over again. We spoke a little, he expressed deep concern about Will, and we parted with a hug, the first since we had been small children; the slender shoulders beneath the uniform seemed those of a child playing dressing-up, and I returned to Bazentin grieving for yet another stolen youth.

My search continued. Whenever I had exhausted one avenue of possibility I simply started down a new one. A trained driver was never turned away, and before long I had visited every clearing station and hospital within twenty miles, giving my services and asking my questions until I could see looks of tired recognition on the faces of the nurses when they saw me.

It seemed everywhere I went I would hear some tale of a shell obliterating a man completely, so that all remained was the twisted tin of his hat, or some part of his uniform ... I could not think of that happening to Will, and so I didn't. I simply took every spare hour that was available to me, often sacrificing sleep, for fear of missing some opportunity. The irony was not lost on me, that when Boxy and I had been training I had searched among the wounded too, with the crawling dread that I would see Will's face there. Now I would give anything to see him, even badly wounded; it would mean he could be helped: that he still lived was all that mattered now.

My determination drove me on, but it also wore away my strength. Even the news that Uncle Jack had returned, and had, as promised, arranged Lizzy's release from prison, took a while to filter through the haze of fear and loss that enveloped me through my waking hours, and plagued me through my fragile sleep. However, seeing Lizzy herself during a brief trip home, and learning that Ruth Wilkins had actually been the one to steal the Kalteng Star, gave me a surge of renewed hope; Uncle Jack should have been my first port of call, even though I hadn't known for sure he'd get my letters, and now he was home he could put his government connections to more good use. He would uncover the truth about what had happened to Will, and all I could do was pray it was a truth I could live with.

I gave the letter to Lizzy to post when she walked into town, and returned to Belgium two days later, throwing myself back into my work with all the guilt of one who'd been away too long and is desperate to make amends. Boxy kept up her usual chatter, carefully avoiding mention of Will, or even Benjy, but my head was filled to the brim with memories, images and dark, terrified imaginings. So, when the unfamiliar officer came to Number Twelve with a sombre look on his face, it was with a sense of complete disbelief that I listened to him stammering out news, not of Will, but of Lizzy.

Boxy and I sat waiting for the officer to return; he was reporting back to HQ and requesting leave to accompany me back to England. Boxy listened in open-mouthed amazement while I tried to explain in as few words as possible.

'Lizzy found out it was one of the Wingfields who'd arranged for Ruth to steal the Kalteng Star. She and Uncle Jack went to the Wingfields' home at Shrewford, but there was a confrontation. Uncle Jack was knocked down by Wingfield's car, and soon after that Lizzy was shot.'

'But she's alive?'

I nodded. The shock of the news, so quickly followed by the relief of knowing they were both safe, had sucked all the breath out of me, leaving me shaking and light-headed. But there was more. I took a deep breath. 'She's alive, yes. And, as of a few days ago, so is Will.'

Boxy gripped my hand tight, for once speechless.

'We don't know where he is yet,' I cautioned, as the officer had done to me when he'd seen my face. 'The Wingfields do though, somehow. I don't understand that part of it properly, all I know is that he's been seen.'

'Is he hiding somewhere?' she managed at last.

'I think so. He must be terrified he'll be accused of desertion.'

'Your Uncle Jack won't rest until he finds him.'

'But what if Will comes out of hiding before he does?' I felt sick at the thought. 'What if he's arrested?'

Boxy put her arm around me, and gave me a squeeze, it was pointless to embrace false optimism; we had both been around the military for too long to believe in miracles, but Boxy's voice, at least, was firm. 'Well, we'll just have to trust that Jack can find him first.'

Royal Victoria Hospital, Shrewford, November 1916

When I arrived I was shown into a room to wait, and found Mary there, looking as white and ill as I felt. We embraced, and Mary told me all that had happened.

'Samuel Wingfield found out where Will was. He had a photograph to prove it, and told Lizzy if she

152

handed over the Kalteng Star he would tell her where Will is. She didn't have it, of course, but she had to get it back to give to Samuel as if she'd had it all along, otherwise the bargain would have collapsed.'

'And she was shot trying to get it?'

'The shot would have hit Jack, but Lizzy burst into the room thinking he'd already been hurt, and she was hit instead.'

I thought about some of the wounds I'd seen and tended, the torn flesh, the shattered bone beneath, the pain in every tense line of the injured man's body and the terror in their eyes ... the knowledge that little Lizzy Parker had suffered the same thing lit a fire of utter fury in me for the Wingfields; if someone had put a gun in my hand right then I'd have gone to Shrewford Hall, and happily returned the violence. I swallowed my tears, with an effort. When I was at last permitted to see Lizzy I didn't want to be red-eyed and distraught, no matter how deeply I felt it.

'There's something else,' Mary said.

'What?'

'Lizzy and your Uncle Jack ... they're, well, they're...' I stared at her, and she sighed. 'I was violently opposed at first, and I told Lizzy as much. But they're so deeply in love, it's the clearest thing in the world.'

I let the idea take hold, turning it over slowly. 'He's twice her age, almost,' I managed at last, but even as my lips uttered the words I felt them lose that dead feeling and curve into a smile that found its echo in my heart. A little flare of pleasure cut through the darkness that had lived with me since

153

July. Lizzy and Jack. Of *course*, Lizzy and Jack ... how could anyone doubt they were made for each other? She was quick, clever and brave, and he was kind and funny, intelligent and occasionally hot-tempered, but if his political ire could be raised by one of my deliberately provocative statements, it could as easily be extinguished by nothing more than a grin from someone he loved. A grin from Lizzy. All those conversations we'd had, the three of us, all the cryptic little comments he'd made, and that smile when I'd told him and Mother I'd chosen Lizzy as my maid...

'No wonder they risked their lives to protect one another,' I said. 'I must tell her I'm pleased for them, she'll be worried sick about telling me.' But even as I spoke I felt yet more tears gathering, and they weren't tears of happiness for the two of them, there was no pretending they were. Hollowed out with loneliness, I walked down the endless corridors, hiding in the crowds and drawing no attention as I let my mind reach out and find Will, bringing him close with memories of laughter and tenderness. I was a willing victim of the sweetest torture; allowing those memories to grow until they seemed real again, only to be snapped back to the here and now by a sudden noise, a shout, or a slamming door ... and be swamped by emptiness once more.

By the time Lizzy was awake I had my emotions under control again, although I almost broke down at the sight of her: small, and almost child-like, her face as white as her pillow. We hugged carefully, and I told her how the officer had come to find me and I'd come right away, pretending to the Red Cross, who'd be asked to supply cover once again, that we were sisters. I saw her swallow hard, and knew what she was thinking.

'We sort of are,' she said. 'Or maybe cousins, at least. Evie, I have to tell you something...'

'I know about you and Jack,' I said, and smiled, seeing her relief and the colour returning to her cheeks a little. 'Mary and I have had quite a talk. I was shocked at first, of course, but I can't think of two better suited people.'

'Except you and Will,' she pointed out, 'and if fate smiles on us just a little longer we'll soon find out where he is.' My heart leapt and I felt my eyes widen. I didn't trust myself to speak. Was she simply being optimistic? But I listened, hardly breathing, as she told what had happened immediately before she had burst into the room where Jack had been trying to stop Samuel from leaving.

'I found a notebook in Samuel's study. I kept going back to it, but I couldn't work out why. All it seemed to be was household accounts. Then I noticed there were two butchers listed, and one was named Davies. Instead of an address though, all there was was numbers.' She shifted on the bed and paled again, and I wanted to tell her to stop talking and rest, but I was shaking more and more, and if she stopped now I knew I would scream.

'I put it in my pocket, then I heard a gunshot next door and thought Jack had been shot so I rushed in. I only remembered about the book a little while ago, and Jack's gone to find it in with all my clothes.'

'Oh, Lizzy! Do you think he'll know what the

numbers mean?'

'He's sure to, I only hope he finds the book, and that no one took it from me – it was all so confusing and frightening, neither of us would have noticed.'

Before I could speak again the door opened, and Uncle Jack came in. I leapt up and hugged him, and he glanced over at Lizzy.

She nodded. 'I've told Evie about the book. Did you find it?'

He sat down on the bed and took her hand in his bandaged one, holding his good hand out to clasp mine too. 'I know where he is,' he said, and I tightened my grip.

'Are you sure?'

'The numbers are co-ordinates. Will is sheltering on a farm just to the north-west of a village called Montauban-de-Picardie in the north of France. He must have wandered south after the battle at Bazentin-le-Petit, missed the patrols by some miracle, and not regained his memory.' He looked at me, clearly troubled. 'He may never regain it, sweetheart. Are you prepared for that?'

But the words rushed over me, swept away in the knowledge that I would soon see him. 'He's still my husband,' I said, 'better to have to start over and win his heart again than to hear of him dead.'

'I've sent Archie to the farm,' Jack said. 'He's carrying a note from me, a photograph of you, and orders that Will must return with his escort or face a firing squad. We can't risk losing him again now.'

He looked at Lizzy for a long moment and something seemed to pass between them, unspoken but clear. He stood up and took my hand

and I smiled up at him, but something in his face made the smile fade.

'What is it, Uncle Jack?'

'Please – you're too old to call me that now,' he said. 'And you may no longer want to in any case. I have to talk to you, and it must be now.'

I gave a little laugh, but it sounded hollow. 'What on earth are you talking about?'

'Not here,' he said.

Uncle Jack quietly closed the door of the side ward behind us, but his expression told me how hard it was for him to leave Lizzy lying there. He looked back at the closed door and I could see the struggle not to go back in, in the tension of his shoulders and the clenching of his hands.

'You're frightening me,' I told him, and immediately wished I hadn't. The face he turned to me was strained and suddenly looked old, and there was an unmistakeable shine in his dark blue eyes as he drew me to a bench and sat down beside me.

'I've not been truthful with you,' he began, 'and it's time to put that right.' I didn't speak, sensed it was better to let him find his way through his tangled thoughts to what he was trying to say, and eventually he took a deep breath, let it out slowly, and began to talk, haltingly at first, then with gathering speed.

'I work for the government, as you know, but what I've never told you, and probably shouldn't be telling you now, is that the branch I work for is what was called the Secret Intelligence Service. I was approached shortly after returning from Africa, and recruited to the service, and that's

157

why I'm rarely home.'

'Is that where you've been since Lizzy was sent down?'

'In a manner of speaking. I was a political prisoner in Serbia.'

'But what–'

'Hush, Evie, please. I have to get this out now or I might never find the courage again.'

I subsided, my stomach churning with fear, and he carried on.

'Before that, when I was in Africa, I was given a mission. There was a spy in the ranks. Someone who was passing our secrets to the Boers, giving them opportunities to fortify their defences, and worse, to attack our own least-defended lines. I identified him, and, as I already knew about him and was something of a crack shot, I was given the task of ... well, of silencing him before he could pass information on our position. You must understand, I didn't volunteer, but neither did I shirk in this; if the information got through, we would lose hundreds of men, there was no question.'

'Of course there wasn't!' I wanted to say something else, to absolve him of the guilt he clearly felt at having to kill a man in cold blood, but his face forbade it and I fell back into silence. He described how he'd had to wait until the spy had been face-to-face with the Boer Kommandant before taking the shot, and that it had been quick and clean, over in an instant. He seemed particularly intent that I should understand that, and then he turned to me and, in a voice filled with the agony of the duty he'd been forced to fulfil, he ripped my heart in two.

'It was your father, Evie.'

I sat in stunned silence, while his words rattled around in my head, and the pain that caught my chest gradually loosened enough for me to breathe. The two of us remained side by side without looking at each other, without speaking, with a past that I could never have imagined in my darkest nightmares forming a wall between us.

Eventually he reached a hand out to me, but I pulled mine away, and saw his fingers curl into a white-knuckled fist which he withdrew and replaced on his thigh. He seemed a stranger to me just then, and it was going to take time to absorb this awful new truth.

Part of that truth was that I barely remembered my father. What I did remember of him was a stern face, not unloving, but neither affectionate. Images flashed through my head of my earliest memories of Uncle Jack; his endless patience, his laughter, his friendship with parents Lawrence and I saw too little of, unless he was visiting. He seemed to soften them, somehow, and whenever he came to stay the house came alive, Mother and Father were more tolerant, quicker to smile and to gather us all together as a family.

When he had brought news of Father's honourable death in service, he had been grief-stricken, that much was clearly true. He told us he'd promised Father he would take care of us should something happen, and he had. But that something had happened by his own hand! How could he have lied to us all like that? I'd only been eight, but I still remembered his white, pain-filled face, and Mother's awful scream – the way he had held

159

her while Lawrence and I looked at each other in mystified dismay at the sudden uproar in the house. And I remembered Uncle Jack sitting us both down in the morning room after Mother had been taken upstairs to bed, and telling us our father would not be coming home again.

'You said he was a hero,' I said now, sounding more like that eight year-old than ever.

'I was at least able to get that much agreed with the Service,' Jack said. 'I couldn't see what good it would do to destroy your family.'

My voice broke. 'You did destroy it.'

He drew a ragged breath, and I looked around at him. He was nodding. 'I'm so sorry.'

I turned away again and thought back to what he'd said, how I'd agreed without question that he'd done the right thing, before I'd known to whom he'd done it. Did that make me a hypocrite?

'Why did he do it?' I had to know how culpable Father had been.

'He was recruited very young, by Samuel Wingfield. The tragedy was that he truly believed what he was told, that our government was corrupt and must be stopped, that our cause was the wrong one.'

'So he chose his path.'

He hesitated. 'I loved your father, Evie. He was my closest friend, you know that. He was an innocent though, and a little weak. Vulnerable, and Wingfield saw that.'

'Vulnerable or not, he chose to betray and kill those he fought with. Friends. Including you.'

'But–'

'No! No more, not now. I need time to think,

160

and I don't know how I feel, not really. But Will's the important one now.'

I slumped against him, drained, and felt him twitch in pain. 'I'm sorry,' I said quickly, moving away, but he pulled me closer again. 'It's all right, it's nothing compared to what ... to...' He couldn't finish, I heard the way his voice caught the words and refused to let them out.

'Maybe not, but it's worse than you've been telling her, isn't it?'

'It's all right,' he repeated. And that's all he would say, but when we began to walk I noticed how his hand crept beneath his coat, and the way his breathing sharpened when he moved too quickly. Every muscle was taut, and his face reflected the deep, bruising ache that had not had time to subside. He must have been struggling so hard not to worry Lizzy, and he was still doing it, but with me it wasn't necessary and I wished I could make him understand that.

He misinterpreted my worried expression, and took my hand as we walked down the corridor. 'Archie should be ready to bring Will across by tomorrow.' He hesitated, then said, 'They'll have to go straight to London.'

A fresh band of terror tightened around my chest. 'You mean he's still being court-martialled?'

'I'm afraid he'll have to be.' His face was drawn, and now it wasn't simply his pain that caused it. There was a dark apprehension there too. 'All I can do is make sure they hear his evidence.' Seeing my face he went on quickly, 'But it will make a difference, Evie, believe me.'

'And what evidence will that be?'

'He'll be thoroughly checked by a medical officer, evaluated by his commanding officer, and I'll draft a supportive statement as a government official.' Uncle Jack looked uncomfortable for a moment. 'It's probably best if you don't see him until after it's all over.'

I stopped, appalled. *'What?'*

'It's for his own good, love,' Jack said. 'If Will is suffering from some kind of amnesia, as we think he is, that will help his case. But if he sees you it might all come back to him. He won't be able to give a convincing performance, and if they think he's lying he'll be found guilty.'

'But it was true!'

'They won't know that. All they'll see is a young man who left his unit, and hid on a farm, scavenging for food. A soldier who clearly remembers everything, but is pretending he doesn't.' He drew me around to face him. 'Evie, promise me you won't try to see him?'

My heart turned over, but his words made a horrible sort of sense at least. 'I promise.' It was no more than a whisper, but he let out the breath he'd been holding.

'Good girl,' he said, and hugged me. We walked in silence for a while, everything that had happened twisting and turning in our minds, and I found the other bright part, quite apart from Will's safety, that had come out of this strange, cold day.

'I'm so happy for you and Lizzy,' I said quietly, and saw him tense, then relax.

'Are you sure? I'm so much older, and she's such a sweet, trusting girl. You must be wondering what on earth she sees in me.'

I smiled, feeling my own tension fade a little. 'I think those are your worries, Uncle Jack, not mine.' I looked at him and saw that, beneath the tiredness and the pain, pushing it away, there was contentment – just to be talking about Lizzy was clearly all the medicine he needed at the moment. But, despite how deeply I loved him, she was my closest friend and he had put her at risk. It wasn't something that sat easily with me.

'I've made my promise, now you make one.'

'Anything,' he said.

I looked at him seriously. 'Promise me you won't put her in any more danger.'

His eyes rested on mine and I saw complete honesty there. 'I promise you I would die before letting any more harm come to her. Just the thought of what happened, what might have happened...' He broke off, but I needed no further convincing; his hand shook, a mixture of exhaustion and emotion, and he let go of mine, but he kept looking at me and I believed him. His own injuries might heal quickly, but Lizzy's would hurt him for the rest of his life.

'Tell me more about Will,' he said, fighting to sound normal. 'I only knew him as the butcher's boy, and you know I didn't get any of your letters. So, tell me how you met. All of it.'

So I did: while he struggled to regain control, while Lizzy slept somewhere behind us, while Will was, maybe at this very moment, being brought out into the sunlight by Jack's friend ready for his journey home, I talked of warmer, brighter times, and about hope and determination. And when I talked about two racing hearts, and the added excitement at the impropriety of their meeting, Jack smiled at last, and I could see the memories echoed in his own.

Two days later Will came home.

Jack had gone back to London to be further de-briefed about the disappearance of Samuel Wing-field, and to give his evidence at Will's trial, and Lizzy remained in hospital in Shrewford. Mother had insisted I come home while I waited for news, and I was glad to go, especially after the way we had parted. It was comforting to hear her express genuine relief that Will had been found, and while I realised it was more for my benefit than for his, she sat willingly to listen while I finally told her everything about the way we had found each other. By the end of my telling she had softened still further, and the sense of betrayal at the way I had excluded her had faded into the understand-ing I had recognised before.

It was those memories that led me to find her on the day of the court-martial. She was writing a letter, and slid it out of sight beneath her blotter as I came into her favourite room; the morning room.

'Evangeline. Hello, my dear.' She sounded extra bright and I eyed the blotter, wondering what she had been so eager to hide. But Will's plight drove the questions from my mind, and I found myself unable to sit still in even the most comfortable of the room's chairs long enough for conversation.

Mother watched me stalking the room, picking things up and replacing them, and repeatedly looking out of the window for the arrival of a telegram. 'Jack will put everything right,' she said at last, quite gently. 'He has influence in the military.'

'Limited, he said so himself.'

'But still more than most young men in Will's position are lucky enough to have,' she pointed out. 'And how is Lizzy?' I heard genuine concern in her voice, which shouldn't have surprised me, but it did.

'She appears to be gaining strength,' I said. 'Mary says she has asked to be moved out of the private room and onto the main ward, which is typical of her.'

'She's a courageous girl,' Mother said. 'I hope she will find a good position when she recovers.'

'But you fired her!'

'I had to, you know that. I just feel terrible that I wasn't able to offer her work when she came out of prison. If I had, she wouldn't have had to go to Shrewford for that interview in the first place.'

'Mother, I think it's time I told you—'

A discreet knock at the door cut my words off and Dodsworth the butler entered; the moment I saw the telegram in his hand my heart froze. He held it out to me, expressionless as usual, and I plucked it from his hand with trembling fingers.

W exonerated stop Returning Breckenhall on 14.15 tomorrow.

Mother saw the colour drain from my face and grew instantly alarmed, but I shook my head; it was relief that was making me feel faint now. I hadn't realised how big a part of me had been convinced of the worst, but now Will would be coming home. I sat down before my shaking legs could pitch me to the floor, and, with a bemused kind of gratitude I heard Mother get out of her own chair and come around to put her arm around me. It wasn't until she spoke that I remembered she had been through the worst herself. But she hadn't had the happy ending that now lay within my reach, and her voice, hardly more than a whisper, was drenched in her own memories of that unspeakably terrible time when Uncle Jack had come to Oaklands with the news that had torn her life apart.

'When he comes home, darling, don't let him go again. Ever.'

Chapter Nine

He was thinner. That much I had expected. He was ghost-pale and I had expected that too, but what came as a shock was his reaction to me. The train chuffed quietly as it sat in Breckenhall Station, and as Will stepped down from the carriage he looked around at his companion and nodded. It seemed he remembered some things, after all, and I felt a rush of relief, but since I had been cautioned against moving to embrace him I remained behind the fence, and breathed slowly to get my thundering heart under control. The officer he was with, Jack's friend Archie, placed a hand on Will's back and guided him to the exit. I took barely any notice of him but felt deep gratitude, nevertheless, for his presence; he hadn't known Will long, and, although merely performing a duty, there was patience and gentleness in his manner.

When they emerged from the station into the little parking area where I waited next to the car, Will caught sight of me. His eyes widened, not with the recognition of a man for his wife, but with the dismay and guilt of someone caught out, and he looked frantically around to make sure no one else had seen us together. His hands rose to cup his elbows, then dropped, then rose again, this time to run his hands through his hair – the movements were quick and nervous, and he seemed unaware of them.

The captain urged him forward but he wouldn't take another step. There was nothing I could do, although his reluctance to even meet my eyes hurt terribly. There was a narrow cut along his jaw that was healing well, but it looked as though it had been made by something extremely sharp, and was perilously close to his throat. I shuddered at how close he had come.

'Will,' I managed at last, and my voice broke on even that short word. He looked at me, but his eyes skittered quickly away. 'Miss Creswell.'

'Mrs Davies,' I corrected with a little smile, but my heart splintered and I smiled distractedly at the officer, through the tears that turned everything into a blur. 'Captain Buchanan, I'm so grateful. It must have been awfully dangerous for you.'

'Don't give it another thought,' he said, shaking my hand, and his voice was as warm and gentle as his touch. His Scots accent was not as thick as Mrs Cavendish's, who hailed from Glasgow, but instead had a gentle Highlands tone. 'I hope the day finds you well, Mrs Davies.'

'Very, thank you. And please, call me Evie.'

'And I'm Archie.'

I turned back to Will, who was looking around and seemed to relax the more he saw.

'Do you remember this place?' I said. I ached to touch him but he looked as though he would break away and run if I did.

'Yes, Miss. I worked in town. Before.'

That word again. Only in Will's case, "before" meant everything up until the moment he had joined up and left his old life behind. Before his orders arrived. Before we had married. All that had happened between then and his rescue was locked away. The naïve part of me had hoped the sight of me might, as Uncle Jack had warned, be enough to reach him, but now I could see the extent of his distress I wondered if anything ever could.

I looked at Archie, troubled, but he gave a slight shake of his head. 'We can talk later,' he said. 'I think it'd be best just to take Will home for now.'

It occurred to me I hadn't even wondered if Will would be happy coming back to Oaklands, but at least his belongings were still there, including all those years' worth of exquisite sculptures. 'Perhaps looking at some of your things might help with your memory,' I said, and now, unable to hold back any longer I stepped forward and took his hand. He immediately pulled it away, but not before I'd felt his fingers tighten on mine, and I took heart from that instinctive response.

Standing so close to him, after these months of fearing him dead, I felt a physical pain at not being able to hold him, and see his eyes resting on mine with the spark of passion that had lit them almost since the day we had met. Instead I curled my fingers against the urge to reach out for his constantly moving hands again, and turned to Archie. 'I do hope you can stay a while,' I said, stiffly polite in the effort to control myself.

He nodded. 'I'd like to help as much as I can, but I have to leave the day after tomorrow. I've already had to rely on Jack's influence too much, and it's not fair on the lads. Not to mention the COs resent it, and quite rightly.'

'I understand, and thank you for everything.' I glanced at Will again. 'I think you've been of more help than you realise.'

I drove us back to Oaklands, and the journey, though short, was a strange one. Archie kept up polite conversation, and I answered his questions, but both of us were hopelessly aware of Will's silence, and willing something to reach into that locked box in his mind and break it open. Nothing did.

I stopped the car outside the front door. 'We don't have a footman any more, I'm afraid,' I said. 'Would you mind bringing your own bag, Archie?' I myself picked up the small bag Archie had packed for Will, it contained very little; most of his things were still in France.

Inside, Dodsworth was his usual, impeccably-mannered self, and nodded without comment to both Will and Archie before taking their bags upstairs. I led them both into the sitting room, relieved to find it empty; Mother was either in her bedroom or the morning room and it would give the three of us a chance to talk. Archie sat opposite me, but Will remained on his feet, his exhaustion not acute enough to overcome his embarrassment and discomfort.

'Were you injured anywhere else, other than your jaw?' I asked him.

He touched a hand to his head and shrugged. 'A small wound. The nurses cleaned it up and said it would soon heal.'

'Are you in pain?' The way he looked at me answered louder than any words might have done. But it was not physical injury that was causing it; he was broken, confused and lost, and terrified he would remain that way for the rest of his life. 'We're going to help you,' I said gently, and stood up. This time when I took his hand he didn't pull away. He glanced past me at Archie, but he didn't look as guilty as he had when we'd been out in the open and might have been seen by anyone. I was aware of Archie rising silently to his feet and slipping out of the room. For the first time in over a year, my husband and I were alone together. I had to try.

'Do you understand we're married?'

He nodded. 'Archie told me. So how is it that I can't remember?' The sudden wretchedness in his voice brought tears to the back of my throat. 'I know we were ... that we used to meet. That we loved each other.'

I shouldn't push him, yet I couldn't help it. 'Do you love me still?' But it was too much. He dropped my hand, and pain sliced through me. 'Will?'

I wished I had managed to choke that question back, but it was too late, and he turned away, his arms folded tight across his chest. 'I *know* I love you,' he said with quiet desperation, 'and that I've loved you beyond reason since we met, but I can't...' his voice dropped until it was barely a whisper, 'I can't seem to *feel* it.'

'It will come back, I know it. It has to, one day,' I managed, trying to convince myself as much as him.

He looked back at me and his eyes glistened. 'I could take hold of you now, and swear to never leave your side again. I could do it, and you would want to believe it, but it would just be words, to make things easier for us both. No matter how much I would wish it, it wouldn't have come from my heart.' He shook his head, bewildered. 'I don't understand it, Evie.'

'Well, you called me Evie, that's a good start,' I said, and was rewarded by his first, faint smile. 'Come on up to the room, and try to get some rest before dinner.'

'I don't think I can eat dinner.'

'Then sleep. You need it.' I held out my hand, and although he didn't take it, he followed me out into the hall, looking around him with cautious, guilty interest, as if he were still the tradesman and he'd taken a wrong turn.

He hesitated at the foot of the main staircase, but I waited patiently, and eventually he gave me an apologetic half-smile and nodded for me to lead the way to the room Mother had set aside

171

for us. Once inside he looked at the bed, carefully made up by Peters, and with two sets of night-clothes folded neatly on the pillow.

He cleared his throat, and his hands fussed mindlessly with his buttons for a moment before falling away. 'I'm not sure about... I don't–'

'It's all right,' I lied. Part of me had hoped the forced intimacy of sharing a bed might re-ignite some feeling, even if we simply lay side by side and talked. But he wouldn't so much as remove his jacket in front of me. 'I'll sleep in my old room,' I said, and tried to smile but felt my mouth trembling. 'Will, listen to me: we're going to find you again.'

'I hope so,' he said, and his eyes met mine at last, and stayed there. In them I read hope and despair in equal measure. I reached up to touch his face, and he didn't move away but neither did he relax or touch mine in return.

'Sleep now,' I said, 'no one will disturb you, I promise.'

Archie smiled a greeting as I went down for dinner, and for the first time I had the opportunity to look at him properly. His hair was thick and very dark, almost black, and he had quite arresting grey eyes; his height and build might have made him seem imposing, but that gentleness was still evident, and I realised it had not simply been brought into play for Will's sake after all. There was something familiar in the lines of his face, too, that I couldn't place, but Boxy and I had met many of the officers stationed nearby, often fleetingly during duties or in the town, so perhaps that was where I'd seen him.

Then I remembered: he had been the one to tell me about Lizzy. He had introduced himself then, and I had steeled myself for the worst news about Will – but the shock of hearing it was Lizzy who lay close to death had been so intense it had wiped away everything else. I had probably been unforgiveably rude to him, but I honestly couldn't remember. I apologised now, just in case, but he brushed it away.

'You were upset and frightened. Really, don't give it a thought, your manners were unimpeachable.'

I doubted it, given the circumstances, but I smiled with gratitude and took my place opposite him, and next to Mother, who had sat at the head since Father died.

During the meal we talked of Will, of course, and while he lay upstairs, hopefully sleeping away some of the terror and exhaustion, we learned how Archie had found the farm from Uncle Jack's co-ordinates.

'It was a shabby wee place, but dry, and the farmer's wife had been bringing some kind of food out to him whenever she could, although it wasn't really enough. They couldn't bring him into the house; if they were caught, by either side, harbouring a deserter...' He caught my stricken expression and shook his head. 'I'm sorry, Evie, but that's the way they'd have looked at it.'

'I know. I just hate to hear it.'

'Go on,' Mother said. 'How did Jack discover where he was?'

Archie took a sip of wine, and I could see him

choosing his words carefully. 'To begin with he had the co-ordinates from Wingfield's notebook. That was down to Lizzy, of course.'

'Lizzy?' Mother looked at me with growing puzzlement but before I could say anything Archie went on.

'Aye, I gather she's quite the brave wee thing. I'm glad to know she's improving.'

Mother frowned at me. 'But didn't you say Lizzy was at Shrewford for an interview? What on earth was she doing with Samuel's notebook?'

'It's ... there's more to it,' I said. 'I'll tell you, I promise. But I want to hear about Will now.' Truthfully, I had no idea how to explain the news about Jack and Lizzy; if she had baulked at my own marriage how would she react to the startling news that her oldest, most trusted friend had fallen in love with her scullery maid, a girl half his age? And eventually, of course, there was the risk that the rest of it, the truth about my father, would come out, and where would that leave trusted friendship then?

'Will was in a bad way,' Archie said. 'He wasn't badly hurt, the cut on his head had all but healed, it must have been a clean one, or the farmer's wife had tended it. But he was starving, and couldn't risk leaving the barn to find anything in the way of food.'

'If he had no memory of why he was there, how did he know he should stay put?' Mother wanted to know. I wondered at her tone; did she believe him to have been lying?

'All he knew was what the woman told him,' Archie explained, 'and that was that he must stay hidden. He was confused, traumatised, and too weak to leave anyway.'

'Thank God for the farmer's wife,' I murmured.

Archie nodded. 'She did her best, aye, but Wingfield had already found out where he was. He has...' he broke off and glanced at Mother, 'contacts in the region.' Spies, my mind supplied, in Uncle Jack's voice. I wondered if Archie was one too, and that was why Jack had turned to him for help. 'As soon as he'd heard Will was missing,' Archie went on, 'he put them to work. They actually found him pretty quickly, but, because Wingfield had his own reasons for not wanting him brought out, they made the farmer's wife work for them. She was to keep Will there until someone came to pick him up, and no matter what, she wasn't to tell anyone. Not the English, not the Germans, not even the French. Only Wingfield's men.'

My voice hardened. 'So she actually betrayed him?'

'You have to think of it from her side,' Archie said gently. 'She'd have been terrified for her life, and that of her family. And she kept him alive, you must remember that. I can only hope she was spared when Wingfield found out, which I presume he has by now.'

Guilt set in for my swift judgement of the nameless, faceless woman. 'How did you manage to get him out without being seen?'

'And how did you know to go in the first place?' Mother added, and I had the feeling she wanted to know more about Lizzy's role, but Archie had sensed my wish to keep that part of it quiet, at

175

least for the time being.

'All I had to go on was a telegram, with the co-ordinates disguised as a series of telephone numbers, and the message: Urgent: remove WD. Take picture of E.' He shook his head. 'Not a lot to go on. But I did already know about Will being missing, I'd been helping to look for him since September.'

I looked at him, startled. 'Had you?'

'I wasn't able to cover as much ground as I'd have liked, getting leave hasn't been easy. And I'd never met the lad, of course, but when I heard about him I did what I could.'

'Thank you,' I mumbled. I wished I'd known before; the looks of pity on people's faces as they recognised my refusal to accept the worst had stung, but maybe if I'd known this earnest young officer had also been asking questions I might have felt less lonely.

'I went back to your ambulance base,' he went on, 'and Barbara gave me a picture of you. It wasn't a good one, but it was clear enough, of the two of you when you first joined up, before you cut your hair.'

'What did he say when you showed it to him?' But I wasn't sure I really wanted to know.

Archie spoke gently, knowing his words would hurt. 'He told me you were the daughter of the house, but that he didn't know you personally, and I was mistaken. Even then, he was trying to protect you.'

I felt a wrenching pain for the golden time when all this had seemed such fun, an exciting secret and impossibly romantic. 'And when you told him you knew the truth, and that we were married?'

'At first he denied it outright, and he meant it. Then, as he accepted there were gaps in his life he couldn't account for, he knew he had little choice but to believe what I told him.'

I nodded. 'Well, he knows it now, but knowing isn't really enough, is it? Not if he's forgotten how to feel.' I heard tears thickening my voice, and took a hurried gulp of water. There was a silence at the table, and then Mother touched my hand before turning back to Archie.

'Was it dangerous? Going out to that farm alone?'

'It was behind our own lines, so that was something. But doing it unseen posed a lot of problems, I admit. The rain was appalling, which actually helped in one way, although it made the going slow. There are patrols out, and I wasn't sure if Samuel had posted anyone to guard the farm itself, but I suppose he had no reason to believe Will would be found. He didn't know the notebook had been stolen, after all.'

'It doesn't feel like stealing,' I put in, a little sharply, 'I don't think it's fair to lay that at Lizzy's feet.'

'No, I'm sorry. Poor choice of words.'

'How *did* Lizzy get it?' Mother persisted.

'It doesn't matter,' I said. 'What's important is that Uncle Jack knew what to do. And it's thanks to all three of them that Will's upstairs now, and not d ... dead or facing a firing squad.'

Mother reached across the table and squeezed my hand again. 'We're so glad he's home safe,

177

darling.' She smiled, and it seemed less of an effort now. 'You must tell him to treat Oaklands as his home.'

I didn't want to tell her we had decided to keep to separate beds, not after she had clearly swallowed every instinct she possessed to accept our status as man and wife, so I smiled gratefully and said nothing, and after dinner I went down to the kitchen. The servants were enjoying a lively discussion over their supper, but they all rose to their feet immediately, which made me feel strange; it had been very different world where I had expected just this kind of reaction, and it had never sat well with me even then. I gestured for them all to sit, and smiled at Peters.

'I'm going to make up my old room, Alice,' I said. 'Will needs to sleep tonight, and I'll probably keep him awake.'

She stood up again. 'I'll do it, Miss Cres ... Mrs Davies.'

'No, I'm quite happy to do it, I just wanted to tell you, and to ask if you wouldn't mind bringing me a cup of cocoa there in about an hour?'

'But–'

'Alice, things are different now,' I reminded her gently, and she nodded.

'As you wish, I'll bring the nightcap in an hour.'

'Who is attending my husband and Captain Buchanan?'

'Mr Dodsworth, Miss.'

I turned to the butler. 'Please see to it that they are both left to sleep as long as they wish tomorrow.'

'Of course.'

'And thank you all, for your help and understanding,' I added, before turning away and stumbling up the little dark corridor to the main staircase. It wasn't until I reached the privacy of my own room, where the memories assaulted me at every glance, that I gave in to the despair that had been trying to break free from the moment I had seen Will at the station. The beautiful, vibrant young man I had known, now hunched and silent, his eyes empty, his hands constantly moving, seeking a grasp on something that remained forever out of his reach. And I didn't know if he would ever find it again.

Chapter Ten

It was two days after Mary and Martin's wedding that his memory came back. We had stood together watching our friends become man and wife, and later we had been with Lizzy and Jack when they had, in typically oblique fashion, let us know they too planned to marry, and yet, amidst all this warmth and love Will still refused to let me touch him in public. He had been home since November and it was now mid-December, Archie had gone back to Belgium, where he was joining the company near us in Dixmude, and although I had begun to sense an increasingly discomforting intensity in his behaviour towards me, I missed his company; we had become good friends. He had also been a buffer between my husband and me. I could never be frightened of Will, but he was quicker to anger than I'd ever known him, and slower to calm. It took most of my energy these days trying to read his mood, and I was still exhausted, and growing more so even as he grew physically stronger. His nervous hand-movements had grown less frequent, and now if he felt himself doing it he consciously stopped himself.

Mary's wedding had been a beautiful occasion, the town draped in softly falling snow, the little church full of well-wishers, and only the absence of a generation of fighting-age men reminded us that there was another world out there, and that it was a bleak and terrifying one. Here, people hugged one another and chatted and, caught up in everything, I had slipped my hand through Will's arm. For a moment it remained there, but then he had stepped away, effectively removing it, and I had just smiled.

I seemed to spend a lot of time doing that, nowadays. Lizzy's romantic news had even brought a fleeting smile to Will's face too, he had known her almost as long as he had known me and they were extremely fond of one another. Uncle Jack looked so handsome and proud, holding her close without fear of what anyone looking on might think, and it hurt when my own husband would not let me do the same.

Still, I smiled.

When it happened there was no flashing moment of brilliance, no bump to the head, no recognition of an old photo or diary, or even the sight of his own carved wooden creations from another time

180

and place. Another life. Will simply woke up, the week before Christmas, and remembered. We still slept in separate rooms, but I had taken to coming into his room with a cup of tea, rather than have him snap at Dodsworth should his waking mood not be a good one. This morning he was still sleeping and I sat on the bed watching him. I could feel a little smile on my face despite everything; in sleep he lost all the tense anxiety he had brought home with him, and was my warm, sweet Lord William again; his face smoothed out, his hair flopping untidily across his brow, one arm flung over his head in utter abandon. I hadn't known him sleep so deeply, nor clearly so well, in any of the admittedly too-few nights we had spent together.

The eiderdown was pushed down around his hips, and I watched the light movement of his chest beneath his pyjamas as he breathed, and instinctively placed my hand gently over his heart; he didn't jerk awake at my touch, he merely opened his eyes and I knew, without a word passing between us, that he was back.

A second later he was sitting upright, his eyes wide and horrified. Then he clutched at his stomach and turned away, and my skin broke into goose bumps at the anguished cry that echoed around the room. Frightened, I reached out to touch his back but he shrugged my hand away, doubling over as he retched, his shoulders shaking. When he finally stilled, I touched him again and this time he turned back, breathing hard, and seized me in a painful embrace. I felt his chest hitch, and, with my face buried in the hollow of his

181

shoulder I just wrapped my arms around him and held him, silently willing him towards calm.

'It was ... they were...' His voice choked off and I soothed him with wordless, meaningless sounds, my hands on his back feeling him tremble in every muscle. He was so much physically stronger now that it was hard to believe he could be shattered all over again by remembrance, but I knew then that I couldn't ask him what he had seen that had driven him away from his unit and out of his mind.

We remained locked together for a long time, then Will's eyes found mine and their bright blue colour was deepened by emotions I had despaired of ever seeing again.

'I'm so sorry,' he said at last. 'I've been–'

'Hush,' I said. 'There's time, we can talk all you want, but not now. And you have no reason to be sorry.'

'I love you,' he said on a sigh, and rested his forehead on mine, relaxing his panicky hold on me and instead taking my hands in his. 'And it's not just words now, Evie, I can feel it.'

Christmas was a strange affair. Lawrence came home on leave, and he and Will went for long walks together; it gave me an odd sort of ache to see my little brother and my husband in the distance, deep in discussion. Lawrence was already a commissioned officer, yet he and Will talked as equals and I could see how it helped them both. When they returned from their walks Will seemed more at peace than I could make him.

I drew Lawrence to one side on Christmas morning. 'I just wanted to thank you,' I said. We had never been particularly close, but our shared experiences had formed the three of us into a tighter group, with Mother watching from the outside. I felt bad for her, but she belonged to a different world, more so now than ever.

'Will's a decent bloke, always thought so,' Lawrence said, 'and he's clearly potty about you.' He poured a large drink and sat down on the chaise opposite me. 'Poor fellow must have seen some terrible things.'

'As have you,' I pointed out, but Lawrence shook his head. 'I've seen it, yes. But it's not the same for our lot. I mean, of course it's awful; we see our chaps killed all the time, lose friends every day, but you don't get the same ... the same...' He struggled to find words that wouldn't offend, and failed to find any at all.

I moved to sit beside him. 'I've seen enough. I know what you mean.'

'The trenches are indescribable,' he said, staring into his glass. Then he looked up at me, his expression haunted. 'The fortifications are partly made up of human remains, did you know that?'

'Lawrence–'

'Don't let him go back, Evie,' he said, echoing Mother, and his eyes were too old for his nineteen years. 'Not if he doesn't have to. He'd be mad to go.'

But, of course, he did go. On a frigid morning in the week between Christmas and New Year we took our leave of Oaklands Manor, and the first, fragile peace we had known in our married life.

I had tried once more, knowing it was hopeless.

183

'You're not ready to go.'

'I have to. I can't leave those boys out there, knowing I'm as fit and healthy as they are, and fitter than most.'

'But they're not making you go yet, so why risk it, after everything you've been through? Please!'

'You'll be going back after Christmas, I take it, now I'm well again?'

I looked away. 'Yes, of course, but–'

'Then you understand.'

But it wasn't just his going, we both knew that. He was different now. The old Will was still there, deep down, but he was almost completely out of reach while this new man, this harder-edged, bleaker man, stood in his place. Now and again a flash of the happy-go-lucky charmer resurfaced, and it was enough to keep my hopes alive, but if he went back to France how much of him would return?

'Please,' I said again, quietly.

'Stop it!' For a moment I heard real desperation in his voice, but when I looked up he had himself under control again. 'We both know I'm not the man you married, not any more.' A muscle twitched in his jaw. I thought he was fighting words I desperately wanted to hear, but in the end the battle was won in his silence. He started up the stairs, and I hurried after him, changing tack.

'So after everything Archie risked to get you out, you're going straight back?'

I immediately regretted my words; Will didn't stop but I saw his hands clench on the bannister.

'Archie's the one you should be with,' he threw back over his shoulder. 'He's the one who risked

184

everything to do what Jack Carlisle wanted him to do.'

'What we all wanted to do!' I reminded him. 'Lizzy and Uncle Jack were able to get him to you, but every single one of us would have gone instead, if we could.'

'Go with Archie,' Will said stubbornly. 'At least he's one of your own.'

'My own what?' But I knew.

'Your own class. And an officer.'

I followed him into his room and slammed the door, making him jump. 'Will Davies, have you forgotten everything we ever said to each other? All those times we sat together on those Sunday afternoons and talked about how our love would overcome all that nonsense? That time you fought David Wingfield for me up by the quarry?'

There was a long silence and I saw him struggling with his determination. Then he sagged. 'No, I haven't forgotten any of it,' he said at last. 'I never did, not that. Evie, I love you still, you must know that. It's because I do that I'm going away again. I can't bear to see the disappointment when I can't be who you want me to be.'

'You *are* who I want you to be!' I hoped he could read the truth in my face because yes, I loved the memory of who he had been, what we had been to each other, but that did not mean I could not also love the man he had become. I touched his cheek and spoke softly. 'When your court-martial was over and I came to take you home, you trusted me. I can do the same for you, if you'll let me.'

He hesitated, and I could see hope flicker in his eyes, then he took my hand and pulled me close

185

again, drawing my head against his chest. 'I'm not right yet, but I will be, I promise.'

'But you're still going back to France now,' I said, my voice muffled against his shirt. He didn't answer, he didn't have to. I couldn't risk fuelling his belief that he was pulling me into his own darkened world, so I continued to hide it. I stayed by his side, every touch reminding him that I loved him and would wait for as long as it took. This gentle persistence had seemed to work; as the time for the departure crept closer he had seemed to revert more easily to his old self. I moved my things into his room, and the first night we slept together he held me tightly but made no move towards any kind of intimacy. I told myself there was time yet, and contented myself with feeling his warmth and his closeness, and listening to the deep, slow breaths of a man finally at peace in his dreams. It was more than I'd dared hope for, for so long, and although my skin leapt at every touch of his hand, and my heart pounded in frustrated desire in the dark, I would accept whatever our marriage had become as long as he was with me.

Our conversations, when not about what had happened or about the war itself, carried some of their old, familiar laughter, although it died away a little more quickly than before. But that he was able to laugh at all gave me further hope, and every time the voice in my head whispered that a renewed closeness would simply make me miss him more than ever, I pushed it away and instead welcomed every little sign that the Will I'd known was ready to come back, to complete the man he had become.

My hand stole into his as the train rattled into the station at Liverpool, where we would part company. Will to the coast, and the ferry back to France, and me to London, where I would spend the evening with Uncle Jack before leaving for Belgium first thing in the morning.

Will curled his fingers around mine, both of us silent in the rising hubbub of passengers gathering belongings and calling greetings through the open windows. I tried to think ahead, instead of dwelling on our imminent farewell, but there wouldn't even be a joyful reunion with Boxy to look forward to; she had left to marry her airman soon after I had come home, and there was a new girl there now, a novice who was being looked after by Anne and Elise in my absence. That was all I needed; some child to train during the coldest, nastiest months of the year, when the chances of her staying were at their lowest. The wretchedness of it all mounted as everyone began spilling out onto the platform, and I couldn't even bring myself to move.

When we could delay no longer Will squeezed my hand, then let it go in order to pull our cases from the overhead compartment, and I curled my fingers over the warmth he'd left in my palm.

He saw, and touched my cheek. 'Won't be long 'til next time.' His voice gave the lie to his optimistic words, but I forced an answering smile.

'It'll fly by.' I stood up and took my case from him, fighting the instinct to grab his hand instead and make him stay at my side. He seemed to share the urge; I noticed his knuckles whitening

187

on the handle before he relinquished his hold.

He looked down at me, his blue eyes darker without their old sparkle. 'Evie, you begged me not to go back, but I had to at some point anyway, I have no choice. Not since conscription came in. You, though–'

'Don't,' I warned. 'I can't refuse any more than you could, so don't ask me.'

To my surprise, he actually smiled. 'As if you'd listen to me anyway.'

'What kind of wife do you take me for?' I said in affronted tones, and added, 'Of course I'd *listen* to you...'

'Ah, the perfect wife, Mrs Davies. Absolute and unquestioning listening.'

Our shared smiles dropped away as we climbed out onto the platform, another of those irrevocable steps towards separation. Bags puddled at our feet, we stood firm against the jostling crowd, hands linked, and eyes on each other, storing up the tiny details for later when we were once more in the midst of our respective chaoses.

I marked the new lines at the corner of his eyes and the shadows beneath them, and the way he already seemed to be looking into a distance I would never see. I reached up to touch the small scar, pink with fresh skin.

'Don't worry about me,' he said gently.

'I won't, if you'll promise not to worry about me.'

His arms came around me then, and I felt his hands smooth down my newly regrown curls, as if by taming them he could tame the ferocious determination that kept me going back.

I tried to keep my voice steady. 'What time is your next train?'

'In half an hour. What about you?'

'A little less.'

Suddenly there seemed too much to say, yet no words with which to say it. I felt him take an unsteady breath and his hands tightened on my back. My own arms were around him pulling him closer still, breathing in the slightly damp smell of his newly washed uniform, feeling the press of his buttons against my cheek and the scratching of the rough material on my skin.

He murmured something against my hair and I drew back to look up at him. 'I said I love you,' he repeated, and I pulled him close again.

'I know that,' I grumbled. 'Why did you make me stop just to hear it again?' I felt his body shaking with laughter, and smiled in response although he couldn't see it. It was so good to hear him laugh again, but it hurt too.

Eventually time had its cruel way. As I bent to pick up my case, I blessed the eager passenger, running for the train from which I had just alighted, for bumping into me and shoving me against Will one last time. He rubbed his thumb across my lower lip and then bent to take it gently between his teeth, sending sparks shooting through me. As we kissed for the last time I felt tears sliding between us and realised there were too many to be mine alone – when he stepped back his eyes were bright once again, as they had been when he'd been the butcher's boy, but for all the wrong reasons.

'Goodbye, Evie,' he said, and, unable to say the

189

words myself, I just nodded. 'I'll come back,' he promised, and I understood he didn't just mean from France. I turned quickly away before I could ruin everything and make us go through it all over again. Fighting my way across the station to the departure platform I was only aware of my mouth, burning from his kiss; my eyes, hot and blurred; and my heart, empty and aching as I left him behind and returned to my own war.

Chapter Eleven

Flanders, February 1917.

I raised my head, and my face stung as it peeled from the rough material of my greatcoat sleeve. The memory of last night's attack on the clearing station was already dimming from shock and out-rage, into dull acceptance and the need to re-evaluate the fuel supply to accommodate the extra miles. Tomorrow, or, more properly, later today, I would check the store we kept in the cellar, safe from stray shells. In the meantime I had to try and get some proper sleep and, as I forced myself to stand up, my eye lit on the envelope on the table in front of me. Stiff and cold, and aching in every muscle, still it was my heart that hurt the most; in the two months since we had been back Will had barely written.

Being back amongst the filth, the fear, and the constant bellowing guns, had obliterated the faintly hopeful tenderness of our parting, and his letters, when they did come, had been like something he might have written to an old school friend, or a casual acquaintance. To my dismay I found my own letters to him were following a similar vein. I could find nothing to say that wouldn't convince him he was right after all, that I was coming undone by his behaviour – every time I tried to express my feelings they came out hysterical-sounding and thin. Easier to match tone to tone, then, and this was what we had become by the time the world moved onwards, into the third full year of the war that should have been over by Christmas 1914.

In a few hours Kitty and I were up and breakfasted, and I was going over Gertie once more to make sure she was fit and ready for another night. She needed cleaning and disinfecting again, and daylight had revealed the extent of the bloody mess in the back, so I fetched a pail and used it to break the ice on the top of the water butt in the yard. As I scoured the floor beneath the benches, the water turning rust-coloured beneath my brush, I wondered how many men Gertie had carried between dressing station, clearing station and ambulance train over the years since we'd brought her over. It hardly bore thinking about, and I scrubbed harder, as if I could eradicate her history along with the blood and waste.

'Steady on, darling!' The voice, with its gentle Scots accent, pulled me back to the bright, icy day outside, and I blinked. A general staff car was parked in the driveway, and two of the four men inside were already getting out.

'Archie! How lovely to see you.'

'Likewise,' he said, and dropped a kiss on my sweating forehead without flinching. I glanced past him and saw the driver smile, but it wasn't a nice smile; it seemed almost like a smirk, and I turned away at once. I'd seen him before, and he always seemed to look at us girls just a little bit too long for comfort, or politeness, and usually with a half-raised eyebrow as if asking a question for which I had a very definite answer. But I told myself not to be unfair; some people just had a way about them that was unfortunate, but not necessarily a reflection of their true nature.

The younger man, who'd now joined us, was holding his cap in his hand and I saw he had hair as bright red as Kitty's and almost as curly. He wore the same uniform as Archie, but with a different coloured flash on the sleeve.

'This is Oliver Maitland,' Archie said. 'He's just joining our lot from Nieuport.'

'Nice to meet you, Captain Maitland,' I said. 'Skittles is doing terribly well, you must be very proud.'

'Skittles?' he sounded amused. 'I am proud, extremely so,' he said, but something about the way he said it made me wonder if that view was shared by the rest of the family.

'And this,' Archie gestured to the fourth man, just climbing out of the staff car, 'is Lieutenant-Colonel Drewe.' He turned to beckon the officer forward. 'Sir, this is the jewel of Flanders I was telling you about. You made it possible for them to set up here.' I blushed at the description, but there was no time to argue as Drewe seized my hand, heedless of the icy-cold wetness.

'My dear girl, all this time and we've never met in person,' he said, a wide smile on his plump, friendly face. He whipped his hat off and gave me a little bow, which made me smile too. 'So sorry, must make more of an effort. I had the honour of knowing your father in Africa. Splendid chap, terrible blow to lose him like that, you and your family have my sympathies.'

With the truth of my father's activities, and his death, so recently discovered, I felt both fraudulent and sad as I acknowledged his condolences, but I smiled my thanks. 'Very kind of you to say, Colonel.'

'Not at all, not at all. D'you mind if I take a gander around? I do so admire the work you girls are doing.'

'Of course. There isn't much to see though,' I said. 'We're not far from Advanced Dressing Stations in two directions, and tried to pick somewhere equally distant between them. We've had to give the cars loaned by the Belgian Red Cross back, but we're hoping for another ambulance in a few weeks so we can split the duties again.'

'Only one bus, eh? Must be a bind.'

'It's hard, but as soon as we have another, Kitty and I will be able to take one each and double the benefit.'

'Excellent, excellent. Well, I shall just stretch my legs awhile then, if I may.'

I turned to Captain Maitland. 'Kitty is around the back fixing the shutter, but I expect she'll be more than happy to stop and make some tea instead.' I raised my voice slightly to extend the invitation to the driver, who nodded, and I tried not to pull a face.

Oliver strode off to find his sister and the driver followed him, leaving Archie and me alone. For once I was glad I couldn't stop work to chat, and turned back to my grisly task.

'How's Will?' Archie said.

'Better, thank you. He's back with his battalion now.'

'Ah, yes. Uncle Jack told me he'd got his memory back,' Archie said. 'I can't tell you how pleased I was to hear it.'

'Well, it's thanks to you that ... did you say "Uncle Jack?"'

'Aye, Jack's my mother's brother,' he said. 'I thought you knew?'

'No! Why didn't you say anything?' It did seem funny though; all these years I had called Jack Carlisle 'Uncle' as a form of affection, and here was the man to whom he really was. 'I know he has a sister, but we never really talked about her.'

'It didn't seem important to tell you, at the time,' he smiled, 'other considerations, you know. Her name's Diane. She moved to Scotland when she married my father.'

'I'll be blowed! At least that explains why he turned to you when he worked out where Will was.' It explained, too, that niggling familiarity I'd sensed, that I'd put down to having seen him briefly once before. Looking at him again, I saw the same determined strength in the jaw, the same square-shouldered bearing, and even the eyebrows were similar; dark and straight above eyes of a

194

different colour to Jack's but equally arresting.

He leaned on the side of the ambulance. 'How's Lizzy, by the way?'

'She's very well,' I said, smiling. 'She's a sparky little thing, always has been, and tough as old leather with it.'

'A lot like young Kittlington there,' Archie observed.

'Very much so.' I sloshed the remains of the bucket over the floor of the ambulance and jumped down. Archie put out a hand to steady me as I landed, but we both knew it wasn't necessary, and I removed my arm gently but firmly from his grasp.

He removed his hat, and it made him look younger and far less authoritative. 'Evie,' he began, but I wouldn't hear it, not now, with Will's words still rattling around in my head. Since our little ambulance base was attached to the division Archie had recently joined we saw each other often, more often than was advisable, perhaps; I kept him at arm's length, but I wasn't blind, and I hadn't given up on Will. I even had my suspicions about Archie's transfer to Dixmude, though I never voiced them.

'Would you like some tea?' I said, adopting a brisk tone. 'I can spare a few minutes, but Gertie needs some attention before we put her through another night like last night.'

'I should think it was pretty grim,' Archie said. 'I hear the clearing station down the road from the railway was hit.'

I told him about stopping to pick up survivors, and about the boy with the shrapnel wounds as we

195

walked back to the cottage, and the momentary awkwardness passed. In the main room Kitty and Oliver were sitting at the little table, each clasping a mug of hot tea, and the driver was sitting in the window seat. His gaze swept over me, too slowly, and then returned to Kitty who was, thankfully, oblivious.

She jumped up to pour more tea, and the way her eyes lingered on Archie was not lost on me. I wished he'd look back at her with clearer eyes; she was bright, hard-working and cheerful, and despite my initial griping about having to train her, I couldn't have wished for a novice with a sweeter temperament. She and Archie would be so good for each other.

The colonel came into the kitchen, and, despite his friendly greeting and informal manner, he was so clearly a man of distinction that Kitty fell silent and slid into her seat. Without her chatter the room seemed very quiet, and I sought to enliven it again.

'How long have you and Archie known each other, Captain Maitland?' I asked, washing my hands in the dribble of icy water from the tap.

'Oh, hundreds of years,' Oliver said. 'We were at school together. He was much older, of course, about to leave when I started. But he coached the first team at rugger and we hit it off, so he ended up staying at the old homestead for holidays a lot of the time.'

'You and Kitty don't sound at all Scottish.'

'We're not, Archie boarded at my school just outside Liverpool, where I was a day boy. He has family there, don't you, Arch?'

'Aye, one or two of my mother's relatives still live there.'

'I remember Archie coming to our house when I was little,' Kitty put in, and blushed as Archie smiled at her.

'I still can't believe what a pretty girl you've grown into, young Kittlington,' he said. 'I know Evie here will take good care of you.'

'Oh, she does,' Kitty said, looking warmly at me. 'I'm learning how to drive at night, and she's ever so good at that.'

'Please tell that to Uncle Jack,' I said drily.

'This would be Carlisle, I take it?' the colonel said with approval. 'Another marvellous chap. No sense of propriety of course, but courageous, and a damn good soldier if memory serves.'

'That's him,' Archie said. 'Been like a father to Evie and her brother since Lord Henry died.'

'Good friends, those two,' Drewe said. 'Always thought they'd come through it, somehow. Terrible shame,' he said again, and squeezed my arm.

'Do you two know each other very well then?' Kitty said, her green eyes going from me to Archie and back again, her expression shadowed slightly.

'Not really,' I said, at the same time as Archie said, 'Quite well.' Then glanced at my face and cleared his throat. 'Well no, not really well, but the circumstances of our meeting were quite intense, so it feels as if we've known each other longer.'

'Archie was a great help to my husband after High Wood,' I explained.

'Husband?' Colonel Drewe looked at my ring-

197

less left hand. 'Lucky man.'

'Very,' Archie said, deliberately misunderstanding. 'I mean, he could have been picked off a dozen times, by either side, but he's back with the 33rd now, managed to get out with barely a scratch.'

I frowned. 'Barely a scratch, yes, but with his mind in shreds.'

Oliver nodded in understanding. 'Still, good to know he's back in harness, eh?'

'Not really.'

There was a tense silence, broken only by the distant boom of shellfire.

'Why don't you wear a ring, Evie?' Kitty asked at length.

I shrugged. 'Lots of reasons. Hygiene, for one. Besides, wives aren't allowed at the Front.'

'How ridiculous, Will is miles away!' Kitty protested, but she looked happier at the reminder that I was married. Her gaze stole to Archie again. He affected not to notice, and I recognised the irony with a little inward sigh.

'Beastly shelling last night,' Oliver said. 'CCS hit, I gather?'

I let Kitty tell him how we'd had to abandon our plans to offload our wounded, while I finished my tea and tried to ignore the way Archie's eyes lingered on me. They were really quite a lovely kind of grey, with shifting, smoky colours deep down that made him always seem to be thinking about faraway places or people, but when they lingered on mine they seemed to still, suddenly, as if his sole attention was on my own thoughts. It was disconcerting.

I thought about Will's face, his fined-down features with the new lines of strain around his mouth giving him at least five years to add on to his thirty. He was due some respite from the forward line soon, and perhaps the chance of an overnight leave; I had already made up my mind to beg steal or borrow a car so I could go to him if he wrote. Kitty had eagerly offered to cover for me if he did.

'You're more than ready to make the night run yourself now, Kitty,' I told her, with a twinge of guilt at my own selfish reasons for suggesting it, but she looked thrilled at the prospect, and smiled shyly into her tea cup.

'Excellent!' Drewe said, patting her hand. 'I'm sure you'll do a splendid job.'

'Thank you, I'll be awfully pleased to be of some real help at last.'

'Watch out for shell-holes,' Oliver said, worried, 'those roads are abysmal.'

After a few more minutes chatting about the state of the roads, Archie turned to Oliver. 'Well, Captain, say your goodbyes, the fun and games await ye.' He turned to Drewe. 'Ready, sir?'

'Of course, dear boy,' the colonel said, and rose and picked up his hat. Kitty hugged Oliver tight; she was so young, and she and her brother clearly so very close, she must be every bit as worried about him as I was about both Lawrence and Will. The driver stood up too, and nodded, replacing his tea cup on the table and thanking Kitty in a rather thick-sounding voice. It was hard to hide a little flicker of distaste as I nodded goodbye to him, and I'm not entirely sure I was successful, but either he was used to it, or hadn't noticed.

Archie squeezed my hand. 'Look after yourself, Evie.'

'And my sister,' Oliver put in, and he looked pale beneath the jaunty set of his cap. 'I'm relying on you.'

'I will.' I searched for my brisk, hearty voice, and stood up, picking up my toolbox. 'Now, you boys go and give Fritz something to think about, and maybe we can all go home.'

When they had left I sat down to open the little pile of letters that had arrived. One from Mother, one from Lawrence, and one, I saw with a little surge of pleasure, from Lizzy. The postmark was Devon, and at first I assumed she was visiting her family in Plymouth, but when I opened it I saw the arrangement was more permanent.

Dear Evie.

I was so sorry to learn of Will's return to France, and so soon. I send you both my deepest love, and my hopes that everyone will soon be safely back where they belong. Particularly you.

As you might have seen, I am writing from a place called Dark River Farm, and that is because, now I have almost completely recovered, I have joined the WLA. It's lovely to be closer to Ma and Emily and the twins, and the Land Army certainly keeps me fit! The owner of the farm is a lovely lady by the name of Frances Adams, and she is fully aware of my limitations and has very kindly given me light duties for a while. By the time the summer comes, and I am needed for work out in the fields, I will be fully fit and able to really pull my weight. In the meantime I'm able to visit home almost every day, as it's a short distance and doesn't tire me too much to walk it.

I'm sorry to say I have worrying news of our friend, Mr Bird. He has been sent to visit his father. We all know they mistrust one another, and I am concerned Mr Bird might be met with some hostility. Still, it does me no good to dwell on that worry, and he told me himself just before he left, that he is determined to return having established a better relationship.

How is the new girl getting along? She's lucky to have you to take care of her. Write to me when you can. If you need anything and you think I might be of some help, do tell me. I am sending, by later parcel, some honey made here at the farm, and Mrs Adams has offered some home-made biscuits too. I will enclose some socks that were given to me by Mary (hush, don't tell her!) they are those lovely warm ones, and I know she has sent you some already, but I think your need is greater than mine.

I will write more soon. Until then I am, as always, Just Lizzy.

I put the letter down, feeling Lizzy's fear pouring off the page despite her assertions that she wouldn't worry. Mr Bird was the name we had chosen for Uncle Jack, since we had learned of his code-name, Goshawk. The use of the word Father could only mean he had been despatched to Germany, and no wonder poor Lizzy was distraught, I felt a little bit sick myself at the thought. But he had been doing this for years and was clearly good at it. Lizzy had told me how

201

coldly efficient he could be when he needed to be, and now I had cause to know it myself, to kill his best friend, even in the pursuit of saving hundreds of lives, required a switch in his mind and his heart he must easily reach and operate. Such a switch might save his life again someday.

I took a piece of paper from my precious and quickly diminishing stack, and wrote back immediately.

Dearest Lizzy,

Please try not to worry about Mr Bird, although I understand completely, and you will miss him while he's away, I know. I hope he and his father are able to reach a better understanding of one another, that will be such good news for everyone concerned.

I'm so proud of you for joining the Women's Land Army, so typical of you! But please remember you are not yet properly well, don't try and do too much too soon. I'm glad your Mrs Adams is understanding of your situation. She must see in you, as we do, such determination to work hard, and she must know you are worth looking after. I have no doubt you will give her your all as soon as you are able. I would love to visit you, I have never been to Devon and it sounds beautiful. Perhaps when I am due some leave in the spring I might write to you and arrange something?

Thank you for the offer of the socks! I know the real reason you're sending them is because they itch dreadfully, but one can never have too many pairs of socks out here! I look forward to some delicious Devon honey, thank you.

Will has written to me since his return to France but

202

I confess (to you and no one else) that his words carry little hope that he is continuing his recovery. He seems distant in more than miles, but I am planning to see him soon, and hope to bring him a little closer to the man we knew before. Please continue to pray for us, and we will pray for you and for Mr Bird.

I knew how Lizzy needed to hear my old, cheerful tones, even in my writings, and so bent to my last paragraph with a determined smile pasted onto my face, in the hope it would translate to the paper.

Gertie, Kitty and I were very busy last night, the town came under some pretty nasty attention, but we muddled through. I think Gertie needs a rest, but like all of us she must press on, and if bits are going to drop off, better they drop off her than us!
Take care, darling.
Yr ever loving
Evie

I picked up Will's last letter and pushed it into the pocket of my greatcoat with the others I kept with me. I had told Lizzy of the distance I could sense in his words, but it was his hand that had written them and so it wouldn't have mattered had it merely been a list of things he needed from home, or an invoice from his days as a butcher's apprentice. It was *his* hand.

A week later he wrote again; he was granted local town leave for a day, and would be able to meet me at the station. I left Gertie with Kitty, assuring her once more of her ability to drive at night, and borrowed a car from Oliver's company under the pretext of fetching supplies. Lieutenant-Colonel Drewe had stepped in and cut through the red tape, bless him, he was so helpful. It seemed predestined to be a perfect trip.

I wouldn't have been half so pleased had I known what my absence that night was going to lead to.

Chapter Twelve

The station was as crowded as always but I saw him right away; straight-backed and square-shouldered despite the weight of the equipment he carried. Our embrace was uncomfortable; bulky and unsatisfactorily clunky, too many layers between us, and our gas masks clashed. I knew his hands were on my back, but I couldn't feel them through my greatcoat and my sweater.

I felt him holding back as he kissed me, as if we were acting a part on a stage and mustn't give in to real emotion; my racing heart was doing the work for both of us. I wondered if he could feel it in my lips and my fingers as I could, but the kiss ended too soon, leaving me with a hollow ache in my chest and a faint feeling of embarrassment, as if it was all one-sided after all.

We walked to the little park beside the railway, and found an empty bench by the cold, grey pond. I couldn't think what to say, whether to ask him outright how he was coping, or whether to simply blather on as I did in my letters, filling the silence with nonsense that neither of us really cared about. In the end I just took his hand and we sat quietly, ungloved against the bitter wind, but at least we were touching. I became transfixed by the sight of impossibly thin ice at the pond's edges, rising and falling gently under the insistent fingers of the wind that rippled the water, until a tiny piece on the very edge broke away, and the whole, lacy-delicate sheet crumbled in front of my eyes. One or two pieces bobbed away to become en-snared by the long, ice-tipped grass, but the rest, insignificant and lost now, simply floated away from each other until the water swallowed them up.

Strangely saddened, my thoughts were trying not to make foolish connections and I jumped as Will cleared his throat. 'Have you heard from Lizzy?'

'Yes!' I told him everything she had said in her letter, so relieved to have something to say that I found myself elaborating, just for the sake of see-ing the tension slowly leaving his taut frame, and the lines in his face soften. 'She's happy, and well,' I finished, 'but she's so frightened for Uncle Jack.'

'Jack's a good man,' Will said. 'He knows how she'll worry. How you both will,' he added, squeezing my hand. 'He'll be more careful than ever.' I almost blurted out the news that Archie was actually Jack's real nephew, but just stopped myself in time: Archie Buchanan wasn't a subject I wanted to bring up, not in such a rare and fragile companionship as this.

'I'm hoping to visit Lizzy soon,' I said instead.

205

'The Red Cross in Kent have raised enough in donations for two new ambulances, and Skittles and I will both go, so she can visit home for a day or two and then drive one of them back. She's coming along ever so well.'

'She seems sweet, from what you've said.'

I nodded, and the conversation died again. It was awful, and so unlike us. 'When do you have to be back?' I asked.

'Next train, to get back before my watch.' He looked up at the leaden sky, as if the gathering dark spoke in his favour. 'I'm sorry it was such a short visit, for all that driving you had to do, but I can't afford to raise the slightest suspicion and people are watching closely, even though I was exonerated.' He was babbling now, in his eagerness to be gone.

'Will...'

He looked back down at me, seeming a stranger in the grey afternoon light. I had known he would become a handsome man one day, and I'd been right, but I'd also believed he'd be someone I knew inside and out, and would be as familiar to me, always, as my own face. We were both enmeshed in this filthy conflict, both struggling daily against dirt, disease, fear and loneliness, but while I took comfort in the knowledge that I was at least doing some good, he had been watching more of his friends lose their lives, their limbs, and their minds, to no discernible gain. Pointless death every day, young men snatched away in the shriek of a shell or the crack of a sniper's rifle, and Will's hesitant return to emotional health was being eroded with every one.

'You weren't ready,' I said, unable to find the words I really wanted to say: that I understood what he was doing, that I would give him all the time he needed, that I had utter faith in the strength of what we had built between us. 'Tell them.'

He turned away. 'I made a mess of things in '16, and risked everything. This time I'm going to stick it out, and if I don't come back ... well, I'll only be one of thousands more, most of them ten times more worthy.'

I could have slapped him for his indifference, if only to shock him back into life. With an effort I controlled my voice. 'And what about my feelings? Don't you care about me at all?'

Will leaned forward with his elbows on his knees and stared at the ground between his feet, as if it held the answer to what should have been the simplest question of all. Then he raised his head and studied me with unreadable eyes, before looking back at the rippling grey water.

'I don't think you should write to me any more.'

I stared at him, too stunned to speak. He wouldn't look at me again, but I saw his hands clenched where they hung between his knees, chapped, raw and bleeding where the skin had split. There was tension too, in his shoulders, in the rigidity of his jaw and in the flicker of a muscle in his cheek, but he didn't say anything else. After a moment he stood up and began walking away, and it was only then that I was able to move. I ran after him and grabbed his arm. 'Wait!'

For a second I thought he was going to shake me off and keep walking, but instead he turned, seized my face in his hands and kissed me. Hard and desperately, and too quickly. He groaned as he pulled away. 'Go back, Evie. Go and do what you were born to do, and try not to think of me any more.'

'No!'

'Please ... you don't understand how I am now. You'll hate me if you get to know me again. I couldn't bear that.'

'How could I ever hate you?'

'I'm not the man you married,' he said, as he had before. 'You deserve someone better.'

'Archie Buchanan.' I'd tried to inject the name with denial, even disgust, but Will only smiled gently.

'I've seen the way he looks at you,' he said, 'he'd be lucky, and proud, to have you at his side.'

'But I want to be at yours!' Why couldn't he see that? If it hadn't been for that kiss, and the urgency in it, I might have thought he was making an excuse, that he no longer loved me.

He touched my face with heart-breaking gentleness, and began to walk backwards, away from me, his eyes locked onto mine. 'I have to go. Take care of yourself, and give Lizzy my love when you see her. Try not to think too badly of me?'

'I could never think badly of you.' I realised it sounded as though I was giving in, but by the time I had found the words to deny it he had gone through the gate onto the platform. I couldn't bear to watch him get on the train, but I couldn't bring myself to leave yet, not while there was a chance he may turn and come back to me. So I stood by the gate, my fingers twisting together with growing anger and frustration; he thought he was being noble, did he, keeping me at arm's length? This man who loved me, as he'd said, 'beyond reason'? Well I wasn't going to let him, and he would just have to–

'Mrs Davies, isn't it?'

I turned to see a soldier, his arm around one of the local women. He looked familiar, and then I remembered him: the tall soldier who'd been taking requests at the hostel almost two years ago, although, for the life of me, I couldn't remember his name. The one thing I'd noticed about him then, as now, was his height; he must have stood six feet seven in his socks.

I forced a smile. 'How nice to see you again.' I nodded to the Frenchwoman, who looked a little irritated that her companion's attention had been pulled away, but nodded back politely enough.

The man looked past me, puzzled. 'Where's Will?'

'He had to get this train back,' I said, my voice surprisingly steady. Presumably this man should also be making his way back, but he didn't appear to be in any hurry.

'Don't know why then,' he said, and winked at the woman, 'we're granted overnight this time.'

His words cut deep but I was determined not to show it. 'Oh, he had something to attend to,' I said. The soldier – Barry something, it came to me suddenly while my mind was occupied – let go of the woman and drew me to one side. He towered over me, but dipped his head to speak quietly into my ear.

'Mrs Davies, I'm sorry to hear about everything.'

'Sorry? Whatever for?'

'Well, that you're parting company,' Barry said. 'It's a real shame.'

'I'm sure I have no idea what you're talking about,' I said. 'We're not parting. He's gone through a lot, you know that, but I'm not giving up on him.'

Barry straightened up and patted my arm. 'I hope that's true,' he said, 'but no one would blame you. It must be very hard for you, what with him being the way he is now.'

'The way he is?'

'Different. You know. Always angry.'

That hurt too. 'He's not always angry. Sometimes he can be just like he was. Before.' Again, that stupid little word that meant everything and nothing at once.

Barry raised an eyebrow, and chose to ignore what he clearly didn't believe. 'He doesn't make things any more, you know. When he joined up he was always makin' things. Out of paper, or whatever he could find. Doesn't do it any more, that's all. Seems a shame.'

'He'll do it again,' I said, thinking with a pang of my paper rose. 'You just need to give him time. It's ... difficult.'

'It's difficult for us too, that anger thing.' Barry said, 'makes him hard to get on with. And when a man doesn't get on with the others in his unit he needs a good friend at his side.'

I swallowed hard, fear squirmed at the implication. 'And are you still that good friend?'

Barry nodded. 'All of us are, that remember him like he was, Missus. Trouble is we lost a hell of a lot in July last year, so a lot of the others are new. They never knew him then. He'd have done anything for anyone. Still would in a way, I suppose; whenever the order comes through he's up and over, before you can blink. Takes a terrible sort of courage, that.'

'What are you saying?'

Barry sighed. 'It's like he has nothing to lose. And to be honest I think that's exactly how he looks at it. Rightly or wrongly,' he hurried on, seeing my face. 'I heard they were looking for volunteer runners. Be just like your Will to step up, the way he is now.'

'Regimental or trench?' I knew the answer, but still I prayed he would say "regimental" – it would be easier to bear knowing Will was relatively safe and carrying messages between HQs. But a trench runner faced instant, invisible death every second he was exposed.

Barry's face gave me the answer I dreaded, and I gripped his arm. 'You have to talk to him!'

'I've tried,' Barry said. His lady friend was tugging at his other arm now and I could see he was uncomfortable talking to me. 'I'll talk to him again, Mrs Davies, of course I will, but, well, he's...'

'Different now.'

'Yeah,' Barry said, and his expression turned sad. 'Look after yourself, Mrs Davies. And keep up the sterling work eh? The lads need people like you.'

I drove back to the cottage in the borrowed car, numbed and silent, not singing as I usually did, not even cursing as the night sky lit up with vivid flashes. In the yard, I dragged the handbrake on

211

with unaccustomed savagery, climbed out and slammed the door. With one eye on the horizon, I hurried inside and made sure oxygen masks were ready, and likewise the few beds we had set up in the cellar. We might not be able to do much, but we could be prepared and help a few, at least, and checking it all gave me something to concentrate on, for which I was grateful; Barry's words were echoing in my memory, and I tried not to think about Will's cool determination to get himself blown up, or shot, in the belief I would be better off a widow than married to someone I could no longer love.

Kitty was still out, no doubt doing a grand job, and once the cellar was made ready I was able to climb into bed, fully clothed against the cold, and try to put out of my mind what I could do nothing about; I would need to be alert for duty tomorrow, and could ill afford the luxury of lying awake feeling angry and sorry for myself.

Sometime around three in the morning, after the big guns had fallen silent, I had drifted into a shallow, unsettled sleep when I heard Kitty come in. I kept very still, hoping she'd think she hadn't woken me, but she tip-toed in, and I breathed softly in relief. Then, as I began to float away again I realised I was hearing another sound: a soft hiccupping and the occasional sniff.

I sat up. 'Kitty, darling, whatever's the matter?'

'Nothing. Go back to sleep.'

'Are you hurt?' I pushed off my bedclothes and hurried to sit beside her.

'No, at least ... no.'

'What do you mean? *Are* you hurt?'

212

'A little. It doesn't matter. Go back to bed, we'll talk tomorrow.'

'We'll talk now,' I said firmly. I might have wished for peace instead of chatter, but this was hardly the same thing. 'What happened? Was it a shell?'

'No.' She hitched another breath, and a moment later she had flung her arms about my neck and was sobbing against my shoulder.

'Sweetheart!' I had no idea what to do. Show me a man with his leg blown off, and instinct overtook thought, but this weeping child had me flummoxed. I settled for rubbing her back and letting her cry, while my mind raced with all that might have happened to set her off like this. I couldn't feel any injuries on her, and her breathing sounded normal, apart from the tears.

Her sobs began to taper off and I started to think more clearly about the questions I would ask, but she surprised me by pushing me away and standing up. She went across to the tiny sink in the corner, and I leaned over to light a candle. The distant, light cracking of rifles had temporarily eased off, and the room was eerily quiet as I watched her unbutton her coat and let it fall to the floor. I got up and picked it up to hang it on the back of the door, and when I turned to speak to her my breath stopped. Her face was a puffy mess from her left eye down to her chin, with blood crusted below her nose and on the side of her mouth, and her right cheek was grazed as well, and oozing blood slowly while she stood, no longer hiding, but silently letting my eyes take in the horror she had probably not even seen herself. 'Who did this?' My voice came out small and helpless as she reached for the cloth.

'It doesn't matter,' she said, and she sounded dull now, and distant, so unlike her usual self it frightened me. I turned away, giving her a measure of privacy while she attended to herself and changed into her one clean set of clothing. I heard the small splashes as she dipped her cloth and wrung it, and then her tiny gasps as she dabbed at her bruised and bleeding face.

'Please let me help,' I begged, but she shook her head. 'Then at least tell me who it was who attacked you.'

She simply shrugged as she climbed into bed. 'How would it help? I'm going to sleep now,' she said. 'I don't think I want to talk about this after all, if you don't mind.'

'But you–'

'No! Thank you, but no. I'll see you for breakfast. Oh, and Gertie needs oil, I'll see to it in the morning. Goodnight.'

And with that Kitty turned away and pulled the eiderdown up to her ears, and didn't speak again for the rest of the night. Anger boiled higher in my blood the more I thought about it. Who could have done this to the poor child? Someone must be quite sure of themselves, and of Kitty's silence, and, to my frustration, it seemed as if their confidence was well-placed.

The next morning I tried once again to draw out the story of what had happened, but all she would tell me was that a soldier had called the empty ambulance to a stop on its way to the

214

dressing station.

'He was walking down the middle of the road,' she said. 'Well, more stumbling, and so I thought he was hurt. He wasn't though, and nor was he drunk, but he wasn't ... steady. His eyes were odd. He wanted...' Her eyes cut away from mine and I went cold. She didn't need to elaborate on what he'd wanted, and I had an awful, creeping suspicion I knew just who that soldier had been.

'Did you recognise him? Has he been to the cottage?'

'No.'

But she said it too fast, and I saw the lie in the turn of her head as she took her coat down and went out to top Gertie up with oil. I remembered the general staff driver with a wave of revulsion, but the accusation had to come from her, I couldn't put words in her mouth.

I followed her, and found her rummaging in the shed. Another suspicion took hold. 'Kitty, you didn't carry on afterwards, did you? I mean, you came straight home I presume?' I presumed nothing of the sort, and her shrug confirmed it. I looked at her with horror, and a surge of something very much like I imagined maternal love must feel. 'You mean you worked on?'

'The convoy is down four drivers since the attack on the clearing station. Why should the Tommies suffer?'

I was floored by her courage. 'You remind me of someone,' I said, 'someone I should very much like you to meet when we go to England.'

'Your friend, the one who was your maid?'

'Lizzy, yes. She's equally reckless, and just as

215

selfless,' I said. I looked at Kitty, so young but with a new wariness in her eyes I would have given anything to take away. 'Sweetheart, you have to let someone know. If not me, then ask one of the nurses to make sure you're not badly hurt.'

'I'm not,' Kitty said. 'Please, Evie, promise me you won't tell anyone. If any word of this gets to Oliver he'll panic and tell my parents. I'll be sent home for good.'

'Your parents didn't want you here to begin with, did they?'

'No, they didn't. It took all my persuasion, and Oliver's, to convince them he would be able to look after me.'

'But he can't!' I said. 'He's a serving soldier, and besides he's stationed miles away!'

'They don't know that,' Kitty said. 'They have a very strange idea of what life is like out here. It's just a picture they've painted out of the few things I've told them, and they've added their own bits to make it easier on them when they think of Oliver and me. Of course, I let them think what they like, if only to stop them from coming here and dragging me back by my hair.' She gave me a little smile and I was relieved to see it, but couldn't help feeling she had not realised herself how difficult it would be for her brother to keep her safe. That was down to me, and I had failed her.

That little glimpse of the old Kitty lasted no longer than the time it took for me to agree not to tell Oliver, and as the day went on I saw her retreat deeper and deeper into herself. Every attempt to draw her out was met with a shake of her head and the view of her hunched back as she turned away to some task, either imagined or real. She refused to go outside until darkness had fallen completely, and was clearly more grateful for the cold weather than any of us; it meant she could wrap her scarf around much of her face when she went anywhere she might be seen and noticed by others. Every time I thought of that horrible driver my suspicions grew, and I had to fight not to try and shake the truth out of her.

Gradually the puffiness subsided and the bruises faded, but when she thought I was asleep I could hear her weeping. We lay without speaking in the freezing darkness, and I wished she would talk to me properly about what had happened. She was frightened to go anywhere alone now, which meant her newly discovered enjoyment of night-driving was dashed, and, I was ashamed to selfishly note, any hope I had of working alternate shifts was thrust aside for the time being.

Two weeks later we were told a driver was available at short notice, and readied ourselves for our trip back to England.

'I've changed my mind,' Kitty said as she hurriedly threw a few things into her kit-bag. 'I don't want to go home. Can I come to the farm with you?'

'Is this because of … what happened?'

She shrugged. 'My face is almost better, but Mother's bound to notice something. So, can I?'

'I can't answer for the farmer's hospitality, but if she can't put the two of us up, I'll find somewhere else and you can have my bed.'

She looked at me, a little coolly. 'Why would you do that?'

'I'd like you to meet Lizzy,' I said, but we both heard the unspoken words: *because I want to make up for what happened to you.* 'And I know she'd like to meet you.'

Kitty observed me for a moment, then nodded and tightened the strings on her bag. 'Thank you.' I hoped her thanks were for the silent part of that conversation, but something told me Kitty's heart was closed off to me now.

The diversion of this particular trip was a welcome one, despite the feeling that I had spent altogether too much time to-ing and fro-ing across the channel since November; my mind otherwise dwelt too long on the fact that I had written to Will every day since our meeting, but that he had not replied to a single letter. I even wrote to Barry Glenn, once I'd remembered his surname, in the cold, panicked certainty that something had happened. He wrote back that Will was in good health, just locked away in his own head and uncommunicative, even with his fellow soldiers. Of course I was passionately relieved to hear he was alive and well, and I knew I must give him time, but it hurt deeply that he couldn't even bring himself to put pen to paper to reassure me. Worry was starting to give way to the beginnings of frustration, and of real anger now.

It was with deep relief, therefore, that I looked forward to getting away from this place, to try and forget everything, just for a few days. It would also be a good thing to be away from Archie Buchanan who was, simply by being his usual gentle, amusing self, starting to seem more and more appealing by the day. In the face of Will's rejection and the pain it caused me, to have an attractive man make no secret of his pleasure in my company felt disturbingly gratifying, and I hated myself for being weak enough to notice it. Better to be away from both of them, and take the time to brace myself for the fight I knew was coming.

Kitty went out to check the shutters one last time, and I finished my packing while we waited for the driver who'd been detailed to take us to the ferry. Tension kept me nervously busy as I considered the possibility it might be the same driver as before, but if it was, Kitty's reaction to him would confirm my as-yet unvoiced suspicions, and I could make a decision as to whether or not to report him.

Anne and Elise were going to replace us for the few days whilst we were away, and I was just musing on what I needed to tell them regarding Gertie's newest failings, when I heard the rumble of a car outside. I took a deep breath, readying myself for coming face to face with Colonel Drewe's driver, but when Kitty came back in her face was showing the first flush of colour I'd seen since her ordeal, and she looked more animated too.

'The car's here,' she said. 'And you'll never guess! The driver's coming all the way back to England with us, he has business there.' I put her new brightness down to the simple pleasure of imminent home comforts, even for a day or two, but when the officer ducked beneath the lintel of the front door I saw the real reason behind the change.

'Hello, Evie,' Archie said.

Chapter Thirteen

Dark River Farm, Devon.

'So then,' Lizzy fixed me with a direct stare. 'Why is he here?'

We were sitting at the kitchen table where we were alone for the first time. Mrs Adams, a tall woman with a strong, handsome face and tired eyes, had greeted us warmly despite the un-expected extra two guests, and waved away any suggestion that I find alternative accommodation.

'You and Kitty can share Lizzy's bed, and Lizzy can bunk in with the girls,' she said. 'Captain Buchanan can have the back room, where Mr Adams keeps all his wet-weather clothes. There's a camp bed in there.'

Putting our bags up in the room we were to share overnight, Kitty had seemed to unbend towards me and I attributed it to the combination of Archie's presence, and the infectious excite-ment of being around three girls of similar age, all of whom treated her like a celebrity, and bom-barded her with questions. Whatever the cause, it was a relief, and I was reluctant to spoil it by bringing the subject up, so I simply accepted it with gratitude. After dinner Archie had whisked her out for a stroll, and Mrs Adams and the other three land army girls had gone back to work, giving Lizzy and me a rare chance to talk.

'It's terribly sad, really,' I said. 'One of his boys, a lad of nineteen, tried to get back to England without leave. He was caught stowing away on a hospital ship.'

'Oh no...'

'His brother had written to tell him their mother was ill and calling out for him. Poor boy was distraught, but otherwise healthy. His court-martial is the day after tomorrow, in London, and he has asked for Archie to vouch for him.'

'So he's not on leave?'

'No, it's army business.'

'I hope he can make a difference,' Lizzy said, but she looked sombre; she knew as well as I that it depended largely on the day, and on the mood of the presiding officer. Uncle Jack had been insistent on Will's medical evidence being heard, but I knew that all too often it was never even presented, let alone considered. And, of course, this boy had no such evidence in any case.

'I know he'll do his best,' I said. 'He looks on them all like little brothers.'

'I'm sure he does. He seems lovely. Very hand-some.' Lizzy spoke with the casual appreciation of a woman who has found her man and would never look at anyone else. 'Are he and Kitty walk-ing out together, do you think?'

'No,' I said. 'I know she'd like them to be though.'

'Ah, and he has eyes for another.' I looked up to see her eyes fixed on mine, altogether too know-ingly. 'I can see how he looks at you,' she said, echoing Will, 'it's the same way Kitty looks at him.'

I began to pick up the plates in readiness for

washing. 'I don't want to talk about Archie.'

'Do you want to talk about Will?' I didn't know the answer to that, so she went on gently, 'How is he?'

'He's well. Healthy in body, at least.'

She nodded. 'I'm glad. But in his mind?'

I put the plates down beside the sink and folded my arms to try and stop the trembling. 'He went back too soon. It's strange, Lizzy; he's so distant, but I can see the man I married, deep down, flashes of him, at least.' I couldn't bring myself to tell even her that he wanted me to cut him out of my life, and I still refused to believe he wanted me out of his. 'I've spoken to a friend of his,' I told her instead, 'and it's as if he's describing a completely different person. An angry stranger.'

'Sweetheart, he'll come back,' Lizzy said gently. 'He's been through so much, it's bound to have changed him, but you know he loves you as much as he ever did.'

I had to change the subject before I broke down entirely. 'Have you heard from Uncle Jack?' I could feel the absence of him in every word she spoke, as if part of her had gone to Germany with him.

'A note routed through London last week, just saying: "Mr Bird is with his father, and they are in conversation." Nothing more. I don't think I can expect anything else, and since we're not married I probably wouldn't hear if anything terrible happened.' She visibly shook the dark thought away, and stood up. 'Tell me about Kitty.'

'She is doing well enough,' I said, helping her clear the rest of the table. 'She had a terrible crossing though, was awfully sick.'

'Perhaps the captain will take her mind off it.'

'I do hope so,' I said, 'she deserves some light in her life.' Then I glanced around to ensure we were alone. 'I have something to tell you and I don't want anyone to hear.'

She frowned. 'That sounds mysterious.'

I told her what had happened to Kitty, and horror stole across her face, quickly followed by fury. 'I think I know who it was.'

'Who?'

'There's a driver with a wandering eye who stopped in at Number Twelve, but Kitty won't name him.'

'Well of course not, she won't want to antagonise him in case it comes to nothing. And in any case, now it's over she won't want to bring all that nastiness back out, what would be the use?'

'But he's just going to get away with it. And maybe even do it again, to someone else.'

'Then you'll have to warn the other girls to be on their guard, but you can't name him without Kitty's word, and you can't make her come forward on her own behalf. As long as she's all right there's no real need for anyone to know, not until she's ready to tell them herself. It's *her* future, *her* reputation you have to think about now. It's not your place to throw a light on it.'

'Well I've promised to say nothing, and she seems so much happier now, so you're absolutely sworn to secrecy.'

'Naturally. Let's hope Archie can keep that spring in her step.'

We both looked up as the door opened and the

223

pair in question walked in. Kitty certainly did seem back to her old self, the sea-sickness just a memory.

'It's freezing out there,' she laughed, clapping her gloved hands together. 'But so gorgeous and fresh.'

'Apart from the smell,' Archie pointed out.

Lizzy grinned. 'Before I came back I'd forgotten what it was like too, living away from Devon for so long, but when you get a good, ripe, farm smell wafting up your nostrils again it all comes back!'

Mrs Adams came in, followed by the girls. 'Chill's in for the night,' she said. 'Would anyone care for a little nip of something to keep out the cold?' We all accepted with pleasure, and Mrs Adams poured glasses of what I assumed was her best whisky.

She handed one to me. 'Here you are, Mrs Davies.'

'Please, call me Evie,' I said, embarrassed.

She nodded and raised her own glass in salute to us all. 'Well I'm glad to have you and Kitty here under my roof, Evie. What you do out there for our boys, well, it don't bear thinkin' about.'

It was a long time since I'd drunk whisky; while wine was still relatively plentiful in town, spirits were not, and the fumes took my breath away. I looked across at Lizzy, who'd taken her first sip with a faraway look in her eyes and a sweet smile of remembrance on her lips. I knew Uncle Jack enjoyed a dram now and again and guessed he was on her mind now. She looked up and met my eyes, and we both tilted our glasses in a silent, secret toast to our absent men.

Much later I finished my drink, and also Kitty's, which she'd tasted and hadn't enjoyed. Lizzy had hugged me and gone to bed ready for an early start in the morning, and eventually the other three girls had gone too, with lingering glances at the tall Scottish captain, who'd blown into their lives like every girl's hero, and would all too soon be leaving again.

Then it was just Kitty, Archie and me. I was feeling the effects of the whisky, and tiredness was creeping through me rapidly, but I had another reason for standing up and announcing I was going to bed: I glanced at Kitty, who was sitting on the edge of her seat, nervously plaiting the fringe on the antimacassar draped over the arm, and just hoped Archie would see they were perfect for one another.

But Kitty came to bed less than ten minutes later, and slipped under the eiderdown with a murmured 'goodnight'. My own tiredness had vanished, quite predictably, the moment I had got into bed, and I lay awake with my thoughts flitting from Will, to my father, to Uncle Jack and then back to Will again, trying not to dwell on the image of him as he might be at this very moment, but to remember him as he had once been. After an hour or more of trying not to toss and turn and wake my sleeping companion, I decided a snack might be just the thing to quiet my racing mind, so I crept downstairs and into the kitchen, pulling my borrowed dressing gown tightly around myself as the chilly air bit through the layers. Reluctant to turn on a light, I tried to remember where the pantry lay, and started in that direction.

'Who's that?'

My heart instantly went up several gears before I recognised the voice. 'Archie? It's me. What on earth are you doing still up?'

'Evie!' He pushed back his seat and lit a match, touching it to the wick of a paraffin lamp that sat on the table. The glow threw strange shadows across his face, but his expression was tender as he looked at me. 'Midnight feast?'

'How did you guess?'

He chuckled. 'Och, well, you seem like a midnight feast kind of a girl to me.'

I could see his whisky glass in front of him but he had barely touched it. I wished I hadn't added Kitty's to mine; my head still felt uncomfortably fuzzy as I picked an apple out of the bowl. 'Couldn't you sleep?'

'Not with you so close,' he said. The baldness of the statement almost made me drop the fruit, but I found my eyes drawn to his, reluctantly, but inexorably. I didn't know what to say, so I said nothing.

Archie spoke softly. 'He doesn't know what he's got.'

'You're wrong.' I tried to make my voice firm, but heard the tremble. 'He's ... he's not well.'

'I love you,' Archie said. 'I'd like to say sorry, but I'm not going to apologise for the way I feel. I love you.' He stood up and came over, plucking the apple from my suddenly numb fingers, and putting his own finger beneath my chin to raise my face.

'No, you don't,' I said shortly. 'You don't even know me.' I couldn't think straight. His grey eyes burned into mine, and before I could come to my senses he had lowered his mouth, pausing just before our lips touched.

'You deserve to be adored, Evie.'

My body was responding in a way I knew to be utterly wrong, but I couldn't help it. 'I love him, not you,' I whispered, even as I felt my eyes growing too heavy and became aware of the tingle of anticipation on my lips.

'I know,' he said, his mouth still brushing lightly against mine. 'I know, and I can live with that. Just tell me you don't want to kiss me right this minute, and I'll stop.'

I surrendered to him then, to his warmth and strength, to the love that poured out of him and into me through the touching of our lips and the mingling of our breath. As the kiss deepened I felt my own self-loathing grow. But this good, gentle man loved me, and Will had cast me away ... didn't I deserve some happiness?

Clarity flared suddenly, and I broke away from him. 'This isn't happiness,' I said, forgetting he couldn't hear my thoughts.

'What? Evie–'

'No, I'm sorry.'

'Listen,' he said urgently, clasping my arms, 'it won't be like betraying Will. I understand your loyalty–'

I pulled away. 'It's not about *loyalty!* I love him, and it doesn't matter if he wants me to or not, it's not a choice I've made. It's a fact. He's in there for good,' I thumped my chest, 'and if I push him out there will be nothing left!'

I had forgotten there were other people in the

house, and footsteps on the stairs shook me into a silence broken only by my harsh breathing, panicked at how close I had come to betraying my own heart, let alone Will. The door opened and Lizzy looked from Archie to me and back again, and, as always, grasped the situation immediately. I pushed past Archie, but he caught my hand, ignoring Lizzy although she took a step closer.

I felt the frustrated anger leach out of me, and turned back to face him. 'I don't want to lose your friendship, Archie. I care for you deeply, you know that. But you understand, don't you?'

He looked at me steadily, and in the silence of the kitchen only the clock could be heard, turning the seconds into minutes, the minutes into hours, the hours into the years spreading before us ... years we might spend wondering if this had been our one chance.

'You won't lose me,' he said at length. 'Never. I can't pretend my feelings are any different though, so don't ask that of me, aye?' He kissed my hand. 'I'll take caring, if that's all you can give me. Now, to bed with you before you catch a cold.'

Lizzy and I turned to go, but at the door I looked back to see Archie staring out of the window at the blackness beyond, and wondered what he was seeing. Then Lizzy slipped her hand through my arm and we went back upstairs in silence. We stopped outside the door of her room and she seemed about to say something, but thought better of it. Instead she hugged me and went to bed, leaving me to creep beneath the covers next to Kitty. It was a long time before I slept, but when I did I dreamed of Will, and woke to find my face tight, and streaked with dry, salty tracks that ran into my hair.

Kitty was already up and dressed by seven, despite the fact that it was still dark outside. Today Archie would take us to Guildford, where we would pick up the train to Kent to pick up the newly donated ambulances, and then he would leave us and drive to London to the court-martial. I had no idea if he'd gone to bed after I'd left him in the kitchen, but a glance out of the window showed me he was already outside, leaning on the fence that separated the yard from the hen-houses, no doubt thinking ahead to how he could best help his man.

I went downstairs to find Lizzy in the kitchen with Kitty. The two of them were chatting quite happily, and Lizzy, who was peeling potatoes at the table, looked up as I came in.

'Good morning, sleepy-head. I hope you're well rested.' She put down her knife and went to pour me some tea from the pot. 'Kitty here was just telling me about all the shenanigans you get up to over there.' Her voice remained light, and she smiled, but there was worry there too.

I shot Kitty a look. 'Don't go filling Lizzy's head with nonsense, she has enough to worry about.' I sat down and took up a spare knife to help. 'Don't worry,' I said to Lizzy, 'we're not allowed right up to the lines.' As Kitty started to speak, I kicked her sharply on the ankle and she stopped. 'We might not be part of the official ambulance corps, but we're very well taken care of,' I went on, quite firmly, 'and hardly ever get anywhere near the shelling.'

Lizzy put my tea down in front of me and resumed her peeling. 'Then how do you get the boys out?'

'We generally go to the dressing stations, and pick up the ones the stretcher-bearers have already brought out. From there it's just a short drive to whichever clearing station is taking in, let the orderlies unload, and we're ready to go back for more. Just like a relay. No cause for worry, I promise. The most difficult thing is trying to remember where the hospitals are in the dark.'

'It's terribly exciting though,' Kitty put in, 'and sometimes we even go out before the shelling stops.'

'Kitty!'

'Leave her alone, Evie, I want to know the truth,' Lizzy said. 'You were cross enough about what happened to me last year, I think it's only fair you should tell me what you're going through out there.'

'There are lots of us,' I said, 'and some are even closer to the lines than we are. Like Elsie Knocker and little Mairi. Jolly brave, both of them.'

'What are they like?' Lizzy said eagerly, putting her potato down and momentarily forgetting her concerns. 'They're always in the papers, and they raise so much money for the cause. I expect they're exciting to be with.'

'Well they do seem to be in the thick of things a lot,' Kitty said. 'Mrs Knocker can be a bit of a tartar, although I do like Mairi...' She stopped talking and swallowed hard, and I frowned as I looked at her properly. She was looking quite pale now.

'Are you all right, Skittles?'

'Yes, I just ... actually I feel a bit sick. Do excuse me.' A moment later she had run from the kitchen, leaving Lizzy and I looking at one another, and the same thought snapped between us.

Lizzy spoke first, her words falling into the silence like pebbles in a puddle. 'You don't suppose ... oh, surely not.'

I felt ill myself. 'It can't still be sea-sickness, surely. Can it?'

'Perhaps it was the whisky?'

I shook my head. 'She didn't drink hers. Maybe she ate something that disagreed with her?' But neither of us believed that. Kitty had led me to believe she had avoided the worst kind of attack, but I hadn't asked her outright. How absolutely, criminally stupid I'd been.

Lizzy sat down. 'What on earth will she do, if she is?' I just looked at her helplessly, questions and answers forming and floating away, as the implications kept making themselves apparent. 'I suppose you have to tell someone now,' she said.

'Yes, but who?'

'Didn't you say her brother is stationed nearby?'

'Yes, Dixmude. It's not far.'

'I know I said it was her decision to tell anyone, but this is different, you'll have to tell him.'

'I can't!' I said. 'Not without her permission at least, and she's not going to give me that.'

'Does she even suspect? She seemed quite happy this morning, but she wouldn't be, surely, if that were hanging over her?'

It was getting worse, I hadn't even considered

231

that Kitty herself might not have realised. 'Oh, Lizzy,' I groaned. 'What am I going to do?'

I sat with my head in my hands, wrestling with the question, but Lizzy's quick mind was already hard at work. 'She can't go back, not if we're correct in our suspicions. Are we agreed?'

I nodded. 'It's far too dangerous.'

'What about her parents?'

'I have the distinct feeling if I so much as mentioned them she would burst into flames,' I said, my voice glum, and a smiled flickered on Lizzy's face.

'Then she must stay here. Or rather, not here, but with Ma. She can have my old bed, and live there until everything is resolved. Perhaps you could give Ma something to help pay for her keep? I'd like to help, but–'

'Of course I will!' I gave a sigh of deep gratitude. 'Don't worry, your mother won't be out of pocket by a penny. But what on earth will she think?'

'She'll be delighted, and so will Emily – I think she's been lonely since the twins have decided she's simply not worth bothering with any more. You know, being a sister and all.'

I took a deep breath. 'I can't tell Oliver myself, it's better if it comes from a friend.'

'Right. You go and find Archie, I'll make sure Kitty is all right.'

'Do you think it's possible it *might* simply be left-over sea-sickness?' But the hope died as soon as the words were out of my mouth.

'No,' Lizzy said gently, 'and neither do you.'

I crossed the yard accompanied by one of the

farm dogs, who'd just been set free from having his paw bandaged by Jane and was eager to adopt a less bossy companion. I absently scratched his ears and looked around for Archie, and found him checking the car.

'That rough track didn't cause too much damage, I hope?'

'The track would have been fine,' he said, looking up with a grin, as if last night's encounter had happened to two different people, 'it's the driver who could do with taking a wee bit more care.'

'You didn't have to let me drive the last part of the way,' I pointed out, relieved to have this familiar banter to delay the inevitable. 'I'm used to urgency, remember?'

'Aye, and this car might look very pretty, but the ambulances are far more suited to that kind of driving. I think she's OK,' he said, giving the nearest tyre an experimental kick. 'Take her easy on the way back up.'

'No fear, you can drive this time, it's nice to have a break.' I looked back at the house, wondering how Lizzy was getting along with Kitty. 'Can I talk to you?'

'Always,' he said, and I could see a flicker of something in his eyes that I knew I must quash.

'I haven't changed my mind, you do know that?'

'I do,' he said, and smiled. 'But after that kiss you can't blame a bloke for hoping.'

I resisted the instinct to touch his arm. 'You're a dear friend, Archie.'

'Aye, well it's easy to be a good friend to someone like you, Miss Evangelastica,' he said, and I found a smile for the humour I was about to wipe out. He wiped his hands on a rag and tucked it back into his belt. 'What was it you wanted to talk about?'

'Not out here,' I said. 'Come into the barn a moment.'

We faced each other in the gloom, and I was glad I couldn't see his face properly. I bent to pet the dog again, just to give me time to think of how to start, but eventually I just blurted it out.

'Kitty was attacked.'

'God!' From the corner of my eye I saw his whole body jerk in shock. 'Who? And when?'

'The night I went to see Will. She was driving alone, and there was a man in the road. A soldier. She thought he needed help.' I battled with the words, and whether or not I had the right to say them. 'I think she's pregnant.' I said it very slowly, and now my eyes had adjusted to the lack of light I looked at him directly.

He went pale and swallowed hard. 'Oh, sweet Jesus.' His voice was taut with a mixture of anger and sorrow. 'Poor little Kittlington.' Then he turned on me. 'Why are you only just telling me this now?'

'She made me promise not to. I owed her that much since it's all my fault, leaving her like that. I swore I wouldn't say anything, but now I have to.'

'You haven't said who.'

'I can't, not yet. Not even to you. It has to come from her, but I have a suspicion.'

'And she's told you this? That's she's pregnant?'

'She doesn't know herself, I don't think,' I said, 'And I don't know for sure either, but Lizzy and I have been talking about it, and we think perhaps that's why she was sick on the boat. She's never suffered from sea-sickness before.'

He looked wretched. 'Aye, you're right, she hasn't. And that would make some kind of sense.'

'She was ill again this morning.' Now I did touch his arm, and it was like iron beneath his jacket-sleeve.

'Archie, I know you've got that poor boy to think about, but I just didn't know who to turn to, or what to do.'

'You did the right thing,' he said, but I could tell he was still struggling with the enormity of the news. 'But you mustn't tell Oliver, whatever you do.'

'Actually I was hoping you would tell him.'

'God no, Evie, we mustn't! Especially since you don't know for certain. He's a wee hot-head at times, and he's enough on his plate just now, don't you think?'

I reluctantly decided he was right; Oliver wasn't the seasoned soldier Archie was, he was still coming to terms with his position in his company and, after all, we were only surmising and might be wrong. Part of me still fervently wished I hadn't said anything, but a bigger part was swamped in relief that I had done so. 'I knew I could trust you,' I said. 'You're very like your uncle, do you know that?'

'Aye, so my mother says. There are worse people to take after, so I gather. I don't know him that well myself.'

'He's an absolute diamond.' Then I remembered how much trouble those particular stones could cause, and gave a rueful smile. 'Or rather, a big lump of solid gold.'

'Then I'll accept the compliment.' He blew out a breath, lifting the hair from his forehead. He had clearly been badly knocked by the news, but of course he had known Kitty since they'd been children; she was like a sister to him.

He held out his arms. 'I'm sorry for snapping at you, sweetheart. How about a hug? No strings, I know how the land lies. But you look as if you could do with one.'

His understanding almost undid all my composure, and while I moved into his innocent embrace all I could think about was how badly I wished it was Will's familiar arms that held me, and his voice I could hear. I was aware of a shadow flickering by the door but paid it no heed. If I had, perhaps I could have avoided the nasty atmosphere that dogged my departure from Dark River Farm.

Chapter Fourteen

'You're wrong!' Kitty glared from one of us to the other. 'I'd know, wouldn't I?'

Lizzy and I exchanged a look over the younger girl's head, but she stayed quiet; this had to be my task. 'Perhaps if you just stayed here for a little while,' I said, 'just until we know for certain?'

'Here at the farm?'

'No, Lizzy has suggested you may stay at her mother's home, which she says is just a short distance away. That way you'd be close enough to visit, you'd be in the fresh air, and this sickness...' I hesitated and glanced at Lizzy again, '*whatever* it turns out to be, might just go away.'

'But you don't think it will,' Kitty said in a dull voice.

'I don't know,' I said truthfully. 'I hope I'm wrong, I truly do. Then in a month or so, if you still want to, you can come back to Flanders and show me how good you are at this night-driving malarkey.' My tone was light, but Kitty gave me a look of mistrust that hurt a great deal.

'And if you're right? What then?'

'Then, I suppose, the choice is yours. Whether you tell your family, or prefer to stay in Devon. If you don't want to tell them you're here, I can...' I hesitated, wondering at the morality of what I was suggesting, then ploughed on regardless, 'I can write to your family on your behalf, tell them how well you're doing, and, if you want to, you, can write to them through me and I'll put your notes in the post from Belgium. Any replies can be posted to you here.'

Kitty remained quiet for a long while, and Lizzy moved carefully around our room, straightening things, waiting patiently for her role in the conversation. At last the girl fetched a deep sigh. It shook on the way out, and the sound seemed to frighten her. She looked at Lizzy.

'Are you sure your mother wouldn't mind? Not even if it turns out...' She trailed away, and Lizzy sat down again.

'Not even if,' she said. 'My sister is around your age, she's a sweetheart, and I know she would be

237

pleased to help you. Ma is the kindest soul you'll ever meet, and my brothers will drive you absolutely mad within ten minutes.' She smiled and took Kitty's other hand. 'I'll be less than an hour's walk away, and you may come here as often as you like.'

'I don't mind helping out, for no pay I mean,' Kitty said, and for the first time since I had broached the subject, there was a kind of weary acceptance in her voice.

'I'll take you up on that,' Lizzy said, and hugged her. 'I'll ask Mrs Adams for leave to visit home this afternoon. You can come with me and meet everyone.'

She left Kitty and me alone, and I picked up the small bag I had brought in from the car.

Kitty looked up at me, her face pale. 'What will you tell Oliver? I mean, you're quite likely to see him before I get back.'

So she was still half-convinced she would be coming back. She might turn out to be right after all. Hope wasn't hers alone, we could all share in that, but it would upset her terribly to know I'd talked to Archie about this already, before speaking to her.

I felt my face heat up as I prepared to lie, and turned away to hide it. 'I should think it would buck him up no end to think you're safely back in Blighty,' I said. 'It might be best to just tell him you were feeling a little unwell after a rough crossing, and that we thought the fresh country air would help.'

'Apart from the smell,' she echoed Archie, and I couldn't help but smile.

'Apart from that.'

As Archie and I prepared to leave, the tension in the little group grew. It had finally sunk in with Kitty that she was being left behind with strangers, as nice as they were. Lizzy made a huge effort to put the girl at her ease, but the sight of our bags by the door kept drawing Kitty's eyes, as if she expected to see her own among them.

I thanked Mrs Adams, and the two land girls who had joined us, for their hospitality and kindness, and embraced Kitty. She clung to me and I could feel her chest hitching as she tried not to cry. Reluctantly, I let her go and turned to take my leave of my dearest friend. 'Goodbye, Just Lizzy,' I whispered.

She pulled me close, eyes glittering. 'Goodbye, Evie. Give my love to that gorgeous young man of yours.' I didn't dare look at Archie when she said that, but I'm certain she intended for him to hear; a not-so gentle reminder, in typical Lizzy fashion.

Archie then said his farewells, and just as we turned to go the third Land Army girl, easily the most vivacious of the three, came in and went straight over to hug him.

'Goodbye, you brave darling,' she said, and turned to me. 'And goodbye to you, you lucky thing. Look after him.'

'Lucky?' Kitty asked, her tone sharpening.

'I'll say! These two are going to have a lovely time going off to the smoke together. No more hiding in smelly old barns, eh?'

'What do you mean?' I said, but I felt my face heat up again.

'I saw you, naughty!' she laughed, and winked. There was no malice in it, but I didn't need to glance at Kitty to know this was the worst possible thing she could have said.

She was having trouble speaking, but managed, 'In the barn?'

'Oh, it was just a friendly hug,' the girl said quickly, catching my expression.

'And now they're going off to London together,' Kitty said dully.

Lizzy stepped in. 'Evie isn't going to London,' she reminded her. But it made no difference. Kitty looked from me to Archie, and from Archie through the window to the waiting car, and her face was flushed with anger.

'That's why you're doing this,' she said. 'You made up that whole silly story, just so I would stay here and you could go off with him!' She realised what she was saying, and went redder still.

Archie took a step towards her. 'Kittlington, don't–'

'Don't call me that!' She pushed him away and pulled open the door. 'Don't you dare go without me!' she shouted over her shoulder, and we heard her thundering up the stairs to collect her own bag.

The land girl stood open-mouthed. 'What "silly story" is she talking about?' She looked quite stricken, and although it wasn't her fault I couldn't help being cross and, worse, I couldn't think of a single thing that would sound plausible.

Thank God then, for Lizzy. 'We told her Ma needed help looking after the boys,' she said, 'but thanks to you she doesn't believe me. Now

240

where's the help going to come from?'

'Oh!' The girl paled, she clearly liked Lizzy a great deal, and was mortified at having upset her. 'I'm so sorry!'

I gave Lizzy a look of heartfelt gratitude. 'Can't be helped,' I said briskly. 'Archie, you'd better follow her, I think you might be the only person she'll listen to now.'

A little while later Kitty was once more reconciled to staying with Lizzy's mother, although still uncommunicative, and Archie and I started our journey up the rough track to the main road. Circumstances aside, I envied Kitty for staying behind; Lizzy was waving madly and I missed her already. I had imagined we'd have had time to talk, and I knew she ached to unburden herself about Jack to someone who not only knew him, and loved him, but who understood the danger he was in.

The way I'd left Kitty laid a veil of discontent and sadness over the rest of the trip, and when Archie dropped me at Guildford I was relieved to turn my mind to trains and tickets, and to be going back to what I knew. The risks, the loneliness and the noise would be more than compensated for by the fact that I'd be near Will again, and doing a bit of good instead of the havoc I seemed to be wreaking elsewhere. But as I posed by one of the new ambulances, smiling for the newspapers, I kept coming back to the fact that it was my selfishness that had led to Kitty's terrible situation. Leaving her alone like that had been unforgiveable, and knowing she had gone on working afterwards only

241

pushed the blade of guilt deeper now I had a fuller idea of what she had been through.

The crossing to France was rougher than the trip out, but I welcomed the unsettling sensation; it meant I could put the churning in my stomach down to the rocking motion and the zig-zagging passage of the ferry across the channel. But it persisted as we docked, and as I drove our new acquisition back up to our beloved little base, and what should have been a triumphant return, my thoughts remained in Devon and all I could wonder was: would Kitty ever forgive me?

Anne and Elise were pleasant enough, as always, but I felt quite the intruder in my own home; I had only been gone a few days and already the little cottage, and the cellar beneath, carried the stamp of their own lives and methods. I couldn't blame them, of course, times were strange, and every little thing that helped you feel at home took on far greater importance than usual. They had worked together from the start, these two, knew each other's habits and dislikes, had their own shared humour, and I was not part of it, it was that simple. There was no room for resentment; Boxy and I had been the same, and Kitty and I would have been too, if someone else had blown in and tried to do things differently. As far as Anne and Elise were concerned I was now the blower-in, but, with Colonel Drewe's help we arranged with their commandant that they would stay on awhile, and pair up in the new vehicle until someone was able to return to Kent and collect the one Kitty would have brought back.

As the more experienced mechanic, I went back to driving Gertie, with no sense of disappointment; in fact it felt quite good to be rattling along the familiar, potted road, and predicting where the next clunking sound would come from. Whenever work allowed a breather, and Will came into my head, I learned to turn my memories to happier days. That little trick he, Lizzy and I had played on Ruth Wilkins in my father's study, the paper rose he'd made me, and his earnest and hopeful promise that he'd never make one for anyone else. I still treasured both the promise and the rose; if someone had offered to return the Kalteng Star to me and demanded that tatty piece of paper as payment, I would have refused.

It wasn't Will, or the rose, that I was thinking of though, as I bumped into the lane by one of the dressing stations one night, two weeks after I'd returned. Instead I was kept firmly anchored in reality at the sound of shells crumping continuously in the distance, and the urgent cries: 'Blessés, blessés!' We didn't usually go out until the all-clear was given, but now and again, as Kitty had told Lizzy, urgency outweighed caution and today the runner had conveyed the need for all hands. There had been no question of lying low.

I pulled open the back of the ambulance, and secured the flap before going into the church hall. Emergency procedures were being carried out by harried-looking nurses and doctors, and VADs were rushing everywhere clutching bowls and bandages; one girl, clearly newly arrived, stood with the dead weight of an amputated leg

243

in her hands, her eyes wide with shock, until the sister snapped at her to put it in the corner and get back to work.

The smell was tremendous. Although I thought I was used to it I was still knocked back every time I went inside; even in this unbelievably cold winter there was the warm smell of filthy, unwashed bodies crammed close together, of excrement and blood, fear and sweat. The air was choked with it, and with the sense of despair and terror that permeated the room. I prayed Will would never have to see the inside of a place like this.

The orderlies saw me, and immediately began selecting those deemed fit to travel. With the ease of long practice they moved into action, and in a matter of a few minutes we were back outside and loaded up. I was almost ready to go, and turned to declare room for a sitter up front, when a familiar face appeared. It was rounded and kind, but without the cheery smile I'd seen before.

'Colonel Drewe,' I said. 'I'm so sorry, are these your boys?'

'Afraid so.' He looked tired and dispirited, not surprisingly. 'I wondered, my dear, might I go with you? I have an urgent message for one of my officers at the hospital.'

I hesitated. It seemed wrong to be taking up the space a wounded man might have taken, even if it would, by necessity, have been one of the more lightly wounded casualties. A loud groan from the back of the ambulance forced the decision quickly; had the situation been different I would have risked the officer's annoyance, and stood my ground and taken a Tommy instead, I think we

244

both knew that.

'Hop in, Colonel,' I said instead, as I closed the flap down. 'And hold tight.'

The road into town had become a mass of small craters and debris, and every journey was a torturous series of lurches and crunches. The shelling was heavier now; the cold, clear air was good for ranging, and Fritz was taking full advantage. Explosions and buzzing whines brought the night to life with their deadly music, and then I became aware of an even more sinister sound; a droning that came from much higher above. My pulse hammered and I made myself take long, deep breaths, but the way Colonel Drewe was craning his neck to look into the sky told me I wasn't imagining things.

We were still only just nearing the outskirts of town when the noise faded and, as relief swept in I realised I'd been hunched into my shoulders, and straightened again. But as the plane veered away I heard another sound, one that struck me in the heart with terror; a high, keening shriek, growing louder and louder until it felt as if it were coming from inside my own head. Through the roaring in my ears, and the furious, unearthly cry from above, my panicked mind turned to how best to protect my charges, and in the split second it took to wrench the wheel hard to the right, and off the road, I knew I couldn't.

Chapter Fifteen

Gertie gave a bone-jarring shudder as she hit the scrubland alongside the road, and then she was flying. The absence of cries from the wounded was more horrifying than their screams had been, and when ambulance and ground crashed together again the impact knocked my teeth so hard I felt one of them splinter, shredding my gum. The floor of the ambulance shuddered as shrapnel tore into her, and I was hit by horrified realisation of the further danger. There was no time to wait for the vehicle to stop sliding; I was already punching forward and out, through her shattered half-windscreen, as she crashed into a half-demolished wall and spun away again. The jerk pulled me halfway back in, and I was dimly aware of a thin, burning pain as a jagged glass edge sliced into my forearm. I heard Colonel Drewe spitting curses as he tumbled sideways into the space I had vacated, and then I was sliding out onto the ground, cool air on my skin and wet mud instantly plastering my hair to my head.

The rumble of the explosion died away and then I heard the groans from the back. Thank God, it sounded as though at least two of the men had survived, but now they had to be pulled out before Gertie's fuel tank went up.

'Colonel,' I shouted, 'if you can move, help me!' I tore open the flap and began to pull the stretchers clear. I tried not to jolt the men more than necessary but haste was making me clumsy; my fingers were slick and slippery with my own blood, and in the jumping light from the nearby burning trees I could see fresh seepage on the newly applied bandages of the soldiers.

Drewe appeared at my side, and together we managed to get all four men out and clear, pulling them behind the half-wall for shelter. I bent over one of them, and Drewe covered two more as best he could, but after a couple of minutes had passed without further explosions we cautiously raised our heads. I realised then that the man whose body I was covering had no further need of help: his wounds, and the shock of the crash, had finally sent him west. Hardened as I'd thought I was to this, the utter hopelessness was too much, and I turned away.

Drewe patted my shoulder. 'Dear girl, you've saved us all,' he said. 'This poor chap was never going to make it, no matter what.'

It didn't matter whether he was right or not, the man had been alive when I'd collected him and now he was dead. And we were stranded out here with no means of getting the three remaining soldiers the help they so desperately needed. I ached in every bone and muscle, and my arm stung horribly. I couldn't see well enough to judge how bad it was, and I wasn't wholly certain I wanted to anyway, I felt quite queasy at the thought of it.

'Do you think it'd be safe to go back?' I said, gesturing at the sorry-looking Gertie lying on her side. Her chassis was facing away from me but I knew it would be ripped apart and completely

247

useless now.

Drewe sniffed the air. 'I should say so, can't smell fuel yet. Do you want me to go and get the first-aid box?'

I sank to my heels, relieved. 'Oh yes, please, if you could. I feel a bit faint, to be honest.'

'Then sit tight.' Drewe rose, but as he took a step towards the ambulance he gave a groan and stopped with one foot raised, reluctant to replace it. 'Dash it all, I don't think I can walk after all,' he said.

I swallowed a surge of nausea, and clambered to my feet, my head swimming. 'Sit down, Colonel, it's all right, I'll fetch it.'

'I'm so sorry, dear girl.' He squeezed my hand, and I dismissed the apology but eyed the over-turned ambulance with trepidation. Best do it quickly. Without allowing myself time to think, I ran across to where the contents had spilled out of the back in our frantic race to get the men out. The heavy first-aid box lay, burst open and spilling snow-white entrails across the ground, and I hastily shoved them all back in and took the box back behind the wall, where I checked the wounded and replaced bandages. 'We must get to the hospital somehow, and borrow an ambulance,' I said, as I worked. 'Do you think you'll be able to walk in a minute or two? I'll have to stay and look after these boys.'

He shook his head and his voice was filled with regret. 'I think I might have broken my ankle. You'd be faster on your feet.'

I looked out at the night, at the flashes that split the sky up ahead, and the awful road we had abandoned. Not for the first time that night, I experienced the cold thrill of fear; the hospital was still at least two miles away.

'Are you sure?' I hated the sound of my own cowardice, but I hurt everywhere and was feeling light-headed and woozy. I wasn't trained for this, as he was. Besides, if I collapsed on the road there would be no ambulance, and doubtless more fatalities among the men, left here in the biting cold.

'Quite sure, I'm afraid,' Drewe said apologetically. 'I wouldn't be half so quick as you.'

Looking at the way he winced with the slightest movement, I admitted he was probably right. I checked the three survivors one last time and, gathering every last bit of courage I possessed, I stepped out from behind the dubious shelter of the wall and back onto the road.

Fear and pain were my dark companions on that seemingly endless walk. I wanted to run, urgency was pushing at me with every step, but the footing was too uncertain, and I still felt sick and dizzy. The hollow boom of guns faded a little, but now and again a shell would whine overhead to strike one of the buildings, reminding me that these three men I was trying so desperately hard to save would soon be replaced by three more, and three more, and three more. And the dead man replaced by countless numbers of the same.

Finally the hospital came into sight, and then I did break into a run until, sliding on the loose rubble of the streets, I slipped and fell. When I got up again, shaken, I forced myself to slow down again to a fast hobble; I'd be no good to anyone if I broke my leg out here. At last I reached the hospital and seized a passing orderly, babbling out my story. After a seemingly interminable wait I was given an ambulance and a VAD, who came with me back to the sorry little group I'd left behind. She helped me load the wounded into the back, and climbed in with them once we'd made the difficult decision to leave the dead man where he lay.

'Can't be helped, my dear,' Drewe said gently. 'He'll be brought in with the others tomorrow.'

'I hate it,' I said, tiredness sweeping through me now the end of this long night was so close. 'It's wrong to just leave him there.'

'Let's concern ourselves with the living,' he said, and limped around to the front. 'And you must get that arm looked at while we're there.'

Despite the number of wounded being tended at the hospital, Colonel Drewe insisted one of the surgeons look at my arm, and when the man eased my coat off, he agreed it was a good job he had. I still couldn't look at it myself, but turned my head away and kept spitting into the little bowl at my side as my mouth watered with incipient sickness. There was blood too, from the shattered tooth in the back of my mouth, but I didn't want to draw attention to that in case they decided to pull it out. I couldn't have borne that tonight, not on top of everything else.

The doctor handed me over to a nursing sister, who cleaned and disinfected the wound. 'The last thing we need is one of you girls going down with gas gangrene,' she said briskly, as she swabbed and dabbed. Once finished, she put in a few stitches and gave me an injection. 'There. Good as new.'

Colonel Drewe, who'd reappeared after delivering his message, looked on approvingly. 'Quite so. And you can prove it by driving me back to HQ if you'd be so kind? I appreciate it's slightly out of your way.'

'Of course,' I mumbled, too exhausted to care now, as long as I could crawl into my bed within the next couple of hours.

I felt a pang of sadness as we drove past Gertie on the way back. She'd been an absolute trouper, and I'd deliberately thrown her into a wall and now she lay, like some kind of exotic dead beast, useless and made ugly by her final sacrifice. This borrowed ambulance would have to go back tomorrow and I had no idea how long I'd have to wait before I could get back to Blighty for the one I'd had to leave behind last time. Perhaps someone might be able to bring it over... I started to think about people I could write to, who might be willing or able to help, but I was too bone-weary to get very far – tomorrow would see me with a clearer head.

I dropped the colonel back to HQ, and was glad to see he was walking quite easily now; he must have not broken that ankle after all. Likely someone had strapped it up for him while I was being tended, and I was glad he'd allowed it, he was such a dear. He waved one last time as he went inside, and I turned my thoughts, and the borrowed ambulance, back towards Number Twelve and the blessed luxury of my cold, hard little bed.

Chapter Sixteen

The next morning I cleaned the borrowed ambulance, ready to return it. I'd already decided I would go via the rebuilt Casualty Clearing Station so the trip wasn't wasted, and since we were down to single-figures in the ambulance stakes, Elise offered to follow me out and give me a lift back. She and Anne had thawed considerably when they'd heard what had happened, and as Anne helped me redress my arm, while Elise made me a fresh cup of tea, I reflected that it was a sorry state of affairs when one had to get blown up in order to fit into the team under one's own roof. Outside, I refuelled the ambulance, and was just dipping the oil when I heard a car crunch into the yard.

'Hey ho!' a cheerful voice called out, and I looked around to see Oliver Maitland, leaning with one arm out of the window of the same car I had driven to France. His red curls, cut short for the military but still rebellious, peeked from under his cap and were caught in the wind that cut through the yard, it made him seem terribly young. We had become friendly over the past weeks and it cheered me no end to see him, despite the gnawing guilt.

'Good morning,' I called back. 'What brings you here?'

'Firstly I came to see if you were all right. I heard what happened.'

'I'm fine, thanks.' I waved my bandaged arm, and tried to ignore the throbbing that set up in the back of my mouth every time I closed my teeth too hard. I would get it looked at, just not yet. 'All sorted, and right as rain. What about secondly?'

'Secondly, Colonel Drewe has said you can use this little beauty for a few days, or until you get the chance to go back for the new bus, if that happens first.'

'How very kind! Won't he be needing it though?'

'Not for a little while, he's got some fearfully important meetings in Paris so he'll be away for a day or two, I've just seen him onto the train. So, I'll follow you to the CCS and you can load up for the hospital. Then we can both come back in this, you can drop me off, and there you go!'

'That's perfect,' I said, relieved. At least I would be able to work, and bringing out sitters would free up space in the ambulances for more serious cases. 'I'll tell Anne she needn't get all togged up for the great outdoors just yet, after all.'

'Now, what news from Kitty?' Oliver asked. 'Beastly girl never writes. How is she feeling now? Has she learned to milk a cow yet?'

'She's ... improving,' I said, hating the lie as I saw relief on his face. His cheery questions hadn't really hidden the worry that went deeper than he cared to show. Again I struggled with my conscience, and as we drove back to the hospital he kept up a running patter of jokes and anecdotes, throwing Archie into a mercilessly stern light, and making Kitty seem quite the little minx – only he himself emerged from his tales with a blameless reputation, and I couldn't help smiling, especially as it was so clear he was aware of what he was doing.

His chatter was designed to pass the journey in fun and friendship, and I allowed it to do so, finding comfort in the fact that I was still able to enjoy amusing company, and even contribute to it. We parted with smiles, and I drove away feeling better and more positive than I had done in a very long time. Then, arriving back at Number Twelve, I found a letter waiting from Kitty and my stomach instantly knotted tight; she would know, by now, if the sickness was what we'd suspected, and I wasn't sure I was ready to find out. But I opened the letter, with shaking fingers, and sat down to read it.

Dear Evie.

Lizzy tells me she has not put the news in with her letter, as she thinks I should tell you myself. The truth has become apparent now, and I write to tell you that what you feared has proven to be the case. I groaned aloud, but at least she hadn't laid it out in writing. *I will just say that I have chosen to remain, for the time, with Mrs Parker. She is, as might be expected, a perfectly lovely lady and very calm.*

Give Oliver a hug from me, won't you? Tell him I'll write soon. And say hullo to Archie for me too. Lizzy has said you feel somehow responsible for what happened. This is nonsense of course.

Kitty.

The throwaway comment stuck in my head, the

insincerity of it came wafting off the paper like a bad smell. There was no 'love', or even 'your friend', on the signature and that was unlike her. That she resented my friendship with Archie didn't help things; Lizzy would be as helpful as she could be, but I could see her getting quite snippy if Kitty kept up that particular and groundless grudge. The horrible smile of the driver hovered in front of my face. He must have known Kitty wouldn't tell, that he would get away with it ... that he would remain free to do it again, to any one of us. I had put the word about that everyone must take special care when out alone, but I couldn't even hint that something had happened, without someone guessing to whom. And without explaining my reasons, the warning merely had the same kind of disciplinary overtones that the nurses were used to hearing – I had no authority, and so who would pay any attention to me? The solution was inescapable: I had to get Kitty to name her attacker, and there was only one person who might convince her.

I had to tell Oliver.

He managed to combine an errand at the hospital with my request to see him, and picked me up a little before lunch two days later. I'd worked the night before, and managed a couple of hours of thin sleep, but my mind would not shut down completely and even my dreams were filled with thoughts of what I had to do. I must have broken the news a dozen times, in a dozen different ways, before waking to the sound of his car outside and a churning nervousness in my stomach.

He waited patiently outside while I hurriedly washed, and boiled water for the Dewar bottle – it was another bitterly cold day, and a drink of hot tea would be welcome later. Then he drove to Furnes, where he carried out his business at the hospital before driving on again a few miles. Apart from my trips home, this was the farthest I'd been from the fighting front, but the dull crump of the guns still punctuated the conversation and it was impossible, even here, to put the war to the back of our minds.

'Adinkerke,' Oliver said, pointing. The town lay to our left, close to the French border, and I felt an unexpectedly sharp pain as I thought about Will, just over two hours away, and Lawrence, only a little further. I'd often thought about transferring to France, nearer them both, but it seemed easier to be at a distance, where I was not frantically searching among the muddied, bloodied, and all-too often unrecognisable faces of the men that passed through my hands on their way to an unknown fate. At least here I was able to give all my attention to the men who needed me.

Oliver glanced across and, noticing my expression, tried to lighten it. 'We're quite close to the coast here, fancy a swim?'

I squinted out at the rolling grey clouds and pulled my coat closer around me. 'Sounds lovely. You go first.'

He grinned, and pulled the car to a stop in a field gateway, and turned to face me. 'Right then, Madame Davies, what was it you wanted to talk to me about? Your wire was intriguing, I must say. I assume this has something to do with Kitty.

Has she decided to stay in England?'

To give myself time to organise my thoughts I pulled the Dewar bottle from my bag and poured two mugs of tea. I could sense his curiosity becoming impatience, but I had to word it carefully. 'I have something important to tell you,' I said at last, 'and I want you to promise you'll listen all the way through before you say anything.'

'Go on.' The friendly, quizzical expression faded slightly into wariness, and I wondered, fleetingly, if I should just make up something else. But the time for lies had passed. 'It *is* about Kitty. She's all right,' I held up my hand as he opened his mouth, and he subsided, his face pale, and my carefully rehearsed words deserted me. 'What we told you, about her being ill, that wasn't true. Not entirely.'

Oliver tensed further. 'Out with it! What's happened? She's got the courage of a charging elephant, that one, it can't be the war that's seen her off.'

'No, it's not. She ... I was, well, she was driving alone one night and stopped to help someone she thought, at the time, might have been drunk. Because of his eyes, she said. He wasn't drunk though, he'd planned the whole thing to catch her. Oli, she was terribly brave and fought back, but–'

'Stop!' His hand crashed against the steering wheel. He lowered his head, and I could see the struggle as he fought to contain his fury. Eventually he took a deep breath and let it out slowly, then he looked at me, and his eyes were cold. 'Who was it?'

'I can't be sure, she wouldn't say. But I do have a suspicion.'

'Tell me!'

My hands were shaking, gloved though they were, and I put my cup on the dashboard and wrapped them together. 'I think it might have been the driver who brought you and Archie and the colonel over that day.'

'I know the one. Ratty-looking bloke. Hardly ever speaks.'

'What's his name?'

'Not sure, but I'll damned well find out.' He bit his lip and looked at me with reddened, worried eyes. 'Is she all right, really? I mean ... I assume this is the real reason she's stayed in England. Is she too scared to return?'

'Perhaps I've understated it so you could absorb it better,' I said, and cleared my throat. 'It was ... the worst kind of attack.' He flinched, and I hurried on, 'I'm so sorry, Oli, I didn't know whether I should tell you.'

'Of course you should have! And before now.'

'Archie said–'

'*Archie said!* She's my sister! *My* sister, not his.'

I didn't say anything, and the atmosphere inside the car was heavy with my helplessness and his silent anguish. The distant crack of gunfire sounded louder in the stillness of the car, and a gust of wind blew a splatter of icy rain across the windscreen. Otherwise the only sound was Oliver's harsh breathing, and the squeak of the leather under us as we shifted in our seats.

'I need your help,' I said quietly.

He was still pale, his hair looked redder than ever in contrast. He ran a hand through it, and I saw the hand was shaking as badly as mine. 'My

258

help? What can I do?'

'You're the only person who might be able to persuade Kitty to tell the truth. To identify him so he can't do it again.'

'More likely to listen to Archie. She's sweet on him, you know.' Oliver looked at me closely, no doubt sharing the belief with his sister that Archie and I were in some way connected beyond friendship.

'She doesn't want him to know,' I said.

'Of course.' Oliver kept his eyes on me and I flinched under their sharp, green gaze. 'She's pregnant. That's what you're telling me, isn't it?'

There was a faint note of hope in his voice, and in the set of his eyebrows, that he had misunderstood. But I nodded and the hope faded. He looked back out of the windscreen and chewed at his lip. 'You think I can get through to her?'

'If anyone can.'

'Not you? You're her closest friend. She trusts you with her life.'

'Not any more.' It hurt to say it, and now I risked angering him all over again. 'It was my fault she was put in the way of danger.'

His tone sharpened. 'How so?'

'Remember the time you and the colonel arranged for me to take this car to see Will? That was the night it happened.' His face twisted, and I reached out to touch his arm but he jerked away. 'I'm so sorry,' I said, longing for him to turn to me with kindness and forgiveness, and tell me I was being foolish. But he didn't.

'You scurried off to patch up some quarrel, and left my little sister to fend for herself,' he said in

259

a tight voice. 'Quite apart from what happened, she should *never* have been allowed to drive alone at night.'

'We all do it!' I heard the protest in my voice and wished I didn't sound so defensive; I knew I was to blame, so why did it hurt so much to have it confirmed?

'She'd been here four months, Evie!'

This was too much, even taking into account my own guilt, and my voice rose to match his shout. 'Most of us do it the first bloody *night!* If she'd joined the regular corps she'd have been driving that road at night, alone and with a loaded bus, before she'd had her first cup of tea!'

'Well, she didn't join them! She came to *you.* And you let her down.'

Oliver shoved open his door and got out, heedless of the rising wind that sliced through even the heaviest of coats, and threw his drink away into the grass. I got out too, it felt as if I should bear at least the physical discomfort alongside him.

'Oli–'

'Don't call me that. That's for friends.'

Stricken, I somehow edged my voice with steel. 'Captain Maitland!' He flinched, and I sensed the approach was the right one and pursued it. 'You're an officer in the British army, and one of your men attacked a vulnerable girl while she was doing her duty to help your men. What do you intend to do about it?'

The silence seemed to go on forever but I held my tongue, and my breath. I'd done all I could. At last Oliver turned to me, and I saw then that he was close to tears. 'Evie, I'm sorry. I shouldn't blame you.'

'You should,' I said, taking a step closer, my voice softening again. 'I do, and so does Kitty. But I blame that driver more, and he's the one who needs to be brought to justice. We need you for that.'

He nodded. 'I may have a day or so saved. I'll talk to the acting CO, and see if I can bring some more forward, enough to go back to England.' He looked at me with a haunted expression. 'Thank you for trying to make this as right as it can be.'

'I owe it to her.'

'You weren't to know,' Oliver said. 'I know you feel badly about it, but you're right; she's not the only girl driving alone at night. It's just ... she's my little sister, and the others aren't.' I nodded. It occurred to me that I had no idea if Will had ever worried about me like this; I don't know if I wished it or not.

'I understand, Oli. And thank you.' My hair was being tugged by the wind, and a fresh splatter of rain stung my cold face, but relief that he had apparently accepted our friendship again gave me the courage to smile hesitantly. 'Can we get back into the car? I've brought a picnic but I'm blowed if I'll sit on the grass and eat it.'

He managed an answering smile, though a strained one, and nodded, and we climbed gratefully back into the relative warmth of the car. To break the faintly awkward silence I delved into my bag and withdrew the bread I'd wrapped in the waxed paper that had accompanied my last parcel from home. I gave some to Oliver, then took out a jar and a spoon.

'Honey from Dark River Farm,' I said. 'Lizzy sent it. Would you like some?'

In answer he held out his piece of bread and I put a dollop of thick, comb-encrusted honey onto it and spread it with the back of the spoon. I needed to get him talking, to break this tense, fragile barrier completely, and help him relax enough to absorb the reality of what had happened. I raised a piece of bread to my own mouth, but then lowered it with regret. I really must get that tooth seen to. Instead of biting, I tore a piece off.

'Tell me about Kitty,' I said. 'About both of you, I mean. She never mentions your family, but I get the impression your parents didn't want her to come out here?'

'They didn't,' he said around a mouthful of bread. He took the spoon from my hand, and dug into the jar for more honey. 'They blocked her application to join the ambulance corps.'

'They must have been worried,' I said. 'My own mother wasn't overly pleased when I told her I was leaving.'

'That's not it. They were delighted when I joined up, told anyone who would listen about their brave son, the army officer. Different matter for Kitty, she was earmarked for marriage to some ghastly oik Father had picked out for her. It's not just one-sided, they can't bear each other. This lad has nothing to him, but his father and ours are in business together.'

'But why would your father try and persuade them to marry?'

'To ensure the business stayed in both families I

262

suppose. Rather an old-fashioned way of looking at things, but that's Father for you.' He licked the spoon and then, as if the honey had sweetened his temperament as well as his bread, he adopted a pompous tone. 'No, Katherine, you will not be running off to chase soldiers around France, you will stay here and marry Alistair, and then spend the next few years popping out lots of little Alistairs.'

My hand tightened on my mug, and his mood changed again as he realised what he'd said. I cleared my throat. 'But she came anyway.'

'Thanks to Archie, yes. I gather the girl who came out with you at the start left to marry?'

'Yes, Boxy. Barbara, I mean. I met her during training. She's the one who suggested we set up alone. She married a very sweet man from the flying corps.'

'Good for her. Well, as you know, Archie and I go a long way back. He was home on leave and came to visit, knew I had completed my training and was heading out soon. He heard Kitty complaining about what Mother and Father had done, and so told her about you needing a new partner.'

I looked at him narrowly. 'You do realise then, she probably only came out here because it was Archie who'd told her?'

'She'd have found a way anyway, somehow. As I said, my sister's a courageous little thing.' His voice choked a little on that, and he fell silent for a moment. Then he went on, 'Archie made it possible for her, after Mother and Father put the brakes on her formal application.' He gave an odd, proud little smile. 'She did the Red Cross training under the pretence of looking for a position on home soil, it was the only thing that stopped her getting pulled out from that too.'

'You're right, she does have enormous courage. She carried on working after ... well, after. Right into the small hours.'

There was another quiet moment while we considered just how much fortitude and dedication that must have taken, then Oliver sighed. 'Thank you for telling me, Evie. It must have been hard for you.'

'Harder for you to hear it.'

'Look, even if she does name him, it will be her word against his. He may only be a private but he's general staff, and they tend to stick together.'

'We have to try, at least.'

He nodded. 'I'll go and see the CO as soon as I get back. It's frustrating as blazes though, I know a couple of the lads who're on the Blighty leave list, and they'd be happy to swap, for a price.'

'Why don't you ask them?'

'Easily done, for local leave, but not for overseas. Those passes are like gold dust, and I imagine the top brass don't want to turn them into currency. No, honesty's the best policy if we don't want punishment duty, or even pips taken off.'

'It's a pity Colonel Drewe isn't here, he'd be bound to understand. Will you tell your acting commanding officer why you want to go?'

'I don't think that's a good idea. It'll raise more questions than we can answer, and cause a hullabaloo that might frighten Kitty into keeping quiet. I'll just say it's a family emergency. Throw myself on their mercy.'

It made sense, and I nodded and started packing away tea things. 'Then I suggest we go back now, the sooner we get this arranged, the better.'

In the early hours of the following morning, midway through a particularly gruelling night, Anne ushered me up from the cellar to snatch a ten-minute break. She set water on to boil to take back downstairs, and then went to the doorway, where she lit up a gasper and pulled on it with almost frantic haste. I pretended not to notice the tear tracks on her cheeks; sometimes, no matter how hardened you like to think of yourself, something will get through to you and tonight seemed full of those somethings.

I sat down at the kitchen table, pen in hand once more. There was blood on my coat-cuff, the blood of someone's son, husband, brother ... and the knowledge that there might be another driver or nurse somewhere with the blood of my own husband on their sleeve gave me a familiar sick feeling. I had lost track of where he was in the cycle of rotation between trenches, and it occurred to me that I wouldn't even know if he was currently operational. I made up my mind to write to Barry again, to ask him to let me know when they might be given a day, or half a day's leave, and to try and get over to see Will one more time before our marriage fell apart altogether.

But this letter was for Lizzy. Although I had written regularly since joining up, she had been right in what she'd said; I was trying to protect her unnecessarily, and it was insulting both to our friendship and to what she herself had been through. It was time to put that right.

My dearest friend,

I write to you now in a moment of rest during a long, dreadful night, and although I have been here over two years I cannot ever remember seeing such carnage. I have kept my letters to you light, not wanting to add to your burden of worry and grief. You have been through so much, Lizzy, and almost lost your life, and I have never been in such danger as you have, never risked anything so selflessly for someone I love.

Tonight I feel helpless and small and weak, and I am ashamed of it. Our boys have been gassed halfway to hell, many of them died in the ambulances, but a few lasted until they reached the cellar before succumbing. It's pitiful, and agonising to watch; bronchitis in the blink of an eye, the fluid rising in their lungs until they drown and die. There were also casualties from the shells that carried the gas, of course, and tonight there seemed to be so many more than usual. Perhaps because the Tommies were exposed as they ran, trying to escape what they could see all around them. These have been taken to the clearing stations but too many of them will go no further and there will be many, many funerals in the next few days. It's endless, Lizzy, and I am heartily sick of it.

I can see you now, reading this, and I know you will have tears in your eyes, but I also know you will have an angry set to your expression because I am the same. I can barely see for crying, but at the same time I feel as if I could walk out into No Man's Land myself and take Fritz by the scruff of the neck. I'd shake him 'til his teeth rattled and he cried for his mother!

266

I must stop writing now, I feel I have poured enough grief into your life. Please forgive me for that, and I promise I shall be back to my old self very soon.

Pass on my kindest regards to your mother and Emily, and the twins, to Mrs Adams and the girls, and, most importantly, to darling Kitty. Tell her again how sorry I am? She will not hear it from me.

Take care of yourself, and I hope you hear from our much-missed Mr Bird very soon.

Your ever loving
E.

I had just finished addressing the envelope, and slipped it into my coat pocket, when the world blew up.

Chapter Seventeen

The impact sent me staggering against the table in sudden, hideously bright silence. A second later the noise came back into the room and I felt as if my head would burst with it. I heard and felt the deadly whisper of glass shards, most unable to penetrate the thickness of my great coat, but some sliced the skin of my face and neck.

The table crashed over and I hit the floor, and through the thunder all around me I heard the scream, 'Cellar, Davies!' Numbed, I tried to remember the training we'd had for just this situation, but all I could do was duck my head and wrap my arms around it. I felt someone grab my arm and looked up to see Elise, blood streaming down her face from a nasty scalp wound. Somehow I stood up, and as Elise urged me towards the cellar I saw a prone figure by the front door and recognised Anne, half-covered in fallen masonry.

I took a step towards her but Elise tugged me on. She was crying but she was, at least, thinking straight. 'Leave her!'

'But it's Anne!' My own voice sounded muffled, as hers did. She sobbed harder but pulled me to the cellar door and pushed me down the steps.

'We'll go to her later, she'll need us in one piece.'

In the relative safety of the cellar I tried to imagine how I'd feel if it were Kitty I'd left alone up there, and I silently raged at myself for letting Elise pull me away. But deep down I knew she was right. Anne was likely already dead, and there would be others who would need Elise and me when this was over. If we survived.

Another shell hit nearby, but this time the cottage itself was spared. I felt blood soaking into the collar of my coat, and raised my hand, dreading what I would find. Elise caught at my fingers before they could touch my neck, and lowered them away; I couldn't see her expression properly, the only light we had was from flickering fire, but I could see her shaking her head.

'Leave it, sweetheart,' she said. 'We'll get you fixed up soon.'

Worried now, I grew more aware of the stinging pain in the side of my neck, but I blinked hard and tried to focus, instead, on the job in hand. The gassed soldiers lay struggling for breath, their nails a livid blue in the peculiar, sinister light of the fire that consumed Number Twelve above us, and despite the oxygen pumps I knew there was little that could be done, beyond trying to ease their passing.

One by one they died, and the shelling around our little cottage seemed less important every time a poor, frightened boy fixed his blinded eyes where he thought mine might be, and choked his last. After two and a half years of watching men die in appalling numbers, this terrifying yet wearyingly hopeless night had reached a part of me I thought I had been strong enough to protect.

The explosions died away. Now I could hear voices outside, water hitting the burning rooms above us, crashing masonry and wood as people broke through the newly created barriers to our cellar, and low sobs as Elise gave herself over to the grief of losing her friend. They would have been closer than sisters, I knew that; our work here made friendships both more important, and more fragile, than anything we had known before, and while we were aware of the risks to ourselves, somehow that was easier to reconcile than the loss of someone with whom we had shared our most terrifying, and our most triumphant, moments.

I felt closer to Elise than I had ever done, and was moved to hold her as she wept, surprised when she let me do so. There was a dull pain in my shoulder and I remembered crashing to the floor as the windows blew in, it was a wonder I had only suffered a few cuts and a bruised arm. The voices came closer, and then I heard a shout.

'Misses? Answer if you can, are you badly hurt?'

'No!' I shouted back.

'Two survivors down here,' Elise called, adding to me, 'You have some glass that needs taking out but you will be fine, I promise.'

'I'm so sorry about Anne,' I said, and she hitched another breath. With the fire put out there was no more light, but I felt her nodding just before she stood back. Then the cellar door crashed open and flashlights swept the small, death-filled room.

Two soldiers descended hurriedly, first-aid boxes in their hands. A light played over my face and I flinched. 'It's nothing, some glass,' I gestured vaguely, then frowned. 'Can you hear that?'

A deep, gurgling sound was coming from above our heads, culminating in a harsh crack, and in the split second it took us all to recognise what was happening, the soldier had seized Elise's hand and mine and dragged us to the steps. The next moment part of the ceiling had fallen in, and water was gushing through, drenching the corpses that lay wrapped in their blankets, briefly bringing the covered features once more to life as the rough wool moulded to the shape of the man beneath.

Then hands were on my back, pushing me, and Elise and I were stumbling up the steps and out into the acrid, smoke-filled rooms above. Elise ran to where a soldier was gently covering Anne's face with his coat. She fell to her knees, heedless of the rubble, and I turned away and hoped she would be able to forgive herself one day, but I doubted it. No matter that she had been right, that she had more than likely saved both our lives by dragging me down to the cellar, she would forever be tortured by the knowledge that Anne might have been alive after all, and might have been saved.

Outside, I looked around at everyone rushing to put out smaller fires, and to find survivors, and the strength just left me. It was startlingly sudden, as if the will to remain upright simply ran out of my legs and out through my sodden shoes, and was trickling away into the churned mud in the yard. I sat down, drew my knees up to my chin and laid my forehead on them. My hands clutched the ground either side of me, scooping up the dirt and squeezing it through my fingers, taking strange solace in the sharp stones that scraped my skin, and the confirmation the pain gave me that I was alive.

'Miss?'

I looked up to see one of the doctors from the dressing station. 'I'm all right.' There was an odd wooziness in my voice, as if I'd drunk too much wine.

But he crouched down beside me, his voice gentle. 'No, my love, you're not. Come with me.'

I sat quietly in the makeshift dressing tent, wearing only my trousers and a blanket wrapped around my upper body that left my shoulders bare. A tense-looking nurse worked quickly, picking slivers of glass out of my hair, and some from my face, and then stepped back to let the doctor through. He didn't speak at first, but looked at me from several different angles as the nurse dabbed at the thin trickles of blood that ran down my arm.

At last he nodded. 'I think it's safe.'

I still had no idea what was going on; I was

numb, in limb and in mind, and the stinging of the glass cuts was a faraway feeling, on skin that didn't belong to me. The nurse eased me back to a lying position, and I grew frightened all over again as the doctor leaned over me. I felt another sting, lower in my arm, and a moment later I was drifting, pleasantly light-headed but still conscious. I felt a tug midway down the right side of my neck, but no pain. The doctor closed his eyes briefly and stepped away, and the nurse took over again.

'What are you doing?' I tried to say, but it came out as an exhausted mumble. A hand on mine drew my attention away: Archie. I felt trembling relief at the sight of him, and his smile reassured me.

'You're talking gibberish as usual, darling,' he said, 'but you're going to be fine.'

'Oh. Good.' I closed my eyes, feeling safe for the first time in too long, and drifted away.

When I awoke Archie was still there. I had been moved to a place I didn't recognise, away from the main tent and into what looked like a recovery area. I ran my tongue over fuzzy teeth, unsticking my lips. I tried to move my arms, but one of them was strapped tightly to my side, and I had been dressed in a clean shirt. My head felt heavy and filled with wool. 'What did doctor do?' I asked, when I had loosened my mouth enough to speak. The hope that they might have spotted my shattered tooth and removed it while I was under anaesthetic, was quashed by a quick investigation with my tongue that resulted in a stabbing pain in my jaw.

'You had a piece of glass stuck in your neck,' Archie said. 'There was concern, for a while, that it might catch your carotid artery, and that when it was removed it'd be all up for you. But I told them you were made of sterner stuff.'

Despite the jokiness of his words, I went cold. I had been walking around, tending the gassed men, and at any moment I might have moved the wrong way... Archie saw my face, and whipped a bowl beneath my chin. I obliged by heaving up the little I had eaten and drunk since that endless night had begun, and he sat, patient and unflinching as I wiped my aching mouth with the back of my hand. 'You'll likely have some pain in your shoulder for a while,' he said, when I had finished. 'The doctor said your trapezius muscle was damaged so you'll have to rest up.'

'Does that mean I've got a Blighty one?' I asked with a little smile, and he smiled back.

'I'll write the ticket myself. But aye, in all seriousness, I think you should go back for a little while. Perhaps spend some time with Lizzy. And Kitty, of course.'

Kitty! I sat up, ignoring the little roll of nausea at the sudden movement, and caught at Archie's arm. 'I have to speak to you, where can we go that's more private?'

'You can't go anywhere,' he said firmly. 'Sleep first, then I'm sure someone will be very glad of this bed once we're certain your blood pressure is stable again. We're already arranging passage back to England.' He raised an eyebrow. 'My CO clearly rates you girls highly, I've been given an overnighter, just to drive you to Calais and see you

273

onto the ferry. We can talk then.'

'No, it has to be now,' I insisted, 'it's really important, it's about Kitty and ... you know.' I looked around but there were too many people within earshot. 'Give me a piece of paper and I'll write it down.'

His face had clouded the moment I'd mentioned Kitty's name, and he gave me a scrap from the notebook in his pocket, and a stub of pencil. With a shaking hand I wrote: *K positive, suspect driver.*

His expression darkened further as the first part became clear. 'Oh, poor Kittlington. She must...' Then he frowned. 'The general staff driver? Drewe's man?'

I looked around again, hoping for privacy, but the sight of the tall officer whispering urgently with the agitated girl was proving too interesting to the others recovering in the small confines of the tent. 'I don't know his name,' I murmured. 'And I don't know for sure it's him. We have to get Kitty's word before we say anything; he can't have the chance to build a defence.'

'Potter, if it's the bloke I think it is. Look, I'll ask around a bit, but meantime get some rest and I'll be back to pick you up in the morning.'

In fact morning was already creeping in through the small, glassless windows, and with it the beginning of yet another unforgettable day.

Chapter Eighteen

Number Twelve was irreparably damaged. Flooded and unsafe, it sat glaring at those who came close, as if ready to bite down on any adventurous soul who dared breach its walls. Those walls were already crumbling though, there were no windows left at the front of the house, just jagged teeth set into the frames, with blackened points where they had been scorched. People moved about, coughing and throwing glances our way, initially curious, then sympathetic, then dismissive.

There was no hope of collecting any of our things from there, whether personal or medical supplies, and Elise and I silently linked hands and turned away. As I did so, the realisation of what I'd lost hit me, and I began trembling, superstitiously fixated on the paper rose, as if to lose it would be to lose Will. I let go of Elise's hand and, ignoring her shout of alarm, began walking quickly towards the cottage.

The doorway was barely an arm's length away when I felt a hand seize my still-sore left arm and pull me to a stop. 'Miss, you can't go in there!' The voice was a friendly, London-accented one which I found comfortingly casual, but when I looked into the sergeant's face I saw only firm resolve. He'd been tasked with making this place safe while the dead men were lifted free, and that did not include allowing hysterical women to barge through, putting themselves and others at risk. But he didn't understand, how could he?

'I have to get something. A black box. It has ... vital paperwork in it.'

He pushed his helmet back and scratched his head; he seemed to be wavering. 'What paperwork, and which room is it in?'

Seizing on this slight fracture in his determination, I forced myself to stay calm. If he thought it was merely something personal he would shut down again. 'I can't possibly tell you the nature of it,' I said importantly, but with a twinge of guilt. 'If you'd just let me go into the back room, the bedroom, I'm sure that part of the cottage was less badly damaged.'

'It may well be,' he said, 'but to get to it you have to go through the front. I can't allow it.'

'But–'

'Describe it to me, I'll go.'

I stared. 'You, you said it's too dangerous,' I stammered. This wasn't what I wanted; the cottage was audibly groaning with loose timbers, and while it had seemed exactly the right thing to do to go in there myself, I couldn't let this earnest young man put himself at risk for something of value only to me.

'And you said the paperwork was vital,' he reminded me, a little impatiently. 'Time is short, Miss, do you need the box or not?'

I needed it. I needed it so badly it hurt, just to see the rose, to feel Will's soul wrapped in its grubby paper heart...

'No,' I said at last, and the word came out of my

276

mouth cracked and hollow-sounding. The soldier studied me for a moment, then let go of my arm.

'Then you ought to leave. This is no place to be hanging around now.' His voice was gentle enough, but his words, said of this place that had been more of a home to me than Oaklands for so long now, sounded cruelly dismissive. I nodded and turned away. The soldier watched as I returned to Elise's side and then, satisfied, returned to his duties.

Elise and I walked to the ambulance. The only one we had left now was the one I'd recently brought back from Kent, but I didn't have to worry about how to bring the second new one back now after all; I'd be able bring it myself, when I returned from my convalescence. Elise climbed behind the wheel, and as I prepared to swing in beside her I tensed with a fresh rush of determination.

'Wait here,' I said, and ran quickly around to the back of the cottage. The movement jarred my shoulder and I swallowed a little grunt of pain and slowed, waiting for the nausea to subside. To my frustration the tiny window of the single back room was closed, and there was still glass in it – which boded well for the condition of the room, but I'd risk further injury breaking in. I glanced around. Lumps of broken masonry were plentiful and I bent down, picking one up and hefting it in my left hand while I checked which side the latch was on. We'd never opened this window, not even in the summer, and I had no idea if the latch even worked. It might have been painted over, rusted in place, anything.

Nevertheless, standing here would not resolve anything. I hit the window hard, turning my head away at the last second as the glass shattered. Eyeing the shards that stuck jaggedly out of the wooden frame I remembered Archie's face when he'd told me about the danger I'd been in last night. I felt the sting, too, of the healing cut in my other arm. More broken glass. I swallowed, suddenly reluctant to put my hand through and fumble for a latch that might not even open.

'Miss!'

I turned; the sound of the window breaking had brought the fair-haired sergeant I'd spoken to before, and he rounded the cottage now, glaring at me.

'I have to get that box,' I told him, and raised the rock ready to hit the glass again, to remove some of the sharpest pieces. But before I could strike, he'd taken it off me.

'Look at the window.'

I looked. I wasn't a chunky build by any means, but even I would never have been able to squeeze in through there, even without my arm strapped.

'I'm sorry,' the soldier said firmly, but not without sympathy. 'Your friend's waiting. You ought to go.'

I nodded, and didn't say any more, but walked to the ambulance and climbed wordlessly aboard. The rose was gone; my precious memento of that magical time when Will and I had been forever and invincible. Gone. Once the cottage was demolished, the box would be buried under rubble and smoke-ruined rafters, it would absorb the rain until its contents were swollen and unrecognisable, and if, somehow, it survived and someone were to stumble upon it, they would see only a twisted piece of old newspaper – they might even unravel it in a moment of historical curiosity, and the last remnant of that gloriously simple, joyful day in the market place would be destroyed.

No. Not the last. I dragged in a breath, and forced myself to count my blessings: Will was still alive, that was number one and the most important. And although Kitty's life was going to be twisted into a new, unknowable shape, she was being cared for. All those I loved were currently safe – it was the best I could hope for, given the peril in which so many of them lived every single day. I had survived two terrible attacks in a very short time, and I was being taken care of by a man who loved me. That I didn't love him back didn't seem to matter just at that moment; it was enough to know there was someone here who knew what had happened and who was as passionately relieved as I was that I was still here to tell the tale.

Will, Archie, Uncle Jack, Lawrence ... all of them might be taken at any moment, one minute warm, breathing, loved and loving, the next moment gone forever. What was a piece of paper next to that?

Elise and I were both thankful we had kept so many layers of clothing on against the night chill, at least we had those to walk away in. My right sleeve, the one with the dark splash of blood on it, was empty and pinned up, and since I couldn't button my great coat, nor fasten the belt one-handed, it flapped open, both annoying me and letting the wind wrap itself around my body and keep my teeth chattering.

The letter to Lizzy was still in my pocket, and I realised I would never send it after all; it had been cathartic to write, but would have been selfish to share such poison. I would soon be able to talk to her, and if our conversation led around to the way life was out here, that was one thing, but to let her open a letter with the anticipation of pleasure, and have her life darkened by it instead, would have been unforgiveable. Besides, she had enough to worry about with Uncle Jack.

Elise drove us both to her Red Cross station, where Archie would collect me to take me to the ferry. Despite my arguing that I was perfectly well, I couldn't deny my neck and shoulder were giving me a great deal of pain now the morphine had worn off, and I would be of little use either as a driver or as a nurse until the muscle healed. Since I had nothing to pack, I spent the afternoon performing light duties, one-handed, wherever I could.

'Captain Buchanan to see you,' a hurried-looking VAD told me, and I put down the newest consignment of gas masks I had been unpacking. Outside, Archie stood looking uncomfortable, and kept glancing at the staff car behind him. I looked there too, steeling myself for the sight of Potter, the driver, but instead I saw Oliver, white-faced and agitated.

I looked defiantly up at Archie. 'Yes. I told him.'

'I told you not to, Evie! Look at him!'

'I had to.' I lowered my voice. 'He's the only one who might be able to persuade Kitty to come

280

forward and get that driver away from other vulnerable girls.'

'He's told me he's going to talk to her,' Archie admitted. 'She'll listen to him.'

I had expected anger, but Archie's discomfort was puzzling. 'There's a problem. Oli hasn't been out here long enough, and can't get on the Blighty list.' He paused, then shrugged. 'But, since Uncle Jack sanctioned my earlier trips under military business, I can. I wasn't going to take it, didn't feel entitled. But I have just under a week.'

'Well, that's no good, you were the one person she couldn't bear to be told about it,' I said with some heat. 'She'll be mortified, and deny everything...' It clicked then, and I stared at him, horrified. 'You're going to let Oliver go in your place? Archie, even *he* said you could lose your commission over this!'

'For heaven's sake pipe down! I'm not transferring my pass. Listen. When I come to pick you up Oli will be with us, ostensibly just to spend a few nights in Paris. When we get to the ferry, he'll take my papers and become me.'

'He looks nothing like you!'

'They never look, not really closely, and you can't tell hair colour. A bit of mud on the photo, and some creases, and as long as they're satisfied he's British, and you can't get more British, let's be fair, he'll be waved on. Too many people for them to worry.'

'What will you do?'

'I'll stay in Calais and lay low, then, in a day or two, when Oli brings Kitty over, I'll drive them back here.'

'And what if Oliver doesn't get back within his few days?'

At this, Archie looked even more shifty. 'I'll cover for him,' he said. When I opened my mouth to speak he raised a hand. 'Just as you're covering for Kitty,' he reminded me.

'It's nothing like it! You and Captain Maitland are serving officers, Kitty and I are volunteers. How dare you compare the two! I will not travel with a deserter.'

'He's not deserting!' Archie looked around, then lowered his voice although we were quite alone. 'He's merely trying to bring a violent man to justice. Don't pretend you wouldn't give anything to see the same. This is for Kitty, remember.'

'I don't even know for certain if I'm right,' I pointed out, wavering slightly under the force of his argument. 'Look, Archie, don't risk this. I'll talk to her, put the name in front of her and see if she reacts.'

'Let Oliver do it,' Archie insisted. 'He'll likely have more chance of talking her around than...' His words faded away but I knew what he meant, and it stung.

'Than the person whose fault all this is?'

'Darling,' he caught my good hand, 'it wasn't you.'

'I played my part. Why can't you go over his head, to his commanding officer?'

Archie shook his head. 'Without Kitty's word they'll just close ranks. Without her there's no crime, and Oliver would be branded untrustworthy, willing to throw accusations around at a time when everyone needs to be unified.' His grey eyes darkened. 'We can't risk Potter getting away with it, when I think of what he did to that poor girl I could kill him myself.' His fury, though understandable, took me aback slightly; he'd always been so calm, seemingly unflappable.

I nodded. 'All right. I owe her this, at least.'

When Archie had gone I went back to my work and, as the afternoon drifted on, I pondered all he had said and reluctantly accepted it was the best, and maybe the only way. Kitty would not respond to me, I was sure of it; not only had I left her alone that night, I had also, in her eyes, foisted her on strangers while I swept blithely away with the man she wanted. And I already had one of my own.

My own...

Will's image danced in front of my eyes, the ghost of his lost smile lighting his beloved face, and I felt again the crushing loss of the life we had dreamed of. I wondered what he was doing now, if word had reached him of the shelling, and if he was worried about me. I still hadn't heard whether or not he had been rotated back to reserve, and wished I had time to go to France before we left tonight, to see him sitting, bored but safe, a mile or more behind our own lines instead of yards away from the Bosche and sinking in an ocean of mud.

I wanted to feel his arms wrapped tightly around me, telling me without words that he was still mine, if I could only wait a little longer. And I wanted to tell him I would wait forever, that he was the same man, deep down, that I'd fallen in love with, that he couldn't push me away no matter how much he wanted to. His heart and soul

283

rested in my hands, but my hands were steady, and always strong enough to hold him.

Dozing in my chair, waiting for Archie to come back, I let my mind drift back to Gretna in 1914 and how he had looked when we married; the seasoned soldier he would soon become already showing through the last vestiges of the charmingly boyish looks, and matching the quiet certainty in his manner. I couldn't give him up, even if he wanted me to. As soon as I was fit and well again I would see him, whether he wanted it or not. I'd camp out in the battalion HQ until he came off the lines if I had to, I'd crawl through all the mud in France just to–

'Wake up, darling!'

I jumped. The car had arrived without my noticing, so intent was I on finding a way back into Will's embrace. I shifted on my camp chair, wincing as my stiffened shoulder protested at the movement. In a flash Archie was out of the car and by my side.

'Are you sure you don't want a nurse to travel with you? I'm sure one can be spared, after all you've earned a little care and attention.'

'Definitely not,' I said, 'they're too important here. Besides, I'll have you to look after me. Won't I?' I said this quite pointedly, and by the way he glanced over at the car I guessed the plan hadn't changed. I didn't know whether to be relieved or frightened; if he didn't get back in time, and Archie was suspected of aiding a deserting officer, he would face imprisonment for up to ten years.

Oliver would be shot.

As we parted company that evening at Calais, Archie hugged me gently, mindful of my shoulder and neck. 'You and Uncle Jack have got almost-matching scars now,' he said with a smile, but he looked concerned. 'I've wired Lizzy that you're coming, but haven't told her you're hurt, or she'd worry. Now try not to overdo things, aye? Oliver will carry anything that needs carrying. And if you pick the new ambulance up on the way over, instead of on the way back, he can drive it down to Devon and maybe get back sooner rather than waiting for trains.'

I looked out over the icy grey waters. 'How are you going to cover for him?' I wasn't sure I wanted to know, not really; the less I understood the better. But if I knew a plan was in place I might relax a little, at least.

Archie glanced around but there was no one interested in us here. 'It's Easter, traffic is heavy. I'll send a telegram to HQ from here on Saturday night, explaining we've had a minor road accident on our way back. He'll only be a day late at most, we're sure just the sight of him will tip the balance with Kitty, and he can drive back right away. Hopefully with Kitty in tow.' He squeezed my hand. 'Remember it's for her.'

'I know,' I said, 'but I can't help feeling–'

'Can we go?' Oliver said, and his face was taut and pale. He actually looked terrified. 'I want to get on this damned ferry before I lose my nerve.'

With one last hug, Archie left for the hospital and I felt very lonely, suddenly. Despite the ease with which he was waved through after his papers were checked, Oliver's fear did not abate as the ferry moved off, and now, as France faded into the darkness behind us, he seemed to grow tighter and tighter with every wave we cut through. After less than an hour he removed himself from sight, and I didn't see him again until we docked at Dover, where there was another shock in store.

Chapter Nineteen

The train to Sevenoaks was due in a few minutes. My shoulder had stiffened horribly during the night, and although I tried to keep it mobile there was a low, throbbing pain that the powders I'd been given didn't seem to touch. Relieved to remember that this time, at least, I wouldn't have to drive, I was looking forward to getting beyond all the business of posing for ... I caught my breath, wondering why I hadn't realised before; I was no Elsie Knocker, but whenever a donation was collected there were photographers and newspaper reporters everywhere.

'Oliver, you can't possibly come with me!'

There was no answer, and when I turned to look behind, where Oliver had been standing a moment before, there was no one there. I looked around, but there were only strangers on the platform. Perhaps he had gone to speak to someone he knew, or to check we were in time for the train? I waited, not wanting to move away from where he knew I'd be, but growing more and more anxious as the minutes ticked away and, when he hadn't

286

returned by the time the train rolled in, I walked up the platform, craning my neck for sight of him.

Passengers disembarked, were replaced, and still there was no sign. I looked into all the carriage windows I could, straining through the glass to the faces beyond but not seeing him anywhere. The guard began slamming the doors shut – I had to make a decision, and I seized my case and scrambled quickly into the nearest carriage just as the whistle blew. The train began to chuff gently out of the station, and I hung out of the window and finally, through the throng of waving friends and relations, I saw Oli. Standing very still, his face turned away, but recognisable by the bright red curls tumbling in the breeze.

Realisation dropped coldly into place; he'd had no intention of either coming to Devon, or returning to Belgium. He had tricked Archie and me, and if he didn't return, and Archie sent that telegram ... it didn't bear thinking about. I felt a helpless, boiling rage at Oliver's selfishness. His nervousness started to make more sense now, the jittery eagerness to get on board the boat, the reluctance to be seen... I thought of how close Will had come to being executed, and compared that to this man using his sister's terrible situation to escape, and I felt like reporting Oliver myself, and hang the consequences.

For a moment I toyed with doing just that, and with getting off at the next station and hoping he would still be here when I managed to get back, but I knew it was hopeless to think he would be. He'd only waited long enough to ensure I got onto the train myself. The thing now was to get

287

word to Archie, to stop him sending that incriminating telegram, and then to somehow track down Oliver and persuade him to go back before he himself was sentenced for desertion. And, almost seeming unimportant next to those desperate problems: how to convince Kitty to give up the name of her attacker now?

The ambulance bumped into the farmyard as the sky was lightening the following morning. Having been awake all the previous night and day, and driven down from Kent alone, I had finally pulled over to sleep as fatigue overtook me, and now felt groggy and sore. But the sight of the early-morning activity, of a widely yawning Land Girl and a brisk Mrs Adams coming out of the kitchen, and the knowledge that I would soon see Lizzy again, gave me a flicker of deep pleasure.

Mrs Adams quickly shook her head and pointed down the lane, raising her voice above the squawking of startled chickens, and the rumble of the engine. 'Lizzy in't here, love. She's back home for a few days. Down there about two miles. Can't miss it, this end of the row of five, just over the bridge. Be sure and come up to see us later, I'll have a bit o' dinner for you all.'

The cottage was small but pretty, with a well-tended garden boasting a few blackcurrant and gooseberry bushes, and windows that caught the early morning sun, shining as though they'd just been cleaned with vinegar; I hoped Lizzy wasn't overdoing things. I switched off the engine just as the front door opened, and I immediately saw that the Lizzy who greeted me was not the same as the

288

one to whom I had said goodbye such a short time ago. She had been just as healthy-looking, and just as cheerful, but there had been a slightly distant look in her eyes then, as if a vital part of herself had been lifted away, leaving her functioning but incomplete. This Lizzy was whole. And it only took two steps into the little kitchen to see why.

Uncle Jack stood beside the table with a piece of toast in his hand, and a look of such surprise on his face that I knew Lizzy hadn't told him of my imminent arrival. For one blissful moment, Archie, Oliver, Kitty, and even Will, were swept from my mind, and there was only the deep relief and joy at the sight of this man, and I knew for certain, and for the first time, that he was forgiven. I was across the room before he had time to speak, and I heard him throw the toast back onto the table a second before I reached him and he lifted me off the ground in a tight hug. I didn't even mind the pain that sliced into my shoulder, and the constant nagging ache from my broken tooth.

'Evie, darling girl,' Jack said, and his familiar voice, with its faint north-western accent, was the undoing of my tightly held composure. I knew his love for me was strong enough to hold me up, so I let go. The moment my feet touched the floor again I laid my head against his chest and began to sob. I heard Lizzy's exclamation of dismay from behind, but Jack spoke, murmuring something I couldn't hear and I sensed he was telling her not to worry.

He smoothed down my hair, just like he had when I'd been a little girl and taken one of my many tumbles. Back then he'd never told me to stop climbing around like an adventurous boy, to ride my ponies with more decorum, or to walk down the stairs instead of running. He'd simply looked at my bruises and scrapes, taken my hand and led me outside to the apple trees where we'd count the small, hard apples on the branches and on the ground until I'd forgotten why I'd been crying. Now it was as if I was that child still, and he still knew how to make me forget my woes.

He drew me out into the little garden Lizzy had told me so much about, and we breathed in the clean, cold air of the early spring morning while I found the calm inside myself again. He had been working here too, I could tell, and as he showed me the shrubs he had planted and the shoots that already poked out of the half-frozen soil, he talked to me. About nothing in particular, mostly the types of plants he wanted to try and grow, but also about the Devon countryside, with which he had fallen in love every bit as deeply as he had with the woman who had brought him here.

I always enjoyed hearing him talk about Lizzy; knowing how she loved him, to hear him speak of her in such wondering tones, as if he didn't deserve her and couldn't quite believe she wanted him, warmed me right through and gave me hope. Eventually his voice faded away, and he waited for me to tell him what had propelled me into his arms with such relief and despair.

'I can't tell you just yet,' I said apologetically. 'I'll talk to you both together. When we're...' I looked around, and couldn't see Kitty anywhere, but I didn't want to risk it. 'Definitely alone,' I finished.

'All right,' he said, and put his arm around me as we walked back to the little house. Lizzy was clearing away the last of the breakfast things, and Jack made me laugh by complaining she had tidied away his toast too soon.

'Honestly, just because I threw it on the table doesn't mean I was finished with it,' he grumbled.

'Too late,' she said smartly, whipping the half-full mug of tea he'd also left to go cold. 'If you can't finish a simple meal without dragging the guests out to show off your garden, you miss out. The birds will enjoy it.'

The look she gave him belied her brisk words, and I glanced away; their eyes had locked together and the gaze remained unbroken. I wondered how long Jack had been back from Germany, and whether they had found privacy to be alone together in what must be a very full house indeed. Which reminded me.

'Where are Emily and the twins?' I asked.

'Gone with Ma, to visit my gran,' she said, and it occurred to me this was a whole side of Lizzy's life I had never even asked about. I felt bad about it and resolved to spend some time talking to her this time. Although, with Jack here, she might be less inclined to natter her time away, and I couldn't blame her for that. It had been clear for a long time that these two were hopelessly addicted to one another, and I couldn't bear to be in the way. My pleasure at being here, while certainly not lessened by Jack's presence, was altered slightly; I couldn't help feeling a bit odd when I saw them touch one another in passing, or exchange a look like this one, that scorched the air between them.

291

It had long been the same with Will and me, but our time together had always been cut short, and so rarely did it happen, that I couldn't help feeling a flicker of jealousy. It soon passed though, when I saw how deeply contented Lizzy and Jack were in each other's company – having found each other, no one else would do, for either of them. But could I say the same about Will and me?

Lizzy seemed to notice the shadow pass across my face as the question popped, unbidden, into my mind, but I wasn't here to talk about Will, as much as my heart contracted whenever I thought of him. It was Archie who needed our attention now, and, though my anger with Oliver still boiled, him too.

'Is Kitty all right?' I said, 'And where is she, anyway?'

'She's fine. She offered to take over from me for a couple of days when Jack came back, since I'm still only on light duties. She's been helping out with the lambing too, she loves that.' She frowned at me then, noticing how I favoured my right arm. I pulled a face and removed my coat, uncovering the padded dressing on the side of my neck.

She and Jack both spoke at once but I shook my head. 'I'm all right,' I said, 'it was just a piece of glass. But it cut the muscle that goes down into my shoulder, so I've been sent back to let it heal.'

Jack's face was grim. 'How did it happen?'

We sat down and I gave them as brief a description of the shelling as I could manage, watching their faces go from concern to horror, and then to determination, and they both began trying to persuade me that going back would be a very poor choice.

'I'm going as soon as I'm able to,' I told them firmly.

'What were you thinking of, driving here alone?' Jack scolded. 'Very very silly, and not at all likely to help your healing.'

I exchanged a glance with Lizzy, who had clearly had the same thought as me.

'Extremely silly,' she agreed, somewhat archly. 'You must never drive when you're injured. Must you, Jack?'

She brushed a gentle finger across his right side and, after a momentary struggle with his sense of parental responsibility, he subsided. 'Point taken. Don't listen to me. But you're a sensible girl, so listen to this,' and he reached out and tapped my head.

'I will, I promise. But I have to tell you something else. Something more important.' I told him everything that had happened after I got back to Number Twelve after seeing Will, and he looked grim at the news of Kitty's situation. The look melted into sympathy, until I told him Archie was planning to cover for Oliver, and then his face darkened again but I pushed on; I was just three words away from fully unburdening myself and couldn't stop now.

'Oliver has disappeared.'

There was a silence in that little cottage kitchen that seemed completely out of place. Not a sound came through from outside, not even the distant noise of animals or birds. Eventually Jack spoke and I could hear the effort of control in his voice.

'I'll kill him.'

'Jack!' Lizzy said, but her voice too was worried and taut. She laid a hand on Jack's arm, and he subsided slightly, but his jaw was still rigid, and his eyes flashed blue fire.

'This is my nephew we're talking about. He's risking his *life* for this bloody Maitland boy!'

'As you did for Will!' I shot back. 'And as Lizzy did for you.'

'That's not the–'

'Please, Uncle Jack,' I said in little more than a whisper, 'you have to help find him, persuade him to go back before Archie sends that telegram.' And he had Archie's papers, too, I belatedly realised. My neck and shoulder hurt horribly and my eyes were grainy and tired. Lizzy had prepared a bed for me in case I turned up late at night, and she stood ready now to help me to my feet, but I couldn't rest until I knew Jack was going to help. His anger was palpable, but he was a good man and I knew he would do the best he could, if only he could put his fury aside.

He exchanged a long, wordless look with Lizzy, and then shifted his gaze to me and his voice softened, although only a little. 'Of course I will.'

It was enough. I felt Lizzy's arm come around me as I slumped in relief, with my head pillowed on my arms. 'I'm so glad you're here, Uncle Jack,' I mumbled into the crook of my elbow. Lizzy drew me gently to my feet, and led me upstairs to Emily's room.

'Do you think he can help?' I asked her as she helped me undress. It was strange, an old ritual, familiar to us both for so long, yet we were different people now. She helped me only because my arm was becoming less functional the longer I remained awake, and when she turned back the eiderdown to let me slip between the clean, fresh sheets, I felt like crying for all we had lost.

But we had gained, too, and Lizzy's trust in Jack gave us both strength. 'I'm sure he'll do everything he can,' she said. 'We'll talk to Kitty later, and see if we can work out where Oliver might have gone.'

'Thank you,' I mumbled, hoping my gratitude was more obvious to her than it sounded to me.

'Sleep now.' She left me alone then, and I closed my eyes as the relief of being among loved ones once more stole through me, and carried me into a peaceful and, for once, dreamless sleep.

When I came awake it was late at night, and the opportunity to talk to Kitty that day was past. For a second I fretted at the passing of time, but there was nothing I could do about it now, and worrying about the wasted chance would achieve nothing, so I lay quietly, relishing the comfort of Emily's bed. The wind had picked up, making a strange, animal-like whine as it cut across the corner of the end-terraced house. I lay for a while, enjoying the sound, comparing it to the hideous shriek of the shells which usually punctuated my nights, making sleep a fitful luxury. As I shifted position to stretch my legs my right shoulder woke up and howled. I bit back a cry and reminded myself to move more slowly, but even settling back down did not lessen this new ache. It set up a sympathetic throbbing in my gum, and I knew I was finally going to have to get something done about that too.

Taking a deep breath, I sat up and eased my legs out from under the covers, the cold moment-arily replacing the stinging tug from the stitches in the side of my neck. I let my eyes adjust to the darkness for a while, until I could locate the Aspirin powder I had brought with me, and then poured a glass of water in readiness. Before I could drink it, however, I heard the murmur of voices from the room next door and realised that was what had woken me.

I didn't want to listen; it would have been like eavesdropping on my parents, but I heard my name, and paused with the glass halfway to my lips.

'It's not just up to her,' Uncle Jack said in reply to whatever Lizzy had been protesting. I could tell they were trying to keep their voices down, but the disagreement had clearly upset Lizzy and her voice had risen.

'You can't go back, not for *that!*'

The echo of my own words, in her scared voice, shook me. Go back where? I carefully replaced the glass and crept closer to the wall between the two rooms. 'It's her legacy, darling,' Jack was saying. 'And he didn't see me, I'm sure of it.'

'And you're absolutely certain it was him?'

Jack's voice was grim. 'Hard to mistake Wing-field, you know that better than most.'

There was a quiet moment and, from the way Lizzy's voice was muffled when she spoke again, I guessed he had pulled her back to lie against him. 'Jack, please, go back for your country if you must, but don't do it for a rock she never wanted in the first place.'

The Kalteng Star? I frowned, my heart speeding up as I strained to catch every word.

'It's not just up to Evie,' Jack said, his voice quieter now too. 'It's a Creswell heirloom, and ... I owe it to Henry.' There was a silence, and I closed my eyes, urging her to convince him not to go, but he spoke again. 'Listen, I'm not risking anything, he doesn't know I've even been over to Germany, let alone seen him. I should be able to find out what he's done with it, and if he *hasn't* got it any more I'll come home. I promise.'

'When will you go?' Lizzy sounded resigned now, and I felt her pain. Just as I had had to accept Will's decision to return to fighting, so she had, equally reluctantly, accepted this.

'I'll leave directly from France, as soon as this mess with young Archie is sorted out. We'll need Kitty's help though, I hope she's up to coming back with me.'

'Jack?'

'Hmm?'

'I love you, you know that, don't you?'

A low chuckle. 'I think you've proved that.' He sighed, and the sound drifted through the wall as I imagined him tightening his hold on her. 'And you know I love you. I'd do anything for you.'

'Except stay,' she said sadly, and then there was no more talking.

In the morning it was as if the exchange hadn't happened. There was no mention of his leaving, and it was only the darker circles beneath Lizzy's eyes that betrayed a sleepless night.

'We'll go and talk to Kitty today,' she told me as

297

she put a bowl of porridge in front of me. It was thick, laced with Dark River Farm honey, and the smell was warm and rich. It made me smile, despite my nervousness.

'Just the two of us,' I clarified, looking apologetically at Uncle Jack. He waved it away, already stuck well into his porridge.

'She's never met me, the last thing she'd need would be some old man rolling up while you three are discussing...' he cleared his throat '...delicate matters.'

I looked at him with some amusement; at a little under forty years old he still looked thirty, square-shouldered and handsome, only the creases beside his eyes and the deepening of the lines around his mouth showing the toll these past few difficult years had taken on him. Judging from the way Lizzy raised an eyebrow I imagined her thoughts were the echoes of mine.

I grinned. 'And what will the "old man" be doing while we're up at the farm?'

'Gardening,' he said with satisfaction, and dropped the spoon into his empty bowl. He leaned back and patted his stomach. 'Any more where that came from?'

Lizzy gave him a look. 'No. There's a war on, you know. Besides, you'll get fat.'

Jack pulled a face and stood up. He leaned down to kiss Lizzy's forehead, and she leaned against him for a moment. I looked away, not quite embarrassed, but feeling like an intruder on their quiet moment together. They both seemed to sense this and broke apart, and once more I felt a pang of envy for their closeness, and the way their minds were completely in tune.

Jack took his jacket down from the peg by the door, and I reflected how well the casual life suited him. He'd never been one to conform to social standards, but here, in this little kitchen with his garden outside and Lizzy within reach, he was more relaxed, and happier than I'd ever known him. 'I'm sorry,' I blurted.

They both looked surprised. 'Sorry for what, love?' Jack said.

'For pulling you away from all this,' I waved my spoon, 'and sending you off to France.'

Jack came over to me and took my hand. He removed the spoon from my grip and drew me gently to my feet. The smell held deep in the fibres of his jacket was a comforting mixture of earth and bonfire smoke, and as I wrapped my arms around him I breathed it in, mingled with the smell of the warm, honeyed porridge. How had we ever lived in such isolated, sterile surroundings before?

'You're not pulling me anywhere, nor sending me,' he said, his voice low and soothing. 'Archie is my family, as are you, and all you've done is let me know he needs my help.'

'Do you think we could send a wire to Archie, warn him not to send the message back to HQ?'

'No, it's too dangerous. We don't know where he's staying in Calais, although I could probably find out without too much problem. But even if we did, as far as everyone's concerned he's in England, and a message would only throw a searchlight onto the whole thing. Better not to draw attention, and trust we get to him first.' I nodded, and he released me with a gentle squeeze. 'How's your shoulder?'

'It's better than it was last night,' I said. The ache had subsided with the aspirin and the water, and I had slept well for the remainder of the night. 'I should be quite fit to travel in a day or two.'

'You will not!' Lizzy protested. 'You'll stay here until you're properly mended.'

I exchanged a glance with Jack and we both smiled. 'Yes, Lizzy,' I said meekly. 'Oh, Uncle Jack, I meant to say; I met someone who remembers you from Africa.'

'Really? Who's that?'

'Lieutenant-Colonel Drewe.'

His expression brightened. 'Ah, yes, I remember him. Good officer. Madly courageous.'

'He said the same of you,' I said, pleased.

Uncle Jack looked surprised, but gratified. 'I remember he was sort of grandfatherly-looking, even back then,' he went on. 'Should think he looks every bit the grandfather now.'

'He does. And he's terribly kind. Not at all the type of brass hat you'd expect.'

'Well, it's good to know he's back in active service. After he was injured at Rooiwal he changed quite a lot, became dependent on morphine for a while. We didn't think he'd rejoin the military so I'm glad to hear things have turned around for him. He runs a tight ship, be a shame for that to have gone to waste.'

'He spoke highly of both you and Father,' I said.

'Did he now? Well, he knew Henry rather better than he knew me.'

I smiled. 'I have the feeling he knew you a bit better than you realise – said you had no sense of propriety.'

'Damnable cheek,' Uncle Jack said, though amiably enough. 'Do give him my regards when you next see him.'

'I will.'

'And don't go overdoing things while you're here, all right?'

'I won't.'

'And remember to change your bandages as often as you need to.'

'I will.'

'And don't forget to write to your mother and Lawrence.'

'I won't.'

'And–'

'Jack!' Lizzy broke in, and he grinned and ducked away from her well-aimed dishcloth, taking refuge behind the closing door. He opened it again just far enough to blow her a kiss, and she blew one back, and then he was gone.

After I'd eaten my porridge I helped Lizzy clear away the plates. She locked the door behind her and the two of us set off up the road towards Dark River Farm. She hadn't for a moment entertained my suggestion that we should take the ambulance, and it was a relief to stretch my legs, wrapped up warm against the stiff breeze, where the only gun we heard was the occasional crack of a farmer keeping down vermin. I turned my thoughts from Will, where they kept trying to settle every time I thought about the way life was at the fighting front, and instead asked about the farm.

301

'It's a lovely place,' I said. 'Where did the name come from?'

'There are woods that back onto it, at the southern edge of the boundary, and in front of that there's a fairly small tributary of the River Dart. The trees cast a shadow over most of its length, and since they're evergreen the river remains in darkness for a good deal of each day.' She shot me a brief grin. 'I know, you were hoping for something a little more exciting, weren't you?'

'Believe me, I've had more than enough excitement for one lifetime,' I assured her. 'And what of Mr Adams? Is he still... I mean, did he...'

'He died, yes. In the first year of the war.'

'Poor Mrs Adams.'

'She's bearing up. She has a lot of help – the girls are a good substitute family for her, and I've seen the man who collects the milk give her the glad eye when he comes over.'

'And does she return it?'

Lizzy grinned. 'She pretends he drives her crackers, but I do think she welcomes it, yes.' She touched my arm, and her voice was gentle. 'Evie, I know things look bleak now, but they must be well again someday, mustn't they? We just have to push through this, and hope for the best.' We were silent for a while as we walked, and I looked across the moors, the woodlands dotted here and there, the valleys spread out below and the occasional farmhouse nestled against the steep slopes. Rain-wet huddles of granite glistened against the green, and the harsh landscape soothed my thoughts, and I began to dare to hope things might just be all right after all.

Chapter Twenty

The chilly wind cut through our clothes as we came within sight of Dark River Farm, and it was wonderful to step into the warm, fragrant kitchen. There was no one there, but we found Kitty upstairs in the main bedroom, stripping the beds. She looked up with a ready smile that died when she saw me; it was clear that, in this case, absence had not made the heart grow fonder, nor had it softened the anger she felt towards me, and it was only going to get harder once I told her what I had come to say.

I looked around at Lizzy, who stood in the doorway, uncertain, then back to Kitty. 'I have to talk to you, is it all right if we sit here?'

'Of course. I hope you're keeping well.'

Her well-bred formality took me aback somewhat, but it was better than the outright hostility to which she had every right. I realised she didn't know about our little cottage yet, nor about Gertie, and groaned inwardly; if only I had some good news to tell her, but it was all absolutely awful.

Lizzy came into the room and closed the door behind her. 'You look a bit peaky, love. Are you feeling all right?'

'It's just a cold,' Kitty said. 'And I'm a bit tired, I was out early this morning with Jane and Sally.'

'Where's Mrs Adams?'

'Gone to the village. She'll be back soon.' Kitty

303

glanced at me. 'She told me she saw you early yesterday.'

I wondered if I had imagined betrayal in that little look, that I'd been here and not come in to see her, and nearly blurted out defensively that I'd thought she was at the cottage. But instead I just said, 'She invited us to come up for a chat.'

'She asks after you often, she'll be glad to see you again.'

'I wish you were.'

She shrugged. 'I'm glad you're safe,' she said, and that was the best I could hope for. 'What did you want to talk about?'

I sat on the bare mattress, wondering where to start. I had considered telling her about Gertie first, then the ambulance base, and only then building up to the terrible situation with Oliver, but in the end I just went straight to the very worst.

'Oliver has deserted.'

'He ... what? *What?*'

'He was on his way back here, to try and talk to you about what happened, but he disappeared from the station.' The girl flinched and swallowed hard, as if she had been on the verge of being sick, but waited for me to go on. 'You have to be the one to name the man who attacked you, or else I'll be accused of putting words into your mouth. But I know who it was. He knew the car was booked to me that night, so of course you'd be alone.'

The way she paled told me all I needed to know, had I still been in any doubt, and I told her about Archie's plan. She looked more hopeful at that, but I had to be sure she understood the consequences. 'Kitty, Oliver might have got away now, but he will be found in the end.' I made her look at me. 'He'll be court-martialled. You know what might mean for him, and for Archie.'

Kitty's eyes were wide and bloodshot in her white face. 'What can I do?'

'You must think hard about where he might be. How we might find him and persuade him to go back. And then you must come to France with us and give your story.'

'What happened to your neck?' she said suddenly.

'There was ... it doesn't matter.'

'I'm not a child! What's happened?'

'We were shelled,' I said. 'Number Twelve is gone. I'm so sorry, darling, Anne was killed.'

She fell silent and her hand twisted in mine but it didn't feel as if she was trying to pull away, so I kept hold of her. Eventually she drew a ragged breath. 'What do I have to say, and who to?'

I sagged in relief, and put my arm around her. 'Come back to Lizzy's house with us. Uncle Jack will be there, he'll tell you what to do. Thank you.'

She pulled away, and her face was suddenly cold. 'I'm not doing this for you. This is your fault as much as *this* is.' She gestured at her belly. 'You seem so nice, Evie, but you just destroy everything. My family will never speak to me again, and now Oli and Archie may both die. You shouldn't have told them, I begged you not to, but *you* knew better! You don't care whose lives you trample on, or who gets hurt. No wonder your husband couldn't wait to get back to the trenches.'

I sat in complete shock, my insides twisting in

anguish, but Lizzy was not going to stand idly by. 'Kitty Maitland, how dare you! Evie has done everything she can to help you; that *one* night she left you, she was trying to save her marriage. Besides, you said yourself, you're not a child! Evie has worked alone on that road before, many times. All the other drivers do, she told me so, and you wanted to be just the same. If something had happened to her, and it might just as easily have done, would *you* have stood up and accepted the blame the way she's doing?'

Kitty stared, her mouth open, but Lizzy hadn't finished, and her voice was pure fury. 'She has taken you under her wing, taught you everything you need to know to save countless lives, brought you here to be safe, and now she's risking her health to make sure you get back to France and put right what your brother has done!'

'Her health?' Kitty managed.

'Oliver tricked Archie and Evie into helping him desert! Evie wanted him to come here and talk to you, persuade you to tell the army what happened. Not just for your sake, you selfish little madam, but for the sake of every single girl out there. And now, when she should be resting, she's putting herself through all sorts on your account.'

'Lizzy,' I protested, as she stopped for breath, 'Kitty's not selfish, she's right.'

'She is not! She had a right to feel a little let down at first, but you have more than made up for your small part in what happened, you know you have.'

I didn't know what to say, and neither did Kitty, we just sat next to one another on the unmade bed, looking at Lizzy who, despite her diminutive stature, seemed to fill the room. Her hands were braced on her slender hips, and her bright blue eyes blazed at the two of us, waiting for one of us to speak.

I was the first to find my voice. 'Well, it's no wonder Uncle Jack is scared of you.'

Lizzy looked back at me, amazed, and then gave a yelp of laughter. Kitty's hand crept into mine, and when I looked at her she was blinking back tears.

'She's right, I'm sorry,' she said in a quiet, hiccupping voice.

'Don't be,' I said. 'Just try and think about where Oli might have gone. And promise me you're going to tell the truth about what happened.'

'I will.'

'It will be hard, and people will accuse you of awful things.'

'My family have already disowned me, I'm ruined. It can't hurt now.' Her words were brave but her voice shook, and I smoothed her hair, the abundant red curls springing back under my hand. I remembered Oliver's hair, so similar, and at the reminder of his youth my anger towards him faded a little. Still, he had abandoned his sister just as surely as her parents had, and the anger did not retreat far.

It struck me then that the three of us in this room had all had our own youth torn away far too soon; by different things, but just as surely as one another. Lizzy to Holloway, myself to the war, and Kitty to the terrible experience that had turned her, at the age of nineteen, into a middle-aged woman with too much knowledge in her sad green eyes.

'We'll look after you, sweetheart,' I said, my voice cracking, 'both of you.'

'But you'll be going back to Flanders, and I'll just be here getting in the way once the baby's born.'

'You won't be in the way, love,' Lizzy said, calmer now. She sat down on Kitty's other side. 'You'll be amongst real friends, just remember that.'

Kitty looked from Lizzy to me and back again, and took a deep breath. 'Do you promise?'

'I swear on Mrs Adams's bread pudding,' Lizzy said solemnly, and was rewarded with a weak smile. 'Right, now let's give you a hand with these beds since we've kept you talking. Not you,' she said to me, as I rose, prepared to help. 'You don't want to put any strain on that shoulder.'

'All right. I'll go and make some tea instead, shall I?'

'Good idea,' Lizzy said, 'and then we'll talk to Jack about where to start looking for Kitty's brother.' She picked up the clean sheet from the basket. 'Right, Miss Kitty, blow your nose, get your thinking cap on, and in the meantime let's get this job done before Mrs Adams gets home.'

Later that afternoon Lizzy looked at me with amused exasperation. 'I don't understand you, Evie. You're out there—'

'Don't,' I warned, but she ignored me.

'Out there facing bombs, bullets, gas, goodness knows what else—'

'Lizzy...'

'You've been shelled, frozen, half-starved, wounded–'

'All right!'

'Are you going in, then?'

'Yes!'

'Good girl.' She held the door open for me and, taking a deep breath, I went in.

The doctor spent a long time looking, making tutting noises, and prodding around my gum. Now and again he would touch a bit of sharp tooth and I would squawk, causing him to draw back and raise one eyebrow; no doubt his thoughts echoed Lizzy's. It was all very well, but when one is in the thick of things there's no time to anticipate pain, which is the hardest bit. Sitting in this chair, however, all I could think about was how it would feel when he picked up the forceps and applied them to the shattered mess at the back of my mouth.

Lizzy picked up my hand, sensing the time for good-natured teasing was past. 'Soon be over,' she said. 'Doctor, it's very good of you to see Evie at such short notice.'

'Glad to be of help. Can't have her going back to fight the Hun if she can't even eat,' he murmured. 'Are you sure you don't want any Procaine?' he asked, before he carried on. 'I know I said it's in short supply, but we do have some.'

'If it's in short supply, then you need it,' I said, trying to sound firm. I'd seen boys put up with infinitely worse treatment without crying out; I must be as strong as I willed them to be, and this must be over soon, in any case.

I could sense Doctor Nichols being careful not to jog my shoulder, but in all honesty a good jolt of pain there might have provided a welcome distraction; I have always loathed, beyond measure, the necessity for dental work, which is why I looked after my teeth to an almost obsessive degree and was glad Will was the same. I turned my thoughts in his direction, picturing his strong, white teeth showing in his dimpled smile. It helped a little.

Lizzy stayed at my side while the doctor bent and picked broken shards of tooth out of my swollen, sore gum. I had my eyes closed but I could hear the breath hissing between her teeth in sympathy whenever he tugged a bit and made me whimper. There were pieces that had driven into my gum, which had begun to heal over the top, and when these came free my whimpers turned to little yelps and Lizzy's hand tightened on mine.

The doctor paused now and again to let me swill my mouth out with tepid water, before pressing me gently back down and setting to work once more. When he had pulled all the shattered fragments out, he put a wad of cotton into my mouth and gradually the coppery taste of blood subsided. It seemed to have taken hours, but a glance at the clock told me it had been less than twenty minutes. Jack would be outside with his car, waiting to take us back to Dark River Farm, and a night's rest before setting off with Kitty in the morning in search of Oliver. I looked forward to just sitting, talking to him and Lizzy, putting the frightening situation to the back of my mind for one blissful night, maybe sipping a warming drop of whisky...

But the doctor hadn't finished. I saw Lizzy catch his eye, and she reluctantly let go of my hand. 'I'm going to tell Jack we won't be long,' she said, but she wouldn't look at me. My clenched hands tightened until my short, ragged nails bit into my palms, and as the doctor picked up the forceps I knew the worst was far from over. The door closed quietly, the doctor leaned in and removed the cotton wad, and I took a deep breath and squeezed my eyes tightly shut.

Chapter Twenty-One

Dark River Farm, April 1917.

Kitty rubbed at her tear-streaked face while Jack and I struggled to contain our frustration. Lizzy sat next to the younger girl, and kept shooting looks of remonstration our way, but things were getting desperate.

'I'm sorry to sound so harsh, love, we're not trying to frighten you.' Jack was pacing, and I felt like joining him. Surely Kitty must have *some* idea of where her brother might have gone? She was clearly unwell, and not all her sniffles were a result of her weeping, but this was Archie's life at stake, and if she really loved him ... but at the expense of her brother? Her dilemma didn't fail to touch me, and to elicit a deep ache of sympathy, but she must do the right thing. She *must*.

'Kitty, please,' I said, urgency making my throat painfully tight, 'Oliver has done wrong, you can see that, surely?'

'He's just frightened!'

I tried not to snap, to keep my voice even, but it was difficult. 'And all those front-line Tommies aren't? Will isn't? Oliver's got it good out there by comparison!'

She gave me a blistering look. 'Good? How can you say that, seeing what you've seen? Don't forget I've seen it too. Just because he's an officer doesn't mean he's safe – officers die too. Every day.'

'But they don't run away!'

'Look,' Jack said, sitting down again and leaning towards her with his hands linked, and I could tell it was in an effort not to reach out and shake her. 'I understand your brother's very young, and if we can get him back soon enough to prove he wasn't seriously trying to desert, he may get away with punishment detail. I'll speak for him, I promise, and your testimony will go a long way too. But if he stays away until they send someone for him, and they will,' he said, fixing her brimming eyes with his, 'he'll be lucky to escape with his life.'

'I'm sure he's just giving himself a good talking to,' Lizzy said, 'time to come to terms with things.' She frowned at Jack, but I was firmly alongside him.

'He doesn't have that luxury, and why should he, any more than any of the others out there? More than that boy whose mother was ill, and who came back to see her?'

Jack looked away and I realised that was a bad example. I'd never even asked what had become of that boy, but it was clear Archie hadn't been able to help after all. I fought down a surge of sorrow, and tried to sound friendlier as I hurriedly pushed on. 'Skittles, sweetheart, you know we just want to give Oli the best chance of putting this right. If you can tell us where to find him, where to begin looking even, Uncle Jack will do his best to help.'

Lizzy touched a wrist to Kitty's forehead. 'You don't look at all well, darling. How are you feeling?'

'A bit achy but it's just a cold. I'm used to it.' She turned to Jack again. 'I know you're both right and I'll try to think, but my mind is so fuzzy.' She concentrated for a moment, while we waited and even Lizzy tensed, then shook her head. 'He'd never go home, I know that. He has friends in Liverpool but I can't remember where they live.'

'Their name?' Jack sat up straight, looking interested.

'Something short. I ... I'm sorry.'

'Don't cry,' Lizzy said, and put her arm around her. 'Jack, she needs to sleep. Maybe she'll remember in the morning.'

'We'll have to leave first thing, whether we have any leads or not,' Jack pointed out.

'I'll be ready.' Kitty coughed and winced, and Lizzy sighed.

'Leave her alone for now, she's doing her best.'

I wasn't convinced, but took a deep breath. 'I'm sorry, I know you are, Kitty. At least you're agreed you must speak up, to name that vile dr...' I caught Jack's eye, and changed the word that had hovered on my lips, '*man* who did this to you.'

She nodded. 'I will do that, I promise.'

'We'll find him,' Jack said, and leaned over to squeeze her hand. She looked surprised, but I wasn't: Jack Carlisle had the forbidding and slightly distant look of the secretive man he'd had to be, but inside that chest beat a heart of pure gold. Lizzy's expression softened to see it evidenced, and she put her own hand over theirs. He raised his face to her, and I saw the apology in the creasing of his brow.

'You're right, and trying to force this is getting us nowhere. Go to bed, Kitty, a good night's sleep might help you clear your head. And try not to worry,' he added, and drew her to her feet. 'We'll find your brother, we'll explain everything, and as long as we get to Archie before he sends that telegram it'll be all right.'

I went with Kitty to her room. 'Are you going to be all right if I don't come back to Flanders with you?'

'Of course. I'll have Elise to take care of me, and your uncle. You need to get some use of that arm back.'

'Not to mention my jaw,' I agreed with a rueful smile. It felt as though I had a tennis ball tucked inside my cheek, but Lizzy had assured me it didn't show too much.

I sat down on her bed and watched as she filled her bowl for washing. 'Skittles, about Archie–'

'I'm sorry about what I said.' Kitty frowned and rubbed at the back of her neck, arching to relieve an ache. 'I understand about you and Will. At least,' she amended, 'I understand how much you love him.'

'I do, and although Archie is a dear friend, and has helped us both no end, I want you to know I could never turn to him ... in that way. No matter what happens with Will.' And what *would* happen? I had no idea, all I knew was that I couldn't give up on him no matter what he said.

I left her to undress and climb into bed, and Jack, Lizzy and myself returned to Lizzy's mother's cottage. As we walked, Jack's hand found Lizzy's and they exchanged a wordless look of understanding for one another's conflicting roles in that evening's conversation; their natural approaches had complemented one another, and I was glad for Lizzy's tenderness, which had also balanced out my own rising frustration.

As for Kitty, my respect for her, despite that frustration, had soared. Not yet out of her teens, and going back to Flanders to face not only shells and bullets, but also disgrace, and the possibility of sending her own brother to court-martial. Courage like that was rare and precious, and I could only pray it would be rewarded.

I was brought awake in the early hours by a hammering on the bedroom door.

'Come in,' I mumbled. The door opened, and although it was still dark, the height and breadth of the silhouette in the doorway told me instantly who was there.

'Uncle Jack? What are you–'

'Is she here?'

'Who?' I struggled to a sitting position, trying not to groan at the chorus of pain that sang from

315

shoulder and mouth.

'Kitty.' Jack came in, and now I could see his face I recognised a mixture of annoyance and worry. 'She's not at the farm.'

I blinked, trying to organise my thoughts, but could only repeat fuzzily, 'Not at the farm?'

'No one's seen her since last night. Has she been in to see you? Said anything about going somewhere before we leave?'

Worry cut through my sleep-addled confusion. 'The last time I saw her was when she went to bed.'

Jack ran his hands through his hair, his annoyance growing. 'I went up to the farm early, to make sure she had plenty of time to get ready. No one saw her leave but she's not there. I hoped she'd come to see you, to say goodbye.'

'No.' I shoved the eiderdown back and prepared to get out of bed.

'It's all right, Evie, stay there, rest. We'll find her.'

'I'll be down in a minute,' I said firmly. 'You can't delay your departure, every minute counts.'

'If I'd thought there would be a problem this morning I'd have insisted on leaving last night.'

'You couldn't have guessed she'd wander off,' I said, then couldn't help trying to raise a smile. 'Although it is starting to look like a family trait.' His brief grin lightened his face for a moment, and I was glad to see it despite the panic gnawing at my insides; if she had, after all, placed Oliver's safety above Archie's, who knew how it might end? I stood up and ushered him from the room. 'Let me dress, and I'll help you look.'

Good Friday was already announcing itself as anything but good. The sun was creeping over the horizon. Lizzy and I searched the cottage and its garden, and the surrounding gardens as well, while Jack took his car to the village. Then, to half-hearted protests from Lizzy, I urged her into the passenger seat of the new ambulance and drove back up to the farm.

We spoke to everyone we could find. Belinda had overslept, and her sister Jane, and the other land girl Sally, both said the same thing: they'd been up early with the lambing and hadn't been in the house to see if anyone had left.

'I hope she's all right,' Sally said. 'Have you checked the outbuildings?'

We had. I was starting to get really worried now, she must have gone in the middle of the night – a thought hit me, and I groaned, wondering why I hadn't considered it before.

'What?' Lizzy wanted to know. I took her arm and led her away from everyone else. It was going to be hard to put into words, but I tried. 'Look, Kitty might be worried about her brother, but she loves Archie too. She wouldn't deliberately put him at risk, I'm sure of it.'

'Then what made her leave?'

'Well, she went through a terrible ordeal with Potter.'

'I know. And I have every sympathy, but...' Her words faded and her mouth tightened as the implication sank in. 'You're saying that sending her off across the country, in the sole company of a man she's never met before, might have terrified her to the point of running away?'

'We know Uncle Jack, we know he'd no more harm her than he would you.'

'He was so sweet to her last night. And surely she must trust us, trust our judgement?'

I grimaced. 'We trusted the army as well, remember?'

'Oh, God.' Lizzy sat down on the low wall. 'How could we have missed that?'

'I'll have to go with them when we find her, or she may not go at all.'

'I could argue with you until I'm blue in the face,' Lizzy said tiredly, 'but it wouldn't make a scrap of difference, would it?'

'No.'

She stood up and put her arms around me. I hugged her awkwardly, one-armed. 'Don't worry, I won't work, and I'll make Uncle Jack carry my bags.'

'Promise?'

'Promise.'

She drew back. 'Well then, all that remains is to find the wretched girl so we can tell her the good news.'

We resumed our search, growing more and more frantic as the day marched on. Jack arrived back from the village, his face grim. 'People don't seem to want to talk to me, not that I can blame them. But I can't delay any longer, I have to leave by three at the very latest, to get the overnight ferry.'

'Then you'll have to go,' I said. 'Find Oli if you can, but Archie comes first. I'll bring Kitty across as soon as we find her.'

Jack looked from me to Lizzy and back again, then glanced at his pocket watch and came to his decision. He crossed to Lizzy and took her in his arms, and she held him as if she thought she might never see him again. His hands went to her hair, pushing it away from her eyes, and as they kissed I turned away again, this time feeling nothing but wretched at being the cause of their parting so soon.

As the sound of Jack's departure died away up the bumpy driveway, we turned back to the problem of where Kitty might have gone. Lizzy went with Mrs Adams and Sally to the village, to search again there, and I teamed up with Belinda and Jane, both of whom were just as interested in hearing about my other life as they were in finding Kitty. Belinda was particularly keen, and I tried to keep my answers as brief as possible without being rude.

'Can I see inside your ambulance before you go?'

'Um, yes, all right. There's not much to see though, just a few bandages.'

'Does it have a bed?'

'Two stretchers. No bedding yet though.'

'How many soldiers have you saved? Do they all fall in love with you?'

'They have rather more on their minds than falling in love, Belinda.'

'Are the injuries terrible?'

'Mostly, yes.'

She was a nice girl, and so bright and bubbly it was hard to get annoyed with her, but worry for Kitty was uppermost in my mind, and before too long I found myself wanting to go off alone and search. Mrs Adams and Lizzy had returned, and the sun was already slipping back down towards

319

the horizon, when I considered the possibility of Kitty having returned to the cottage. I started across the yard to the ambulance, already gritting my teeth against the prospect of driving again, but plucking my collar away from my shoulder I realised I'd already strained my stitches, and there was fresh blood on the bandage. I hissed in frustration and turned back; I'd need help for this.

In the farmhouse kitchen, I sat quietly while Mrs Adams began to carefully cut away the bandage that covered my shoulder and half of my neck. She was a quiet woman by nature, and I'd already come to appreciate that, when she did speak, it was because she had something of import to say, so her constant trickle of chatter and casual questions took me by surprise, until I realised.

'She'll be all right, Mrs Adams,' I said quietly.

Mrs Adams gave a little sob, and put down her scissors in case her shaking hand caused them to snag my skin. 'I know I'm being silly. But she's such a dear girl. Too young to be in this awful situation.' She sighed, and pulled herself together. 'We've looked everywhere, I don't know where else to try.'

'We'll find her,' I promised. 'Lizzy and I were worried she might have been scared at being sent off with Uncle Jack. You know, after what happened.'

But she shook her head as she picked up the scissors and resumed her careful cutting. 'I don't know the man myself, only met him a few times but he seems trustworthy. Young Lizzy has a sensible head on her shoulders, and you've known him all your life. I can't imagine Kitty would think twice about going with him anywhere, if *you* trust him.'

'She's had cause to doubt my judgement before,' I reminded her, 'and she's only just forgiven me for that. She hated me for a while.'

'What on earth makes you say that?'

I told her how Kitty had reacted when I'd seen her, and of the row with Lizzy, and as she gently lifted the bandage away Mrs Adams shook her head. 'Well, that might be what she was thinking right at that moment, but let me tell you, Evie, that girl barely spoke of anything else when you were gone, except what an amazing person you are.'

For a moment I thought I'd misheard, and just looked blankly at her. 'I'm sorry?'

'Oh yes, she might have had a flash of temper, and I'm sure she did feel a bit betrayed. Seeing you when she'd just found out she was pregnant knocked her for six all over again, but after you left last time, and she came to take over from Lizzy here, all she would talk about was what you'd taught her, how you gave everything to the job, and how you'd never give up on a Tommy if there was the slightest breath of hope left.'

'But I'm not a doctor, nor a nurse.'

'No, but you saved lives nevertheless. And when you couldn't, Kitty said you just sat there, keeping them comp'ny. Made them feel less alone.' Her voice roughened. 'I wish my Harry'd had someone like you there at the end.'

'Mrs Adams, I–'

'Frances. Don't talk now, just let me get this cleaned up.'

The door opened and Belinda and Jane came

321

in, followed by Lizzy, who gave a little gasp of alarm when she saw me.

'It's all right,' I said quickly, 'it's just time to change the bandage and Frances kindly offered to help. No luck, I take it?'

Lizzy shook her head. 'Do you think she caught the train back to her parents?'

I'd like to have believed so, but shook my head, biting my lip as the movement tugged at the stitches again. 'She was scared to go home, her parents don't sound the type who would take her in anyway, once they found out.'

'Poor girl,' Frances said, and she sounded angry as well as sad. 'A girl should have people who love her around at a time like this.'

'She did,' I pointed out, 'and she ran away from us.'

'I don't know where else to look,' Lizzy said, accepting a mug of tea from Belinda. Another was placed on the table at my elbow, and I smiled my thanks. Frances finished cleaning the side of my neck, and rummaged in a tin before finding a fresh pad of wadded lint and placing it on the wound.

'Belinda, dear, fetch me the first-aid box.'

'I was going to go back to the cottage,' I said to Lizzy. 'I thought she might have gone back there while we've been out.'

'Good idea,' Lizzy said. 'I'll go instead.'

'Finish your tea first,' I ordered, and she smiled and saluted me with her cup. 'Yes, My Lady.'

'Where are all the bandages?' Frances said with some exasperation. 'I was sure we had two brand new ones in here.'

'I used one on Sally's ankle when she turned it last week,' Belinda offered. 'But I don't know about the other.'

'The dog,' I said, remembering. Four faces turned to me in surprise. 'The last time we came, Jane had just bandaged the paw of one of your dogs.'

Jane's face brightened. 'Of course! He'd got caught in some chicken wire, don't you remember, Mrs Adams?'

'Well, it's no help knowing that,' Frances grumbled. 'Evie needs this covering up sharpish.'

'Oh, I know!' Belinda exclaimed, and pulled open the back door. 'Wait here!'

'I do hope she's not going to take the bandage off the dog,' Frances sighed. 'It's just the sort of thing she might do, bless her. She's not the brightest of buttons.'

'Where do we look if Kitty's not back at the cottage?' Jane asked, but no one had an answer. We'd gone into every shed and out-house, and every barn on the farm, we'd even checked the pigsties and the hen houses, in case she'd sacrificed comfort and fresh air for the security they'd afford her.

'Maybe she's found her own way back to Belgium?' Lizzy ventured.

I nodded. 'She might be trying to get to the docks by herself. Did she have money for the train?'

'I don't know,' Lizzy said. 'I still think we should try and contact her parents too, just in case.'

'I think so too,' I said. 'I have their address, and I expect we could find their telephone number from that. My address book is in my bag in Emily's

323

room, I can drive you back down in a few minutes, as soon as I'm patched up.'

I twisted to pick up my tea, rather awkwardly with my left hand, but a distant cry from outside made me drop it. It was Belinda.

'Come quick!'

After a startled glance at one another we all surged forwards at once, and Lizzy reached the door first. Belinda was still several yards away across the yard, and running towards us, but she stopped and gestured behind her at the ambulance I'd parked haphazardly by the wall.

'She's hiding in there!'

With one hand holding the lint against my neck, aware of the pain only as a very distant thing, I ran across the yard, outstripping the others by several paces. My heart was thudding with a mixture of relief and infuriated embarrassment; I had driven the blessed thing here all the way from the cottage this morning, and she'd been in there all the time! The flap at the back had already been loosened by Belinda, and I flung it aside, words of angry remonstration ready on my lips, but they never fell.

Kitty slumped in the corner, her eyes closed, her breathing harsh and uneven. I crouched beside her, holding my hand out behind me to keep everyone else back.

'Skittles? It's Evie.' I gently touched her leg, and she moaned and jerked away. Then she opened her eyes and looked at me in the gloom, and the fear I saw there struck me hard. 'It's all right, darling,' I said, still quiet, trying to appear calm, as if my heart weren't racing to climb out of my chest through my throat.

'I'm sorry,' she whispered, then she leaned forward and grabbed at my hand, her eyes widening. 'Swain!'

'What? Never mind, let's get you–'

'Swain, the name of the family in Liverpool. I remembered in the middle of the night and came to tell you.'

'Hush, sweetheart. Uncle Jack has already left, we'll try and reach him later. We need to get you back to bed, you're too ill to be out here.'

'I wanted to tell you right away,' she broke off, choking back a sob. 'But I started to get cramps. I thought they'd go away if I could only lie down...'

'Cramps?' My hand had been outstretched to help her to her feet, but when she put her own hand out I withdrew it, a sick feeling creeping through me. 'No, don't try to stand.' Without thinking, I shifted my own position and slipped one hand behind her back, the other beneath her knees, and even as I lifted I heard Frances Adams exclaim loudly behind me, and felt the pain shriek through my neck and shoulder. My vision darkened and I stumbled, but strong hands held me up and then the burden of Kitty's limp body was taken from me. I sank to the floor trying not to be sick, or to faint, and then Lizzy was there, her familiar voice telling me off in the strongest possible terms, but her arms warm and gentle around me. Eventually she helped me to my feet and I saw we were now alone; someone had taken Kitty inside to warmth and safety, but I felt stickiness on the hand that had tried to lift her, and knew it was too late.

Chapter Twenty-Two

The doctor closed the bedroom door gently, and ushered Frances, Lizzy and me ahead of him down the stairs. Back in the kitchen, he regarded us with a serious expression, and it was Frances he turned to eventually. 'Were you aware the young lady was in the family way, Mrs Adams?'

She nodded. 'She was ... treated most roughly while on active duty.'

'I see.' His face softened in sympathy.

'There was blood,' I said, and my voice wavered. 'When I tried to pick her up to carry her back here.' I kept my eyes on him, and he cleared his throat but didn't reply immediately. 'Doctor Nichols, the blood?'

'Yes. The young lady is no longer expecting.'

I let out a shaking breath; of course I'd known, but it was hard to hear it.

Nichols pursed his lips. 'I've done all I can for her, now it's your turn.'

He looked at me now, and held out a hand to Belinda, who placed in it one of the bandages she'd gone out to the ambulance to find. 'You do understand the concept of rest, Mrs Davies? As opposed to trying to lift young women off the floors of ambulances?'

'I do,' I said, feeling foolish again, and the pain in my shoulder was throbbing madly, as if in reproof. 'It was instinct. Kitty's ... well, she's like a sister to me.'

'What caused it?' Frances wanted to know.

'It was very early days,' Dr Nichols said. 'Who knows why these things happen? Nature might have taken a hand, or the young lady might–' He broke off, embarrassed to say it aloud, but we all knew what he'd been thinking.

'No,' Frances said with quiet conviction. 'She wouldn't. Not Kitty.'

'What can we do for her?' I said, to steer the conversation towards the positive.

'She'll need plenty of fluids, and she's lost some blood so keep her still for a while. No travelling, no exertion. Other than that,' Nichols finished tying off my bandage, 'there's very little you *can* do.'

He made me open my mouth before he left. 'Still gargling with salt?' I made a strangled sound of affirmation, and he nodded, satisfied. 'Healing nicely, Mrs Davies. But stay off the toffees for a while, eh?'

When he'd gone, Frances went back upstairs to see Kitty, telling us to stay put; good intentions or not, the girl didn't need to be crowded. Lizzy and I waited, and Lizzy cleaned up the spilled tea and made fresh, which we didn't drink. We couldn't think of a thing to say, and both looked up with relief when Frances eventually came back down.

'Is she in pain?' I asked.

She shook her head. 'Not now. But she's heart-sick, the poor dear girl. Thinks it was all her fault.'

Lizzy looked as appalled as I felt. 'Why ever would she think that?'

'She says it's because she wished it. She wanted

327

it gone, and now it is.'

'But that wasn't because of anything she did,' I said, feeling even more wretched. I could only hope she wouldn't continue to believe it, or she'd punish herself forever.

'She's been ill for a few days,' Lizzy said, and her musing tone made me look at her closely.

'Do you think it's connected?'

'I don't know. Do people usually become sick?'

'I don't know either,' I admitted, 'but it seems quite likely the other way around. If she has some kind of illness it might have affected her badly enough.'

'We'll see how she is in the morning,' Frances said. 'If she's no better we'll call Doctor Nichols back.'

I nodded. 'She was saying she had a cold, but yesterday she was rubbing her neck as if it was aching, and she's got quite a temperature. Maybe it's 'flu.'

'Stay here tonight,' Frances said to me. 'I'd like to keep an eye on you. And you, Lizzy, you're looking done in, girl. You're not back to full strength yourself.' She looked from one of us to the other and back again, then raised her eyes to the ceiling. 'Goodness sakes, girls, will one of you please learn to take care of yourselves, then teach the other two?'

Kitty was no better by the following morning. The doctor called around again after breakfast, and spent a long time with her while we waited in the kitchen. Eventually he came back down, and pronounced her suffering from influenza, on top of everything.

'Keep her rested,' he said, 'and don't let her go back out in the cold until she's fully better.'

Belinda sighed. 'Does that mean *I'll* have to help with the lambing now?'

Nichols looked up sharply. 'Eh? What's that?'

'The lambing,' Belinda said, and licked some butter off the knife. 'Kitty enjoyed it ever so much, and she took my turns. But if she's not to go out in the cold I expect I shall have to do it.'

'You mean that child has been...' Nichols shook his head. 'Well, that puts a different complexion on things.' He turned to Frances. 'Mrs Adams, it might very well not be the 'flu at all, more likely that Miss Maitland has contracted a disease from the sheep. It's very dangerous for expectant mothers to come into contact with livestock, I thought that was common knowledge.' He picked up his bag, a little crossly. 'With that in mind, I shall now go and examine her again.'

We all looked at one another in stunned, guilty shock. Frances and Lizzy clearly felt responsible for letting Kitty work with the lambs and not being aware of the risks, and Belinda had cheerfully given over her share of the tasks. As for me...

After Doctor Nichols had left a little while later, having confirmed his new diagnosis, we were still helpless to find the words to ease each other's remorse, and eventually Frances reverted to her brisk, businesslike self. She despatched the three girls to their jobs, told Lizzy to take me back to the cottage, and prepared to nurse Kitty through the fever that had taken hold. Unable to contribute anything useful, Lizzy and I agreed,

329

and before long we were pushing open the door to her mother's cottage, feeling the peace and familiarity like a comforting cloak we could pull around us and shut everything else out.

Lizzy took a dark bottle from the cupboard under the window-seat. Uncle Jack's favourite single malt whisky. She poured a generous measure into two glasses, and we drank in silence, each lost to our own thoughts. Hers, clearly, to Jack, and mine to Will. My own Lord William. I felt again the clenching loss of the paper rose that symbolised everything we had meant together these past six years, but made myself remember that the hands that had made it were still living, still strong, still able to create, even if they no longer wanted to; he was so much luckier than he might have been, so much luckier than countless others.

I sipped my whisky and let my head rest against the back of the armchair, and the low, insistent throb in my neck and shoulder gradually faded. My heartbeat slowed for what seemed like the first time in days, and with the warmth of the whisky loosening my limbs into blissful relaxation, the pictures of a dark, frightening future were gradually replaced by memories. They were safer; they couldn't change. They could hurt, but they could not kill.

Chapter Twenty-Three

I was brought back to reality some little time later, as the sun began to dip, spilling orange light into the little front room of Mrs Parker's cottage. Lizzy was sitting opposite and looking at me with an odd expression. I blinked and roused myself, and noticed she was holding a piece of folded paper.

'What's that?' I sat up straight suddenly, panicked. 'News from France? Already?'

She frowned. 'No. News from Belgium. Specifically from you.'

'What on earth do you mean?' Then I recognised it: the letter I'd written in the depths of unaccustomed despair, and had been so glad I had not been able to post. 'Lizzy–'

'This is ... well, it's terrible.' I saw then that she'd been crying although she was dry-eyed now and just looked haunted. 'Why did you never unburden yourself like this before?'

'I shouldn't have done it now,' I said. 'I'd decided not to post it, it was unfair of me to throw this kind of thing at you.'

'Why?' She stood up and turned away, pretending to straighten the antimacassar, clearly agitated even beyond what she was willing to let me see. 'If writing to me helps you, as this must have done to some degree, then why not do it?'

'Because you have your own worries.' I levered myself off the chair with some difficulty, and tried to take the letter from her, but she lifted it away and scanned it again.

'"*I must stop writing now, I feel I have poured enough grief into your life. Please forgive me for that, and I promise I shall be back to my old self very soon.*" Well, there you have it,' her voice cracking slightly, 'Lizzy can't possibly be expected to shoulder the grief of her dearest friend, and must be protected from reality at all costs!'

'That's not what–'

'The point is, you *are* my dearest friend. You were so keen to hush Kitty when she was trying to tell me what it was like. But I think of you out there all the time. *All* the time. And all I have to base these thoughts on is what you've been telling me in your letters. So now I'm to understand it's all been a lie?'

'No! We do have fun sometimes. It's hard to imagine, with all of that going on, but it's true.' I sighed. 'Why don't I make us a cup of tea and we can sit down and talk. I'll tell you all of it. The good, the bad, the frightening and the just plain absurd.'

'Promise?'

'Absolutely. Everything.'

'All right. But you sit down, I'll make the tea.'

'Don't be silly, I can do that much. My shoulder feels much better already.'

She looked at me for a moment, and her eyes flashed with a hint of their old humour. 'Doubtless, and I'm glad to hear it, but the fact remains you make horrible tea.'

We talked. For perhaps the first time since New

Year 1913, we sat down together and put everyone else out of my mind while we learned about each other all over again and I told her everything. I didn't hold back on the horror, and more than once she paled and swallowed hard, but I made sure she also knew of all the interesting snippets that went on day to day: we had been known to raid the town's abandoned wine cellars on trips ostensibly taken to stock up on necessities; we would regularly ignore warning signs and sentries outside crumbling buildings in the pursuit of fresh, clean bedding, and we'd often send up to HQ for cigarettes and rum for the patients, pretending they were for us.

'And Boxy once dressed up as a Tommy to see how far into the support trench she could get; she was only discovered when she stumbled over...' I sobered; the funny aspect had quickly dissolved when Boxy had relayed the incident too.

'Over what?' Lizzy's voice was gentle.

'It was, well, a man.' I met her searching look, and shrugged. 'Part of a man. Sticking out of one of the trench walls.'

She blanched, but her gaze was steady. 'They'd left him there?'

'They have to. So many fallen. No time to recover them all.' I shook my head. 'Hard to know who's the luckier of the dead; those killed quickly during an advance, but left alone out in No Man's Land, or those who make it back to the clearing stations in the most awful agony, but are at least given a funeral of sorts when it's over.'

We were silent as we considered, but of course we would never know. The question itself was too dreadful to contemplate.

'For the families, it must be better to know their man had a decent send-off,' Lizzy ventured.

'It's not that decent,' I pointed out. 'Barely individual. Row upon row of plain boxes, when they're available. More often just a huge hole in the ground, and boys wrapped in their blankets. There's a chaplain, of course. And a bugler, most of the time. But the funerals go on all day long, and "The Last Post" sometimes wobbles so much you wonder if the poor chap is going to get through it yet again, but they always seem to.'

Lizzy touched my arm. 'I know this has been horrible to hear, but I'm glad you told me.'

I was, too; it was a relief to shake off some of the dark burden which I never felt able to put onto Will's shoulders, and know that it was received, if not happily, at least willingly.

I took one of Lizzy's home-made biscuits from the tin, and bit into it, then pulled a face. 'My tea might be terrible, but at least it would have softened this.'

Lizzy smiled, as relieved as I was at the lightening of the tone. 'Jack hates them too. He used to pretend he didn't, but when I caught him putting one in his pocket to feed the birds with, he had to admit the truth.' I couldn't help laughing at the picture she painted, and then, of course, our thoughts were with the man in question, hardly daring to hope he would find Oliver, and that they would reach Archie in time to stop him sending that potentially lethal telegram.

The early April evening was fully upon us now; there was still a bite in the air, and although it was already Easter it still felt like winter. We'd had above average rainfall, the papers said, but we didn't need to read those to know it was not yet even near time to think about shedding layers of clothing. Lizzy set to making up the fire, and banished me upstairs in case I offered to help.

'If you want to write to Will, there's paper in Emily's room. I have some letters too, I can post them in the morning before I go back to the farm.'

'You're going back to work?'

She sighed. 'Well, Kitty's in no fit state. Mrs Adams will need someone to help.'

'Is there anything I can help with? Something I can do one-handed maybe?'

'Your left arm's not exactly up to working either,' she reminded me. 'No, you're here to convalesce, and convalesce you shall.'

'I can go to the village,' I said, putting on my stubborn voice. 'I'll take the letters, and pick up anything you need from the shop.'

'I need a bag of potatoes and some coal,' Lizzy said, and I glared at her.

'Stop being difficult!'

'Go and write to Will.'

I went.

My dearest Will,

I am just scribbling a short note in case you have heard about the shelling of Number Twelve, and might be worried. It's true we were hit quite badly, but I am only slightly hurt and have been sent back to England to recuperate. I am staying at Dark River Farm with Lizzy, who is quite determined I must not lift a finger and so I think I will recover very quickly.

I hope this letter finds you in decent spirits, and not too down about it all. Easter is here, and our weather is perfectly horrible, I shudder to think how it must be in the trenches. I hope your funk hole is kept away from the water and that you are getting at least a little sleep despite the noise.

I hated the thought of him tucked into one of those ghastly little holes, scraped out from the side of the trench and just big enough to sit in and cover himself with his greatcoat. But not even the most comfortable bed would provide a good night's sleep, with the constant bombardments going on night after night ahead of the next push. I bent to the letter again, determinedly not mentioning our last meeting and his insistence on pushing me away. Nor, of course, could I tell him I had lost the rose.

I will send a parcel soon. Is there anything you would like in particular? I will put Oxo cubes in, of course, and socks and chocolate. I will also send some of Lizzy's home-made biscuits, and you may choose whether to eat them, or to throw them at Fritz and hope they hit square; there would be plenty of broken heads if so! The effort of trying to sound normal was giving me a headache, but I pictured him smiling reluctantly as he read the letter, so I continued. *Perhaps we could send them to Lawrence to throw beneath the wheels of his tank and make the mud less of a problem!*

In case you think I'm being mean, I have said nothing here I have not already said to Lizzy, and made her laugh by saying it. I pondered on my closing, but determination seized my hand and wrote, *I miss you terribly, Lord William, and only wish I could prove it, so you will no longer even consider I might be better off without you.*

Take care of yourself as best you can, and I will do the same until we are once again able to take care of each other.

Your ever loving wife
E.

The letter I wrote to mother was even shorter. I had not visited her since my return to Belgium after Christmas, and neither of us suggested it in our notes to one another. I had long since stopped trying to sound bright and breezy; she had seen some of the truth now, more than she'd ever wanted to, and the pretence of all being well was insulting to us both. So I simply asked after her health, and that of Mrs Hannah and the others, and told her I was likely to be moving to a different station soon, and that any mail should be directed to HQ until I had more information for her. I didn't tell her about the shelling, or that I was injured – she would see the Devon postmark and simply assume I was visiting Lizzy, and she would understand. I closed by sending her my love, and hoped she knew I meant it. We might have grown distant in the years since the war began, and she might not yet have come to terms with who I was now, but we were still mother and daughter, and we still had memories of happier days that, I desperately hoped, would someday return.

Finally I wrote to Lawrence, who was having the devil of a time at Courcelette; the Germans had recently withdrawn, but everyone said it was a struggle to hold the trenches and although I couldn't mention that, I tried to communicate how my thoughts remained with him. I remembered the little brother who'd taken such an awed shine to Will, despite the difference in their stations, but I also remembered the way I'd seen him last Christmas too, and it was as if I were thinking of two different people. This war had done so much to our young men, and even those who returned would never be the same again. I felt a familiar surge of anger, but anger would help no one; I just had to straighten my backbone, give thanks for each day that passed with no terrible news of a loved one, and play my part.

I gathered up my letters, and took them downstairs where Lizzy was at the sink washing her hands. I could see a pan on the stove with the lid set just off, and heard bubbling from within it. Immediately my stomach began to grumble, and Lizzy heard it and laughed.

'Won't be long.'

'Smells heavenly.'

'It's basic, but filling. Have a piece of bread while you're waiting.' She waved me towards the bread bin, and as I nibbled on a crust I watched her work. She had grown up in this house, and it showed in the easy familiarity of her quick, comfortable movements. I couldn't help feeling a pang of envy; I had never felt at home in any kitchen, until I'd come here. At Oaklands it was a risky business even going in there, and on the few occasions I had, I spent most of my time worrying someone would tell mother.

In this kitchen though, where Uncle Jack had clearly been absorbed into its history as effortlessly as he had at Oaklands, I felt I could just get on with things. I hoped it would be the same when Will and I found our own home together after the war. To beat back the fear that such a day might never come, I affected a stern expression and tapped the table.

'Right then, Just Lizzy. Your turn.'

She looked blank. 'My turn for what?'

'Well, I've told you all the awful stuff. The cruel stuff. The stuff I wanted to shelter you from. Now you can jolly well tell me everything. Prison, the Wingfields, all of it.'

She protested, but I was relentless; I'd felt so much better once I'd unburdened myself, and I wanted nothing less for her. 'I mean it, I want to hear it all. But let's not have any biscuits this time.'

Lizzy laughed, but it was hesitant, and very short. 'I haven't bottled everything up the way you have,' she pointed out. 'I've been able to tell Jack.'

'But you haven't told him all of it, have you?'

I could see my guess was right; she bit her lip. 'Not all, no.'

'Then it's time you told someone,' I said gently. 'And who better? Come on, sit down.'

With the stew making the occasional blupping sound, and the cosy smell of it wafting around the kitchen, it was hard to imagine a world like the one Lizzy described. But her words, plainly spoken, blunt even, painted a picture of which little detail needed filling in by the imagination. Her stories of

339

violence and terror in Holloway were delivered without emotion, yet I could feel the weight of reality behind every one. She had struggled, those years, far more than I had realised, and far more than even Jack knew. This girl had been through fire as punishment for something she had not done, and if my admiration for her grew as a result of learning of it, so my loathing of the Kalteng Star intensified with every word she spoke.

She didn't mention Jack's having seen Samuel Wingfield in Germany, and I remembered their murmured conversation, overheard in the haze of discomfort and exhaustion, and wondered if I'd dreamed it after all. But the thought was swept away as she moved on to describe how she and Jack had crept through the cold darkness at the Wingfields' home, not knowing what lay in store for them, and I felt my own flesh rise into goose bumps.

'How on earth did you both manage? And with Uncle Jack hurt too.'

'We had Will's safety to spur us on,' she reminded me. 'And it turned out well in the end. Here we all are.'

'Thanks to you,' I said, and squeezed her hand. 'Will might not have survived at all if you hadn't found that notebook.'

'Have you written to him?'

I showed her the little pile of letters. 'And Mother and Lawrence too. If you have anything for me to post I'll take it and go in the morning.'

'Just something for Mary.'

'How are Mary and Martin?'

'Struggling, like everyone else, but getting

through it. Poor Martin feels it dreadfully that he can't go over and fight, especially now Mary is doing so well in her nursing. I think she'll be a sister one day, they seem to think highly of her up in London.'

'They should think themselves lucky Martin can't go,' I said. 'There's no glory in it, Lizzy, none at all. It's just a mess, and a tired and terrible waste.'

Lizzy nodded. 'I know, darling. But if those boys hadn't had the spirit to go and fight, where would we be now? We can't demean their sacrifice, and their bravery, by letting our disillusionment show. All we can do is try to keep the country safe and comfortable for their return. When they've won it for us.'

I marvelled a little at her quiet certainty, and decided she was right, up to a point. No matter what my own feelings, my own disgust and cynicism, our fighting men deserved our support, whether it was binding a wound, knitting a pair of socks, or providing food for the people at home. We were all in it, every last one of us, and all we could hope for was to come out of it alive.

Chapter Twenty-Four

There was a heavy frost two days later, on Monday morning. Easter Sunday had passed with no news, of course, but in quiet companionship and unspoken hope. Uncle Jack should have reached

341

Calais on Saturday morning, it just remained to be seen whether he'd been able to find Archie before the telegram was sent that same evening.

I watched Lizzy make her way up the road towards Dark River Farm, picking her way among the puddles with their thin crusts of ice, and then turned away to follow the road to the village. My shoulder was stiff, and still ached, but as I walked I flexed my arm carefully and by the time I arrived in Yelverton I was moving more freely, and the stitches had stretched a little so they hurt less with each movement.

I wondered how long it would be before I was fit to return to work, and felt a little surge of sadness as I remembered Number Twelve.

'Well, I wish you a good morning,' the postmistress huffed, 'since it don't look too much like you're 'avin' one of those yet.'

I smiled. 'I'm so sorry, I was just remembering something.'

'You'll be the lady then?'

'Pardon?'

'Young Mary's friend. From Cheshire.'

I was none the wiser, until I remembered Lizzy's real name. 'Oh. Well, yes.' Word clearly spread quickly here.

'Then you'll be wanting this.' She handed me a telegram and my blood froze, but she had seen the same look on too many faces since 1914 and her voice softened. 'It's not from the war office.'

She moved away to serve someone else, and, with fingers that shook so badly I almost dropped it, I took a deep breath and read the telegram:

Calais successful stop No sign O stop Keep hopeful

'Everything all right?'

Once again I barely realised the words were directed at me, but this time it was because of the thundering relief, and the sudden need to sit down that must have shown in the way I braced my hand on the countertop.

'Yes,' I managed. 'Thank you. It seems it is a good morning, after all.'

'Glad to 'ear it. Now, are those letters for posting, or just to decorate your glove?'

I'd forgotten them, in my relief, and passed them over with a still-shaking hand. Now it was simply a matter of finding Oliver and getting Archie's papers back, and all might be well after all. Surely he couldn't stay hidden for long.

'I see the Americans have joined us,' the other customer piped up, waving his newspaper.

The postmistress nodded as she glanced through the addresses on my letters. 'And not a moment too soon if you ask me.'

They both looked at me, trying to draw me into the conversation in a friendly enough way, and I supposed I should have agreed, but I couldn't help thinking that yet another country would now be sending its finest young men off to that filthy mudhole to die ... more families ripped apart, more young lives blighted. Of course it'd mean a fresh injection of strength, and perhaps some respite for the longest-serving men, Will included, but rather than the buoyant mood that seemed to have gripped everyone else, it actually filled me with a strange, dark sorrow. Was no one to be spared?

It was almost a week later that I was finally pronounced fit for travel. Uncle Jack had returned to continue his search for Oliver, but the Swains in Liverpool claimed not to have seen or heard from him, likewise his family. It was too much of a risk to try and contact any friends; no one could be sure of their discretion. Kitty had taken the lack of success with surprising calm at first, but Lizzy told me she'd heard her weeping alone in her room. I remembered those nights after the attack, the soft hiccups, the anguished, tight-throated little moans, and my heart twisted for the girl; it seemed she, Lizzy and I had much in common when it came to concealing our grief from one another.

I allowed Frances to dress my shoulder once more, and she gave me a fierce hug and helped me on with my newly-washed greatcoat, then handed me a bag, into which she and the girls had put some spare clothes and a couple of old, many-times mended sheets.

'Where will you stay?' Lizzy asked as she pushed a packet of sandwiches into my pocket.

'Elise has a new partner, and one or two others have joined them. She wired me a few days ago. They've got a place just outside Dixmude. A bit closer to things than Number Twelve, by all accounts.'

'How much closer?' Her voice was sharp, and I smiled.

'Not right up, but you know, quicker for getting them out. Mrs Knocker and Mairi are still at Pervyse, I think, and still doing amazing work.'

344

'Elise and the others will be sure to take care of you, won't they?'

I hugged her. 'Of course. The doctor will be whipping these stitches out any day now.'

'Will you see any Americans?' Belinda wanted to know. She, Jane and Sally had arrived to see me off, and it seemed she might need to be forcibly restrained from climbing into the ambulance beside me.

'I have absolutely no idea,' I said. 'I don't know where they're stationed.'

'Americans are so dashing. I do envy you, Evie, out there, doing such great things.' She looked longingly at the empty front seat and I was glad she'd had no training and couldn't come; she was such a bubbly thing, so full of romantic ideas about what she thought we were doing, I hadn't the heart to wish the reality on her at all.

I drove out of the farmyard on the morning of 16 April, and there was snow still lying along the edges of the road, although the worst of it seemed to be over now. Behind me, Lizzy, Frances and the three Land Army girls waved frantically but I couldn't lean out and wave back; my shoulder was immeasurably improved, but not to the extent where I could flail my arm around without causing fierce language to leap to the fore.

Rumbling off the ferry at Calais, I glanced with no more than casual interest at a group of soldiers gathered there awaiting transport, but one of them looked up and waved, and broke away from the group. I slammed on my brakes in surprise as he came closer.

'Well, here's a sight!' Archie smiled, and hefted his kit-bag. 'Any chance of a ride back?'

I gestured to him to get in. 'What on earth are you doing here?'

'Spent a couple of days in London after all,' he said, swinging on board. He dropped his bag comfortably between his feet. 'Uncle Jack stepped in and smoothed over my lack of papers,' he went on in a lower voice. 'He wanted me to help look for Oliver. I hate like hell to say it, but that laddie's going to cop for it now, even if we find him.' He looked at me anxiously, before I could question the coincidence of his being here. 'How's Kitty faring?'

'A little better. Not well enough to travel though. You heard about ... what happened?'

'I did, aye.' His voice shook a bit. 'Poor little Kittlington. I cannae believe all that's happened to the poor lass, and her so sweet. So trusting. I'd like to get m'hands on that scrawny–'

'And end up court-martialled anyway? We need *her* word, Archie, or all we've got is you in prison.'

He sighed. 'I know, I'd be no good to her locked away. Anyway, how are you?'

'As you see. Much restored, and spoilt rotten by Lizzy and Frances. Is Jack still in England?' I wondered if he'd already left for Berlin, but relaxed when Archie replied.

'Aye. He's doing everything he can to trace the young idiot, but drawing blanks at every turn I'm afraid.' It wasn't until we were well on our way, and I couldn't rescind the offer of a lift, that he cleared his throat and said, somewhat sheepishly, 'Actually I knew you'd be here. Uncle Jack told

346

me which crossing you were hoping to make.'

I felt a little lurch of apprehension, but reminded myself that knowing I was there wasn't the same as deliberately choosing the same crossing. I took a quick glance at him before returning my attention to the road. He'd turned away and was watching the landscape fly by, but I could see the faint flush on the back of his neck.

'I'm glad Uncle Jack was able to get to you in time,' was all I said.

'You and me both, lass.'

The road had been badly shelled since the last time I had travelled it, and I failed to notice a new hole in the road until the last moment. I pulled hard on the wheel to avoid it, and almost managed, but clipped the very edge and wrenched at my right arm. I felt an all-too-familiar warmth at the side of my neck and had to stop, hissing in exasperation.

'Right, that's it,' Archie said, and opened his door. 'Slide over, I'm going to drive. I knew I should have suggested it before,' he called out, as he crossed in front of the ambulance, 'but I also knew what you'd say.' As he climbed into the driver's seat he looked over to continue his scolding, but stopped.

'Ah, you silly wee girl,' he breathed instead. He reached out to turn back the collar of my coat, and I winced. 'You'll need to get this looked at again before you go out to the new place.'

'It's fine, I just keep pulling the stitches, that's all.' I moved away from his hand, wishing he wasn't so gentle, so obviously caring. Wishing he wasn't him. Why couldn't it be Will sitting here

347

with me? I blinked away more tears, but this time they weren't born of frustration.

'Sweetheart, you're back too soon,' he said, and I heard the echo of my own words to Will, and the tears would not be held back. Archie misread them, and pulled me close. 'You'll be fixed up properly in no time,' he murmured, and I shook my head against his shoulder, wanting to explain without hurting him or making him feel foolish. In the end it seemed easier to let him think it was the pain of my healing wound that had undone me.

I sat back as soon as it felt as if doing so was not an insult, and wiped at my eyes. 'Go on then,' I said, and forced a smile. 'Let's see you do a better job at getting this bus back to Dixmude.'

'That's not why I–'

'I know, silly,' I said, and now my smile felt more natural as he blushed again and started off. Unable to untangle the conflict in my own mind, I thought, instead, about Oliver Maitland. Twenty-one years old and facing the worst scenario he could ever have concocted in his own mind, as he left home to fight. I had to trust that justice would prevail, and that, whatever Oli's punishment might be, he would at least be spared the horror of the firing squad, but it was becoming less likely with every passing day.

Archie handed the ambulance back to me at HQ. 'At least come in and see the medic,' he said, when I slid back behind the wheel.

I shook my head. 'Elise or one of the others can sort me out when I get there. I'm not going to take up someone's time for the sake of a bandage

348

and a dab of iodine.'

He gave in, kissed his finger and touched my cheek, and told me he'd come and see me later, when I'd settled in. I wished he wouldn't, but I smiled and waved, and made him promise to bring a loaf and some wine. I drove on, out past poor, shattered Number Twelve, over the pot-holed road, avoiding the worst bits from a memory I hadn't realised I'd engaged; my mind was still on Oliver, and what Uncle Jack might be doing to prepare a solid defence. Eventually I saw the wooden board by the side of the road, pointing up a track: 'Ambulance post #22.'

Elise heard me pulling to a stop outside the cottage and came out to meet me. She had a broad smile on her face, but looked a little bit secretive as she hugged me. 'Jolly good to see you again, Davies. How's your neck?'

'Tons better,' I said. 'I just need help to clean it up, I pulled the stitches again.' I looked at her closely. 'How are you, though?'

She still sported a bandage on the side of her head, but she knew exactly what I meant, and shrugged, the smile fading. 'I miss her, of course. She was the best out of us, you know.'

'Nonsense. You brought out the best in each other. I'm so terribly sorry, Elise, and what's worse is that I don't think I even told you that.'

'I wouldn't have expected you to.' She looked at the ambulance, and nodded her approval. 'This will do splendidly. Come in, let's introduce you. We've a few extra hands for a week or two before we all move on and leave you to it.'

'What's the new girl like?'

349

'Not nearly as new as I led you to believe.'

'What?' I followed her into the cottage, and was nearly knocked off my feet by a laughing girl who threw her arms around me and began jumping up and down, taking me with her.'

'Careful!' Elise cried, but although my shoulder and neck protested the treatment, I couldn't help laughing too.

'Boxy! What in blazes are you doing here?'

'Oh, I got utterly fed up at home, you know how it is. How are you, poppet?'

'Tired,' I confessed, disentangling myself from her enthusiastic embrace. 'And I could do with a fresh bandage before my coat gets ruined. It's marvellous to see you though. You must tell me all about how married life has treated you.'

'Likewise,' Boxy beamed, taking my hand and leading me to the table to sit down.

'Davies, this is Sarah Johnstone,' Elise said, gesturing at a thin, slightly nervy-looking girl in a woolly hat. 'She came out with her friend Alice Kelloway last week.'

'Hello, Johnstone.'

'Kelloway is out today,' Elise said. 'It's her turn for the town run.'

'I was supposed to go with her,' Boxy put in, 'but I just had to see you.'

'Take off your coat,' Elise ordered, putting a large tin on the table in front of me. As Boxy helped me ease my coat down over my arm I reflected, a little sadly, that even our old familiar first-aid tin, with the bumps and scrapes that told a hundred stories, was now gone. Elise set to work and, with a little slump of relief I let her get on with it.

It was all a little bit overwhelming, and I was glad to relax and accept a mug of hot, overly-sweet tea. Elise put a pile of letters in front of me, and my heart did an extra-hard thump as I recognised the neat handwriting on the top one. Will. More than anything I longed to take myself off somewhere quiet and read it, but I couldn't leave just yet; Boxy was determined to hear everything she'd missed and, in between asking me dozens of questions about Kitty, which I fielded as best I could without giving any actual answers, she told me all about her wedding, her new home and why she couldn't bear to stay in England another day.

'Honestly, Davies, you know I love Benjy to absolute bits, but I was in danger of saying something extremely blunt to that mother of his. I mean, she's a poppet, of course, but so very exacting! And since they were talked into opening up the house as a convalescent home, she's become a nervous wreck and come to stay at ours, claiming all kinds of highly suspicious ailments she might catch. And she complains about the food, the dogs, the lack of grandchildren...'

Her commentary provided a soothing, familiar and much-missed background noise, and I felt myself smiling at the sound of it, although most of the words faded into a hum. I kept looking at the letter, and when Elise had finished and pronounced me fit for anything, I made my excuses and took myself off out to the ambulance with my little stack of correspondence. No one followed me; we all knew how precious these letters were, and how we preferred to read them in private, at least the first time.

Dearest Evie.

This will be hard for you to read

All my days are spent marching from trench to trench

and waiting to take my turn back on the front line, where I might find myself in a position to help advance our position. The censors had blacked out the next sentence too, and I wondered if there was something in the offing. I took a deep breath, gave up trying to see what lay below the thick black lines, and continued to read.

I shan't burden you with the names of the good men who have gone West in the past day alone, but it can only be a question of time now, until I join them.

Even worse would be to survive this war in such a state as I have seen too many men returned to their families. I have seen the looks on the faces of their wives and sweethearts when they see what has become of their loved ones – raving, some of those men, made violent and angry by circumstances over which they have had no control. I feel that anger in me, and have done since

and I can't bear the thought of unleashing it on you. Much better to hope for a quick, clean death. Please understand, I am not looking for it, but if I must go, then please God let it be quick, impersonal, and that you never have to see my body.

When I think of you alone and grieving it makes the wait all the more painful, and I would give

352

anything to spare you that. Archie Buchanan cares for you, I could see it when we were at Oaklands, and he's a good, honest man. As an officer he is far more likely to make it to the other side of this madness (if it ever ends) than I am, but of course you must choose for yourself. I must beg you to release what you have felt for me, say goodbye to me now while I am alive to hear it, and do not ask, ever, what became of me.

Your much saddened, much older, and much wiser Lord William.

It was a long time before I felt able to go back into the cottage.

Chapter Twenty-Five

Alice Kelloway turned out to be a bit third-rate, sadly. I was used to people who worked tirelessly and single-mindedly, and both Boxy and Kitty had been a joy to partner up with. Kelloway and Johnstone drove rarely, and helped with cleaning and repairs even less frequently, but, to be fair to them they knew their way around a first-aid station. Kelloway and I didn't really get on from the start although I don't think either of us really knew why.

The cottage hadn't been evacuated long, and there was still work to be done fixing it up so I joined in where I could, reminding a disapproving Elise she'd said I was fit for anything.

'She meant you'd be absolutely fine digging a

353

trench, or firing a sixty pounder from the front line, not scrubbing this ghastly muck off the floor,' Boxy grumbled. 'Honestly, the boys have got much the easier job!'

I flicked water at her, and went back to work, my mind on Will's letter. There seemed little doubt that it was really me he was thinking of, but not once had he said he still loved me. Was that because he thought it might weaken my resolve? Perhaps... I swallowed hard, and it hurt as my throat was so tight, suddenly. Perhaps I was wrong after all, and that he no longer loved me and was looking for an escape.

I had changed too, I knew that. As evidenced by my impatience with poor Kitty that night, I was bleaker in outlook, less ready to please others, and although the optimism Will loved in me hadn't really disappeared, it had certainly faded. I'd tried so hard to be the same old Evie whenever we met, but just as I could see past his smiles and still love what he had become, so he would have been able to peel back the layers of my own good humour. Perhaps the difference, though, was simply that *he* did not like what he saw beneath. The thought panicked me and, worse, it made me question my persistence; if he wanted to relieve himself of the burden of my love, how could I possibly force him to endure it?

Boxy seemed to sense my need to keep working, and she and Elise stopped nagging me to take things easy. Thanks to Elise's superb dressings I felt as if I could keep going all night, but when Archie arrived, with the promised bread and wine, we all downed tools and the others took themselves off for a walk, urged by Boxy who looked at me with a rather too-knowing expression.

Archie poured wine into two tin mugs, and produced some biscuits, and told me how Uncle Jack had found him at Calais where he'd been staying in a small hotel by the dock.

'I was pretty surprised to see him, I must say,' he said. 'He certainly knows how to use his contacts to good effect.'

'I wish he was having the same luck with Oli,' I said. 'I'm so glad he found you though, we were all so worried you might send that wire.'

'Aye, it was a close run thing, a couple of hours to spare. And it was good to see him in any case. I've not seen him in a long time, we communicate by letter, mostly.'

'You're very alike,' I said, studying him again. 'I can't think why I didn't notice it when I first saw you.'

'You had Lizzy and Will to think about.' He paused, then cleared his throat. 'How is Will, by the way?'

'He's ... uh, he's well,' I managed, but my voice wobbled and a moment later Archie was on his feet and around the table.

He knelt at my side. 'Come on, Evangelastica, he'll be absolutely fine, try not to worry, it's not fair on him.' The way his words echoed Will's own plea struck me; I had also used the same argument, when Mother had been so worried about Lawrence. How could I now dismiss it?

'He wants me to leave him.'

'I see,' he said carefully.

'Should I?' I looked at Archie, pleading with

him to tell me no.

'Do you want to?'

'Of course not!'

'Do you think you should?' That was the wrong question. I struggled to find a reply that wouldn't rip my heart right out of my chest, but couldn't find one. I nodded. Archie didn't say anything, but stood up and drew me up with him. I looked up at the kind, handsome face, echoes of Jack Carlisle in the strong bone structure making him seem even dearer and more dependable than ever. His strength seemed to flow through his hands as he held me to him, and it was so like leaning against Uncle Jack that I unthinkingly let myself relax against him.

After a moment I became aware of his breath stirring my hair, and that his heartbeat was heavier beneath my cheek. His head moved slightly as if he were about to speak, and I pulled back, remembering who he was, and who he was not. I was being unfair.

'Nothing's changed,' I said, searching his tired grey eyes, looking for understanding in their depths.

'I know, darling.' He kissed my forehead. I missed the feeling of being cherished, but what I felt for Archie Buchanan was the wrong kind of love. 'I'm sorry,' I whispered. And I didn't know if I was sorry for wanting to accept his love, or sorry for rejecting it, but he nodded.

'Aye. Me too.'

'There's something else. He wants me to ... he doesn't want me to be alone.'

'I can understand that.'

'He likes you.'

Archie looked at me for a long, quiet moment, then nodded. 'You can tell him whatever will give him the most peace.'

'Thank you. I mean it, you're the dearest–'

'Friend. I know.' He smiled and squeezed my hand. 'Write to him now, Evie. Give him what he needs.'

Voices heralded the return of the others, and Archie stepped away as Boxy came in brandishing a bunch of wild flowers and looking for a jar to put them in. I turned on my brightest smile and put the water on to boil for Bovril, and Archie exchanged a few words with Elise and the new girls before picking up his cap.

'I'm away now, ladies. Thanks for the hospitality. Be sure and let us know if you're in need of anything. Supplies, mechanics, extra hands, wine.' He said that last with a wink at me, and grinned, but those lovely eyes were shadowed still. As we said our goodbyes he brushed my cheek in a gentle kiss. 'Take care of yourself, Evie. And please tell young Kittlington I'm thinking of her.' Again, I detected a tremble in his voice, and there was a tightness in his fingers where they closed on my arms. Then he was gone, and in front of me lay the awful task of writing my final letter to my husband.

I kept it short; I wanted a swift cut, as painless as possible. Which is to say it only hurt like the slice of a blade for a few moments, and then it subsided to a deep, low throb that nevertheless eclipsed any pain I'd ever known.

My dearest Will

I hated to read your words, but hate even more to be a burden to you. I once told my mother the same thing as you have told me, that it is a weight on your heart you would better be without if you are to give your full attention to survival. As you wish then, I will stop writing to you and will no longer come to see you when on leave. I cannot keep fighting two wars at once, so I write to tell you that you have won. The next time I am in England I will begin divorce proceedings.

I will take such support as I find here, and Archie is a dear friend and keen to comfort.

E.

I placed the letter in the pile on the little table by the door, and by the next morning it was gone, and Will would soon know he was free.

After breakfast Elise, Boxy and I set to work preparing the cellar, and when the mail arrived there was sad news from Pervyse. Even Boxy was silenced as she digested it.

'Poor little Mairi Chisholm's fiancé was killed,' Elise said as she flicked out the end of one of the sheets Frances had donated.

I caught it and we pulled it tight between us. 'I didn't know she was engaged.'

'It was a private thing. Dorothie told me last week, but you're not to say it around.'

'Poor child. Mrs Knocker must be a great strength to her, at least.'

'She's not there, apparently. Mairi was alone, so

Dorothie's been staying with her.'

Dorothie Feilding thought even less of Mrs Knocker than I did, particularly after Elsie had published her memoir. Dorothie had really been incensed by the whole thing. I'd not read the book myself and so couldn't comment, but the consensus was that it was very much a story of how Elsie Knocker, now a Baroness, was the bravest woman at the Front. Mairi was so sweet, and every bit as brave, and it was a terrible shame to learn of her bereavement.

'How did he die?'

'It was the most awful thing,' Elise said, scanning her letter. 'Apparently his machine came down with engine trouble, when he was flying over the aerodrome.'

I caught her eye and jerked my head towards Boxy, who had paled. 'What freakish bad luck,' I stressed.

Elise cleared her throat. 'Well, yes. That sort of thing can't be at all common.'

'You needn't be careful on my account,' Boxy said. 'Benjy and I talk about the likelihood of things going wrong all the time. If you talk about it, it stops being such a worry somehow.'

I could see that wasn't entirely true, but didn't push the matter. 'Poor Mairi,' I said again, and we worked in silence for a while. Thinking about the little Scots girl at Pervyse, and what she was going through, helped convince me I had done the right thing. If I heard something had happened to Will, my cutting him loose would not soothe me in the slightest, but it would help him if he believed me to be taking comfort elsewhere.

I pictured him reading the letter, tucked into his awful little funk-hole, or sprawled out with his division in the fields further back, and I imagined the burden of care lifting from his shoulders. Yes, I had done the right thing.

So why did it feel as though my life had disintegrated?

Over the next few days I got back into the swing of things, and it was a relief to be distracted, even by a seemingly endless stream of trench foot cases, and heavy lice infestations. However, once my stitches were checked and pronounced to be 'doing the job nicely', I went back to driving. It was a relief to be away from the cottage, and to have something to take my mind off both Will and Oliver and, although the work was grim and our contribution often felt inadequate, I seized every chance to work. Boxy and I fell into our old routine easily; we had always worked well together and it was a deep and genuine pleasure to have her back. And Boxy was happy to take her car right up to the lines and then let me know if it was worth me taking my bus up, or if it was better relying on the horse-drawns.

I think Kitty might have been pleased to do that too, but despite her obvious courage I'd always hesitated to suggest it and so, on day runs, she'd always go up to the train station and take the wounded from there. I never had to worry about Boxy the same way, which left me free to worry, instead, about how Will had received my terse little note and if it had given him the release I'd intended, or if it had actually hurt him further. It was driving me mad, not knowing, and I prayed for one more letter from him to indicate how my seemingly quick acquiescence to his wishes had been interpreted. I didn't even know whether I hoped he believed me or not, and part of me, despite knowing it would work against what he needed, wished he would read between the pathetically few, sharp lines and see the pain there.

'Where are you off to?' Boxy said, coming out of the cottage after breakfast, and catching me climbing into the ambulance. 'The convoy's not due for hours yet and I'm not ready to go up the line, I've got to replace the plugs on the car first.'

'I'm going back to Number Twelve,' I said. 'Just for a look around. See if I can find ... anything useful.'

She looked steadily at me for a moment, her lips pursed. 'And if you find "anything useful", will you risk your life to go inside and get it?' She knew, of course, what I was hoping to find.

'I'm sure it's quite safe there now,' I said evasively. 'Anything that was going to fall down would have done so by now.'

'And what if you don't find it? Or if it's mashed beyond all recognition, or burned? Would that be worth the risk?'

'I have to try. You do see that? It's all I have left now.'

'Then let me come with you, you might have an accident, trip on something.'

'You have the plugs to do,' I reminded her. 'You have to be ready for tonight, that's far more important. It's all right, I won't do anything silly, I'm just going to be in and out again in a few minutes. I know exactly where it is. If I'm not back in an hour, come and find me.'

'Be careful, poppet. Promise me.'

'I will. Go in, you'll catch your death out here.'

I began the long, frustrating task of starting the cold engine. Boxy watched me for a while, clearly struggling with her conscience, then blew me a kiss without smiling and went back inside.

I parked the ambulance on the road just across from Number Twelve, and sat quietly for a while, listening to the distant sound of the bombardment and knowing that, when it stopped, we would not celebrate, but instead feel that hollow, sick anticipation of the whistles summoning us to bring our men back from yet another hopeless push. The rain beat steadily down, turning the last of the late snow to grey-brown mush where the hundreds of tyres had churned up the mud. There was a good deal of traffic on the main road, but none of it pulled into the yard any more; Number Twelve was useless now, where it had once been a bustling haven of hope to so many. The cars, ambulances and horse-drawns simply rumbled carefully past on their way to the clearing stations and hospitals, and in the other direction they sped, empty, to the aid posts and dressing stations up near the lines.

I peered through the downpour at the cottage, seeing it in its ugly quaintness, as it had been for our first years out here, before my vision accepted the rain and allowed me to see through it to what was really there: just another of the countless, shattered ruins that had once graced the landscape, and now marred it beyond all recognition.

I pushed my hat more firmly onto my head and climbed down, sloshing through the puddles and mud that were all that remained of the once-neat yard, stepping over small holes and skirting larger ones until I reached the doorway where Anne had stood, smoking what was to be her last cigarette. I closed my eyes for a moment in memory, then stepped into the ruined main room, looking ahead through the gloom to where the bedroom door hung half off its hinges.

There was debris everywhere, but the roof looked sound enough, and nothing was creaking or groaning. A few tentative steps across the room and my confidence and excitement grew; I would go straight into the bedroom, find the little black box, and be out of the cottage and back to Number Twenty-Two before Boxy had time to spare me another thought.

But a noise from the cellar changed everything.

Chapter Twenty-Six

I stopped, my heart pounding so hard I was sure it could be heard. I turned my head, trying to analyse the sound. Had it been a shuffling step, as I'd thought? Or might it have been a simple shifting of some masonry down there, disturbed by my passage through the room above? The sound did not come again and I decided on the latter, and let myself breathe again. I took a couple of steps, concentrating on where my feet fell; I didn't want Boxy's worries to become a reality, and even a sprained ankle would put me out of action for tonight's work.

I pushed at the awkwardly hanging bedroom door and looked in, seeing the window I'd broken, and the thin curtain hanging limp and sodden as a result, and was hit by the horrible irony that I might have destroyed the rose by my own impatience, letting all the damp in. If the box had been even a little bit open...

The noise came again. This time I was certain: it was a footstep. On the cellar stairs. A sliding scuffle of a boot, and now I could hear another, and another. What if it was Potter? He might have seen me park up, and followed me in, knowing there was no way for me to get out once I was this far into the room. But what was he doing in the cellar? Scavenging? There might still be some medical supplies down there, and anyone who could attack a vulnerable young girl would be just the type to try to seize them and sell them on.

My skin rippled into terrified goose flesh, and I looked around for somewhere to hide. If I could only make him think I'd gone, he'd go back down-stairs and I'd be able to make a run for safety... I ducked down behind the broken door and list-ened, holding my breath, letting it out oh, so slowly, before drawing another and holding it until I felt dizzy. The sounds stopped. I didn't know whether that was because Potter had reached the main room, or because he had gone back down to finish what he'd been doing. It was likely still flooded down there, and I couldn't hear the swish of water as he walked through it ... but neither could I hear any sound from the next room. Perhaps he'd seized the opportunity to escape unseen, while I cowered back here like a frightened child?

Slowly I rose to my feet, careful not to dislodge any of the broken sticks of furniture or loose bricks that lay strewn across the floor in the semi-darkness, and peeped into the main room. Right away I could see it wasn't Potter; this man was taller, and an officer. I could only see his left shoulder and his head as he'd begun to descend the cellar steps again, and he was hunched with cold and fatigue, but the colour of his hair, unkempt and escaping the confines of his cap, was unmistakeable.

'Oli!'

Oliver turned in shock at the sound of my voice. He was a terrible mess; exhausted and terrified, his face no longer clean-shaven but dark with two weeks' growth, and filthy. His eyes flew wide at the sight of me stumbling across the room towards him, and he held out a defensive hand.

'Don't, please...'

I stopped, worried he might turn and run. 'What are you doing here, you bloody fool? We've been all out trying to find you, to give yourself up before it's too late.'

'It is too late,' he said, and his voice shook.

'No, it's not. Look,' I stepped closer, carefully so as not to scare him, 'Jack Carlisle is doing everything he can to fix things. We're going to get Kitty out here to tell her story...' I hesitated, unsure whether to tell him, then decided he ought to know. 'Oli, Kitty lost the baby.'

He caught his breath, then came back up the stairs. Framed in the front doorway, his hair caught the light and he looked so much like his sister I could have wept for them both. 'Is that the truth?' he asked quietly.

'Yes.'

'Then I suppose I should be glad,' he said, but he didn't sound it. 'A child born of violence can't have a happy life, one would assume.' He gave me a sad smile. 'A child born in love has no guarantee either, evidently. Poor Kitty. Is she all right?'

'She's being well looked after. Look, we all want to help, but they'll find you eventually and it'll go badly for you if you wait until they do. Oh, you have to come back with me.'

'No!'

'Please! There may still be time to put this right, when you explain why you wanted to go to England.'

'And why *was* that?' he said bitterly. 'To speak to Kitty? That was how it started, but I didn't do that, did I?'

'I understand you were scared—'

'I can't come back with you, it's too late.'

'Why do you keep saying that?'

'Because he's dead!'

I fell silent, wondering if I'd mis-heard. He backed out of the door, almost losing his balance on the loose stones, his green eyes on mine and his face a twisted mask of fear and misery.

'That's why I ran away, Evie. I killed him.'

Before I could find my voice, or any words, he had gone. The doorway stood empty, but afforded me no other sight than a shattered yard and the distant road. Oliver Maitland had vanished again. Numb with shock, it was almost as an afterthought that I turned back to the bedroom; even the black box didn't seem as important as it had just a few minutes ago.

Until I saw it had gone.

'What do you mean, "gone"?' Boxy said, when I told her.

'Exactly that.' I couldn't tell her about Oli, and so the vanished box became the focus of my thoughts until Archie responded to my urgent wire. Not giving myself time to agonise over the choice, I'd gone straight from Number Twelve to the field post office, and now every time I heard a vehicle outside I prayed I'd done the right thing.

'Someone stole it? Was there anything else missing?'

'Someone must have decided it looked interesting enough,' I said. 'Probably one of the soldiers who helped move the bodies out after the flood.' I'd already considered, and dismissed, the hope that Oli might have thought the box was Kitty's and taken it; he had nowhere to put it. Sorrow stole through me again; when whoever took it opened it, and saw nothing inside but a collection of letters and a tattered paper rose, they would discard it in disappointment and it would lie there in the mud, and eventually become part of the landscape. No matter how much I told myself it was just a piece of paper, it symbolised so much more and now its disappearance fell into neat symmetry with the loss of Will. Like the world at war, everything was falling to pieces, everything was dying.

I slept late after a particularly gruelling night, and emerged from my flea-bag just before lunch to find, not Archie after all, but Uncle Jack, in uniform, sitting at the kitchen table, chatting amiably with Elise and Johnstone. I'd not seen him wearing his uniform in years; he cut a dashing figure though, and I couldn't help smiling at the way Elise was staring at him.

He looked around as I came into the room, and rose to his feet. 'Sweetheart, you look exhausted. How are you holding up?'

'I'm well,' I assured him, and accepted his unselfconscious hug with relief. 'And so pleased to see you, but what are you doing here?'

'I came over yesterday, on government business rather than army, but it's surprising what difference a uniform makes. Archie couldn't get away, but he showed me your wire. Shall we go for a walk while you tell me what's so urgent?' He had obviously sensed it had to do with Oliver, and I nodded gratefully and took my coat off the back of the door. Boxy thrust a piece of toast at me in lieu of breakfast, and then we were outside, glad to find a rare clear sky and even the glimmer of the sun behind scudding clouds. It was a relief to explain everything, and the words tumbled out, in the wrong order and punctuated by distractions as I went back to try and correct them, but he grasped what I was saying.

'Poor boy must be beside himself,' he said when I'd finished. 'Look, try not to worry, darling. Now we know he's around here, we can concentrate on finding him.'

'But what about Potter?'

He shook his head. 'I don't know. No one's reported having found him, it may turn out that Maitland only believed he killed him.'

I snatched a sudden, hopeful breath. 'Is that likely?'

'Well, it's most odd that a body hasn't turned up in over two weeks. He might just have been put out of action for a while. I'll check the field hospitals and the clearing stations, in case he's wandered in looking for medical help. Don't worry, I'll be discreet.'

I shook my head, almost ready to laugh. 'I can't believe I didn't even consider the possibility!'

'You've a lot on your mind,' he said. 'Besides, I don't want to raise your hopes. Unless Maitland stole his papers Potter would have been identified by now, if he did go for help. Then again, HQ would have been informed if he made a complaint against Maitland, so that's another possible bit of good news.'

I needed that, and held onto it, hugging his arm in relief. 'Thank you. How are you, anyway? I'm so sorry, I never remember to ask.'

He patted my hand where it lay in the crook of his arm. 'Don't worry about me, love, I'm fine. How's Kitty?'

I could see that wasn't really what he wanted to ask, and said, 'I'm sure she's being very well fed, and will soon be up and well.' Then I added casually, 'I expect Lizzy has made some biscuits for her.'

The smile that swept across his face could have lit St Paul's Cathedral. 'Lucky Kitty,' he said, and pretended to check his teeth for breakages.

I laughed. 'She misses you like a lopped-off limb,' I told him, and his smile faded a bit, but the warmth was still there.

'I worry about her doing too much,' he confided. 'I'm not able to spend enough time watching her, what with zipping off all over the place, and she does tend to try and do everything herself.' He bumped me with his elbow. 'A little bit like someone else I know.'

'I'm learning,' I assured him.

'And how is Will?'

This time I was able to hide my emotions quite well; it wouldn't be fair to pile my cares onto shoulders that already bore so much for the sake of others. 'He wrote a few days ago, and I wrote back,' I said evasively, 'it's all rather the same as always. His unit's in Arras now, so the grapevine tells me.' Archie, of course, being the grapevine; letters between units were now almost as strenuously censored as those travelling back home, and more and more I had been left with a few bland words between the heavy black smudges. But I would have treasured another one nevertheless.

'He's a good man,' Jack said, and I heard genuine approval in his voice. 'He'll keep you in check once all this is over, goodness knows you need a strong bloke to keep you on the straight and narrow.'

'Uncle Jack!'

He grinned at my protest, and his teasing helped ease the ache. For a while we talked of inconsequential things, but soon the conversation drifted back to Oliver.

'He's just twenty-one,' I said, 'surely they'll go

370

easy if he gives himself up?'

'If Potter's alive, maybe. It'll still be the desertion charge, and that's bad enough, but once we get Kitty over it might just go in his favour. Plus, he's an officer, and, anecdotally, if not officially, it's less likely he'll be shot for desertion. But if someone finds Potter's body, and they realise he's not a military casualty...' He didn't have to complete the sentence, and we didn't discuss it any further as we turned to walk back, and I bitterly regretted all the times I'd taken our leisure for granted.

We said goodbye in the yard, and Jack paused with his hand on the car door handle.

'Evie?'

'Yes?'

He didn't smile, but I felt his strong, dependable love reaching across the cool air between us. 'You did the right thing telling me.'

I nodded, but watching him drive away, I felt very young, and suddenly quite lost. What if all our hopes came to nothing? How would Kitty survive that, knowing what had spurred Oli into violence?

'Come inside, poppet,' Boxy said, coming out of the cottage. 'Elise has made lunch.'

I turned and smiled. I could feel it wobbling, and knew she could see it, but moments like this weren't unusual, certainly nothing to dig over. The trouble was, I could feel the expectation of many more 'moments' to come, and it was getting harder and harder to pick myself up. The morning of April 23rd 1917, St George's Day, would prove to be one of the worst.

Chapter Twenty-Seven

It started at around four a.m.

I'd left everything in the ambulance after the last run; I hadn't even given it a cursory clean, but had fallen into bed, unable to think beyond closing my eyes and resting my aching muscles. But, naturally, I lay awake for too long while my mind played over the news I'd had that afternoon from Uncle Jack: *O located. Confessed. Trial noon 23rd. Will send staff car.* All I could think about was Oli's haunted eyes as he'd pleaded with me, and how I could possibly say anything that might save him now he'd confessed. Despite being physically worn out, it was a long time before sleep crept in and smothered my racing thoughts.

Shouts and whistles, and sounds of panic outside, brought me struggling upright out of a disjointed and fractured dream. I blinked into the darkness, then realised what was happening and lunged for my gas mask. It wasn't there, and, with a groan of fearful dismay, I pictured it quite vividly, sitting on the seat of the ambulance. I had gone to bed half-clothed, as was usual, and now seized a jumper and my coat, and hunted about for my boots. Boxy was doing the same, and we stumbled into the yard together, trying to hold our breath until we could pull open the ambulance and get our masks, for once cursing our good fortune in having a vehicle with a closed-in driving seat. Boxy coughed, an innocuous enough sound under ordinary circumstances, but one which filled me with unease now.

'Here!' I threw her mask to her, and she fumbled it, dropping it into the mud. I dragged my own mask on and hurried around to where she was scrabbling about in the dark, and between us we managed to get it fixed in place. Her eyes, when I saw them up close, were wide and frightened, but she was breathing all right, thank God. In the light of my torch her freckles stood out on her pale face, but she had that determined look about her, and I knew I could rely on her as always.

The gas was coming in waves down the street from the front lines, and we could hear the distinctive, double-explosion of the shells and canisters as they dispensed death with horrific regularity. I clambered on board the ambulance, and Boxy took the car and we drove up to the lines, waiting with growing impatience as the orderlies loaded as many as they could, before lurching over mud and rocks to the road, and the re-formed group of clearing stations.

I kept glancing at Boxy whenever our paths crossed, worried by that initial, harsh cough, and the realisation that she would, quite naturally, have taken a deep breath immediately afterwards. She seemed unaffected though, and I didn't say anything to worry her; I didn't need to. She knew the dangers as well as any of us. I had a moment to thank the heavens Kitty was not here, and then all my thoughts were for those hit by the attack.

We worked non-stop for the first few hours. I drove between ADS and CCS, and on one fuel break I found Boxy replacing a wheel on her car, a job made hideously difficult by the mask she wore, so I stopped to help. We'd almost finished when we heard the crunching sound of another vehicle coming into the yard and, seeing the staff car, I only then remembered today was Oliver's court-martial. Boxy and I looked at one another, and she straightened, waving me away. 'You have to go, if you don't your friend's brother might as well kill himself.'

'But how can I just–'

'Don't be a blithering idiot, Evie! Just go!'

'You take the ambulance. I'll be back as soon as I can,' I said, trying not to give in to the guilty feeling that I would rather see these boys safe, and my girls too, than fight for a foolish young man with a hot temper. I knew as soon as I saw him I would feel differently, but my instinct was towards anger, unreasonable or otherwise.

The driver was friendly-sounding, but I had no wish to talk about anything; my mind was on Oliver and what I could say to help him, so I let the conversation remain more or less one-sided as we drove. He'd just returned from two weeks' leave, after a two-week secondment in France, and closer to the lines than he was used to. 'Shook me up proper,' he confessed, before moving on to happier things: his wife had hopes that this time she might be pregnant, that'd please his little boy; a brother or sister to look after. I murmured polite things in return, wishing he'd hush, but at the same time soothed by the obvious pleasure in his voice when he spoke of his home life.

'I thought I'd resent leaving there to come back,'

he said, 'but it sort of feels like home here too, if you get me?'

I did, and told him so. He nodded. 'I can't say I like this business though, Miss.' He gestured to his own gas mask and I agreed again. Wordless little grunts, he must think me most rude. 'Dirty game,' he went on. Then he was back to talking about his boy again and I couldn't help smiling, although of course he couldn't see my face. 'Reckon you're all right to breathe here, Miss,' he said as we pulled up outside HQ, a splendid-looking hotel in a former existence.

I waited until I was inside to gingerly remove my mask, however, and immediately heard a voice calling. 'Miss? Come with me, your clothes will be full of gas.' The hurried-looking adjutant kept his distance but gestured to me, and I looked around anxiously for a sign of Uncle Jack, but the lobby was full of hurrying people and I couldn't see his distinctive, tall figure anywhere.

'Excuse me, is Jack Carlisle here?'

'I don't know the name. Rank?'

I had to stop and think; Uncle Jack had not re-signed his commission when he took up his work for MI6, but he never referred to himself in relation to it. I thought back to his uniform, and remembered the crown on the insignia. 'Major, I think.'

'If he's anything to do with Captain Maitland's court-martial, he'll be incommunicado until it's over,' the adjutant said, and directed me to a room where I could wash, and where I was able to borrow a smallish-sized army uniform. Looking in the mirror, with my short blonde hair up in

375

sweaty spikes, and the khaki jacket and trousers that were still too big, I looked like nothing so much as an under-aged boy soldier. A very tired one. I sighed, and rubbed cold water over my face and into my hair, acknowledging I would not cut a particularly glamorous figure but hoping it wouldn't diminish my credibility.

In the end my part in the trial was very small indeed, and over in less than ten minutes, giving me little time to do or say anything of any real help. I was called in early, asked about Oliver's return to England, and about his disappearance at Dover. Not once did the question of the murdered driver come up, all they were interested in from me was information about the desertion. It seemed Oliver had not mentioned I'd seen him at Number Twelve, for which I sent him silent thanks: if it came out that I'd seen him and not reported it, I would be accused alongside him. He looked back at me, eyes expressionless beneath the peak of his cap, but his clenched teeth evident in the tenseness of his jaw.

I explained what had happened at Dover, while omitting Archie's part in the plan, and I also said I was certain Oliver had planned only to be away long enough to persuade Kitty to return and tell her story. I was given a telling-off for saying that, as the prosecution insisted I could only suppose it and didn't know for sure, but words once uttered cannot be undone, no matter how firmly one is told to disregard them. I had to trust they had done their work.

After that there was little more I could do. The defence's questions allowed me to repeat my impressions of Oliver as a splendid officer and a protective brother, and to explain all Kitty had told me and what I had seen for myself. I told them Potter had been lurking around the cottage and kept giving Kitty longing looks, and noticed the puzzled glances flickering around the room ... he must had made himself quite popular, for them to be surprised. Finally I was able to make it quite clear that Kitty had wanted to give her own evidence, but was currently too sick to do so. Instead she relied on me to relay her side of things. No mention was made of me not being there that night, to my great relief, at least I would not be put in the position of telling the court that Colonel Drewe had allowed me to borrow the car; it would have been unfair to drag him into this. I wondered if he had any notion of the true nature of the man who'd been driving him around, and how he would feel when he found out.

While I would have desperately wished to stay and see it out, or at least speak to Uncle Jack, I was equally relieved to be dismissed just after lunch, and permitted to return to my station to assist where I could. I was still wearing the borrowed uniform, and when Boxy saw me she grinned at the sight. It was an exhausted grin, but it was real, and I was relieved to see it, but I just gave her a withering look and asked how we were doing.

'There were several waves,' she said, smothering a yawn, 'but the worst seems to have dissipated now, though the ADS is still filling up all the time. The trenches were evacuated, and Fritz ran at us, but he was pushed back and we held the line, thank God.'

'Do we know about losses?'

'No numbers, but both sides. The Germans copped it from our fire, and we took some prisoners. Also I think the wind shifted, and some of their men went down under their own gas.' She rubbed at her eyes with a grubby hand.

'Right, you're having a break now,' I told her firmly. 'Go and bathe if you can, get out of those clothes and soak them. And,' I handed her my own bundle of dirty clothes in their protective bag, 'if you wouldn't mind doing these at the same time?' She took them off me with a sigh of mock annoyance, and I grinned, but as I drove out of the yard and looked back I saw her holding the bag at a distance; the attack had clearly shaken her more than I realised.

I drove long into the evening, taking men away from where the heavy gas had lain the longest; the attack had come so swiftly many had not been able to don masks in time to avoid taking a deep lungful. We had to take some who had been exposed but seemed fine, as well, since chlorine gas had a nasty habit of often holding off a day or so before making its effects felt. These men looked at their comrades with ill-disguised fear, seeing their own future in blue lips and bloodied phlegm.

When I arrived back at the cottage the cellar was once again full, and the oxygen masks all used up, reminding me strongly of the night Number Twelve had been hit. I wondered if we should expect the same again; the Germans disabling as many as they could with gas before launching their bigger, further-ranging guns. It seemed likely, and when I fell into bed in the early hours I was still wearing my clothes and boots, just in case. Boxy was asleep, but her breathing sounded harsh and laboured and I didn't like it.

I closed my eyes and thought back to the sight of Oli, alone and terrified in the huge room at HQ that had been the site of his court-martial. My anger towards him had, as I had known it would, vanished immediately I saw him, and all I could think of was how he was really just a child who, by now, would know whether he was to live or die. It seemed ominous that Uncle Jack had not come over to tell me the verdict, but exhaustion was creeping in, making a nonsense out of any coherent thought and, with the sounds of Elise and the other two girls moving about downstairs, administering treatment where they could and comfort where they couldn't, I drifted into a light, troubled sleep.

Around five a.m. I was woken again, this time by a hand on my shoulder, shaking me roughly.

'Boxy!' I sat up, horrified by the sound of her breathing. My own chest was tight, and I fought the urge to cough, knowing it would hurt, but she was in a much worse way.

'Can't breathe, poppet,' she gasped, and tried to smile, but it turned to tears and her fear transmitted itself to me through the grip of her hands on my arm.

'Ambulance. Now! There are no oxygen masks left.' I pulled her outside and she staggered to the ambulance, her head dropping as she struggled for breath. Somehow we got her on board, and I drove in the faint light of dawn towards the base hospital. All the way, I could hear her dragging short, agonised breaths, and I kept up a steady patter of nonsense that was worthy of her own non-stop talking. A glance at her now and again showed her staring fixedly at me, nodding, understanding what I was trying to do. When we reached the hospital it was all I could do to keep her on her feet, and an orderly came across to help us. His expression, when he looked at Boxy, made me feel sicker than ever.

I hugged her, as best I could with her sagged against me. 'I'll wire Benjy and tell him you're in the best possible hands,' I said, and forced a smile as we handed her over to the tired-looking Sister. Boxy looked as if she wanted to answer, but I shook my head. 'Just do as the nurses tell you, and don't be a nuisance. Let them get a word in, at least.'

'Leave her with us,' the Sister said. 'You look as though you might benefit from some fresh air yourself. The courtyard's through there.' She jerked her head in the direction of a double-door. 'I'll send someone if there's anything you can do.'

I felt roundly dismissed, but the ward was almost full and I would only have been in the way, so I watched from the doorway while the Sister and a nurse helped Boxy into one of the few empty beds at the other end, and then pushed open the door and went out into the chilly early morning. Snow was drifting lazily around in the air, falling wetly to a sodden ground and vanishing instantly. I felt the odd flake alight on my cheek and wondered if this winter would ever end; it had been the bitterest one I'd ever known, and surely by now it should have given way to spring. But, as the war grew older the weather stayed harsh to match it, and I could barely remember how it felt to be warm, comfortable and happy.

I'd intended to walk awhile, but my chest still felt tight and when I turned my head too quickly I became dizzy, so I sat down on an iron bench beneath the big beech tree at the far end of the path and, despite the cold, and the hard discomfort of the seat, I dozed and drifted. My thoughts were mangled and dark, twisting around themselves with divided fear for Boxy and Oliver, and the ever-present ache of missing Will. I don't know how long I had been there when I eventually raised my head, but the sky had lightened and there were more people coming outside now. Patients and nursing staff leaned on one another as tiredness, injury and long nights took their toll, and lifted their faces to the sky as if to soak in the hope that we all sought in each brand new day.

One man, tapping a cigarette on his case prior to lighting it, caught my eye and nodded in casual greeting. I peered closer and my breath froze. It couldn't be... I stood up and took a couple of steps closer. It was! Oli hadn't killed him after all! Oh, thank God...

'Private Potter?'

He looked up again, squinting against the flare of his match, and looking a little nervous at the way I was staring at him. 'Miss? I hope you're all right?' He shook out the match, leaving his gasper unlit. 'How did it go at your friend's trial yesterday?'

The voice shocked me even more; those friendly,

conversational tones that had lulled me during the drive to the court-martial. I felt the first wave of doubt; could this really be the man who'd done that terrible thing? This proud, devoted family man? Then I snapped back to reality and stepped away. This was obviously how he'd done it: lulled poor Kitty into dispensing her typically eager comfort and sympathy, before trapping her in the back of the ambulance and destroying, not only her life, but that of her brother too. I was about to shout for someone, anyone, when I heard my name called, and turned to see a familiar figure rounding the corner by the double-doors.

I almost melted with relief. 'Archie! It's him, don't let him get away!'

'Hush, Evie–'

'Grab him!'

'Miss? Sir?' Potter sounded bemused and frightened, barely remembering to salute, but Archie spared him no more than a glance.

'Evie, listen to me!'

I stopped, my heart chilled suddenly. 'Is it about Oli?'

Archie's face was pale through worry and lack of sleep, and there were dark circles beneath his eyes. He put his bag down at his feet, heedless of the damp ground, and took my hands. 'The news isn't good. I'm sorry.'

'But Potter's not dead! It can only be a desertion charge, and Uncle–'

'He wasn't the one, sweetheart.' He shook at my hands. 'Potter didn't do it. Oliver knew who did. And that man *is* dead.'

'Who, then?'

'Colonel Drewe.'

Everything darkened around me, and my balance shifted sickeningly, but Archie steadied me. I tried to stop my voice from shaking when I spoke. 'What happened?'

'Sit back down, I'll tell you all I know.'

'I've been sitting too long. Tell me now.'

Archie looked at Potter, who had been staring from one of us to the other, fascinated. 'Dismissed, Potter. Be ready to drive me back in an hour.'

Potter saluted again, a quick, not very smart salute, and looked reluctant to leave, but Archie waved him away. Then, alone again on the path by the door, we stood, heedless of the whispering snow that continued to drift around, and Archie told me everything, exactly as Oliver had told it to him.

About an hour after Oliver and Archie had seen me in the CCS, Lieutenant-Colonel Drewe had summoned Oliver to drive him over to the shelled cottage, to see what might be salvaged and to make his report. 'He took a great interest in these places,' Oliver had said to Archie, 'and everyone thought what a wonderful bloke he was for it. Anyway, he needed a driver, since Potter was still on secondment, and all the others were busy after the shelling the night before. I volunteered instead.'

He told Archie how he and the colonel had been walking through the rubble outside the cottage, and he'd been unsettled to notice Drewe's eyes, bloodshot and skittering around in their sockets; the man was clearly done up on something. Something had jolted his memory then, something Kitty had said about her attacker's eyes. And, more tellingly, the realisation slipped into place that Potter was with another unit, in another country ... it *couldn't* have been him! Oliver's mind raced, putting things into the neat little boxes from which they'd spilled in the fury of hearing the accusation levelled at the driver: Drewe had been the one who'd made it so easy to borrow the car that night, Drewe was a respected officer, someone Kitty would have been both familiar with, and eager to help when he'd been stumbling up the road that night. She would have been most reluctant to name him; who would believe her?

Oliver's suspicions began gnawing harder, and he'd studied Drewe's amiable, grandfatherly face, searching for a hint of anything dark. Drewe had abruptly turned away but Oliver had seen guilt in that gesture, and spoke bluntly.

'Was it you? Did you rape my sister?' He wanted the colonel to express puzzlement, even anger at the insubordinate tone, but he hadn't. He merely turned back and studied Oliver's face in return, drawing himself up even straighter. There had still been others there at that time, stretcher-bearers wading through the floodwaters, and negotiating the stone steps to bring the gas victims back out for burial, and as Drewe walked away, and Oliver followed, the tension flared between captain and colonel and several heads turned to watch with interest.

Oliver called out, anger sharpening his tone. 'Don't walk away from me!'

Drewe spun back. 'Raise your voice to me again,

Captain Maitland, and you'll be up on a charge.'

'Do it and be damned! Answer me!'

Drewe had ducked into the cottage unchallenged. Denied further entertainment the stretcher-bearers closed the ambulance flap and drove slowly away, but Oliver knew talk of the altercation would be all over the company inside an hour. He shook his head, annoyed with his own fragile temper, and went inside. He still didn't know for sure, and vague suspicion was not enough to risk an insubordination charge over. Inside, the front part of the cottage was ruined but it looked as though the back had escaped the worst of things; perhaps some of Kitty's belongings might be saved after all, he'd look later. The water had been turned off, and the air was thick with the smell of burning and, as he headed for the cellar, to make sure everyone was indeed out, Oliver took shallow breaths to avoid inhaling too much soot. It made his heartbeat race uncomfortably, and was evidently having the same effect on the colonel; Drewe's face was reddening, and his eyes seemed to be getting smaller and smaller. He was looking longingly at the door already.

Oliver's disdain kindled again. 'Look at you! Fought in two wars and yet the biggest coward I've ever met.'

'Coward?' Drewe snapped. 'You have absolutely no notion, boy, of the things I've done in the name of king and country!' He pushed past Oliver to the cellar.

Oliver followed him. 'I know what you've done in the name of greed and cruelty. And it takes a yellow man to force a sweet, trusting girl who

385

only wanted to help.'

'Not as sweet as she'd have you believe,' Drewe said, making Oliver's breath halt in his chest. 'None of them are.' He turned, and smiled up at Oliver, and it was such a familiar, kind smile, that Oliver had trouble accepting what he was hearing, the words were so incongruously mismatched to the expression. Drewe carried on down the steps, stopping just short of the floodwater. 'It's why they come out here,' he threw back over his shoulder, 'haven't you realised that yet? All the girls love a Tommy, and your sister was no different. She was the lucky one though, bagged herself an officer instead.'

Oliver's rising rage carried him several steps down before he realised Drewe had turned back and was coming up again. He had felt his own fist bunching but found enough control to hold back, and instead of lashing out he had taken a step backwards, deliberately putting Drewe out of reach.

But Drewe pressed closer until his face was level with Oliver's chest. 'Move, boy.' And with a speed and brutality that Oliver might have found terrifying if he hadn't been so furious, he drove the tip of his swagger stick into Oliver's stomach. Oliver stumbled and gasped at the pain, but a second later his still-curled fist was up and smashing into Drewe's jaw. The colonel lost his footing on the waterlogged step and crashed backwards, spinning to land face-down in the filthy water. Breathing hard and swallowing a wave of nausea, Oliver had waited in vain for him to get back up, and eventually he had waded down the last few steps to Drewe's side and rolled him over. Drewe's eyes were wide open, the late afternoon light fell on them through the tiny, ground-level window and gave them the appearance of life, but an appearance was all it was.

'He came to find me, as soon as he realised,' Archie said. 'He didn't tell me what he'd done, but he was obviously keen to get on the road to Calais before someone found the body.' He hesitated, then said gently, 'No matter what the provocation, or how freakish the accident, he killed a superior officer. He's been found guilty, and sentenced.'

'Sentenced...'

'He's to face the squad tomorrow.'

Bright hatred washed over me as I recalled the cheerful, friendly face of the Lieutenant-Colonel. I remembered the way he had let me half-run, half-stumble into town the night Gertie had crashed, claiming a broken ankle; how terrifying and dangerous that journey had been ... and how quickly that ankle had healed.

I wrapped my arms across my middle, and heard my own voice escape in a little moan, and Archie took my shoulders and made me look at him. 'Listen, Uncle Jack is still working on this, he's calling in every possible favour he can. Pulling strings all over the place. We'll just have to trust him, aye?'

I nodded, unable to do anything else, or to find anything to say. Jack had been able to make sure all the evidence was heard at Will's trial, but this was different: Oliver had killed Drewe, he had even confessed. 'I don't think I should tell Kitty just yet,' I said reluctantly. 'It'd destroy her to know it's going to happen and she can't do anything.'

'Aye, that's best,' Archie said, when I told him. 'She'd be frantic to get here, and she's not up to the trip yet, poor wee girl' His voice was tight again, and a distance had come into his expression. I was about to ask what he was thinking, when he swam back.

'Oh, I almost forgot.' He bent to open his knapsack. 'This was dropped off at HQ yesterday, just after you left.' He moved aside a spare set of puttees, and brought out something that made my heart stumble and then race. I stared at it, expecting it to vanish, half-convinced I was dreaming, but when I reached out to take it, it remained solid and real in my hands.

'Who dropped it off?' I asked, running my fingers over the battered black box as if it were covered in the most precious gold leaf.

'A Sergeant Blunt. He was the one who found Drewe's body.'

Blunt? It took a moment, but then I remembered. 'Did he have blond hair and a London accent?'

'Aye, that's him. He said he'd seen you the day after the base was shelled, and you seemed distressed about the box when you left, so when he was off duty, he went back and found it. Of course, you'd gone back to England by then, so he couldn't give it to you. Anyway, he took some lads back there the other day, to see if they could recover some of the stretchers and so forth as well, and that's how they found Drewe. Blunt

388

hoped to see you at the trial, but you were gone by the time he arrived, so he asked me to give it to you.'

I held my breath, blessing the sergeant silently, and lifted the lid. There, right on the top of the pile of letters, lay the paper rose.

The words we'd spoken on that day in Blackpool sounded as clearly now, in my head, as they had done when they'd flowed between us, punctuated by the clacking of the train wheels that carried us home.

'...*I will never, ever give up on you, and I want you to promise the same.*'

'*I pledge my life on it.*'

How quickly we forget promises made in the rush of relief and happiness, when a face you love is looking at you with earnest devotion, and all you want to do is kiss it and forget the doubts ever existed.

I looked at Archie and said bluntly, 'I've got to go.'

'Where?' Archie reached out to take my arm, but I jerked away from him and started walking towards the door.

'Arras.'

'To do what?'

I walked faster. 'To tell him I didn't mean what I said in my letter.'

Now Archie did seize my arm, and pulled me to a stop just outside the door. 'What letter?'

'I told him I was setting him free, but I can't. I don't want to. And deep down neither does he, he just thinks he's doing what's best for me.' My chest was still tight and my breathing thin, but the burning in my eyes had nothing to do with gas.

Archie shook his head. 'Look, I understand, but think for a minute. There's a push on, you'll not get anywhere near him.'

I pulled away and yanked on the door, pulling it open. 'I don't care, I'm going anyway. As soon as I've checked on Boxy.'

I walked into the stale warmth of the ward and flinched. No matter how much cleaning went on, nothing could disguise the mingled reek of disinfectant and decay, and I automatically began to breathe through my mouth again, longing to be back out in the fresh, cool April air, and on my way.

I would see Boxy for a minute or two, explain where I was going, then leave her to rest. If I left now I should reach Arras well before teatime, even on the terrible roads and with stops along the way. I would not sit by and let Will fall out of my life. I needed him, and, more importantly, I needed him to know it. If it put pressure on him, that was just too bad; he'd only be the same as every other man out there.

These thoughts whirled through my mind in the time it took for me to adjust to the gloom in the ward, get my bearings, and look over towards where I had last seen Boxy. The nursing sister who was stripping the bed saw me, shook her head slightly and turned away. I stared at her for a moment, at the empty bed, at the little dolly bag hanging at its end. Her things. It must have happened just moments ago.

Archie came into the ward behind me and

followed my stunned gaze. 'Oh, sweetheart, I'm so sorry,' he said softly. I couldn't answer; numb from the heart outwards, my lips would not move, nor my brain comprehend what had happened. She had been here, now she was gone. Her lively chatter, sometimes interesting, often exasperating, but always welcome, had been silenced. I struggled for something that would help me understand, but found nothing.

'I have to go,' was all I managed to repeat in the end, and those pathetic words came out strangled and small. Dimly, through a strange rushing, roaring sound, I heard Archie pleading with me to wait, to talk. But wait for what? Talk about what? I felt my head shaking 'no' although I wasn't aware of making it do so. I felt my legs moving, although it didn't feel as though I had enough strength to make them do so. Everything I did felt as though some ghastly puppeteer was above me, jerking my limbs in a dance to some discordant music only they could hear.

'You can't save everyone,' Archie was saying now, and his voice filtered clearly through the din. I turned to look at him, and saw only genuine sorrow; he hadn't meant to sound harsh.

'I know,' I said bleakly. 'But I used to think I could save those I loved, at least.'

'You can. You have.'

'No. I've let them all down. First Lizzy, then Kitty and Oli, and now Boxy. I can't destroy Will too.'

'Don't go. Please.'

'You can tell Uncle Jack if he asks, but not until I've had the chance to get well away. He'll only

391

come after me and he's needed here.'

'Wait!' Archie caught up as I walked away. 'All right, if you insist on going, then I'm going with you. You have no idea what you're driving into.' I choked a dry laugh, and he shrugged. 'Yes, I'm sorry. Of course you know. But I can't let you go alone. If something were to happen, and you by yourself–'

'You have duties here.'

'Your ambulance is attached to my division. You *are* my duty. Besides, you'd get nowhere near Will without me, you wouldn't stand a chance of getting a pass.' He touched my face with a large, gentle hand, and gave a rueful little smile. 'You might be dressed like Tommy Atkins, but you're far too pretty to pass off as him.'

Despite everything, I found a watery smile. 'Thank you.'

'Come on. We'll take my car, it'll be faster than the ambulance.'

'I'd have crawled if I had to,' I told him, and he nodded.

'Aye, I know. He's a lucky man.'

'Archie–'

'It's fine, Evie, it's sunk in, don't worry.'

I squeezed his hand, and together we left the hospital, heading for France, Will, and a single, snap decision that would change everything forever.

Chapter Twenty-Eight

The roads were cluttered, but mercifully free from attention from the Teutons. Cars and buses carrying troops and equipment to the Front, and ambulances coming away, edged past each other on the pitted, broken surfaces, and all around was the sound of grinding gears and struggling engines, shouts, and orders to keep moving. I'd have recognised the grim signs of a push even if Archie hadn't warned me.

Will's unit had been in reserve during the first battle at the Scarpe, but this time he was not so lucky. I waited in the support trench while Archie went into the command HQ dugout, ignoring the curious glances of those who hurried past, and trying not to resent every soldier I saw for not being Will. Eventually he came out, and told me what he'd heard. 33rd Division had gone over yesterday, with the Suffolks and the Seaforth Highlanders. Seeing my bleak expression, and unable to ease it, Archie took refuge in the familiarity of military details.

'They had two objectives, d'ye see? One lot were sending hate down the Hindenburg Line,' he gestured, 'and Will was with those who were attacking in the open, towards the copse.'

'I can't hear any bombs.'

'No, the barrage stopped when the first object-ive was gained, and the troops made it further in.

Sent some prisoners back, but...' He trailed away.

'But what?' My heart was as cold as my voice. 'Where is he, Archie?' He sighed, and tried to take my hand, but I wouldn't let him. 'Is he dead?'

'No, not... They were cut off, that's all. The Bosche got in between the copse and their jumping-off line. They're digging in.'

'So you're saying they're trapped.' My hands shook and I thrust them into my pockets, trying to calm my frantically hurrying heartbeat.

'For now, yes,' Archie said, and went on quickly, 'but the enemy fell back early this morning, and our boys secured the German front-line trenches. As soon as it was safe, they relieved the 1st Middlesex, and after nightfall it'll be C and D company. Will's turn.'

I digested the information through a twisting mess of fear, and found something to hold onto. 'So all he has to do is sit tight?'

'They're holding off well, they've even taken prisoners,' Archie said, but I thought he sounded evasive.

'But they're still having to fight to hold the captured ground.' It wasn't a question, I could see it all too clearly but I needed to know every detail. 'How well are they dug in?'

'I don't know,' he confessed. 'Look, I don't have any more answers, I just wanted to tell you what I found out. We'll just have to wait until nightfall and hope for the best, aye?'

I looked up at the sky; it was hard to tell if it was darkening with cloud, or with the natural advancement of the evening. The journey had been long and tiring, and although we had started early it had taken the best part of the day. Night couldn't come fast enough.

'Let's get something to eat,' Archie said gently. 'You must be half-starved.'

It wasn't until he said it that I realised I hadn't eaten since I'd snatched a crust of bread before falling into bed last night. My stomach immediately growled, and I nodded. 'So must you,' I pointed out. I turned to look out towards where I knew Will lay entrenched, I hoped, and unhurt.

'I could do with something,' he admitted. 'There's a wee place in the town. If we hurry we'll make it before curfew.'

We drove back a few miles until we reached town, and Archie found the café, where we were able to melt into the background and accept thin, faintly greasy cottage pie and a bottle of Claret. I tried to eat, I honestly thought I'd have wolfed it down, but the first mouthful stuck in my tight throat, and I raised streaming eyes to Archie and shook my head. I replaced my fork and took a big swallow of wine, which helped, but I couldn't bring myself to eat anything after all, not knowing Will was out there in the gathering dark, awaiting a rescue that might come to nothing after all.

When we left the café I felt light-headed; drinking was easier than eating, and it had seemed to fill me up. As soon as the fresh air hit me I knew it had been a mistake; I'd been exhausted, tense, I hadn't eaten for hours and hours ... the wine had been rich and comforting, but now I just felt queasy.

'There's one other thing you should know,' Archie said, and he sounded hesitant now. 'Will got your letter. It was delivered on the 22nd, they

395

went over the top on the 23rd. I'm so sorry.'

I nodded, feeling dry and husked out. It had been a faint hope that he hadn't, after all. 'We'll go back to the dugout,' Archie went on. 'At least there we'll get news on how things are going.'

'Fine, yes.' I swayed, and once again his hand was there to stop me stumbling. He eased me onto the seat of his car. 'Just sit there for a minute, there's no rush just yet.' I let my head fall back against the leather, and closed my eyes, wishing the world would stop spinning, and awoke much later to a gentle touch on my shoulder. It was pitch-black outside, and only the dim pulse of light from a flare lit the night sky. I struggled upright, and ran my tongue across my fuzzy teeth.

'Here,' Archie said, and I jumped at the sound of his voice. He lifted my hand off my lap and put a biscuit into it, and I bit into it gratefully. It helped break the thickness of my mouth, and I washed it down with water from his canteen.

'Thank you,' I said hoarsely. Then I remembered, rather shamefully, how I'd fallen asleep. 'I'm sorry,' I added, and he chuckled. He sounded so much like Uncle Jack when he did that, it made me smile despite my worry.

'No need to be. Are you ready?'

I nodded, then realised he probably couldn't see me. 'Do you think he'll be back?'

'Let's find out.'

The car moved off, lights out, of course. I found it comfortingly familiar, and a welcome distraction from worrying about Will, to be peering through the darkness and feeling the car jolting over potholes and mounds of blasted earth. When we arrived back at the dugout it was just after 11 p.m., and there was a noticeable buzz in the air.

Archie ducked inside, and after another agonising wait, during which I couldn't remember drawing breath, he emerged with a grin. 'They've reached the sunken road,' he said, 'they're safe!'

The relief almost sent me to the floor, and I sagged against the side of the trench. 'Where?'

He pointed out towards the roads in the distance, crossing the flat landscape but affording some shelter, where the rest of Will's battalion waited. 'I can't believe they held out for forty hours,' he added in a voice tinged with awe. I felt a massive surge of pride and love as I pictured a muddy, tired, but smiling Will, rejoining his battalion in a chorus of triumph and congratulations.

'How long 'til they're back?'

'I don't know, I'm going back in to find out more details. Will you be all right out here?'

I nodded. Archie squeezed my arm and handed me a tin hat. 'Put this on. You're quite safe back here, but you'll attract less attention.' He ducked back inside, and I walked a little further on, wanting to be first on-hand when any news came back. No one challenged me, or questioned my presence, I felt as invisible as Lizzy had said she'd always felt at Oaklands; it wasn't a sensation I was used to, but I welcomed it. My life had always been lived in the full glare of attention, both at home and in Flanders, and here I was just a shadow like so many others. It was extraordinarily liberating.

Archie was gone a good long while, and I strained for any news among the muttering men who came and went along the trench, taking messages, delivering provisions and ammunition under cover of darkness ... now and again a couple of stretcher-bearers would hurry past, returning a few minutes later, laden, to slip and slide in the mud on their way to the aid post behind me. I hadn't realised I'd wandered so deep into the trench system, until someone shoved me in the back in their hurry to get past and I realised my surroundings had shrunk considerably. I had passed through the support trench, with its rows of dugouts and the sense of order, into the much narrower, forward-travelling communications trench. I stopped, a new fear worming its way through me at how close I had come to arriving, unchallenged, at the front line.

I'd never been so far forward; it gave me a horrible, sick feeling to think of all the men who'd lost life and limb here, right where I stood. Boxy's story of tripping over the remains of one such boy suddenly became more real, vivid and horrifying than ever. Now my mind was on poor Boxy herself, and relief for Will was tinged with, not sorrow, as I'd expected, but anger. I remembered writing to Lizzy that I could quite happily stride out into No Man's Land and shake the Hun until his teeth rattled ... but shamefully I had to admit the anger was not enough to quell the fear, and I turned back.

Voices were drifting out of the dark, a constant mumble of different accents and tones, some warm with low laughter, some raised in annoyance ... two of them came closer and brushed by me, still talking.

'Not 'til daylight, orders say.'

'Seems a bit ... disrespectful though, given what happened.'

'Can't risk it.'

'First light, then.'

'Yeah.'

Half-listening, I followed the two men a few steps, eager to get back to the relative safety of the support trench, then froze.

'Of course if that tall bugger hadn't been so damn keen to get his souvenir it'd never have happened. His fault, I reckon.'

'It's the other one's missus I feel sorry for. I mean, he's well out of it, but she's got to live with it. She's one of them independents over near Dixmude I think. Landed gentry an' all.'

My heart was starting to race, fast and loud, and I tried to swallow but couldn't. I kept step by trembling step with the two men as they reported to their CO.

'Two men down, sir. Glenn and Davies.'

I sank down onto my haunches, unable to support my own weight on legs that felt like twigs. Through the roar of rushing blood in my ears I heard the details.

'C and D Company relieved, sir. Private Glenn went back to retrieve a weapon from a dead Squarehea ... uh, German, sir.'

'What happened?'

'He got hung up on their wire. Credit to him, sir, he didn't shout, but Private Davies realised and went back to get him. They was got by a sniper, sir.'

I moaned into my gloved hands, squeezing my

eyes tight shut as if by blocking out the light I could block out the words.

'Can't get them tonight, Corporal.' The C.O.'s voice was regretful.

'No, sir.'

'First light. Not leaving those boys out there for the bloody crows, not after that siege. Bloody heroes, the pair, even if Glenn botched it at the end.'

Botched it. Barry Glenn had killed my husband. *Botched it.* The scream in my head did nothing to drown out those words, and I only vaguely heard the corporal explaining how the grenade had been thrown after the sniper's second shot; that Will had, at least, lived long enough to take the enemy with him. My chest and stomach felt like rocks, my throat hurt with the effort not to let the scream loose, and all I wanted to do was strike someone. Hurt them. I didn't even care who. The urge was almost overwhelming, but I fought to control it and as a result my fingers cramped, the pain sudden and breathtaking. It gave my mind the chance it needed to clear, to comprehend, but not to accept; I could not leave him out there alone.

Somehow I rose to my feet, and stumbled away from the three men, back the way I had just come. A fragment of my mind skittered towards Archie, wondering whether I should go to him for help, but he would only stop me. The movement of troops was increasing, carrying me along in its wave towards the Front, meeting others coming the other way; shattered to the point of collapse, but relieved to have made it through another push alive.

Unlike Will.

Reality kept trying to force its way through; unthinkable numbers of men and boys, and serving VADs and nurses too, had died in this hideous conflict. Will was not a special case, he was just another in that awful number. Hundreds of thousands. Millions. I realised now, how innocently speculative had been my conversation with Lizzy: it wasn't a question of whether it was better to die or to suffer; too many suffered, struggled, fought for every breath, experienced gut-wrenching fear of death, and then died anyway, with no more understanding of why than when they had joined up. But those who died quickly were no better off, bodies that had been full of life and energy, minds that had sung with intelligence, humour and kindness – snuffed out, destroyed and then left to rot. A job to be done at first light. A task to be performed "for decency's sake", but no one to hold their hand, no one to lie with them in the dark while the cold, wet ground stole the last of their warmth.

But Will *was* special. He had died trying to save his friend's life. *As have others!* He had taken down his enemy before he died. *As have many!* He was ... he was my own Lord William. I wondered when the tears would come, and only realised they were already coursing down my face when they began to run into my hair as I stared upwards at the black night sky. I was not sobbing, my breath was coming evenly, clear and steady, but the pain was threatening to pitch me to the duckboards beneath my feet.

We burst into clearer space, and the troops be-

401

hind me dispersed in different directions. The trench was now running the other way, and with a cold sense of triumph that eclipsed my former fear, I realised I'd made it to the front line. The parapet rose in front of me, sandbagged and filthy, and I could see the tiny loopholes that permitted sight out into No Man's Land. I was about to climb up onto the fire-step to look through one, when someone bumped me and I staggered against the side of the trench.

'Sorry, mate,' the soldier mumbled, and hurried on. I levered myself off the wall, feeling my elbow sink into the mud, and began to walk. It didn't matter which direction I went in; I couldn't see more than a few feet ahead. My eyes had adjusted a while ago to the darkness, and whenever a flare rose in the distance it took just a few minutes blinking to readjust, but the trenches zigzagged and dog-legged across the landscape and I never knew what I would see when I rounded the next bend. Time and again I slipped on the wet boards, but I kept walking, my head down, thankful for the tin helmet although my mind kept hissing the savage question; *whose was it, Evie, before?*

A sign hung, haphazardly, on one corner: 'to centre of section'. An arrow pointed the way I was going, and every few steps I looked for an unmanned fire-step. But it was a clear night and there was an expectation of retaliation. Ladders stretched up the side of the parapet, and I saw the scuffs of countless muddied boots on them, and wondered how many of the men who'd made those marks had lived beyond the next few, un-speakably shocking minutes.

402

I passed through the centre section, again un-challenged. The trenches were busiest at night in any case, and while I wasn't trying to blend in, it seemed I had managed it anyway. My thoughts went back to the gas attack that had caused my clothing change, and the worry of an evacuation that had persuaded me to remain clothed and booted when I went to bed. It was all I needed to convince myself I was doing the right thing, and I pushed on, acknowledging, but not accepting, fate's apology for stealing my love, while provid-ing me with the means to go to him.

The further I went, the fewer people I saw, and the rougher the ground became. The overhead wooden struts that shored up the sides were sag-ging and off-kilter, and then the duckboards abruptly ended, leaving me floundering in mud al-most to my knees. I realised this end of the trench was unoccupied now. There were a couple of dugouts but they were shallow and empty, and the ladders opposite were broken. Shattered, in fact. This had probably been the scene of an enemy attack – burst shells and discarded bayonets, evi-dence of hand-to-hand fighting, was everywhere I looked, and no attempt appeared to have been made to repair this section; it seemed the troops had consolidated their efforts where they could do most good, up near the centre.

I eyed the ladders, trying to decide if one of them might bear my weight, and then, just up ahead before the solid wall of earth, I noticed another, very narrow, entrance running off at a right-angle. Another sign, broken but readable, pointed down it: 'LP'.

I took a deep breath, and it shook quite audibly. The listening post, abandoned or not, would be quite some distance out into No Man's Land. I could feel my trembling getting worse, but the thought of Will lying there in the dirt was too much to bear and I glanced behind me; no one was in sight although I could hear voices, quite clearly, just around the bend. One of them made the breath catch in my throat. It was angry, low, and unmistakeably Scottish.

'What the bloody hell do you mean, you don't know? She's a woman for Christ's sake!'

'Ain't seen no women, sir,' the nervous Tommy stuttered. 'They don't belong down here.'

I melted silently down into the sap leading to the listening post, my heart pounding. If one of those people I'd passed was forced to think, they'd remember an extremely short boy, stumbling along as if the layout was completely unfamiliar, and, more tellingly, carrying nothing. That would be enough for Archie.

I fought my way up to the sap-head, and it took forever for each step; pulling my foot clear of the sucking mud, and feeling my other foot slipping beneath me, finding no strong purchase in the waterlogged ground. My hands braced either side of me in the narrow space, pushing against the sides and sinking into the earth, and my gloves peeled off in turns, sticking there in the walls of the trench and leaving my hands icy-cold and filthy. I strained through the night to hear what was going on in the main trench, but professionalism had dampened Archie's fury and there were no more raised voices.

And there was the ladder. Unbroken, waiting. I closed my eyes briefly, pictured Will, and began to climb. As my head rose above the parapet I had to swallow a surge of nausea; terror took hold and threatened to push me back down and propel me back into Archie's safe, comforting arms. But Will lay out here, just up ahead by the copse, Archie had said. My gentle, clever, courageous Lord William. Dead. And he'd died believing I had broken my promise and given up on him.

My hands slipped on the ladder, and I felt the sting of a splinter from the rough wood but managed not to hiss aloud in pain. No one had taken a shot at me yet; it seemed the rumours were right, that Will had managed to take out the last remaining sniper before he died. *Died* ... oh God... Could I bear to see him, after all? See those beautiful, clear blue eyes staring up at the sky, the mouth I had kissed now falling open, slack and cold? I stopped, holding on to the last part of the ladder, almost praying for an invisible bullet to take me too. Then self-preservation took over and I threw myself forward, flat onto the torn and blasted ground of No Man's Land.

Chapter Twenty-Nine

The first flare almost made me shout. A hiss, a whine, and I shoved my face into the dirt before the light spilled across the land and could catch my white, terrified face. I pulled my frozen hands back up my coat sleeves and, lying there, breathing in the wet filth, I waited for the shot that would reunite me with Will, but it still didn't come. I lay still, unable to see when the light had faded, and finding it harder and harder to breathe as the mud got into my nose, and I began to feel as if I was suffocating.

I knew for sure then that I wasn't yet ready to die, despite the pain of grief that ripped at me, and the absence of anything hopeful to cling to, and I twisted my head to the side far enough to drag in a breath through my mouth, then turned back into the ground again. I had no need to rush, but at the same time every moment I wasn't at Will's side felt like someone was gradually unravelling me from the inside out. Only touching him now could stop it, and leave me with some part of myself intact.

My head still down, I concentrated until I had my bearings, picturing the location of the German trench in relation to my outstretched hands, and then began to inch forward over the pits and boggy mounds. The patches of grass that had survived the barrage were like little oases of cleanliness, and I used them to wipe mud from my eyes so I could see at least, but I had to fight the strong urge to do the same with my face and hands. The former German stronghold was silent, but a good distance before I reached it I saw the first huge coils of barbed wire. It was of a heavier gauge than the wire the British Expeditionary Forces used, and near my hand lay a set of wire-cutters, no doubt cast aside in frustration at their inability to cut through it. The bombardment didn't seem to have done much to it either, the same sorry story as the Somme offensive last year; were lessons never to be learned?

A shadow moved up ahead and I bit back a cry and turned my face back down, heart thudding. From the corner of my eye it had looked as though a man were standing beside the wire, swaying from side to side as if he rocked a troubled child in his arms. I waited for a challenge, or the snap of a rifle and then oblivion, but heard nothing except the wind rustling in the trees of the nearby copse. Slowly, I raised my head again and looked properly. The shadow was in fact a silhouette, a darker patch in the darkness of the night, and he swayed because the wire did: the two were now one.

He was tall. Extremely so, and I realised who he was and couldn't stop a moan from breaking free because at his side lay another shape, face down, his pack hanging open where he'd fumbled for his grenade with dying fingers. Behind me I heard a whisper, and it registered somewhere that it was urgently speaking my name, but I couldn't turn to look back; Will lay a few feet in front of me and that awful unravelling was happening faster. If I didn't get to his side I would die too.

I crawled to him, over mud and stones, feeling my skin tear as it fell on the twisted metal of spent shells; my hands and knees were a mass of blood by the time I reached him. I tried to roll him onto his back, desperate for the sight of his face, praying I would recognise him, that he hadn't been hit there, at least. But he was heavy. His uniform and pack were weighed down with equipment, and water-logged by his lying out here in the wet for hours, and I couldn't roll him over, I had no strength with which to do it.

I sobbed aloud then, throwing care to the bitter winds, what did it matter if I was heard?

'Evie!' the voice came again but I still didn't turn.

'I can't move him, Archie. Help me!'

'Damn you! What were you thinking?' But he crawled up beside me and when I finally looked at him I saw his face was not angry at all, but desperately sad. 'What are you trying to do?'

'I couldn't leave him out here,' I said, my voice hitching. Will's hat had fallen off as I tried to roll him, and the sight of his familiar dark hair, and the vulnerability of the back of his fair-skinned neck, lit by the sliver of moon, sliced through me like a blade. 'Help me take him back, Archie? Please?'

A second later we both threw ourselves flat as another flare went up. Archie stirred first, after an age it seemed. 'It's all right,' he said, 'the Bosche are well back, they've abandoned this post. The flares are just proof we've shaken them.'

'Then say you'll help me,' I begged again. He looked at me, then at Will, and nodded. I realised I'd been so lost in my own grief I hadn't spared a thought for his; he and Will had been close for a while, he must be feeling the loss acutely too. I touched his arm, but didn't say anything.

Together we took hold of Will's shoulder and rolled him. There was a sucking sound as the front of his uniform came free of the mud, and where he had been lying with his head turned to one side, the right side of his face was plastered in it. His eyes were closed, the lashes dark against the white of his clean cheek, and matted on the dirty side. His mouth was only partly open, showing a glimpse of half-muddied teeth, and he looked pale and very, very young.

'Wh ... where was he hit?' I managed to say, and Archie patted his hands down Will's body. 'In the side, I think,' he said. 'Hard to say until we get him back into the light.' He added more softly, 'Don't worry, I'll see the mortuary treat him with respect.'

Despite the gentleness of his tone, I hated the words he spoke, and looked back at Will's beautiful, achingly familiar face. The thought of him going into the ground threatened to push aside all reason, and I realised how close I was to hysteria. I forced the image of him in one of those awful plain coffins from my mind; I'd think about it later, would have to, but for now I had to get him back behind our own lines where I could make sure his body was cleaned and cared for.

Archie was eager to get back now, too. I could see him looking worriedly around, peering through the dark. 'You take his arms, I'll take his feet. For heaven's sake keep low.' He spared me a look before picking up Will's feet, and his voice was exasperated but full of affection. 'Uncle Jack was right about you. Just don't get yourself killed, he'll never forgive me.'

After my terrified crawl through the shattered landscape alone, I felt almost nonchalant about the journey back, as though I could just stand up, throw Will over my shoulder and march back to the sap-head in full view of anyone who cared to take a pot-shot. But we bent low, inching our way, with me holding Will under the arms and Archie supporting his feet. My back screamed with the effort, each foot we covered felt like a mile, and it was hard not to grunt or exclaim aloud as our muscles strained and our breath shortened. I could feel the stitches at my neck pulling, but they held, and there was only the harsh, fiery pain of the healing wound, no fresh blood.

I went first, and backwards – Archie insisted, in case of enemy sniper fire which would find him before me – and stretched my foot out behind me at every step, knowing a mis-step could send all three of us tumbling into a shell-hole. The terror of mines was something I couldn't afford to dwell on.

At last we reached the sap-head again, and Archie told me to go down the ladder first. 'I'll lower him down to you, you just guide him, aye?'

'It'll be even more difficult carrying him through that mud,' I whispered back. 'There's no duck-boards there, remember?'

He hesitated, then nodded. 'OK, once we're down I'll go and get a stretcher-bearer, I'll need help to get him up to the collecting post.'

I climbed down the ladder, wincing at the press of the splinter I'd received on the way up a million years ago, and Archie carefully lowered Will to me, lying flat and holding onto Will's webbing, grunting with the effort of controlling the slide. I felt Will's body slither into my arms, and sank to my knees with him, holding his head up so it didn't fall into the mud. It felt more vital than ever now to keep him clean, as if allowing more

410

dirt to collect on his skin were a form of burial. I wasn't ready.

I smoothed his hair from his eyes, wiping at the dirt as best I could, and Archie briefly squeezed my shoulder and went in search of some means to carry him away. I was only aware of the water lapping over my knees in a distant sort of way. The stinging cuts from shrapnel and stones hummed quietly in the background and I didn't even think about how lucky I was to still be alive, beyond the ability to hold Will again. His head rolled back in my arms and I instinctively cupped my hand beneath his cheek and jaw, gently lifting it again, so I could look down into his face until the time came when I would have to surrender his body. As I did so I felt my skin tingle. All over. Every part of me suddenly leapt to life and, with my heart triple-thumping, I pressed my shaking fingers against his neck, just below the angle of his jaw.

I hadn't imagined it. I opened my mouth to scream for Archie, then remembered how close we were to the German lines. Instead I lifted my fingers from Will's cold skin, and then replaced them, suddenly terrified it had been my own thundering pulse I had picked up. It wasn't.

'Will?' I whispered. There was no response, but I lowered my face to his parted lips and felt the faintest brush of his breath on my skin. 'Will!' A sound behind me in the trench made me turn in sudden terror, but it was only Archie and two stretcher-bearers. 'He's alive!' I said, through lips that suddenly felt numb. What if this was the last breath in him? We had dragged him across that rocky, ruined ground ... we might have killed him.

Archie dropped to his knees beside us, heedless of the water, and took Will in his own arms, feeling, as I had done, for the faint, thready pulse. He looked up at me, then around at the stretcher-bearers. 'Right, quick, you two. Get him down the line and out. Now!'

Between us we got Will onto the stretcher, and then Archie's arm came around me as we watched the men round the first difficult bend into the main trench. I slumped against him for a second, trying to make sense of the swift turnabout of emotions that rendered me utterly useless, then plunged after them, desperate not to lose sight of Will in case I never saw him again.

Archie and I followed the ambulance in his car, and my eyes were fixed on the hurriedly fastened canvas that flapped in the wind. Neither of us spoke... I wanted to thank him again for helping me, but when I rehearsed the words they sounded insulting and self-indulgent; he had helped Will, not me. He had risked his life to come after me, it was true, but in the end it was Will's life he had saved.

By the time we reached the Clearing Station, Will was conscious. Sheet-white, and sweating, he breathed in short, shallow bursts, his eyes closed, his hair matted to his head and with one shaking hand he held a wad of dressing against his left side. Word of his return from the dead had flashed around, and the corporal I'd overheard delivering the news arrived, in a state of guilty relief, to tell his story again.

'He was trying to lift Private Glenn off the wire.

He had one hand up, see?' He raised his left arm in demonstration, 'and the sniper got Glenn, and then him. He managed to get to his grenade before he fell, and sent Jerry off. We was all sure he'd copped it too.'

The nurse cut away Will's filthy, mud- and blood-covered jacket and jersey, glanced up at her VAD and snapped an order for fresh bandages and iodine. The VAD hurried away and I looked back at Will's face; tight-jawed, eyes closed, brows drawn down. The bullet wound was visible only as a small, neat hole, but I had seen enough casualties to be able to guess at the truth behind that seemingly innocent mark. The bullet had hit him midway between hip and ribcage, and travelled across his body, but there was no exit wound, and when the sister gently palpated his abdomen he groaned. I grabbed his hand, but he didn't open his eyes.

'Well, it looks as if your little act of negligence has cost this young man dearly,' the sister said to the corporal, with some heat. 'Leaving him out there has done him a good deal of harm.' She looked at me, at my muddied state, at my clothes, and then at my hand holding Will's. Her eyebrows went up.

'My husband,' I managed, and after the first flash of disapproval, her voice softened. 'We can do our best for him here, but he's going to need better care than we can provide. Surgery, obviously, and the sooner the better, but the after-care is going to be vital. Infection's the biggest danger with abdominals, and he's been lying out there a long time. We'll get him as comfortable as we can,

413

and give him something for the pain, then as soon as he's fit to travel he needs to get out to the hospital.'

With his shirt cut away I could see scratches and scars I'd never even known he had, and once more I was hit by the realisation that our lives were utterly separate, joined only by our past. To pray for a future together felt like too much, all I could bring myself to hope for was that he had any kind of future at all. He opened his eyes at last, and looked down to see our hands still linked, and it seemed he wanted to say something, but the sister was cleaning his wound and laying fresh padding over it, and each gentle brush of her fingers seemed to slam into him like a hammer blow. His fingers ground into mine but I held on, taking comfort in the strength I could feel in his grip. Fighting strength. The sister finished applying the bandage, and prepared a morphine injection which he eyed with frantic hunger. As she slipped the needle beneath his goose-flesh-rippled skin he turned once more to me, and his face relaxed. 'Thank you,' he breathed, and then he was away.

'Who told him you went out after him?' Archie wanted to know, his voice sharp. 'No one knows as far as I'm aware, and there could be trouble if anyone finds–'

'That's not what he meant, Arch.' I stumbled over the words, trying not to break down. 'He was thanking me for letting him go.'

We watched in silence as Will was lifted away, only to be replaced by another soldier, his face swathed in blood-soaked bandages with small, whimpering sounds coming from behind them. A

414

shock of blond hair was all I could see of him, but the sound was very young, and the slight body trembled, drowning in a uniform that hung on a frame shrunken by hard work and poor diet. I felt terrible that my thoughts barely drifted across him before following the stretcher carrying Will; every one of these men deserved someone to hold their hand, to soothe their fears, to murmur comforting words as they fought their own intense battle against encroaching darkness ... but I had no strength left, I could only be that person for one man now.

The hospital at Arras was underground. A labyrinth of roughly-hewn tunnels, accommodation for soldiers, signs pointing to exits and different areas, new tunnels joining up with existing ones, quarried hundreds of years before. There was electric light, running water ... these things should have struck me with awe, but all I could see was the mud-encrusted soles of Will's boots as they whisked him away from me and into one of the operating theatres, and all I could think about was whether that brief glimmer of life had been his last.

Archie walked beside me as we made our way back up to the surface. Both of us pushed up against the walls as groups of soldiers clattered past, heading for the exits on their way to the trenches, and surgeons and nurses hurried by on errands on which life nearly always depended. Once again I tried to make myself remember that Will was just another nameless face to them, a young man to be tended and, hopefully saved

415

ready to send back out there again, but all I wanted to do was scream at them that he was more than that, he was more important than all the others. But of course he wasn't.

Archie was becoming more and more agitated; his replies to my questions were growing shorter, and his face was tense, his eyes dark and haunted-looking. It wasn't until we emerged into the night and his face immediately looked to the sky that I realised why. It had been creeping into the small hours by the time Archie and I had got Will back to the sap-head, and although it was not yet growing light, it was late April and soon the sky would be brushed with the first light of dawn.

'Archie?' I spoke gently, but he jumped, and turned a white, strained face towards me.

'I know Oli did a terrible thing,' he said, his voice husky with the effort of control, 'but he's just a kid, Evie.'

'I know.'

'He doesn't deserve to die.'

'No.'

'For God's sake, it was his *sister!* If I'd known, and got to Drewe first, I'd likely have done the same thing.'

'No!' I grabbed his arm. 'You wouldn't, you know you wouldn't. And if you had, well, you wouldn't have gone off and left a friend to fight your battles for you.'

'That's just it, though. I *am* his friend. And what am I doing? Hanging around this place–'

'You saved Will's life,' I reminded him, trying not to be stung by his words. 'If it weren't for you coming out to help me I'd just be lying beside him out there now, not knowing he was even alive, let alone unable to get him back.'

He subsided with a little sigh. 'I'm sorry, sweetheart. I'm just... I feel so helpless.'

'Uncle Jack is doing all he can.'

'Aye, but what can he do? The fact's the thing; Oliver killed his superior officer and then deserted. He's going to die, Evie, and then what'll become of Kitty?'

Archie walked away a few steps, then spoke over his shoulder without turning. 'I'm away to get a bit of air. Come and find me if you hear anything about Will.'

I watched him go, wondering if being alone really was the best thing, and decided it probably was. For him, at least. For me it felt as though everything that had been holding me up had suddenly been yanked out from under me; I couldn't bear the emptiness, I felt stranded and hopeless, and I turned to go back down into the hospital – at least there I might be of some use to someone while I waited for news.

Within a few minutes I had been given a role in one of the long-term wards, and having cleaned myself as best I could, and borrowed yet another uniform, I set to work changing beds and cleaning floors alongside the grateful, overworked VADs. The only uniform available in my size had been a nurse's one, hurriedly plucked from the sewing basket, and, creased and holey-pocketed though it was, I found myself smiling faintly at the thought that Will would have found it extremely funny to see me dressed as a nurse at all; I'd always hated the idea of women fussing over

417

uniforms, instead of getting on with the work of helping people.

'I know what I'd rather, if I was in a sticky situation,' I'd written, exasperated when, during training, I'd received yet another warning for slovenly dress, 'between someone coming towards me dressed in rags with a first-aid tin, and someone telling me to wait while they fix their cape properly and straighten their cap!'

'It's good for discipline,' he'd said, amused, but of course he'd already become used to army life and could see both sides. To me it still felt like pointless posturing, and I'd sworn he'd never see me in a nurse's uniform, but seeing the smooth way the hospital was run, and the way the patients relaxed when they saw a neatly-turned-out nurse approaching, looking calm and capable, I allowed there might be some merit in the almost military attention to detail.

It was good to put myself to work; the tension of my emotions was eased by exhaustion. But I'd not been there more than half an hour when I heard something that stopped me in my numbed, mindless tracks, and set my brain racing once again.

Chapter Thirty

'The morphine's going to be what does for him in the end,' the nurse murmured to me. I looked back at the patient she was referring to, sitting up in bed after we'd replaced his bandages. He'd endured another fitting for one of the masks that were growing more lifelike and detailed all the time, and, just as Will's had last year, his hands were clenching and unclenching on the bed next to him, and I didn't think it was pain that was causing it; the movement was jerky, unlike the rhythmic, determined focusing on something to take one's mind off physical discomfort.

'Does for him?'

'Look at him. Eyes all over the place. Next stop opium, and probably soon after, heart attack. Poor boy.'

'Really?'

'Not his fault, of course, but he won't have access to morphine. It's the family I feel sorry for. When he goes it won't be as a hero, it'll be as a drug-addled mess. Better if he'd died out there in the field, sorry to say.'

My thoughts were jumbled and tired, but they quickly sorted themselves into neat parcels of information: Uncle Jack's remembrances of Colonel Drewe's morphine addiction, '...*he changed quite a lot, became dependent on morphine for a while...*'

Kitty had said the man who attacked her had seemed drunk, but had not been. His eyes, though, had been 'odd'. Oliver's own telling of the events in the cellar at Number Twelve had told a similar tale, and I remembered how he'd said the necessity to take short, shallow breaths had made his heart race, and had affected Drewe even more severely.

And finally, the expression on Will's face as he'd looked at the syringe of morphine that would, temporarily at least, lift him away from his pain

419

and give him some peace. He had looked as though, if anyone had stood between him and that peace, he might have killed them without a second's thought.

I dropped the cloth I was holding back into the bucket by my feet and, ignoring indignant shouts from the ward, I ran. Back out into the tunnel system, up into the cool breeze of the thankfully still pitch-black early morning.

I found him right away. He wouldn't have gone far, I knew that, but in the dark only his height and stillness gave him away against the others travelling to and from the underground city.

'Archie!'

He turned, saw the urgency that propelled me towards him, and came to meet me, clasping my arms as I fought for enough breath to speak clearly. 'We have to telephone Uncle Jack *right now*. Where can we go? How can we find him?'

To my relief he didn't ask for answers then and there, but caught my hand and dragged me to the nearest field telephone. 'If we can just get a stay of execution,' I urged. 'We need to check the cause of Drewe's death.'

'Got it. Hello! Yes, Captain Buchanan. Vitally important this message gets to Major Jack Carlisle...'

He left the message, with the rather worryingly determined, 'Evidence to follow,' and all we could do then was wait. We stayed next to the field telephone, but my eyes kept straying to the doorway, and eventually Archie touched my hand.

'Go back, darling. Be there when he needs you, I'll come to you with any news.'

Electric light was a wonderful thing, but it couldn't tell me if dawn had come. Archie's continued absence was worrying, but as soon as I heard the operation was over, all thoughts of him, and of Oli, were swept from my mind. There was only Will.

'The bullet took him just below the lowest rib,' the surgeon said, his voice tired and his eyes tireder. 'Thankfully missed the aorta, and lodged at the bottom of the pancreas.'

'But is he–'

'He survived the operation, yes,' the surgeon said, and my knees almost gave out. He held up his hand as I opened my mouth to express my relief and gratitude. 'He's got a long way to go, Mrs Davies. He's extremely lucky to have survived this far, please don't get your hopes up.'

His caution did little to quell the fierce elation that ran through me; I would see him again, speak to him, have the chance to tell him I never really gave up on him. I wasn't allowed in just yet, however, and paced the tunnels with a twisting, aching need that grew stronger with every minute that passed.

I thought back – was it really only a few short hours? – to the moment I had seen him lying by the wire up by the German trench; clinging on to life, not trying to throw it away. His body had been fighting, every bit as hard as the instinct that had caused him to turn his face to the side as he lay there – an echo of my own instinctive desperation to go on. I wondered how long he'd been conscious, frightened and in terrible pain, before the darkness had closed in, and if he knew he would see daylight again or if he believed that to be the end.

My musings were interrupted by a low voice in my ear. 'Don't hope for too much, but they've agreed to postpone the execution, pending evidence that Oli didn't kill the colonel.'

'Oh, thank God!'

Archie nodded. 'How is Will?'

I told him, and we leaned against one another in shared relief. Both outcomes were shaky at best, but we would have a little time, at least, to gather ourselves and make sure we did all we could. Breathing space. Time to sleep, even.

But no. Archie had switched back into briskness. 'Right, where's this evidence?'

It occurred to me that I hadn't told him anything of any substance, and that he had just potentially committed a grave offence based only on my frantic babbling. 'It's just ... I think Drewe might have had a heart attack, not drowned at all.'

'You *think?*' He shook his head and blew out a heavy breath, then calmed himself 'Aye well, a post-mortem will confirm if that's the case,' he conceded. 'I doubt if they'd considered one necessary, what with Oliver confessing to murder. So, what have we got to go on?'

I told Archie everything that had flashed through my mind while listening to the nurse's musing. 'She said morphine addiction can lead to dependence on opium, and that a big risk is heart-failure.'

'She's right, of course,' Archie said. 'Seen it happen. Tragic. Especially when it's nearly always a result of a courageous act, or following orders.'

'Well, Oli said Drewe was very red in the face, and quite breathless, when he went into the cellar. If he thought Oli might go to the authorities with what he knew, might that have brought on a heart attack? He hadn't denied it, after all.'

'It's possible. Oliver said he waited a moment before going down the steps to roll him over.'

'But we don't *know* he drowned.'

'Not conclusively. But it's still likely Oliver will face the firing squad. Even striking a superior officer carries the death penalty.'

'The question then, even if we can prove Drewe died from natural causes, is whether we can also prove the provocation. Maybe we can get the sentence commuted to life imprisonment. We just need to borrow some time! Time to get Kitty out here.'

Before Archie could reply, a VAD approached and touched my arm shyly.

'Mrs Davies? You can see him now.'

Archie squeezed my hand. 'Go on. I'll give this some thought and work out what to tell Jack.' I nodded gratefully, and followed the VAD back to the ward.

'You mustn't tire him,' she began, then subsided with a little smile and gestured at my uniform. 'Well, you know.'

'Thank you. And I won't.'

I approached his bed, more nervous than I had ever been around him, even on our wedding night. My heart pounded and my hands felt clammy, and I wiped them on the front of my apron. He slept, still, but I was glad; it gave me a chance to compose myself and I sat down beside him, marvelling in the reality of him, and comforted by the sight of his chest rising and falling gently as he breathed. I felt as if I tore my eyes away from him it would all stop, that the next time I looked he would be waxy-looking and still, and a hand would fall on my shoulder, eyes looking at me with sympathy mingled with faint impatience: I should move away, let them free up the bed...

'Evie?'

So fixated had I been on watching him breathe, I hadn't seen him open his eyes. They looked at me now, calm and familiar, and once they locked with mine I couldn't look away. I'd told myself his life was all that mattered, only that he should survive to hear my last plea, and then make his decision, but now I knew I'd been trying to fool myself. I would give anything to see the same tender, hopeful look of love in his face as I knew must be on mine.

'I never meant it,' I whispered. 'That letter. I was coming to tell you.' He nodded, and his hand turned palm-up on the bed. I laid my own in it, feeling his fingers closing over mine and it was as if he'd folded my entire body in his arms just by that one small gesture. But it was the giving and taking of comfort, nothing more. The need for a human touch during a moment of deep fear and regret. The last touch of a love that was broken and burdensome.

I couldn't tell him about what had happened out in No Man's Land; hated the thought that it sounded as though I had hopes of winning him back through obligation, but I remembered something else, and fumbled at the dolly bag I wore at my hip. 'Look.'

I pulled out the torn, battered paper rose, and laid it on his chest. He picked it up with his free hand, and closed his eyes briefly as the movement caused a spasm of pain. It took a moment for his breathing to settle. Then he said, with the tiniest hint of a smile, 'As I thought. Shocking mess.'

'Shocking,' I agreed. There was a long, difficult silence.

'I'm sorry,' he said at last, on a sigh. 'You shouldn't have come. You needn't have.'

I looked at him, my answering smile fading. 'What are you talking about?' He shook his head, then carefully lifted his hand away from mine. My fingers closed on empty air. 'Will?'

'All this,' he said. 'It's exactly why,' he winced and swallowed hard, 'why I said what I did.'

'And you think *all this* is going to make me want to leave you?'

'You'd be a fool if you didn't. And you're no fool, Evie.'

'Oh, aren't I?' I folded my arms across my chest. 'I actually think I must be, to think you had half an ounce of common sense about you, Will Davies.' I leaned in close, hardly raising my voice above a whisper, but pouring every ounce of frustrated anger into it. 'Do you know what I think?' Without giving him time to form an answer, I went on, 'I think it's *you* who's stopped loving me.' His hand clenched on the covers and he looked stricken by the ferocity in my voice. 'You're not the only one who's had to build a wall between the past and the present!' I paused to wipe a furious tear. 'We knew we'd change, Will. We even talked about it, but you

425

promised me...' I realised I was beginning to raise my voice, and dropped it low again. 'You *promised* me that wouldn't matter. If you don't like what I've grown into after all, I think you should just tell me the truth. You owe me that much.'

'Now, nurse, let the patient rest,' a voice behind me said, and I turned to see the sister bearing down on us, a tray in her hand that drew his eyes away from mine, leaving a cold fear snaking through me at the desperation in that look.

'I thought about you,' he whispered, still looking at the syringe the sister was preparing; his face was milk-white and greasy-looking. 'When I was lying out there. I couldn't move, or even open my eyes, but I remember, I thought I heard your voice.'

'Will–'

'Come along, nurse,' the sister said. 'God willing there'll be time for talking later.' She stepped forward and, with despair taking hold once again I moved aside, but Will gripped my hand and pulled me back.

There was a new light in his eyes, one of realisation and trembling awe. 'I didn't imagine it, did I?'

I didn't reply, but he must have seen the truth in my face, and in the guilty way I looked over my shoulder.

'My God, Evie,' he breathed. 'You thought I no longer loved you, and you still did that?'

'It didn't mean my own feelings had changed.'

'You're rarely wrong,' he managed, 'but when you are, you are spectacularly, ridiculously, unbelievably wrong.'

'Does that mean–'

'It means you are spectacularly, ridiculously–'

'Unbelievably wrong,' I finished for him, my heart beginning to thump hard with relief. 'We're well-matched then. You finally accept you're burdened with me for life?'

He was becoming tired, and his words were mumbling across his lips, but every one of them sang. 'How could I not, with the sacrifices you've made?'

'Nurse!' The sister was growing impatient, but Will and I ignored her and kept our eyes on each other.

'I couldn't leave you alone out there.'

'I'm not talking about that,' he said, and, from somewhere, a smile crept across his face, banishing the pain just for a moment. 'I'm talking about this.' He flicked the collar of my uniform. 'You even fixed your cape properly and straightened your cap.'

'You remembered that?' I was trying not to laugh now but I couldn't help it, the relief was thundering through me and banishing every last ache and doubt. He laughed too, then gasped and held his breath. I clutched at his hand and he let out the breath slowly, his eyes closed tight, and accepted the sting of the needle with gratitude. After a moment he looked at me again, and I could tell by his expression that he was going to say something important. I leaned in closer so he wouldn't have to raise his voice.

'You've got a hole in your pocket,' he murmured, and then his eyes closed, and he went gratefully into whatever awaited him in the darkness.

At that moment I wished, above everything, that I could follow him.

427

Archie found me a little later. I'd been told Will would sleep for a good long time; he needed to let his body begin the healing process and if I returned too soon and disturbed him, let alone made him laugh again, I would be given extremely short shrift and bundled back outside. So I went of my own accord, and stood watching the light streak across the sky, lightening the day until it felt like another world.

I was able to look around for the first time properly, and see my surroundings, the personnel coming and going, the endless chains of supplies of medical equipment, blankets and ammunition that was unloaded and carried away from the lorries. While watching one team of men unloading a consignment of mortars I caught sight of Archie, looking around for me. I waved and he came over.

'Uncle Jack has swung it,' he said, before I'd had chance to ask. 'They're going to do a full post-mortem, and if it turns out Drewe did have a heart attack, the charge will be altered. There will be another trial, another chance for Oli to tell his side.'

'And for Kitty to do the same,' I said. Relief peeled the last weight from my shoulders, but, conversely the release of that weight stole the strength I needed to stand up any longer, and I looked around for somewhere to sit.

'Get some sleep,' Archie said instead. 'Here, use the car again, I'll find a blanket.'

'But Will–'

'Is in good hands. And needs his rest.'

'He understands now,' I said, tiredness turning

my own words into the same mumble I'd heard in Will's voice. 'He knows.'

'Of course he knows,' Archie said gently. 'He's a sensible lad, aye?'

'Aye,' I said, and he smiled.

'Cheeky.' He guided me towards the car. 'I'll bring you a hot drink and a blanket, all right?'

I slid gratefully along the wide front seat of the staff car, and waited for Archie to come back, letting my mind envelop the knowledge that Will was safe and still loved me. As the world drifted away I found time, at last, to whisper a few words to my poor Boxy. I told her I missed her and I hoped she hadn't felt frightened and lonely at the end, that it had come swiftly, before she had realised she wasn't going to see her beloved Ben again. I laid my head back and gave myself over to the memories of our meeting at the hospital in Rugby, to our first arrival in Belgium, and to all the hundreds of little moments we had shared that had cemented our already sturdy friendship.

I didn't see Archie bringing the blanket, but when I struggled to wakefulness a little while later I realised he'd draped it over me. I saw the cup of cold tea on the dashboard and swilled my mouth out with it, then blinked up through the windscreen at the sky; the sun was quite high, not mid-day yet, but not far off.

Will! I knocked over the cup in my haste to get out of the car, but Archie would understand. Flicking cold tea off my hand I scrambled out of the door, feeling the muscles in my legs seize solid after their crouching scramble back across No Man's Land. I grunted and clutched at the

429

car for balance, and a moment later felt a strong hand beneath my arm.

I steadied my trembling knees and forced myself to stand very still. 'Thank you, Archie.'

'Try again.'

'Uncle Jack!' Relief swept over me, and I accepted his embrace.

'That's better. Now, what's wrong with your legs?'

'Nothing,' I said, rather too quickly judging from the look on his face. If he found out what I'd done ... well, I don't know what he'd do, but telling mother would have been the very least of it. 'I've just been sleeping, and locked up a little bit. It was a long night.'

'I'll say. Look, Will's awake. And he's doing much better from what the sister says.'

The sister was right. Will's colour was back to some extent, he had lost that waxy-white look, and his eyes were brighter. He still lay flat and would not be sitting up for some time, but he twisted his head as if he sensed it was me coming down the ward, and the smile that spread across his face warmed me right through.

'No making him laugh,' Jack warned, low in my ear, but I could hear amusement in his voice.

'He started it last time,' I said with mock indignation, then put on a haughty tone. 'Might we be left alone, please, Major Carlisle?'

He withdrew, and I sat down close to Will once again. This time there was no hesitancy between us, and I lifted his roughened hand to my lips and kissed it.

'Back to Blighty soon. The minute you're able

430

to travel.'

'I've been thinking, do you suppose there's a chance I could go to Dark River Farm to convalesce?'

'That sounds like a perfect idea. Lizzy would love to see you again, and I'm sure Frances would be delighted to have us. The girls will fall over themselves to take care of you, and all that fresh air will be a great help for healing.'

He grinned. 'That all sounds wonderful. But I was thinking more of avoiding your mother.'

I turned to see if Uncle Jack was near, so I could point out who'd started the laughter.

Dark River Farm, May 1917

'How long do you think it'll be before he realises?'

I looked up from my diary, and saw Will gesturing at the window. Outside in the courtyard I could see Archie and Kitty deep in conversation.

I raised an eyebrow. 'Realises what?'

'That it's really been Kitty all along, not you.'

'You could hurt a girl's feelings like that, Lord William,' I said, rather archly, but Will's grin told me he wasn't fooled. He shifted carefully in his armchair, and I eyed him critically; it had only been a few weeks but he was already itching to get back to some kind of work. I pushed aside the niggling worry that he'd try to rejoin his unit again – even if he'd wanted to it would be a long time before he was fit for that. 'It's pretty obvious,' he said, 'even you know, don't you?'

'Of course.'

Lizzy looked up from a letter she was writing. 'Really? How?'

I put my pen down and thought about it. 'I've had a suspicion since ... what happened. With Drewe. Archie would tense up every time I mentioned her name, and when he found out what had happened I thought he was going to go right over and tear Potter limb from limb.'

'Good job he didn't,' Will pointed out. 'Poor bloke wouldn't have known what was going on.'

'How did *you* know, then?' I asked Will, curious.

Will levered himself out of the chair and came over to stand behind me at the kitchen table. 'Same reason as I know you and I are forever,' he said, putting his hands over my shoulders to clasp mine. I almost leaned back against him, but felt him withdraw slightly and just stopped myself before my head bumped his midriff.

'And how's that?'

'He gave up on you too quickly,' Will said. I twisted in my chair and looked up into his face. He smiled down at me. 'I'm serious. He swore his devotion to you and I'm sure he meant it, but as soon as you said "no", he accepted it.' He jerked his head at the window. 'Not so with Kitty. He's been writing and talking to her for weeks now, but she's having none of it.'

'She loves him though,' Lizzy put in, sounding as exasperated as I felt. 'I wish we could convince her she's worthy of him.'

'He's an idiot,' I said shortly. 'They're as bad as one another. He's known her nearly all her life, and only just realised she's anything other than Oli's little sister.'

432

We jumped as the front door banged and Archie came back inside, nodded to Will, and put the kettle on the stove to boil.

'How's Oli?' I asked, to try and banish the glower from his face.

'As you'd expect. Doing time in a civilian prison isn't the most fun in the world.' I glanced at Lizzy, and Archie realised what he'd said, and groaned. 'I'm sorry, sweetheart. Didnae think, as usual.'

Lizzy waved the apology away. 'At least he escaped with his life,' she said, gently taking Archie's hand off the metal handle of the kettle before he could burn himself.

'Aye. Cashiering's the best we could have hoped for, but not the worst we expected. He's lucky to have had Uncle Jack on his side, right enough.'

This time Lizzy's face clouded over, and Archie glanced at me with an apologetic grimace, and went upstairs before he could say anything else out of place. I touched Lizzy's hand but said nothing; Uncle Jack had gone back to Germany a few days ago and we all felt his absence but none, of course, as deeply as Lizzy. I made our excuses, drawing Will outside into the yard to give her some time alone.

Kitty saw us, and gave us a tiny smile before hurrying back into the house. I sighed and looked after her. The poor girl had lost a great deal in such a short space of time: her family wanted nothing to do with her; her brother was serving a sentence he'd be lucky to see the end of for at least two years; her work in Belgium was over – she was terrified to go anywhere alone – and now she had convinced herself she wasn't good enough for the

433

one man who could bring her back to her former, glowing life. The one positive thing to have come from it all was that Frances Adams had brought her into her own little family, and was more of a mother to her than her own had ever been.

Will was looking out towards the woods. 'Go for a walk with me tomorrow?'

'If you like.' I followed his gaze, and instinct made me look down at his hands. Fine, strong hands, artist's hands. Sure enough, the long fingers were flexing in readiness. 'What will you make first?'

'A box, I think. Just about big enough to hold a single paper rose. Make sure you don't lose it.'

He reached out and cupped the back of my head, pulling me towards him for a kiss. Through the brief touching of lips and teeth, I felt him smiling, and smiled back, and then the smiles fell away as we melted deeper into one another, our hearts remembering what the war had tried so hard to make us forget. Yes, we had changed, Will and I, but deep down we were the same two people who had fallen in love in 1912, who had been little more than children at the start; playing tricks, defying my mother, running away to Blackpool and then to Gretna Green ... and who had finally grown up apart, on different ends of the allied front lines.

And now our war was over.

The publishers hope that this book has given you enjoyable reading. Large Print Books are especially designed to be as easy to see and hold as possible. If you wish a complete list of our books please ask at your local library or write directly to:

Magna Large Print Books
Magna House, Long Preston,
Skipton, North Yorkshire.
BD23 4ND

This Large Print Book for the partially sighted, who cannot read normal print, is published under the auspices of

THE ULVERSCROFT FOUNDATION